Harbo

Katie Flynn has lived for many years in the north-west. A compulsive writer, she started with short stories and articl...   ...were broadcast on Radio M... ...She c... ...to write ...rpool series after hearing the reminiscences of fa... ...embers about life in the city in the early years of the t... ...th century. For many years she has had to cope with M.., ...ut has continued to write. She also writes as Judith Saxton.

Katie Flynn

writing as
**JUDITH
SAXTON**

Harbour Hill

arrow books

Published by Arrow Books, 2014

6 8 10 9 7 5

First published in Great Britain in 1991 by New English Library Hardbacks

Arrow Books
The Random House Group Limited
20 Vauxhall Bridge Road, London, SW1V 2SA

A Penguin Random House Company

www.randomhousebooks.co.uk

Addresses for companies within The Random House Group Limited can
be found at: www.randomhouse.co.uk/offices.htm

The Random House Group Limited Reg. No. 954009

A CIP catalogue record for this book
is available from the British Library

ISBN 9780099598718

Penguin Random House is committed to a sustainable future for
our business, our readers and our planet. This book is made from
Forest Stewardship Council® certified paper.

Printed and bound in Great Britain by Clays Ltd, St Ives plc

For Simon and Holly,
Dino and Zak, with
love and huggles.

Chapter One

If it had not been a fine day, Henry would probably have slumbered until noon but a slender finger of sunshine, persistent as a searchlight, sought out a gap in the curtains and fell across his face. It brought him reluctantly up from deep sleep, first into the golden shallows and then, crossly, into wakefulness.

A glance at the clock told him that it was not yet time to get up. And furthermore, what was the sun doing, shining on his face from this particular angle? Hell, where was he?

Henry opened his eyes but memory returned before his glance had taken in the ill-fitting curtains at the windows . . . so that was how the ray of sunshine had got in . . . and the bed in which he lay, an island of comfort on a sea of bare boards. Of course! He and Keith had moved into the Ambleside Hotel yesterday, and today the rest of their stuff would be arriving.

Henry sighed and glanced again at the clock. Ten past six – how annoying that he had woken. Normally he would not have been up at this hour because the offices of all the various people concerned with this rambling great house – estate agents, solicitors, even accountants – did not open until nine and he and Keith usually let the staff settle in before they descended.

However, estate agents and solicitors were no longer their concern. Now Ambleside was officially theirs they would have quite enough to worry about.

The idea of buying a hotel and running it as a resident sailing school had been born out of Henry's experience of working on yachts and Keith's search for a gap in the market. Sailing was a popular sport in Norfolk, yet Haisby, with its big marina and thriving yacht club, had nowhere for aspiring small boat sailors – and it could be such a money spinner! For years Henry had bummed around the world on other men's yachts, putting money by, dreaming of the day when he would settle down somewhere and perhaps have a boat of his own. And in a way the same went for Keith; he had worked in hotels for several years but had never been able to make the jump into management, though he was sure he had the capability. Both single and living largely at the expense of various employers, both men had dreamed of the day when they would have sufficient capital put by to start a little business of their own.

They had met as the result of Henry's accident and Keith's forethought. Henry's current employer had berthed his yacht in Haisby marina whilst he and his party explored Norfolk. And Henry, that experienced sailor, had slipped on the wet deck and fallen into the gap between the boat's side and the harbour wall. The wind had crowded the vessel on top of him, crushing Henry like a living fender between itself and the great, weedy stones. He had been lucky to escape with his life.

Now, Henry moved his right arm and twinges of pain shot from wrist to elbow. He would never crew on an oceangoing yacht again, and while he was recovering in hospital he seldom thought past a rented flat, part-time work in a boatyard and perhaps a small dinghy just for fun.

But it hadn't come to that, because one day he had picked up the local rag and seen Keith's advertisement; *Wanted, person familiar with small sailing boats to put capital into business venture centred at Haisby-on-Sea.*

Curiosity had made him ring the telephone number, idleness – and interest in what Keith had revealed during that conversation – had made him agree to a meeting. He had limped into the suggested rendezvous, the wreck of a once tall and husky man in his mid-forties, his tan faded to an unhealthy yellow, his arm a mass of puckered purple scar tissue, and despite the odds he and Keith had got on at once, had realised that each had something the other would need in the venture which Keith was proposing.

Did it worry me when I realised Keith was gay? Henry asked himself now, as he had asked himself often over the past few months. But the answer was always the same. It had not mattered because this was to be a business partnership. When Keith's father had died Keith had used his inheritance to buy an attractive harbourside cottage. The property had simply leapt in value and suddenly Keith realised he could sell the cottage and start his own business, free from the fret of an employer who would never give him a free hand within the medium-sized hotel in which Keith was happiest. The idea of a residential sailing school seemed sensible because in Haisby there was such an obvious gap in the market.

But he was sensible enough to realise that he needed a partner and Henry, of course, was to teach sailing whilst Keith dealt with the hotel and catering side of the venture. And their combined resources would enable them to buy somewhere big enough to spread their wings as the business expanded.

So Henry, who had been living in a one-roomed flat in Cloister Row to eke out his money until he found congenial work, moved into a larger flat in Harbour Hill, the long road which led from the yacht marina to the top of the cliffs. Keith continued to work at the Miramar Hotel and both of them spent hours viewing property.

And in the end they had found Ambleside, the very last residence on Harbour Hill, right at the top of the cliff before the road began to wind down again. Henry saw it first, a great white elephant of a house perched on the cliff, but had never thought twice about it until the day the sale-board went up.

Then he rang Keith at work, almost incoherent with excitement, and rushed round to the agent to collect the keys. The hotel had been abandoned years ago as being too far out of town, but in recent years Haisby, as if regretting what it had done to Ambleside, had begun to creep up the hill towards it, apologetically reaching out shops, an amusement arcade and small guest-houses until the big hotel was no longer solitary on its cliff. Even so, the solicitors acting for the owners had been relieved as well as pleased when the two men had decided to buy the place. And for their part, Keith and Henry were well satisfied. Ambleside was structurally sound and the position ideal.

During the waiting period Keith and Henry spent most daylight hours together and though they were very different, they got along well. Henry's meals improved with Keith doing the cooking – the younger man had been trained as a chef – and both men read up on interior decorating and enjoyed using this new skill.

3

Would it be different now, though? Having Keith around the flat and working on the hotel had been fine but this was real sharing. Here, it would just be Henry and Keith, until they began to take bookings.

No, it won't be any different, Henry decided. If Keith wanted boyfriends he would have them, but he had said he never mixed business with pleasure so it should be all right. Henry snuggled down, firmly shutting his eyes against the sunlight.

This tactic worked for a bit, until the shaft of sunlight moved across his lids. Then Henry sneezed and sat up. It was no use trying to go back to sleep, he would get up and have a go at cooking something simple; he could start with breakfast. Half reluctantly, he got out of bed. He stood in the shaft of sunlight, yawning, stretching, then went over to the window and drew the curtains. The window faced the sea and he blinked at the strength of sun on water, then stood back, knowing he was grinning like a fool and not caring. The sun edging up out of the sea was dazzling, a brilliant sight. Guests would be bowled over by it, Henry was sure.

And what a view! The smooth downward curve of the shaggy grass, groups of trees planted to frame the edge of the cliff, and all the brilliance of the blue and silver early-morning sea. The cliffs were high here, forty or fifty feet, so he could not see the beach, but he could imagine it. The big pebbles, ridged up by the harsh attack of the North Sea in winter, the pale, firm reaches of sand, the low-waters and the wooden groynes, all colour sucked out of them by the relentless waves, shaggy with seaweed, thickly sown with mussels. Like a child, he suddenly wanted to be out there, exploring!

Why not? I can go down to the shore and be back in plenty of time to make breakfast, Henry assured himself.

To think, in this instance, was to act. Henry hitched up his pyjama trousers – he never wore the jacket – and reached for his sponge-bag. There was a bathroom on every floor though none of the rooms were en suite, but that would be remedied slowly, as the money came in.

Henry set off along the corridor heading for the bathroom. A tall, rangy man, broad-shouldered but with the neat movements of one used to living in confined spaces, he could move silently when he wished, and he did not want to wake Keith now. He slid into the bathroom, locked the door behind him and turned on the cold tap. When the water was running he found the box of matches Keith had balanced on top of the geyser and turned on the gas. He had struck three matches without success, poking them cautiously through the very small hole which one was supposed to use to light the thing and was just beginning to think nervously that he had best turn the gas off when the geyser ignited with frightening suddenness, the flames jetting two feet from the cracked white enamel. Henry unpeeled himself from the opposite wall, heart thumping, and approached the bath. It was a very old, very grand bath, with cloudy brass taps, a deep tub decorated with blue poppies and ears of corn and with four feet shaped like lion's paws, one on each corner.

The handbasin was equally magnificent, with room in its depths to bath a five-year-old child and, incongruously perched above it, a soap-dispenser leaking nasty pink mucus across the crazed porcelain.

Henry, whilst distrustfully dabbling a hand beneath the warming water, examined the rest of the bathroom. A cork-covered floor, warm to the toes but stained and freckled with dirt, a lavatory on a pedestal with a red mahogany seat, more blue porcelain in the bowl and a chain with a porcelain pear to serve as a handle. A large sash window, the bottom part frosted – and cracked from corner to corner – and the top part stained glass, with an improbable-looking coat of arms surrounded by meek lions and fierce lambs.

Neglected? Weird? Ancient grandeur? Henry supposed it was all three but as he stepped gingerly into the tub and immersed himself in the hot water he reflected that he would vote for ancient grandeur every time if it meant a choice between wallowing in this tub or sitting, primly upright, in a modern bath's measly four inches.

It was a good bath, too, the hard water refreshing in a way which was lacking in softer, southern water. Presently he climbed out, turned off the geyser and rubbed himself dry, going carefully still round his scars. Then he plugged in his electric razor and began to shave, grinning at his square, ugly mug with its greenish-grey eyes, bumpy broken nose, pepper and salt hair. You may not look it, but you're a lucky guy, he told himself. First, you had the sort of life most men secretly want – yachts, adventure, tropic seas. And now you're settling down in a town you already love, full of people who have already proved themselves very willing to befriend you. There had been the nurses at the hospital – one of them had found him his first flat, helped to move him in, even advised him how to tackle Gilbert Patani, their mutual landlord. A pretty girl Suzie, happy to introduce him to her friends, taking him to the yacht club to a dance so that he could meet the boating crowd. Confirming his own feeling that Keith was trustworthy, that Haisby could indeed support a sailing school. You've landed on your feet, Henry told his reflection. This is what you need, an outdoor life, the sea, and a friendly relationship without any of the difficulties which always seem to enter Eden when sex rears its head. Why, even if you met the perfect woman and wanted to go to bed with her, you and your partner aren't going to compete for her interest. Imagine that – a pal to whom you can introduce your best bird without fear!

There had been girls, of course, from the very first one who had sent him guiltily off to sea when she had announced she was pregnant. He had not wanted to settle down before he had seen the world, enjoyed the pleasures of a single man. He had enjoyed them so much that it had been twenty years before he came home to England for good, driven by the accident perhaps, but content with this small town that he had happened upon by chance but would not now exchange for the Bahamas or the Seychelles or any of the other exotic places he had once thought contained all a bloke wanted from life.

Shaving with finicky care, he remembered one particular girl. Fluff, he had called her; odd that he could no longer remember her real name. But he had always called her Fluff and never quite forgotten her simplicity and sweetness. But that had been years ago, since then there had been no one special. Just holiday romances, not expected to last.

And now? Since the accident he had scarcely thought about women. In your mid-forties, Henry had discovered, sex simply isn't the main thing on your mind – you can take it or leave it. In fact the thought of displaying his twisted leg and scarred arm to a stranger was a complete turn-off.

I think I'll give women a rest, Henry decided, and almost laughed at himself. Who on earth did he think he was? Some Adonis? He was a burnt-out case, he had done all the things most men dream of, had all the experiences the young Henry had yearned for. Now he would rest and be satisfied with simpler pleasures. A North Norfolk beach in winter, with gulls shrugging their shoulders against the cold and a boat nosing into a little marina, breaking the cat-ice with her bows. And Ambleside waiting for him to relax in the big old kitchen with a mug of hot tea at his elbow and toast browning beneath the grill.

And you never know, I might find a homeloving lass just yearning to settle down with a beat-up, ugly bugger who lives in an old-fashioned hotel and sails small boats for a living, his thoughts continued. Women were a wonder and a marvel – and a closed book. But he supposed such a woman might exist, might find burnt-out Henry attractive!

Grinning at his own optimism, Henry finished shaving and, towel-girt, left the bathroom. Once in his room he dressed in slacks and a tee-shirt, put on his trainers and headed for the hallway below. It was a gloomy place at the best of times but now, with the shrouded shapes of such furniture as they had brought with them bulking at one end, it looked positively sinister. Though at least the half-light hides the dirt, Henry told himself, turning the key in the front door and slipping outside. The freshness of early morning greeted him and he skirted the house, walking round it until he stood on the lawn outside his bedroom window. At least, it had once been a lawn, but now it was an area of rough grass, grey with dew and winter. And on either side the beds showed roses half-strangled by weeds, trees with ivy clambering up their trunks, and unkempt bushes. Henry set off across the grass, scattering dew with each step.

He noticed an orchard to his left and a great almond tree, the buds already showing colour, but he had come outside to see the shore so he hurried to where the stunted, sideways-leaning trees framed the cliff-edge and found when he reached it that it was a sheer drop to the beach below. He squinted sideways but could see no way down which was a nuisance, since he and Keith had both assumed there would be a private path to the beach. Still, there was a lane further along which they could use.

But before he left, Henry glanced narrowly at the cliff-edge. A fall had produced that knifelike finish to the sweet turf, he decided grimly. It was clearly not safe to go near the edge and look, but he would be surprised if he did not find the evidence on the beach below.

Was that why the hotel had been within their means? They had assumed it was because the house was in such a bad state of repair, but perhaps the locals knew that the cliffside here was eroding away? He and Keith must erect a sturdy fence which would prevent the unwary from tumbling over and would also help to stop further erosion, since people walking near the edge must increase the likelihood of cliff-falls.

Henry stood back to plan just how he would fix such a fence: at least, he concluded, it would not be a costly undertaking, unlike the work on the building itself.

Have we been fools, Henry wondered as he turned towards the lane which would lead him down to the beach. When it came down to it, a chef and a yachtsman are not exactly businessmen and it would be an enormous job to bring the hotel back to profitability, but he believed it was possible. Neither he nor Keith was afraid of hard work and Henry was encouraged by what they had achieved already. All the floors downstairs had been sanded, dyed light oak and polished. They had stripped paper and colour-washed walls in pale primary shades. If we can do that ourselves, with very little experience, then surely we're capable of setting up a small sailing school, he told himself, crunching down the lane and emerging onto the beach. We'll make a go of it in time.

The sun was half out of the sea now and white-fringed waves hissed against the wet sand. Henry's smile broadened. With this on their side, how could they fail?

'Any more marmalade, Henry? And I *won't* mention diets, because I'm starving and you must be, too.'

Keith smiled sweetly as Henry, without comment, pushed the marmalade jar across the table. He did adore it when Henry was preoccupied and kept giving him those lowering glances which seemed, Keith thought hopefully, to promise violence if he did not desist. Violence, he knew, could easily be the start of the sort of liaison he wanted, though Henry had made it plain that he was a heterosexual with no interest whatsoever in guys. But Keith had noticed that his partner seemed fairly indifferent to women, and now that they were living under the same roof – well, you never did know, did you?

8

'So? You went down to the beach and what did you find?'
Keith asked next, spreading marmalade. He had noticed the
cliff-fall on his first visit and had made it his business to find
out about it because it was half his money which would be
going into the place. And the solicitor had done his searches
and pronounced himself satisfied. The cliff-fall had happened
in the nineteen-twenties, almost seventy years ago, and nothing had slid away since though the gales of last winter had had
ample opportunity to wreak havoc, had they been able.

'I couldn't find any sign of a recent fall,' Henry admitted,
when Keith had told him what the solicitor had said. He
reached for another piece of toast. Keith longed to remind
him that he had sworn to lose weight before the summer, but
decided it was not the moment. Henry, he guessed, was a bit
twitchy about sharing accommodation, and the weight gain
had been the result of the accident, when Henry had not been
able to take proper exercise. Pointless as well as silly to make
him feel self-conscious over the few pounds he had gained.
Besides, Keith liked cuddly men . . . not that Henry was
cuddly. Very tall and big-boned, was Henry. Keith hugged
himself inwardly. Just let things happen, he thought. Softly,
softly catchee monkey . . . he knew that was his only chance
with Henry. If he was sensible and pulled his weight in their
new venture, who could tell? If there was a latent gay lurking
in Henry, secretly longing to come out of the closet, then that
was the way to lure him forth. Because, despite knowing that
he himself was gay, Keith had not actually done anything
about it. It was only recently that he had begun to long for a
proper relationship with a like-minded guy.

'Then you think we're safe enough?' Keith said. He had
been touched and delighted when he entered the kitchen
earlier to find Henry hard at work making breakfast, but he
knew very well, really, that it was prompted by friendship
and not by the sort of affection for which he longed. Hal really
isn't the type at all, he told himself now. Once he's got over
the accident he'll start fancying women, and anyway it's
always a mistake to mix business with pleasure. But Henry
was so lovable that he, Keith, could not help himself. Against
all the odds, because Henry was plain as a boot and the wrong
side of forty, Keith loved his partner – and acknowledged that
Henry had no suspicion of it and would not be flattered if he
knew.

9

'Oh, we're safe enough,' Henry said now, as crossly as if he could read Keith's thoughts. 'But that drop will have to be fenced off. I don't suppose many small kids will come to the sailing school but even an adult could go over the edge as things stand . . . I mean there's not even a warning, and it's a pretty sheer drop.'

'You're right,' Keith said soothingly. 'Tell you what, Henry, why don't we make it an attraction? We could call it Lovers' Leap and print a booklet telling tourists how these star-crossed lovers had jumped to their death. How about that?'

He knew it would make Henry laugh and it did, then until breakfast was over they talked about advertising and which periodicals and newspapers were likeliest to bring in customers.

Later, when Henry had limped off to watch for the removal van, Keith began to clean the black and white tiles in the big old reception hall. They were filthy, with the rubber backing of cheap carpet still stuck to them in places and a dappling of dirt everywhere.

Keith scrubbed away and used a knife to scrape off the worst of the muck. He thought about their new venture as he scrubbed, and smiled to himself. A sailing school! He had always loved the outdoors, and taking care of people, so he would adore this! Eventually they intended to staff the big old hotel properly, but for a while they would do most of the work themselves.

Good thing I kept my eyes open and helped out in most areas as well as the kitchens, Keith mused now, breaking into song. He had a nice light tenor and a good sense of pitch. At least it means I can do the bookwork and wait at table as well as cook. Good thing Henry's a first-rate sailor, too, because if I'm here, cooking and seeing to the guests and keeping the hotel part of our venture going, then I can't be sailing as well. He had told Henry that he was an experienced yachtsman but this was more wishful thinking than fact. Many years earlier, when he had been at the grammar school in Norwich, he had crewed for a cousin aboard a small yacht all through one summer holiday. He had loved it, but it had been a long time ago. Keith, who admitted to twenty-eight but was actually six years older, could still remember the pleasure and companionship of that sailing summer. Life had been simple then, uncomplicated. Keith had been a boy like any other, it had been before . . .

But he never thought about his life pre-Terry, and did not intend to start now. He was too happy for regrets, or what-might-have-beens. Live for the moment, Keith, he advised himself, scrubbing away. Live for the moment, my dear!

The removal men were finished and gone by four, the furniture stood around in unhappy little groups, you could almost see normal-sized dressing-tables and nice sensible chairs casting terrified glances at the vaults which they were now supposed to inhabit.

'They'll look better when we've got some carpet down,' Henry said, his tone almost apologetic. He felt sorry for Keith, looking at the miniaturised furniture standing in this giant's castle. But his pity was wasted.

'I don't see what's wrong with the stuff, myself,' Keith said cheerfully, turning the hall light on and, in Henry's opinion, promptly shrinking the furniture further as the shadows sprang into play. 'All it needs is a few more pieces and we're away.'

'Ye-es,' Henry said, loth to ruin the younger man's optimism. The furniture was all from Keith's cottage; Henry had not lived ashore for long enough to acquire such things. 'Quite a lot more pieces, wouldn't you say?'

But Keith was not to be put down.

'No, not really. We'll have to buy some huge wardrobes and Welsh dressers and things, to fill in and lend atmosphere, but for practical purposes we've got most of what we'll want.'

It was true that the kitchen was adequately equipped, and the hall, Henry supposed, was probably meant to be fairly empty. But the vast, echoing dining room, and the living room where guests would sit in the evenings . . .

He voiced the thought to Keith, who nodded.

'Well, yes, we'll have to pick up some cheap tables and chairs from somewhere, and some comfy sofas in the living room, because our guests are bound to want to relax after a hard day on the water. But once we've done that, and got beds for the guests' rooms . . .'

'We're home and dry,' Henry said, meaning to sound sarcastic. But it didn't come out like that, it came out enthusiastically and to his surprise he realised that was how he felt – as though he and Keith were at the start of an adventure and looking forward to every minute of it.

'That's it,' Keith said gleefully, when Henry told him. '*Life must be an awfully big adventure* – wasn't that in *Peter Pan*? Now we've done all we can for a bit, so how about popping into town, having a look in Jake's for some cheap carpets?'

Jake's was generally agreed to be the cheapest place in Haisby but Henry had heard stories of carpets which had looked like bargains until they revealed their motheaten innards and furniture which crumbled away at the first breath of wind.

'I'd rather have a word with Archie,' he said firmly. 'Yes, I know he sells antiques but he goes to all the sales and when I needed a table for the flat he picked one up for a song. We can be in the Arcade in ten minutes if we walk briskly.'

It was an interesting walk, too. Down Harbour Hill past the big, decaying houses, then the smaller ones, and finally the terraces. Over the swing bridge between the fish wharves on your right and the yacht marina on your left, then into Lord Street with its banks and travel agents and the gates to the little Arcade.

We'll pass Lavengro of course, Henry thought almost wistfully as he fetched his coat and put walking shoes on, for the sunny day had turned chilly with typical March unpredictability. Those two girls moved into my flat a few days ago – I wonder how they're getting on? Of course the hotel was a dream of modern convenience compared with Patani's awful conversion, but Henry had enjoyed living in Lavengro, particularly after first occupying a Patani bedsit. He thought of cheery little Ceri and the pretty blonde he had seen coming out of the house with her the previous day. Gilbert the Grope, as Ceri had nicknamed their landlord, would love to get his hands on the blonde, but Henry thought she looked quite capable of coping.

'Ready? Come on, then,' Keith said, running lightly down the stairs in his oilskins and sou'wester to where Henry waited. He looked cuter than ever, Henry thought resignedly. 'What are you doing down here?'

'Thinking,' Henry said, buttoning his anorak. 'Those girls who took over my flat; I was just wondering how they're getting on. And there's a nurse called Jan on the floor above, she's a decent sort. The hotel's marvellous but I miss having

12

a full house around me. I'll be glad when we get some guests.'

Keith shrugged and tugged open the heavy front door.

'The girls will cope; girls always do. And we'll soon have to start employing staff because there are things we'll need help with, if we're to succeed. Come on, we don't want to miss Archie.'

Chapter Two

'Ceri, there's a pigeon in the kitchen!'

Nicola had returned from a tiring day at work to find Ceri already established in their sitting-room with a newspaper spread out before her and a slice of bread and jam in one hand. Nicola, who had shed her cinnamon-brown coat and the elegant but crippling court shoes which she wore to work, sighed deeply and approached the kitchen, intending to put the kettle on.

And now, on entering the room, what did she find? A fat grey pigeon perched unconcernedly on the wooden draining board, apparently having found something edible thereon to judge from the single-minded way it was pecking and its complete lack of interest in Nicola's arrival.

'Ceri, did you hear me? It's a *pigeon*! Can you come? I hate birds . . . I'm scared it'll touch me.'

'It won't; they hardly ever do. Don't say it's in the fridge! I hate finding shitty little footprints in the butter.'

Ceri's voice was abstracted. Clearly she was still reading her wretched paper, Nicola thought vengefully. Whatever was she to do? She had a 'thing' about birds . . . Ceri could jolly well come and help her shoo the blasted thing out the way it had come. The window was open at the top, the pigeon must have flown in whilst the two of them were out and having grown accustomed to the place, was obviously not going to leave, or not until it had finished its feast, anyway.

'Ceri, I mean it – do come! Oh damn, it's done a plop in the sink!'

'Nasty,' Ceri said. 'Did you know Mick Jagger is going to give an interview after the nine o'clock news tonight?'

The pigeon seemed to take heart from Ceri's patent lack of interest in its presence. It gave a fat and wobbly hop and got up on the piece of slippery board euphemistically known as a 'working surface', then had to flap its wings to keep its balance. Nicola's heart promptly leapt into her mouth and her stomach heaved in sympathy . . . feathers, birds . . . ugh, ugh!

'Ceri? Are you coming through or shall I . . . ?'

There was no sound from the other room save for the turning of a page. Nicola, made bold by fear, flew into the living-room and snatched the paper from Ceri's grasp.

'Ceri, if you don't come and help me this minute you'll never see the *Sun* again!'

It sounded bloodcurdling put like that but Ceri, getting to her feet, gave a tolerant chuckle. She was a small girl with curly auburn hair, green eyes and a great many freckles and so far as Nicola had discovered she feared nothing. Which is a good thing, Nicola thought now, when you consider the mire of indecision and self-doubt in which I flounder. Still, the person at Marriage Guidance had told her it was a common feeling amongst women whose husbands had been unfaithful, so she might as well get used to it. Now, she followed as Ceri walked towards the kitchen, talking over her shoulder as she went.

'Wouldn't it go out of its own accord? Bloody thing, perhaps it wants to take up residence with the mice!'

She laughed but Nicola, who wasn't keen on mice either and had greeted signs of their presence with real dismay, could not find it amusing. Their landlord, Gilbert Patani, forbade pets or they could have kept a cat, but even a cat, she thought, could not have dissuaded that damned great pigeon from scuttling around the kitchen as though it owned the place!

Nicola had shut the door behind her as she left the kitchen but Ceri flung it open, clearly not at all afraid that the pigeon might get out and infest the rest of the flat with its presence.

'Where is it? Don't say you made me leave my paper just for . . . Oh no, there it is.' Ceri and the pigeon stared at each other, the pigeon rolling its small, chalk-rimmed eye until it focused on them whilst its head was nearly screwed off its shoulders with the effort of looking at someone directly behind it. Nicola saw that it had found a half-full tin of sweetcorn which it had tipped over and was demolishing enthusiastically. For a moment the pigeon and the two girls stared at one another and then the pigeon, apparently considering them harmless, returned to its meal.

Ceri, however, was not putting up with this.

'Out, you!' she said briskly.

Nicola really admired her. Here was she, twenty-four years old, married for two of them, separated for six months, yet she was scared to death of a pigeon. Ceri was four years younger and a babe, experience-wise, yet her red curls seemed to stand up like a dog's hackles as she approached the bird and although Nicola could not see her face, she could tell that Ceri was hideously scowling, every freckle standing out the way they did when she was in a rage. Ceri was not a girl to cross lightly, particularly if you were a pigeon.

The pigeon seemed to realise this. It looked over its shoulder once more, this time with a distinct look of alarm in its beady eye, then it tottered plumply along the draining board looking like the Queen Mum trying to run in a too-tight skirt, and rammed its big, soft breast briskly but uselessly against the window pane.

The window was a sash one, with the bottom firmly closed and the top open. The pigeon had flown in and could fly out, but it could not stroll; it must be persuaded to fly. Ceri, with her usual bluntness, pointed this out.

'Get airborne, you bugger,' she said. 'Move!'

She clicked her tongue in exasperation when the pigeon only gave a strangled coo and pressed its breast yet closer to the glass. Then she charged towards it.

To an extent, this tactic worked. The pigeon abandoned the window pane and belted down the draining board, taking off just when it seemed that death by drowning was to be its fate. It clattered clumsily into the air and gained sufficient height to avoid Ceri's vengeful swipe. Then it flew straight into the clothes pulley up by the ceiling, causing tights and frilly knickers to rain down upon their owners' heads.

'Damn!' Nicola said, untangling her best black tights from her hair and trying to ignore Ceri's rich oaths. 'It's near the window, it's going out . . . oh, blast!'

The pigeon headed for the open window, turned at the last moment, zoomed across the room and went straight into the clothes pulley once more. Staggering, but still on the wing, it seemed to recover from the blow the pulley had delivered, only to fly head-on into the wall. It crash-landed this time, cockeyed and lopsided, on the Welsh dresser which contained the meagre oddments of crockery which the landlord

16

provided for his tenants' use. As luck would have it a large willow-pattern dish toppled, caught the bird another stunning blow, and they descended to the floor where the plate broke dramatically in two pieces. The pigeon lay ominously still.

'It's dead!' Nicola said. She might not like birds, but she would never have harmed one. 'Poor thing, it only wanted to get out and we've gone and killed it.'

However, she was not afraid of dead birds, or at least she did not think she was; she often had roast chicken when it was on the menu.

'Pick it up and put it through the window,' Ceri advised. 'I'll get the bottom pane up.'

Nicola would have liked to raise the window and let Ceri deal with the bird but the younger girl was already tugging at the sash so she went cautiously over to where the pigeon lay with its little pink claws curled and its eyelids closed, looking totally harmless, even pathetic. She picked it up, feeling the warmth of it and a horrid, squelchy softness. She held it rather firmly just in case it suddenly came to life and flew in her face, flapping its disgusting wings and digging at her with its beastly little claws, but it remained supine in her grasp.

'Push it through the gap,' Ceri recommended, scarlet-faced, for the window was stiff and had only moved up about four inches. 'Can you get it through?'

Nicola, now shaking like a leaf in a gale, dumbly shook her head. She felt it would be unwise to open her mouth. The pigeon might be a bit large to seek shelter therein but she knew ill animals crawled into dark holes to die; she had no wish to find the pigeon trying to cram its way between her teeth.

'You can't? Oh, hang on, then.' Ceri released the right-hand side of the window and began to struggle with the other side. It moved up a bit. 'Will that do?'

'Not wide enough,' Nicola muttered through clenched teeth. Ceri struggled, panting, to get it wider and managed another inch or so.

'That's it,' she announced crossly. 'Shove it through or it'll stay here for ever.'

Obediently Nicola began to shove the fat and feathered body through the gap. It was half out when she felt it begin to struggle and to her horror the eyes opened, fixing themselves with what looked like beady pleading on her face. So

17

must an axe-murderer's victim look at the axe seconds before it descends.

Revulsion gives one strength. Nicola remembered she was touching a live bird – ugh, ugh! – and pushed harder, skinning her knuckles, but the bird was out, it was on the wing, making off in the direction of the yacht marina, unable to scream murder and mayhem but doing the best it could with a series of sore-throated, passionate coos.

Ceri let the window descend again and flopped against the draining board. The rich colour faded from her face and she smiled at Nicola.

'There you go, you got rid of him,' she said cheerfully. 'I wonder if we ought to close the top of the window in future and leave the bottom bit open? Imagine coming back here and finding a whole family in here!'

'I think we ought to keep the windows closed in future,' Nicola said with a strong shudder. She walked over to the sink and rinsed her hot and dirty hands. 'I can't think what I'd have done if I'd been here alone, and . . .' She turned from the sink and saw the state of the room. 'Oh, my God! And Mr Patani's coming to see . . .'

The front door bell rang even as they turned to look at the wreckage of the plates, the wet clothing festooned about the floor and the feathers, still floating.

Ceri sighed and headed across the kitchen.

'It's him, it's bound to be,' she said. 'Just shove everything out of sight; he only wants to see the larder.'

Ceri left, closing the kitchen door behind her.

Nicola began frenziedly tidying. Plates, broken and whole, were jammed into cupboards. Clothing was squeezed, wet as it was, into the fridge. Feathers were clutched in Nicola's damp hand. She was stretching up and trying to straighten out the clothes pulley, which was threatening to spill its remaining clothing over the cleared floor, when the door opened and Ceri ushered a man into the room.

Nicola had not met Mr Patani since it had been Ceri who had taken the flat, but she had heard a good deal about him. Ceri had been a tenant in another building owned by Mr Patani and knew him better, she had said darkly, than she liked. In view of his proclivities, for he was not known as Gilbert the Grope for nothing, Nicola thought it was noble of Ceri to engage him in chat for so long, so she smiled winningly at the man who came into the kitchen, talking over his shoulder to Ceri as he did so.

'So you see, dear Ceri, that in matters of . . .' He broke off with a well-simulated start and headed for Nicola, both hands outstretched, a wall-to-wall smile bisecting his coffee-coloured countenance. 'Ah, now I meet my other tenant, the charming Miss Wharton . . . I am enchanting, my dear young lady, enchanting!'

Nicola had reverted to her maiden name after Roger and she had split up, so now she allowed her hands to be seized and smiled too, though guardedly. But Mr Patani was quite a surprise since she had got the impression from Ceri that he was a Shylock-type person, mean, treacherous and two-faced, as well as an inveterate grabber of young women. Yet he was an extremely handsome man and young, too, probably in his early thirties, not at all the typical Pakistani landlord she had envisaged.

'You aren't enchanting, Mr Patani, you're *enchanted*,' Ceri pointed out righteously, but this only drew a broader smile, a more roguish glance.

'Ah, how you tease me, Ceri! Now, Nicola, to my tenants I am Gilbert, for we are to be friends. I shall call you Nicola, you see.'

Nicola, hands still held captive, tried unobtrusively pulling; Gilbert Patani retained his grip. Nicola was just beginning to wonder whether they would stand there all night, grinning like idiots and hand-fasted like lovers, when Ceri put her spoke in.

'Now, Gilbert, about these mice . . .'

In order to pantomime distress, disbelief and concern, the landlord released Nicola's hands and Nicola hastily shoved them into the pockets of her skirt. What with pigeons and landlords, her hands were having quite an eventful hour! Then she turned back to Mr Patani.

'. . . Never before in my years of owning this property has anyone complained of a mice,' Mr Patani was assuring them. 'You say you see a mice . . . you are young girls alone, vegetarians perhaps, you have imagined a mice.'

It was tempting to wonder why a vegetarian should imagine a mouse more easily than a carnivore, but Ceri clearly knew a red herring when she saw one.

'We've both seen mice,' she said firmly, 'there are signs all

19

over the place.' She flung open the larder door and pointed dramatically to the lowest shelf. 'See?'

Mr Patani edged forward, peering. All over the lowest shelf unmistakable signs of mouse-occupancy were scattered. The landlord touched, clucked. Then he straightened, the huge smile firmly in place once more.

'That is caused by the damp,' he assured his doubting tenants. 'It is brown rice . . . the tenant before you was also vegetarian, very fond of brown rice . . . see, the damp causes the rice to darken, even to swell a little . . . not that it is damp as such, my properties are never damp, it is condensation, that is all.' Mr Patani chuckled richly, sweeping the mouse droppings neatly off the shelf and into the palm of one lean brown hand. 'Now we'll throw it away . . .' he crossed the kitchen and threw the mouse-droppings out of the window with a swift, underarm bowling action, 'And you will worry no more, eh?'

Nicola shook her head, hoping that the back garden of Lavengro was untenanted right now, save for pigeons. That would be justice, if a pigeon got the mouse droppings.

'. . . and tomorrow I shall send my sister-in-law, a good woman, to make sure there is no more rice and to block up any little holes . . . not that there is mices on my property, but we cannot be too careful, eh, girls?'

Nicola mumbled something but Ceri spoke up, determined that Gilbert should not have a total victory.

'It's good of you, Gilbert, to block the holes so that brown rice can't sneak back into the larder. I wonder if they sell brown rice traps?'

But landlords are not so easily put down.

'Don't worry, Ceri, my sister-in-law will make all right. I'll see you another day, girls. My property will never lack for repair, never shall a tenant's wishes be ignored. It is in my best interests to keep my property in good repair, so that my tenants are happy peoples.'

The 'happy peoples' stared disbelievingly at each other as Gilbert's footsteps clattered down the stairs.

'Brown rice,' Ceri said wonderingly. 'Does he think we're mad, or is it him? I just hope he doesn't try to charge us for his sister-in-law's shit-shovelling, because that I won't take.'

'Brown-rice-shovelling, you mean,' Nicola said, beginning

20

to remove the china – broken and whole – from the cupboards. 'I say, that bird broke our only meat-dish.'

'We'll stick it with glue and put it on the top shelf and swear we've never used it, which is true as I'm standing here,' Ceri said with relish. 'Damn the man, he always seems to win . . . Oh lord, look at the time, and we haven't even started to cook a meal.'

'Some of this washing's dirty again,' Nicola said, pulling the wet clothes out of the fridge. 'What a weird bloke Gilbert is – you never said he was quite dishy.'

'He isn't. Smooth, perhaps, and slimy, but most definitely not dishy. He came to see a leak in the ceiling at my bedsit in Cloister Row and I climbed the stepladder because he pretended he couldn't see the huge damp patch and next thing I knew he was on the ladder too with his hands in unwanted places. I couldn't kick or jump in case I fell fathoms onto the floor, and he maintained he was helping me keep my balance . . . Oh, it was horrible! All I could think of was the drawers I was wearing – I just sort of *knew* it was the old holey ones with the weak elastic – and of course in the end I willingly agreed the leak was just my imagination so that I could get down the ladder as pure as I went up it.'

'I'd die if that happened to me,' Nicola said with conviction. 'Look, it's a bit late to cook a meal, shall we get a takeaway? There's Chinese or Indian, or we could have fish and chips, if you'd rather.'

'Let's have Chinese – I just fancy sweet and sour pork and masses of flied lice,' Ceri said brightly. 'By the way, you know the chap who had this flat before us? I don't believe he's a veggie.'

'I wouldn't know. I've not been in Haisby long enough to know anyone much.'

'Of course, I was forgetting. Well, Henry and I followed one another around, you could say. First he had a room near mine in the Cloister Row house and then he moved into this flat, and now he's living in upper Haisby. He and his partner have bought an old hotel right at the top of this road. I've got to go up there tomorrow, to the new *Chronicle* offices, to see old Mullins. I've a good mind to pop over and ask Henry if he's really a vegetarian.'

'Why should Patani lie, though? It seems a silly thing to do.'

'Nature of the beast,' Ceri said cheerfully, hooking her coat off the back of the door. 'Shall we both go? If so we'll walk, but if I've got to go alone I'll bike.'

The bike lived downstairs, in the tiny square of hall on the ground floor. Nicola couldn't help thinking wistfully of the terraced house she'd left behind in Norwich, of Roger hopping into the car and roaring up Kett's Hill to the Heartsease roundabout, where the fish and chip shop specialised in fresh-caught skate and never used old fat to fry the chips. She could have stayed there, she supposed, had it not been for the shame – everyone knew Roger had been having an affair with Milly Coppack except for Nicola herself. And anyway, Roger had cheated by simply moving Milly in whilst Nicola was staying with her parents and trying to come to terms with the break-up of what she had supposed to be a successful marriage. When she got back and found Milly there it had seemed simpler to gather up the shreds of her pride and go. Move right away. She had answered the advertisement for a secretary to an accountant in Haisby, moved into a guesthouse a week later, and started looking for a flat-share after her first week with Gregory Paulett.

I never appreciated how comfortable married life was, compared to being a single girl, Nicola thought now. Before, I lived at home with Mum and Dad and had the use of the car and lots of friends and a whole past all of my own which I never even thought about. Then I met Roger and we married and I came from Acle to Norwich to live, and I made another life for us both. There were two of us for everything, dinner parties, tennis or squash, two of us to eat a meal, two of us in bed. And now? Ceri would be a good friend, but she had a social life which she would not think it necessary to share with Nicola. And right now, it was chilly and dusk was falling fast, and someone had to get a meal.

'We'll both go, then we can choose a dish each,' Nicola decided. 'It's not far to the Chinese, is it?'

'No, not far. Just down the road, over the swing bridge and onto Lord Street. It's on the prom at the far end, it'll be quite a pleasant walk.'

It was a pleasant walk, once they had grown used to the windy dusk, and by an odd coincidence they met Henry and his partner as they went up Lord Street. Ceri hailed them since

Nicola had never met either man before, and introduced them.

'Henry, Keith, this is my new flatmate. Nicola, that's Henry Johnson and the other one's Keith Fell.'

Nicola murmured her greetings, eyeing the two men covertly as she did so. Henry was middle-aged and ordinary, Keith Fell young and handsome. But Roger had also been – was, presumably – good-looking, so in future Nicola intended to go for character. And anyway I'm right off men, she reminded herself. Ceri, however, having observed the conventions, came out with the question she was plainly bursting to ask.

'Henry, were there mice in the flat at Lavengro when you had it and are you a vegetarian?'

'Umm . . . there *were* mice until I got Solomon. And neither Solomon nor myself is vegetarian. Why do you ask? What's Gilbert been up to this time?'

'Oh, he swore there were no mice and said the previous tenant was a vegetarian who had left some brown rice behind. Of course we knew they were really mouse-droppings and I'm sure he knew . . . and knew *we* knew, what's more, but you know what he's like.'

'None better,' agreed Henry, whilst the younger man stared from face to face, clearly both fascinated and baffled by the unusual turn the conversation had taken. 'So what are you doing about the mice? Because if you leave it to Gilbert . . .'

'He's sending his sister-in-law in,' Ceri said gloomily. 'I say, what was Solomon? Not a cat, surely? Because Gilbert said we couldn't have pets.'

'Solomon is still a cat,' Henry said cheerfully. 'I told Patani that if he could get rid of the mice then I'd get rid of the cat. Not another word out of him . . . and no more mice, either.'

'Where is he now? Solomon, I mean,' Ceri said, for all the world, Nicola thought, as though she expected Henry to pull the cat out of his pocket. 'Could we borrow him, do you think?'

Henry laughed, but shook his head.

'No, sorry. I left him with Norrington & Frazer, the vets, whilst we moved in but we're fetching him tomorrow, and it wouldn't do to confuse him by letting him go back to Lavengro. Tell you what, though, I got him from the vet in the first place, they get strays brought in, so just have a word with John Norrington.'

'Well, we could,' Ceri said. 'Only I'm not sure we'd be good cat-owners, we're out so much. Still, we'll think about it – you don't suppose the vets would *lend* us a cat? Just until the mice were all eaten?'

'Cats keep mice at bay whilst they're in residence, they aren't really a magic cure-all,' Henry observed. 'Otherwise it's poison – or traps.'

Ceri shuddered and turned back towards Nicola, who shook her head violently at both the latter suggestions. She had never been shy before, but found now that she needed time with people before she could be natural. It was as though Milly had stolen not only Nicola's husband but also her self-confidence. Once she had taken her effect on the opposite sex for granted, but not any more. If Roger could find her anathema then so could any man.

Ceri laughed at Nicola's expression, then turned back to the two men.

'No, neither of us approve of poison or traps, it'll have to be something else,' she observed. 'Thanks for your help, Henry. See you!'

Making their way along the promenade presently, to what Nicola thought of as 'the chippy end', where in the season the seafood stalls would have queues and the amusement arcades would buzz with people, the two girls discussed the pros and cons of getting a cat, how they would deal with Mr Patani's sister-in-law if she ever arrived, and whether there was a mouse-repellent on the market, which seemed to Ceri to be quite possible, though Nicola was more doubtful.

'Well, I don't think we want to actually keep a cat,' Ceri said at last, when they were warmly ensconced in the Slow Boat, sitting on a comfortable upholstered bench and waiting for their order. 'But I wouldn't mind a sort of permanent kid-napping situation – we'd nick a cat each night off the street and let it free again before we went to work in the morning.'

'That's theft! And, it's daft,' Nicola said. 'I longed for a dog when I was little, even recently I thought . . . but the trouble is we're not allowed to keep any animal at all. I'd hate to get on the wrong side of Mr Patani and risk being slung out on our ears. Why don't you want a cat, though? You don't strike me as the nervy type!'

24

'I'm too young for the responsibility,' Ceri said. She sounded serious. 'I'm only twenty and I'm still trying to fight my way up in the newspaper world, that takes me all my time and energy, I don't have any left over for a cat.'

'Does a cat take so much energy and time?' Nicola queried. 'I'd have thought it was relatively easy to keep a cat. Now a dog is demanding, I grant you. Besides, a dog really would be out of the question in a flat.'

But Ceri thought it immaterial which type of animal was in question. To her, a responsibility was a responsibility.

'I know dogs need taking for walks and cats don't, but cats wander, and we'd never have an easy moment, wondering whether it was crossing Harbour Hill and being pancaked,' she explained. 'Cats have tiny brains, they simply can't see danger. Oh no, I'm not giving my heart to a cat to tear. That's a quotation,' she added, as Nicola raised her eyebrows. 'It's Kipling . . . *oh brothers and sisters, I bid you beware, of giving your heart to a dog to tear.*'

'You said dog that time,' Nicola pointed out. She knew she had recognized the quotation but, distorted by Ceri's rendering, she had been unable to pin it down.

Ceri scowled.

'So what? Dogs or cats, whichever. You'd still cry buckets when you saw it being used as a frisbee.'

'But cats are quite sensible, really they are. Not when they're kittens, I suppose, but a mature cat can be quite clever about roads and things. Besides, why ever should it go onto the road when it's got loads of gardens to play in? I'm not saying I'm in favour, but I really don't like mice. They're a health hazard.'

'Mm. Well, we'll think about it,' Ceri said, just as the little Chinese girl popped out from the kitchens, saying brightly, 'Two king prawn swee' an' sour, two fried rice . . . ?' and gazing hopefully at them. 'Yes, that's us.'

Later, walking back up the road with their little brown carrier bag full of delicious food, Ceri began to sing beneath her breath. Nicola, listening, sighed and then smiled. Her flatmate was incorrigible. Yet there was an endearing warmth about her . . .

Sharing accommodation is always a risky business and Nicola had been doubtful, at first, about sharing with someone as ebullient as Ceri. But suddenly, she was sure she had done the right thing. The two of them would muddle along and become real friends in the process. She shook her head at Ceri, who promptly began to sing louder.

'Oh mummy dear, what is that mess
That looks like strawberry jam?'
'Hush hush, my child, it is papa,
Run over by a tram.'

Chapter Three

The question of whether or not to keep a cat had still not been settled next morning, when Nicola and Ceri set off at high speed for their respective places of work.

Usually they walked together into town but today, because Ceri was going to the newspaper headquarters and not to the reporters' office, they parted at the gate.

It was not far from Lavengro to the *Chronicle* offices but Ceri took her bicycle anyway. She wanted to go straight to Queen Street after seeing Mr Mullins so she would need her bike and besides, Cambridge people are as at home aboard a bike as others are in cars. Ceri, a true child of Cambridge, rarely went anywhere on foot.

Accordingly, she mounted the bike, glancing down at herself as she did so. Green anorak, charcoal grey skirt, black shoes. She could not see her white blouse or grey cardigan, but she hoped they made her look what she was – a businesslike reporter, a proper little Lois Lane.

However, there were times when Ceri doubted her ability to rise in the world of newspapers. It sometimes seemed that she would spend her whole life struggling to make her mark at the *Chronicle*, which left little time for Fleet Street as a pathway to the stars. Of late she had been seriously considering trying to get into local radio with a view, one day, to joining a television news team.

There's only one Kate Adie, Ceri told herself now, but there must be lots of minor roles. Surely it was possible for someone as dedicated as herself to get a job on radio or telly, in a purely background capacity of course? Ceri had no illusions about her looks, it was her news-getting abilities in which she had faith.

At this point in her reflections Ceri saw a gap in the traffic coming from her right. She hurried across the road, dodging a maniacal motorcyclist and a couple of delivery vans, and gained the further shore. Here, she mounted her bike once more and urged her trusty steed to greater effort by standing up in the stirrups – pedals – and cycling hard until the slope of Harbour Hill became really steep, when she had to stop daydreaming and slog.

Trust Mr Mullins to choose to get me out here on a day when I'd planned to be in town, Ceri thought as she bent over her handlebars. The estate was on the left, and as yet it consisted only of the very modern newspaper offices, a small printing works, a paper recycling firm and a group of grubby little garages where a number of mechanics spent their time hammering things and eating sandwiches. Or that was what it looked like, but Ceri was a friendly girl and shouted to them as she cycled past.

'Morning, all! Hello, Sid, got me a car yet?'

Once or twice she had arranged advertising for one of the garages and consequently was on first-name terms with the owners. Several of them were looking for a suitable car, which showed optimism since Ceri had very little money and would be on the doorstep of anyone who sold her a bad 'un.

'I've sin a likely motor,' Sid growled. He waved a half-eaten sandwich at her. 'Come you down later, gal, and I'll tell you woss on offer.'

Ceri agreed to see him later and shot past the front of his garage and down the side of the *Chronicle* offices, where she left her bicycle and hurried into the foyer.

It was an imposing place. There were a great many potted palms and ferns, a number of large and squashy armchairs upholstered in cream-coloured leather, and low tables scattered with copies of the wildlife and high life magazines produced by the group.

However, all that interested Ceri right now was how soon she could get the interview with Mr Mullins over so that she might return to Queen Street. There was a court case due to start today which might well prove to be both juicy and interesting and Ceri, uneasily aware that in some respects she was much too naïve for a newspaper reporter, was relying on the case to . . . well, to *worldify* her a little. The only child of ageing parents, one of them a Cambridge don, is seldom as experienced as her contemporaries and Ceri was trying very hard to remedy this lack. But knowing her luck, some already worldly reporter would bag the court case first and she'd be left out in the cold, to deal with weddings, funerals or the trials and tribulations of the pier theatre, which was annually threatened with closure and annually saved by either philanthropy or ego, depending on whether a townsperson or a theatrical plunged a hand into a pocket.

Ceri headed for the lift; it was all very well to go on about using the stairs for one's health's sake, but people who said that hadn't just bicycled miles and miles, with their hearts banging and their knees going like the coupling bar on a steam-train.

Ceri was not at ease in lifts, having sufficient imagination to see herself trapped but not enough to envisage an escape-route. So she stood, eyes raised worshipfully to the indicator board as the arrow sped upward . . . first floor, second, third . . . top.

Despite her fears, the lift opened, revealing the doors which hid not only Mr Mullins but also a great many staff – up here the tele-ad girls reigned supreme, gossiping, bickering, phoning their friends when times were slack, clocking up huge sums in advertising revenue, planning new methods of persuading Joe Public to eat at Bloggs', or buy at Figgs'.

Poor souls, Ceri thought indulgently, walking past the doors which led to Sin City, as she called tele-sales. Thank God I'm not cooped up there five days a week, I'd go mad! She strode forward and knocked on Mr Mullins's door.

'I'd rather leave!'

Ceri glared across the desk at her boss. Mr Mullins, usually a mild sort of man (Who would have guessed, Ceri thought in wild parentheses, that mild-mannered Mr Mullins was really Superman?), glared right back.

'What makes you think you're any different from the other girls, Miss Allen? I warned you months ago that we didn't really need another reporter, we were keener to recruit tele-sales staff, but you said you needed experience and . . . well, anyway, matters have come to a head. Our cash-flow situation is such that I can no longer allow this state of affairs to continue. We're short of at least six people in tele-sales and I've no choice but to insist that you work there from today. However, if you choose to leave . . .'

'But I'd go mad shut in that place all day,' Ceri said, jerking a disdainful thumb towards the wall which separated Mr

Mullins from tele-sales. 'What about the woman's page? I could work for them, though I'm sure I don't know how the guys will manage without me.'

'My staff will manage very well, I expect,' Mr Mullins said acidly. 'And to be honest, Ceri, I'm not sure you're woman's page material. Certainly Louisa Foster doesn't think so and she's the expert.'

'She's your daughter,' Ceri snapped, casting caution to the four winds and quite enjoying the surge of adrenalin which followed. 'She knows all about clothes, I grant you, but nothing whatever about anything else! She goes on and on about hemlines and how to make butterscotch cream for that special party, but she never reviews a book, or comments on current affairs, or . . .'

Mr Mullins's mildness had long fled; his eyes seemed to crawl closer and his mouth tightened into a rat-trap, then opened as wide as a pillar-box. The butterscotch cream had been a blow beneath the belt, Ceri knew, since the recipe had lacked a vital ingredient and for weeks afterwards Louisa had fielded, in her mail bag, scores of complaints from those whose cookers would never recover from the quatermass properties of the butterscotch.

'That is untrue, Miss Allen! I agree that Louisa is my daughter, and very proud of her I am, very proud, but our relationship has never influenced me in my dealings with her. She's a gifted journalist, gifted! I tell everyone how lucky we are to have her, but we shan't keep her long! She'll be off to Fleet Street and the nationals – she would have gone long ago but she'd feel she was letting me down. So don't you forget it, young lady.'

'If she goes, then I could do the woman's page,' Ceri said brightly. 'Not that she will, of course. You may think I'm not woman's page material, Mr Mullins, but I *know* that your daughter will never make Fleet Street.'

She had made a lightning decision. She would be so rude that Mr Mullins would sack her, and then she could claim unfair dismissal, the dole, all sorts of options reared their heads. Because she knew she could never admit to her parents that she was no longer the ace-reporter – or the budding ace-reporter – they loved, but a mere salesgirl. Father had been so good over having produced an unscholarly child, a dimwit, in fact. But he had wanted her just to have a shot

30

at university, he was even willing to see her waste her talents on red-brick. Only her desperate insistence that what a newspaper reporter wants is experience had reconciled him to a child who left school at eighteen with low-grade A levels, one in English but the other, shame shame, in art!

If Mr Mullins sacks me, Ceri thought craftily, and I get the dole, then no one need know I'm not still a reporter . . . Cambridge is a long way off and Mother and Father won't come and visit me until the summer vacation and by then I'm bound to have come up with something better. She stared challengingly at Mr Mullins therefore, and waited for the blast.

But Mr Mullins seemed to have some idea of what she was up to; he started to swell, toadlike, then suddenly deflated and almost smiled at her.

'You may have a point,' he conceded. 'Fleet Street isn't exactly falling over to employ folk from the provinces, not even editors.'

'No . . . well . . .' Ceri said awkwardly. She liked the opposition to crumble but she did not want to have to feel sorry for it; the grapevine had recently buzzed with the news that Mr Mullins had been applying for jobs elsewhere. 'Look, Mr Mullins, I'd be no good in tele-sales, I'm not cut out to sell things to people. Let me stay with the reporters, please! I'll work ever so hard, I'll prove I can do it, I'll . . .'

'You'll have a go at tele-sales,' Mr Mullins finished for her, falsely smiling. 'Be honest, Ceri, you can't afford to turn the job down and the pay's good – better than you were getting in the newsroom.'

Were getting! Ceri could have wept, but provided she was still earning she could keep the bad news to herself. Wild thoughts of freelancing for the *Guardian* or the *T.L.S.* freewheeled through her mind. Father's beaming face, Mother's bright, secret smile . . . but it was the stuff of dreams, not reality. What was more factual, if she just handed in her notice she would be in no position to pay her half of the rent, and she did like the flat. It was not exactly a luxury apartment, but her previous home had had what Mr Patani euphemistically called 'shared facilities', which meant one kitchen and one bathroom between ten, and the loo had been in the bathroom. Many a day a desperate Ceri had trodden the boards, creaking up and down the dark landing outside the bathroom,

31

begging her fellow-tenant to get a move on. After discovering that the men simply piddled out of the window or into an empty bottle, she did buy a large white enamel bowl with a blue rim, but she didn't enjoy using it and was relieved in more ways than one when Henry told her his flat on Harbour Hill was up for grabs, and even more relieved when Nicola had answered her desperate plea for a flatmate and had turned out to be all right, so far.

'Well, Ceri? What's it to be? I'm waiting.'

'I'll have a go at tele-sales,' Ceri said grudgingly. 'But if they need someone in the newsroom, sir, could I be considered before they advertise the job?'

'I'll see what I can do,' Mr Mullins said.

Ceri, thanking him and leaving the room to go next door and speak to Karen Poole, a brisk, hard-faced blonde whose unenviable job it was to hire and fire for tele-sales, could understand his reluctance to commit himself, much though she deprecated it. It was very hard to fill tele-sales vacancies despite the good money because it was such a devilish job. But you only had to mention the word 'reporter', and everyone was lining up to have a go.

Including me, mug that I was, Ceri told herself as she opened the door and walked into the long room filled with telephones and girls. Karen was at the far end, in a glass cubicle. It was said she never took her eyes off her staff and had such long ears that a telephone call which was beginning to sound friendly as well as good business meant her immediate arrival on the scene with a telling-off for the sales girl concerned.

Karen stood up as Ceri made her way between the desks. She might appear to be a pretty woman, Ceri supposed disdainfully, trying not to stare at the peroxide hair and false eyelashes, to say nothing of the amount of scarlet, shiny lipstick Karen wore. Karen looked like a good-time girl, whereas everyone in tele-sales knew her for the tale-bearing, fault-finding liar that she was.

'Ah, Ceri.' No greeting, no attempt at friendliness, Ceri noted sourly. 'You'll be with Bettina for a week, she'll make sure you understand the drill. She's at the far end of the room, beside the empty desk. Bettina will start you off and you'll get some proper training next week, if we can spare you by then.'

'Okay,' Ceri muttered shortly. She turned and began to walk the length of the room, determined not to show the yawning sense of misery which had engulfed her. She would not stay here! It was March now and unemployment was rife but when the season started she would find something to do which wouldn't turn Father's hair white over night, even if it wasn't newspaper reporting!

'It's beginning to look all right, wouldn't you say?'

Keith stood back and gazed around him, then turned an interrogative glance on Henry. The two men were standing in the television lounge looking at the furniture which they had just rearranged on the new carpet.

'It's marvellous,' Henry admitted. 'You've got quite a flair for interior decoration, old lad.'

Keith smiled modestly at the huge, old-fashioned sofa, so much too large for a modern house that Archie had got it from the salerooms for a song.

'Yes, I've always been keen on furniture. If you choose something old but good you won't go far wrong. We were lucky that we needed big stuff, which isn't fashionable.' He moved a chair shaped like a huge cockleshell a fraction to the right. 'Luckier that Archie managed to lay his hands on some plain carpeting – nothing looks better. And since we're admiring our handiwork, let me congratulate you on your paper-hanging. This room looks professional, and I do love that shade of paint.'

'Hint of peach,' Henry said. 'It's warmer than plain white and more unusual than cream.'

'It's perfect in here. Now tomorrow's Saturday, we've toiled like two *slaves*, Henry, and we deserve a break. How about taking a look at that hotel in Yarmouth which offers sailing lessons? I'd like to see what boats they use, and later we could eat out . . . does that appeal?'

'It does,' Henry admitted. He was really beginning to enjoy his new life, even to believe that the new life would prove, in the long run, preferable to his previous existence. He could see that he was his own man in a way he had never been before and he liked it.

'Right. Then who'll drive, you or me?'

'Me,' Henry said at once, for Keith was a dashing rather than a decorous driver and the old Sunbeam Talbot which

33

they shared was the pride of Henry's heart. 'Unless you'd like to?'

Keith smiled and patted his arm. He was looking tousled today, with several large smuts adorning his countenance. Henry sometimes daydreamed that one day Keith might take a shine to a girl and become as heterosexual as Henry himself, but it seemed unlikely – Keith was so very pretty!

'No, Henry, you drive. Then I can have a teeny g and t, whereas you'll have to be a good boy.'

'It's worth not drinking, to drive the dear old Sunbeam,' Henry said, ignoring Keith's flirtatious tone. He reckoned the bloke couldn't help it, it was a part of him. 'And whilst we eat, we can discuss what sort of craft to buy.'

'Lovely,' Keith said breathlessly. 'What about a bit of a do to celebrate once we're ready to roll?'

'Why not? Though God knows who we'll ask!'

'We've loads of pals,' Keith said. 'That's the nice thing about a small town, we all know each other.'

'True, but we mustn't overdo it,' Henry agreed. 'And now we must tackle the bedrooms, there are ten doubles with no beds in 'em . . . Back to Archie? Or do you feel that second-hand beds . . .'

'My dear chap, if it was bedding I'd agree that we needed to be careful, but beds . . .'

The two men left the room and began to climb the flight of shallow, curving stairs.

Chapter Four

When the weekend came Ceri, who had spent the week in tele-sales, woke up on Saturday morning and saw that the sun was shining. It did not shine in her heart.

Misery, thy name is Ceri Allen, she said to herself as she climbed out of bed. Be thankful for the sunshine.

Right now, however, the sunshine only seemed to bring her unhappiness into glaring prominence. It might light up the distant marina, shining on the yachts' masts, on the water, on the wings of the gulls swooping casually overhead, but it could only marginally lessen her gloom. She had been so pleased when she had got the reporting job, her parents had been so proud when she had told them about it. All their disappointment over her inability to gain a university place, all Father's bewilderment over his daughter's lack of academic brilliance had dissipated beneath the warmth of her excitement. My daughter's a press reporter, our girl's gone into journalism . . . they were two of the expressions suddenly very much on the lips of Mr and Mrs Godfrey Allen. Ceri's father knew she would do well. He was even glad it meant she must leave home, because he believed in young people making their way in the world at an early age. Of course if she had managed to get to university – but to be a newspaper reporter, at eighteen . . . ah, that really was something!

And Ceri loved them so, admired them so! To disappoint them, to have to admit she had not been up to the job . . . it was unthinkable. She loved Cambridge, had vowed to return there as a successful journalist, one day. She certainly did not intend to go back as a tele-sales girl, no matter how well paid. Father thought money was nothing compared with job satisfaction . . . she would never tell them what had happened. And it was not going to be easy to face other people. It was all very well saying that the *Chronicle* had made her redundant, but

35

who would believe her? They would all assume that she had been demoted as not quite good enough and, frankly, she could not blame them. It's what I'd think, Ceri told herself unhappily, even though I know Mr Mullins sent me to tele-sales because they were short-staffed.

Still, the money was very much better in tele-sales, Ceri thought now, clutching the loaf to her bosom and slicing uneven chunks off it. She had already earned quite a large bonus despite her dislike for her work. And in a way, she supposed, it was a challenge. Having to put on a sugary voice and be nice to people you really hated, having to kowtow to supervisors and trainers, all this was distasteful to a Free Spirit, like Ceri Allen. But . . . she would be able to keep the flat, and her secret, too.

Not that anything could make up for the misery of losing her job. She had adored being a reporter. Nothing had pleased her more than the announcement: 'Press!' and the writing itself had been marvellous. Choosing the right words, making a fairly ordinary experience into something exciting and newsworthy – it had all been such *fun*, and totally different from sitting at a telephone correcting someone's English and working out costs.

They wouldn't even let her invent a nice 'In memoriam' for a client who kept getting halfway through a dreadful little poem and then bursting into tears. Ceri had the neatest ending all prepared, when her supervisor had glanced over Ceri's shoulder and nearly had a fit.

'They don't write the poems themselves, stupid,' she said crossly, when Ceri tried to explain that she was helping the bereaved. 'They're all standardised. It ends *never never more to part* whether you like it or not.'

'But it doesn't rhyme,' Ceri pointed out. 'And it didn't sound like that at all.'

But Bettina wouldn't discuss, far less argue. She had simply waited until Ceri had finished off the four-line piece as she had been told, and then moved on.

The only advantage, really, was that she was not actually obliged to tell anyone that she was no longer reporting. She didn't even have to tell lies to her parents, she just didn't tell them the whole truth.

But I'm living a lie, Ceri reminded herself, staring unseeingly out across the patch of weedy grass to the gleaming waters of the harbour. I'm letting people believe I'm a reporter, when all I am is a salesgirl.

Even Nicola believed it. That was to say, she thought that when Ceri said 'work' she meant the newsroom in Queen Street. I'll tell everyone when I'm sure there's no chance of getting back into reporting, Ceri told herself now, rescuing burning toast from under the grill. First I'll tell Father and Mother; she envisaged the Georgian house in its neat garden, the cedar tree casting its shade – and a good many tiny pine needles – over the side lawn, the magnolia lording it in the front. They would sit her down in the living-room with piping hot China tea and crisp wholemeal toast, well buttered. And she would talk about Haisby and her life there, and Father would smile into the fire and every now and then shoot her a proud and loving glance . . . Oh God, I can't possibly tell them, not now, not ever. But I'll tell Nicola. Not that she tells me much, her thoughts continued, because she jolly well doesn't. She had asked Nicola where she worked before she came to Haisby and it had been like getting blood out of a stone.

'Norwich,' Nicola had said shortly, not looking up from the newspaper she was reading.

'Oh? Whereabouts?'

'Prince of Wales Road.'

'Oh? Who for?'

There was a perceptible pause, this time, before Nicola said, 'A firm of advertising agents.'

'Which one?' Ceri said baldly. At the time she had felt quite cross with Nicola; she kept no secrets herself, so why should her flatmate be so . . . so buttoned up?

Nicola looked up from her paper.

'Why? I mean, it's past, so what does it matter?'

Put like that, Ceri had to think quickly for a logical reply, otherwise she would have had to admit to being nosy, and no one likes to be thought that.

'Umm . . . I just wondered because the obvious next move up the ladder, for me, would be the Eastern Counties Group. Did you have many dealings with them?'

'Yes, quite a few.' Nicola put her paper down and stood up. 'Want a hand with the washing up?'

It was like that whenever Ceri tried to get through the barrier which Nicola had erected round herself; just about impossible to find anything out about Nicola without seeming rude and pushy. And though I'm probably both, Ceri thought defiantly, I don't want to *seem* either. Nicola's such a beautiful girl, too, so she can't have a dreadful secret. But there's something . . .

Whatever it was, though, Nicola plainly did not intend to confide in her flatmate. Which means, Ceri told herself now, trying to scrape toast quietly, that if I don't want to tell her about my job then I jolly well don't have to. But whatever could Nicola have to hide? A career in crime? Or perhaps she had been a high-class prostitute in Norwich and had come to Haisby to put her past behind her and find a rich husband.

But Ceri knew that was just romancing, because if there was one thing which had struck her at once upon meeting Nicola it was her air of innocence. She's twenty-four years old and I don't believe she's had a boyfriend, Ceri told herself now. It was almost unbelievable, for someone so lovely, but she had seen how Nicola behaved with men, and it was as though she wanted to crawl under a stone and hide. She looks so sophisticated, Ceri thought wonderingly, yet she's got no self-confidence at all!

The kettle boiled so Ceri made herself a cup of instant coffee, spread butter on the scraped toast and sat on the table to eat. She saw Nicola in her mind as she saw her every day. Long, primrose-coloured hair, clear blue eyes, flawless skin carefully made up, and that air of deceptive fragility which, Ceri supposed, would make men want to cherish her.

She must know she's beautiful, Ceri reasoned, so why doesn't she use her looks? I would, if I had them!

But conjecture was useless, and so was endeavouring to enjoy toast burnt to a crisp. Ceri abandoned her meal and padded into the living room. She swished back the curtains and sunshine flooded into the room.

Outside, the road looked unusually busy. There was a chapel opposite, and judging from the number of well-dressed people hanging about outside, a wedding was about to take place. Like most women, Ceri adored a wedding. She leaned on the sill, squinting sideways, trying to see whether she could pick out the groom, whether the bridesmaids had arrived yet. I ought to go down, she told herself now, as the party of people disappeared into the chapel. Suppose I have to do the wedding report on Monday, then I'll wish I'd gone down so I could describe the dresses properly and . . .

The bubble burst. Ceri Allen, cub-reporter, shrank to Ceri Allen, tele-sales girl. The sunshine dimmed, the warmth of the morning turned chilly. Ceri padded back to her bedroom, conscious suddenly of the cold lino beneath her feet, the stale smell of burnt toast and an enormous reluctance to face the day.

But it was stupid to cower in the flat when outside the sun shone. Ceri reached for jeans and a shirt, and headed for the bathroom.

Because she felt miserable, Ceri abandoned the idea of surviving on toast and made herself a cooked breakfast. The smell brought Nicola out of her room, sniffing hopefully.

'Sausages! Gosh, and an egg . . . and tomatoes? What's got into you?'

'I'm hungry. This is breakfast and lunch . . . brunch,' Ceri explained rather unnecessarily.

Nicola, in a full-length pink nightie and the sort of negligée only film stars wear, came across the kitchen, trod in spilt fat, and swore as she slid into the table.

'Damn! You are careless, Ceri, I might have done more than stub my toe. Can you put an egg on for me? I never eat breakfast, but the smell's made me hungry.'

'Okay,' Ceri said easily. So far as was possible they combined resources to buy food, though mostly they got convenience food, pre-packed, pre-frozen, pre-cooked meals which only needed twenty minutes or so in a hot oven. But what Ceri called staples, eggs, milk, margarine and so on, were bought out of a common fund.

'Thanks. Shall I make coffee? Or tea?'

'Tea, I think, because I had coffee earlier. And we seem to have drunk most of the milk.' Ceri juggled more sausages into the pan. 'I'll cook you these, too.'

'Thanks. I'll get some milk later, when I go out.'

Nicola bustled round getting the teapot, warming it, finding teabags. Ceri watched her curiously.

'It's all right. I'm going out myself when I've eaten,' she said. 'That's a very glamorous outfit!'

Nicola, who had been humming to herself as she made the tea, cut her tune off short.

'Yes. Is there any stale bread? If so, we could fry it to go under our eggs.'

'There's a loaf in the bin. I find pyjamas more convenient for flat life, myself.' Ceri splashed hot fat over the eggs. 'They're warmer, and less embarrassing if you have to go to the door. Mind you, that lot's awfully pretty; honeymoon gear, I'd have thought.'

She glanced sideways at Nicola. As she watched, a pink flush gradually turning the pale skin to rose. But Nicola continued to pour water steadily into the teapot, then she turned her attention to the two white pottery mugs, carefully sharing out the milk left in the bottle.

'There's your tea. Shall we have it here or in the living room?'

'In here,' Ceri said. 'I'll serve up, shall I?'

'Might as well.' Nicola pushed a mug of tea towards Ceri and took one of the plates from her. 'My, this really looks good!'

'So it should. Nicola, there's something I've been meaning to ask you . . .'

Nicola, knife and fork poised over her plate, looked up. There was something in her expression, a sort of patient pain, which went straight to Ceri's soft heart.

'What?' was all Nicola said, but her tone was heavy with foreboding.

Ceri, with a million questions, all of them personal, on the tip of her tongue, swallowed hard.

'Oh, I wondered whether you'd rather have tea in the morning, or coffee? I usually make coffee if I'm up first, but I'd be happy with tea, if you'd rather.'

She watched as Nicola's expression softened, as the hurt, guarded look left her eyes.

'Oh . . . tea's just fine. And . . . I think you're right about pyjamas, they are more practical. I'll buy myself some as soon as I can afford it.'

For the rest of the meal the two girls chatted desultorily, Ceri carefully keeping her distance, Nicola seeming more relaxed. But it isn't easy to talk when wherever your eyes rest they fall on 'keep off' notices, and Ceri was glad when the meal ended with Nicola getting to her feet and going through to her room to change.

40

I was right, she thought as she washed and dried the dishes. There *is* a mystery there; not a very big one I don't suppose, but a mystery, nevertheless. And at some time in the past, Nicola has been very unhappy. Over something a lot more important than losing one job and getting another. I wonder if she was one of those brides left waiting at the church? That would account for that lovely negligée. But I suspect I'm being over-fanciful. Probably she misses her friends, that's all.

It was odd how someone else's troubles, even when you don't know what they are, can make your own seem trivial. Washing up and putting away, Ceri suddenly saw the sunshine, felt its warmth. She sang as she worked, and began to look forward to her lovely free Saturday.

Ceri enjoyed her morning despite her early depression. She left the flat before Nicola had re-emerged from her bedroom, shouting that she'd be back for the evening meal, and then mooched a bit further up Harbour Hill and took the little lane near the Ambleside Hotel which led down to the beach. The wind was chilly despite the sunshine and when she reached the end of the lane she saw the tide was in. The sea was a flurry of foam, the waves crashed against the shingle ridge and the beach was deserted save for a couple of hardy dog-owners, exercising their pets.

Ceri watched for a bit, then turned back and walked down Harbour Hill in the direction of the town. She passed Lavengro, then Bridge House which was derelict. Tramps sometimes bedded down in the outhouses and Ceri worried about such a feckless existence.

After Bridge House came two guest-houses. The largest belonged to Emily Raison and was just holiday accommodation which made her a nice bit of money from May to September though it was empty the rest of the year. Miss Raison had curled grey hair and cold grey eyes and blue-rimmed spectacles which hung on a gold chain round her neck most of the time. She wore twinsets and sensible tweed skirts and was thin and precise, with a refined laugh. It was said that her laugh frightened holidaymakers more than anger would have done.

After Miss Emily's guest-house, inaptly named Clovelly, Ceri passed an amusement arcade, a café, a general store and a couple of gift shops. After that the small terraced houses began, mostly turned into offices or dentists' surgeries. There was an acupuncturist, someone who dealt in herbal remedies, a lady who sold various diets and a vet's. After that Ceri turned onto the swing bridge, with the marina on her left and the fish wharves on her right. She usually closed her eyes crossing the bridge due to a conviction that one day it would swing round and dump her abruptly in the gleaming oil-patched water.

However, today she got across safely and headed into town the long way, which meant walking beside the marina and gazing enviously at the yachts, then passing the yacht club and finally reaching the sea itself, with the Harbour Way cottages on her right.

It was a marvellous day for such a walk. The beach was clean from the recent heavy rain and Harbour Way, which would be crowded with sightseers in the season, was deserted. Should I have *that* one, with the blue shutters and the brass dolphin knocker, Ceri asked herself, peering at the little houses as she passed. Or should I have *that* one, with the tubs of daffodils and the green-painted door?

But the game could not last for ever and Harbour Way ended at Beach Road which eventually led to Queen Street, home of the reporters' office, and even thinking this brought Ceri to an abrupt recollection of her circumstances. She hastily banished the thought, however. She would not think about it, she would enjoy herself!

Only what should she do? She tried to banish the recollection of her busyness as a budding newspaper reporter. Ceri the newshound had never lacked something to do, she had been down at the harbour hoping a Russian trawler might come in and provide her with a story, or going round the villages, attending fêtes so that a piece might be written up about it on Monday morning.

But now? Suddenly, she had time on her hands and nothing much to do with it. She had made no close friends in Haisby apart from Nicola, since you could not count the reporters. Besides, she could not bring herself to look any of them up; they knew her guilty secret.

Ceri crossed the road and went into the covered market. It was busy in here and smelled good what with a fine display of spring flowers and all the vegetables and fruit mounded up on the stalls. She wandered over to the secondhand book stall and browsed until she found a very old copy of a book entitled *How to Write for Radio*. Ceri was about to replace it amongst the others when something made her flick it open. Oh, what the hell, it was only ten pence, she might as well buy it and have a laugh. She was no longer a working writer, but she could still dream.

Nicola came out of the flat when Ceri had been gone an hour or so. She was wearing a long navy skirt with a matching jacket, navy court shoes and an emerald green necklace. Her fine blonde hair was tied back from her face with a navy silk scarf and from her earlobes hung two tiny, emerald green leaves. Nicola, who loved good clothes, had gone to a great deal of trouble over her appearance. She had bathed and scented herself, put on pretty undies, added the navy blue outfit and fine navy tights and matched a deep rose lipstick carefully with deep rose nail varnish.

For what, though? Out of a deeply rooted terror of becoming a slut, a woman in a dressing-gown who, having lost her husband, could not attract another man? Or from boredom and a sort of self-despair which might be lifted by telling herself that even if no one else loved her, she did? It might not make sense, but it was a reason for living, for making up one's face, wearing pretty clothes, painting one's nails . . . It was a way of saying, without words, so I wasn't good enough for Roger, eh? What does it matter? I'm good enough for *me*, and *me* matters.

So Nicola let herself out of the flat, locked the door behind her, and hurried down the communal stairs and across the communal hall. She passed doors belonging to other flats – one contained two female hairdressers, another a young couple; upstairs lived a nursing sister in her thirties. Nicola practised looking like someone who knew where she was going, who was glad it was Saturday, enjoyed a day to live her own life.

But she was only acting. Because she was afraid now, most of the time. Not afraid of a person or a place or an event, even. She was just afraid of facing life without Roger, afraid of people finding out, pitying her, probably sharing Roger's opinion, seeing his point of view.

I'm boring. She tried to deny it, tried to keep the bitter little phrase out of her mind, kicking it under the mat of memory whenever it reared its hideous head, but it would not be kept under for ever. Now and then it would sneak out and confront her. Nicola Wharton, who had been Nicola West for two years, was boring. So boring that she had driven Roger, who had once been desperate to marry her, into the arms of another woman. Milly Coppack.

Milly was not boring. She had frizzy black hair, snapping dark eyes, a big nose and mouth. She was energetic, with hands that flickered and gestured all the while she talked, as though they, too, had a message, more important, perhaps, than the one her mouth was telling.

Milly was artistic, but her clothes! Bright, jarring colours, all mixed up. Dreadful flat-heeled shoes which she insisted on wearing because they were comfortable. A disreputable old jacket, pearl-grey, with big, sagging pockets and a hood which Milly hid in when she felt like being private and alone.

Milly hadn't wanted Roger. She had been polite to him but Nicola had known how Milly felt because she and Milly had been friends for years and years, since they had met at infant school. Tiny Milly Coppack, frizzy hair in bunches and no front teeth and small Nicola Wharton, blonde plaits and a brace which made her lisp. Firm friends because they had been put at the same sand-table and the boy who shared it had spat in the sand.

Ugh! He spat! Did you *see*? Are you my friend? I'll never touch that sand. No, I won't either. Never. Not if I'm a hundred. Ugh! He spat!

A little, frail link, forged early, strengthened with the years. Shared joys – walking home from school in summer, laughing at each other, at themselves, mocking the stupid boys who fell in love with Nicola's blonde looks and with Milly's forcefulness. Shared sorrows – the teacher who died in childbirth, failures in exams, Milly's inability to throw a ball straight, Nicola's complete lack of talent with the fat wax crayons or the coloured pencils or the lovely, sloshy poster paints.

It's an odd thing, real love. The sort that transcends different backgrounds, different personalities. Milly was often alone, her parents indulgent but busy, both talented, both working in their own way. Milly's father a financial genius, her mother a writer. Milly got her frizzy hair from her mother, and her sallow skin, too. But her dark snapping eyes and her eager personality came straight from Ben Coppack. Her intelligence and her talent were just Milly, who could draw well enough to be published and could write like a dream. She had gone to London, to work on a glossy magazine. Then her short stories and articles had begun to appear in the national press, some funny, some sad, all beautifully written with the sharpness of vision and the keenness of wit which had always characterised Milly.

Nicola had been terribly proud. She had collected Milly's work and pasted everything into a big scrapbook. She and Milly wrote, exchanged visits and long, long telephone calls. When Nicola met Roger Milly was the first person she told . . . when they got engaged, Milly was at the engagement party. She would have been a bridesmaid but at the time of the wedding Milly was off on assignment somewhere in India, from whence she sent exciting postcards covered in her big, scrawly writing. She had seen the Taj Mahal by moonlight . . . A young man had held her hand and told her she was beautiful . . . She had gone through the jungle on an elephant and had seen a tiger crossing in front of her as though small dark girls on elephants were scarcely worth a second glance.

A year after Nicola and Roger married, Milly came home. She got a job with a television company. She was not pretty but she was lively and intelligent. She became a presenter, when she smiled you wanted to smile back and Roger remarked, one night, that the whites of her eyes were whiter than anyone else's; how did she do it?

Nicola glowed with pride. My friend! She invited Milly to the little house on Kett's Hill and Milly came and loved everything. In the end, even Roger.

Nicola came out of her reverie to find herself simply standing outside the flat, staring at nothing. She felt the hot colour rush into her face – what a fool she must look! How long had she been standing here, for God's sake, reliving her wretched past? Oh Milly, Milly, it must have been easy as taking candy from a baby, to steal my weak, beautiful lover from me, because I never guessed, never grudged . . . not until it was too late and he had seen me for what I am – blonde, empty-headed . . . boring.

There was a wedding at the chapel. A bride was just floating down the path on her man's arm. Cameras were clicking, there was an excited little buzz of conversation. No one, thank God, was taking any notice of Nicola, standing as though turned to stone on the other side of the road, seeing the bridal party through a blur of tears.

Besides, you're supposed to cry at weddings, Nicola told herself. She fished a hanky out of her jacket pocket and applied it to her lower lids, one at a time. She felt the hanky grow damp and was once more able to see the scene before her. Thank goodness . . . And now stop thinking about Roger and Milly, stop regretting, start deciding what you intend to do with your day off.

It was easier said than done, of course. It was too cold for walking on the beach, too sunny for frowsting indoors in shops or cinema. She had money though, she could take herself out for a meal, have a glass of wine . . .

She knew she would not do it, though. She could no more walk into a restaurant alone now than fly – what would they be thinking? *Poor thing, not a friend in the world, just a clothes peg, no looks at all really, you only think she's attractive because of that lovely pale hair – and that's probably bleached.*

The bride, with a hand resting lightly on her husband's arm, was disappearing round the corner of the chapel. Going for the photographs, no doubt. Nicola looked across the road and saw that other idlers were beginning to disperse. She had better follow suit, or begin to look conspicuous. Already, she realised, Ceri was more than a little suspicious, what with the glamorous nighties and Nicola's shyness with men. If only I could make myself talk about it, Nicola mourned. But if I do I'm afraid to see people's faces change, grow cold. To be a failure in one's own eyes was bad, but to be a failure to the rest of the world was unbearable, a humiliation she simply could not face. Any more than she could face being conspicuous, so she had better move away from here.

Nicola walked down Harbour Hill towards the town. She passed the vet's with its shiny brass plate – Norrington & Frazer, Veterinary Surgeons. Despite the fact that it was Saturday morning, there was a surgery going on. She could see, through the speckled glass, that the room was crowded with people and animals.

The door was opening; a man came out with a moth-eaten greyhound. It wasn't on a lead, he was holding it with a short leather strap on its collar. It saw Nicola looking at it and sneered, lifting one side of its lip to display yellowing teeth. Nicola was not used to dogs; her parents thought them dirty, Roger had refused to take on what he termed 'additional responsibilities', so Nicola walked round the dog, then slowed to look down into the harbour as she crossed the bridge. She enjoyed looking at the yachts and she loved the sounds, too, the slap and slurp of water against the hulls, the soft bell-like clunk and tinkle of the wind in the rigging. And the fish wharves were fascinating, the smell so strong that a number of cats tended to hang around, jumping up onto the fish boxes, always hopeful. And then there were the gulls, wheeling and squawking, attacking one another, milling round the fishing boats in an untidy, squabbling skein of wings and raucous voices.

Thinking about the nice part of living at the seaside kept Nicola occupied until she reached the T-junction at the end of Harbour Hill. If she went to the right she could go to the bus station; she could catch a bus and be in Norwich in an hour. She could go and spy on Roger and Milly, living in the house on Kett's Hill.

But this was just the sort of thing she was determined not to do. You've made your home in Haisby, she reminded herself fiercely; now you must start living here properly, not just . . . just roosting before you fly away! Meet people, make friends! Don't prove, with every breath you take, that Milly was a fool for twenty-odd years to prefer you to the dozens of others who wanted to be friends with her. Don't let Milly down!

The thought made her smile even as she turned left, onto Lord Street. How could she be such a fool? Hadn't Milly let *her* down, in the worst way possible, when she had stolen Roger? But the habit of all those years was too strong; Milly had not been at fault, it had been Roger, greedy for Milly's bright, bubbling personality, as greedy as he had once been for Nicola's blonde beauty, who had been unfaithful, had broken her heart. Milly had been free, even though she had done wrong by poor Nicola.

As she strolled along with the wind tugging at her hair, Nicola thought how odd it was that she missed Milly more than she missed Roger. Not physically of course, but with her mind and heart. If it seemed disloyal she was sorry, but Milly had been her dearest friend for twenty years, she had known

Roger less than four. Which was why, she supposed, she found it so difficult to blame Milly, except for the deceit. If Milly had told her how she felt they might have worked it out, between them. But by the time she found out it was too late. Roger was infatuated, Milly was in love and she was the unwanted third.

Presently she crossed the road and turned into Felbrigg Street, finding herself outside the offices of Sneap, Paulett & Franks. It was odd to see the bay window empty, with her typewriter covered and no neat figure sitting behind the reception desk. Reception duties were shared between Nicola herself, Wendy Barlow and Helen Gerrard but because the other two girls had worked together for four years, Nicola always felt the odd one out. How long will it take, Nicola asked herself dismally, before I feel at home in Haisby?

No answer being forthcoming, she walked slowly on past the office, suppressing an urge to go inside. Silly fool, no one wants to work on a day off! Instead, she hurried on and presently found herself in the bus station.

I'll go along the coast, she told herself, sitting down on a bench. Whatever I do, I shan't go to Norwich.

Chapter Five

An hour later, she was in the city. She got off the bus at Castle Meadow, waited with a crowd of other would-be shoppers to cross the road, and plunged down Davey Place steps. She would go to the market, buy something for her tea tonight and return to Haisby on the next bus.

Halfway down Davey Place, between the man selling roast chestnuts from a mock-Victorian vendor's cart and the posh shoe shop, she found that she had stopped in her tracks. She knew very well why. If she went back to Castle Meadow and hurried, she would just about make the little bus. After all, she had come to Norwich intending to go up Kett's Hill; why not give in, do it?

She turned. Waited a moment, feigning interest in a pair of swooningly beautiful leather shoes in soft shades of fawn, tan and gold, then began to retrace her steps. She had not been here for two months, had not visited the house on Kett's Hill for ages. Suppose it was all a ghastly mistake, suppose Milly wasn't living there with Roger, suppose, suppose . . .

She reached the bus stop in a daze. The little red bus came along, room for twelve sitting and a further six standing. The driver took her money, smiled, switched his eyes from her to the next passenger. Nicola took the last vacant seat, next to a wheezy but cheerful pensioner with electric-blue hair and a scarlet coat. The woman had a huge carrier bag on her knee. It appeared to contain a great many cabbages and some pungent fish. Standing passengers squeezed on and Nicola was pressed closer and closer to the fish; she just knew she would smell of it when she got off at . . .

You aren't getting off, she reminded herself. You're going to the terminus and then you're going to buy a ticket back into the city again. No *way* will I allow you to make a fool of yourself by getting off, walking down the hill, stopping with a hand on the wooden gate, opening it, going up the path, knocking on the lovely blue door . . .

There was a brass knocker in the shape of a slender hand. Roger loved that knocker, loved the deep blue of the paintwork, loved the polished step, the well-swept path, the wallflowers and daffodils she had planted, nurtured. Would Milly nurture them now? Would she dead-head the roses when summer came, put out the bedding plants, take up the bulbs and dry them in bunches in the garden shed? Would she weed and plant, sowing seed and reaping not only beauty but also Roger's fond smiles?

They were crossing the river now, by Foundry Bridge, the bus was lurching round into Riverside Road. Nicola tried to interest herself in the boats tied up alongside the towpath, watched out for Pull's Ferry, that star of a million calendars. It was too early in the season for many holidaymakers on the river but there were half-a-dozen boats moored alongside. And over the heads of the bare-branched willows which edged the bank she could see the spire of the cathedral against the pale grey sky.

The bus reached the end of Riverside Road and turned right at the roundabout into Kett's Hill. Kett's tavern, the homemade bread shop, a car park . . . the houses. She could scarcely take her eyes off them as the bus toiled up the steep hill and when it stopped she was on her feet and halfway down the aisle before she had remembered she was most definitely not disembarking here.

She got off, people following her so that she could scarcely turn back. She stood at the bus stop for a moment, then, with a sigh, set off down the hill. She would walk past the house – she had little choice – and then cross over the road and catch the next bus back to the city. It had been sheer madness to come here, she could not imagine why she had done so. When I get back to Haisby, she told herself, I'll go home to the flat and I'll tell Ceri I want to join that club she mentioned once . . . I'll ask her to introduce me to people, I'll stop looking back over my shoulder and start looking ahead. And I won't look when I pass the house, I *won't look* . . .

She drew level. She looked. The house looked back, blandly, innocently. The door knocker twinkled despite the overcast sky, the blue paint shone. Had Milly cleaned the windows? Apparently. At any rate, they shone, too. And the daffodils were almost over, the hyacinths which smelt so sweet were in strong flower, sending out their fragrance every time someone brushed against them.

I wonder if they're in? Nicola thought. It's Saturday, of course – they've probably gone to the city, shopping. Dear God, I might have walked straight into them . . . what a good job I came up here, instead! It occurred to her that she could open the gate, walk up the path and press her nose to the window, look inside, spy on their lives in their absence. Probably, knowing Milly, the bed isn't made and the breakfast things are all over the place, she thought sourly. Roger won't like that – he likes the house immaculate.

Or did he? He had said he did, paid lip service to her good housekeeping, but perhaps it had been she who liked the house always to look its best? Perhaps what Roger liked was washing up piled in the sink and paperbacks flung down where Milly had last read them, perhaps he enjoyed Milly's typewriter on the dining room table, sheets of paper everywhere, tights dripping over the bath because it was easier than putting them on the line, hair in his comb, his precious razor blunted from being steered over Milly's dark and furry legs. Perhaps what Roger really liked was lying naked between those dark and furry legs . . .

Nicola caught the thought, aghast at herself. She was not only blonde and boring, she was absolutely filthy, to think such things! But inside her head the thoughts bubbled on, each more terrible than the last. Milly lying on her back amidst the clutter of her possessions, Roger on top of her, fumbling, feeling, sliding back and forth, and both of them laughing, Roger burying his head in her warm, furry armpit, snorting, slobbering, whilst Milly bucked and leapt and shouted, clutching Roger's shoulders and digging in her short, practical nails, biting his neck, arching her back to lock her legs around his waist . . .

Nicola's hand was actually on the gate when she came to herself. Sickened by her wickedness she snatched her fingers from the wood as though it had suddenly become red hot. Oh God, she was going mad, that must be it! She had never behaved like that in all of her married life, how could she ever suspect Milly of such animal behaviour?

Because it's natural, a little voice in her mind said smugly. Because Milly's got more sense than to lie quietly on her back in bed with her nightie folded neatly back to her waist, wondering whether this will mean more sheets in the washing machine tomorrow.

I didn't! I never did! I was very responsive, I enjoyed it, I really enjoyed it very much! And besides, it was what Roger liked to do so of course I had to enjoy it . . . though I would have, anyway, because I'm not cold and undersexed, I'm not, I'm not!

Oh no? the little voice said provocatively. Then why wouldn't you do what Roger wanted when he suggested . . .

Because it wouldn't have been right; it was an awful thing to suggest. Awful. And he didn't mean he wanted to do that, not really. Roger was very upright, just not the sort of man to . . . to . . .

But you wouldn't undress in front of him, the little voice reminded her. He complained that he had never seen you naked . . . was it wise to say he never would? Just you think of all the things you didn't like! Kisses anywhere but on the lips. Any attempt to open your mouth with his. Hands which wandered below the waistline. Any attempt to rouse you into a response. Putting into words how he felt about you sexually. Why, even a hand on you, in the kitchen or the living room, was slapped away pretty briskly, wasn't it?

But I let him do it in bed whenever he wanted, so long as . . . Every night it was, at first. Only of course he couldn't possibly go on like that all the time, so after the first ten, twelve weeks he got more reasonable, more loving and less . . . well, less lustful I suppose.

The little voice sniggered. Bet Milly doesn't slap his hand away if he touches her up in the kitchen; bet she's bending backwards across the table, letting him have what he wants where he wants, laughing, enjoying it . . .

Nicola's hand fell from the gate. She felt sick, she ached as though she had been forced into doing all the distasteful things the little voice had talked about. Was that where she had gone wrong? But surely not? Surely Roger had understood her feelings, respected her for them? Surely the fact that she had let him, freely and often, work his will on her should have been enough? And anyway, she *had* enjoyed it, she just couldn't ever quite see what all the fuss was about!

She was turning away when the front door opened. For a moment she couldn't believe it, could only stand, open-mouthed, and stare. Then she dodged behind the lilac bush which grew beside the gate, but she still stared through its barely budding branches.

Milly stood there, hair a bird's nest, in a skimpy blue cotton dressing-gown which she was clutching inadequately across her chest. She was yawning, bending down to pick up a milk bottle on the step, turning to go back into the house.

From inside the house, a figure appeared; a long arm reached out towards Milly and just for an instant she saw Roger. He was wearing a pair of pyjama trousers at half-mast, clutching them with one hand whilst the other curled round Milly, clasping her breast. Milly squeaked and tried to shut the door and the dressing-gown flapped open for a moment, revealing Milly's nakedness in the split second before the door closed.

Nicola turned away from the house. For a moment, rage flowered, gloriously real. Then came the sort of sodden, useless misery which had haunted her ever since she and Roger had parted. Roger and Milly were happy, with a happiness so sublime that it had made Milly look different, her face, her body, everything about her seeming bathed in a rosy glow. Nicola knew Milly as well as she knew herself yet she had spotted the differentness at once. Milly wasn't pretty but standing in the doorway, softened, gentle . . . Oh God, they did not care about her, they must have forgotten she existed! Roger had laughed, teased, the whole tiny episode had shown, above everything else, the couple's simple, radiant happiness.

And Nicola was boring and not only boring, cold. Unable to understand the so-called joys of sex, unable to allow Roger to teach her because she honestly thought that what he wanted was wrong, she had ruined her own marriage and killed Roger's love.

She began to plod down Kett's Hill again; she could have a wider choice of buses if she walked some of the way down Riverside Road. It was raining now, a fine drizzle, and the tears which ran down her cheeks seemed in tune with the day, mourning for her loss, not of Roger nor of Milly, but of her shaky self-esteem. You don't value yourself because there's nothing to value, she told herself bitterly, stumbling along with her head down, seeing nothing but the rain and her own feet. Better get out of here, go back to Haisby, try to start a new life there. A sensible life, without wanting what

53

you can't have, which is a happy marriage. After all, hundreds of women never marry, why shouldn't I be one of them? I can live very happily on my own or with a girl friend, I'm sure.

But she was not sure, not really. She acknowledged that her attitude to the intimacies of marriage might have been wrong, but she had still loved being married, being a two-some. To put all that behind her, to embrace spinsterhood, seemed a bitter thing at twenty-four.

When the bus came she was soaked to the skin, but it seemed a fitting punishment for someone who had ruined her own marriage and then grudged her dearest friend for trying to pick up the pieces. She sat and shivered her way into the city, then got out at Castle Meadow and consulted the time-table. The next bus for Haisby didn't leave for an hour; what should she do in that time?

I could ring Milly and tell her I'm sorry, try to explain, she thought. But knew she would do nothing of the sort. Instead, she would go to Jarrold's, see if she could dry herself off a bit in their ladies' room, and then have a pot of tea and some toast in their restaurant on the top floor, overlooking the market.

She did as she planned, loitering over tea and scones and then hurrying back to Castle Meadow in time to catch her bus. She sat in her seat, steaming gently, and watched the rain fall and the people scurry about their business until they left the city behind and then she watched the rain fall and the grass and trees bend before the wind, watched dusk thicken. By the time she reached the bus station at Haisby it was full dark, the street lights casting a golden glow onto the steadily falling rain. She had dried off a bit in the bus but got wet all over again walking back to Lavengro.

I must tell Ceri what's happened, she thought as she let herself into the flat. It's just stupid to be so miserable, and I do like Ceri; she wouldn't think less of me. But Ceri was still out and the rain beating on the windowpanes discouraged her from sallying forth again to search for the younger girl. In the end she had a bath, hating her own pale body as it lay in the warm water, got out, dressed in slacks and a sweater, and snooped round the pantry.

Nothing. Ceri had some Vesta dried food in packets but even though she was sure her flatmate wouldn't mind, none of them appealed to Nicola. She burrowed in the bread bin. No loaf. She went through the vegetable rack. No potatoes.

In the pantry she found a tin of baked beans, another of soup
. . . but without toast or bread?

Damn and bloody and bugger and shit, Nicola said child-
ishly, in her mind. She rarely swore, believing it to be the
prerogative of those with an inferior vocabulary to her own,
but suddenly she felt the need. Bums and tits and dicks and
willies. I'm hungry . . . I'm *bloody* hungry, and anyway, why
should I starve as well as feel guilty and miserable as hell?

Her soaking jacket hung on the back of the kitchen door.
Her hand went out to take it down, then hesitated. It was
silly to put it on again, she would get her mac and umbrella
and go along to the Chinese takeaway down on the prom.

Duly clad, she set off. As she went, misery suddenly
gripped her again. All alone on a rainy Saturday evening, to
eat her solitary meal at the kitchen table and then go to bed.
What else was there to do? They had a very small black and
white telly which they hardly ever watched, and a radio set
which Ceri said had been tuned in to Radio Norfolk for so
long that it refused to get any other station. Nicola, an avid
local radio listener Monday to Friday, never listened at weekends, so had no idea what was available tonight.

Harbour Hill in the rain was the epitome of dreariness. The
streetlamps were few and far between, their greenish glow
casting only a modest circle of light. One or two windows
were lit but otherwise it was jolly dark and somehow dangerous, the big houses standing too far back from the road to
be a comfort, the sound of the sea, which should have been
pleasant, menacing. Nicola hurried along, over the swing
bridge, down the road, along Lord Street, following it round
until it joined Beach Road which led directly onto the promenade. In summer the prom would be alive with lights and
people, in March it was deserted, the sand and shingle re-
flecting what light there was in the cloudy sky, the sea rest-
lessly pounding the beach.

But the Chinese takeaway was doing fairly good business,
so Nicola joined the queue, gave her order, and went to the
waiting area.

No room. Not a seat, only family parties watching the telly
in the corner as though they had never seen a set before,
young couples giggling and whispering, heads close, and a
tall, dark young man hiding behind a newspaper.

Nicola had been told by the cheerful little Chinese girl

behind the counter that her order would be twenty minutes; it was a long wait but Saturdays were always busy not only with the people who came in, but with telephoned orders. She could stand here and wait . . . or she could go home and come back in half an hour, to be on the safe side. Or she could just walk – was it still raining?

She went outside to find out and to her relief the rain did seem to have slackened off to a fine drizzle. She walked slowly along the prom, looking down on the rain-pitted sand by the streetlights. The tide was coming in and it was an angry sea too, what with the wind and the rain it was really roaring tonight. Even through the darkness she could see the white lines of surf as the waves crept inshore.

She also saw a small group of lads down on the sand. They were looking out to sea, pointing, jostling. Nicola wondered if someone was in distress out there . . . but then realised it could be nothing as the youths, still arguing, turned and came up the beach towards her. She waited until they were almost up to the prom, then dropped onto the sand. One of them, smaller and younger than the others, saw that she intended to walk down to the sea and stopped.

'Don't go near the groyne, gal – there's a package – the lads reckon that might be a bomb!'

'Well, it might be,' one of the youths said sheepishly. 'Reckon we'll go onto Lord Street and find the fuzz – wouldn't mind seeing one of them blown sky-high!'

'It won't be a bomb . . . where thass bin put that wouldn't harm no one and terrorists, they want to see carnage,' another youth observed shrewdly. 'Box of old clothes, more like, or rotten fish . . .'

'Where is it?' Nicola asked. It was raining again and though she could see the dark line of the breakwater she could see no package.

'There – see!'

She followed the pointing finger and picked out the dim shape of a box. The waves were halfway up it already . . . it appeared to have been tied to the breakwater, probably at low tide several hours earlier. Now, though, the waves were hitting it hard, sending it back and forth like a pendulum, soaking whatever it contained.

'Thass nothing,' the largest of the youths said definitely. 'C'mon, let's get some chips.'

The boys argued and cuffed each other up off the beach but Nicola set off for the waves' edge. She peered through the dark . . . it would soon be too late, if she did go out to it she would be wet up to the waist . . . was it worth it? Probably the boy was right and it was just rotten fish.

She almost turned back, almost made for the promenade once more. But something, some perverse little imp of curiosity or unhappiness or just sheer pigheadedness, made her kick off her shoes, roll her slacks up to the knee, and make her way to the breakwater.

So she'd get wet — so what? She'd got wet so often today already that a bit more wouldn't hurt her. But the sea was freezing cold and the force of the waves was quite frightening. The water dashed against her legs, filled with gravel and pebbles, she could feel them striking her shins.

She reached the breakwater and climbed unsteadily up onto it. Now the sea tugged at her but at least she was above it so that the skirts of her mac and most of her slacks were splashed by the salt water rather than soaked. She worked her way along and when she was within touching distance of the box a surprising thought occurred to her.

This was the sort of thing Milly would do, not sensible Nicola! Nicola would have watched Milly, squeaking encouragement and urging her to take care, but she would never have climbed out along that breakwater just to see what was in an old cardboard box, not in a million years!

It nearly made her turn back, nearly shamed her into giving up, but perhaps there was more steel in her nature than she knew, for she settled herself astride the wooden bars, feeling the discomfort of barnacles and seaweed almost with enjoyment, and reached for the box.

It was securely tied. She could not move it. And it was quite light, too . . . no bomb then, but not rotten fish either. She sighed and tried again to heave the box free from the rope, tilting it up into her arms . . . and heard, from within the soggy cardboard, a light, scratchy sound as something slid from one end of the container to the other.

The cardboard was soggy. Nicola managed to get the box more or less onto her lap and then she simply tore at the cardboard until she made a hole. Oddly she, who was afraid of so much, pushed her hand into the box without a second thought. And drew it out again, her fingers closed around the limp body of a tiny puppy.

Not moving. Soaked, small . . . Oh, what had it done to be treated like this? What sort of monster lurked out there, in the dark, to put this pathetic scrap to such a cruel and lingering death? And she had arrived too late, had hesitated too long – she was no more good to this little puppy than she had been as a wife to Roger. She might as well tip off into the sea right now, and drown, and cause no one any more heartache.

In her hands, the puppy moved. Not much, just a tiny twitch. And then it sneezed and she saw, by the faint light from the thick cloud-cover overhead, the flash of an eye as the lid lifted for a second.

There was a chance! It might still live if she hurried!

Without a second thought Nicola dropped into the sea, the puppy cradled against her chin. It was so small, so light, that it was no effort to hold it thus. She felt the drag of the waves and fought briskly against them, hurrying to shore, and now the tide was coming in, the water pushing not pulling, as though anxious to see Nicola and her burden on shore as soon as possible.

Halfway up the beach, she remembered her shoes, glanced round, abandoned them. What were shoes, after all, compared to a life? Her Chinese meal forgotten, she did her best to run on her frozen feet, up the beach, onto the prom, running along the pavement, slipping and stumbling on her cold bare feet. Hurry, hurry! Get home, into the warm, where the puppy might stand a chance!

She was on Harbour Hill and hurrying past the terraced houses, the puppy still warm against her skin but beginning to shiver, when a door opened and an old man came out. He had a cat basket swinging from one hand and must have thought she was bound for the vet's surgery when he saw her hesitate because he held the door open.

'Just in time,' he said breezily. 'Mr Frazer, he saw my Tibs, then he was agoin' to shut up shop. Go you in, my dear, and he'll see your puppy.'

Your puppy! Nicola muttered her thanks and went past him, into the warm, brightly-lit waiting room.

It was empty, of course. No receptionist behind the desk, no customers waiting. But there had to be a vet here somewhere or the door would have been locked. She went towards the door marked 'Surgery' and pushed it open. Empty, no lights. There was another door, similarly marked, opposite. This one was closed but she could see a line of light under it. She rapped sharply on the panel, feeling the warmth of the puppy under her chin but knowing that it could just be her warmth – the little animal had not moved since that one twitch and sneeze.

The door opened and a man stood framed against the light. He was tall and dark-haired, in a white coat and grey flannels. His shoes looked as though he had been wading through farm-yards in them and the white coat, Nicola saw, was somewhat scruffy, too. He frowned, looking not at the puppy but straight into her eyes.

'Yes? I'm sorry, surgery's over, I was just about to leave, but if there's anything . . . oh!'

Nicola had thrust the soaking puppy into his hands and now she began stammering her explanation but to her horror even as she spoke tears began to rain down her cheeks and sobs fought for release, fought to turn her rational explanation into howls and hiccups.

'Hey, hey,' the vet said soothingly. 'What's the matter? Being out in the rain . . .' He stopped. 'Did someone try to drown it?' he said sharply. 'This chap's been in the sea . . . he's cold as ice.'

'Th-that's what I w-was trying to t-tell you,' Nicola said through chattering teeth. The cold, held at bay by fear and indignation, was beginning to make itself felt. 'S-someone had tried to d-d-drown him!'

The last words were a wail. The man was rubbing the puppy between his hands, holding it close to his white-coated chest, but now he knelt on the surgery floor and flicked the electric fire on.

'Fetch me the towel off the back of the door,' he said briskly. 'He's breathing, on and off.'

Glad to be doing something, Nicola grabbed the towel and handed it down, then watched as the man massaged the small body with the rough material until even she could see signs of life. Blinking eyes, opening mouth, the small struggles of a baby animal suddenly warm, suddenly come out of darkness into light.

Five minutes later the pup's coat was dry, his eyes were wide, he actually emitted a small yip. Nicola beamed as the vet got to his feet and held the pup out for her inspection.

'There! Well, you saved his life, but I'm not quite sure what for – want me to try to find a good home for him?'

'No,' Nicola said indignantly. 'I mean no, thank you. He's coming with me.'

She felt the small, squirming body between her hands with love and thankfulness – one good thing, one mark in her favour. A little, little life.

'Good.' The vet was brisk now, switching off his light, moving beside her over to the surgery door. 'Got some bread? Milk? He's no more than five or six weeks old and he won't need much other than bread and milk for forty-eight hours. If he lasts the night you can bring him to morning surgery and I'll give him a 'flu jab . . .' He hesitated, sighed, then turned back to the surgery. 'Better play safe, I'll give him one now; he's suffering from cold and exposure, if he lives . . .' He glanced shrewdly at her face. 'Anyway, hold him still whilst I fill a syringe,' he finished.

Nicola held the puppy whilst wave after wave of warmth and thankfulness broke over her. The pup was alive, presently she would give him something to eat, and he would last the night because she would make sure he did. A 'flu jab was just a precaution . . . oh, but he was pretty, stirring drowsily in her arms. Black on the back and head, goldy-fawn on belly and legs, with big, milky blue eyes blinking up at her, trustful as a child.

The injection administered, she remembered two things: she had not paid for the treatment the puppy had received, and she had neither bread nor milk in the flat. Did vets sell dog food – or rather, puppy food? She asked for the bill and the information and the man passed a hand across his forehead, looking worried, tired, even perhaps a little cross.

'The money will do if he survives, because then he's going to need more than a 'flu jab, he'll need parvo-virus and so on. Bread and milk . . . well, you could go to the Paki shop out where Felbrigg Street becomes Felbrigg Road, they're open till midnight.' He hesitated, glancing from the puppy to her face and back. 'Where do you live?'

'Flat 2, Lavengro, further up Harbour Hill,' Nicola said. It was the first time, she realised, that she had given her Haisby address without a pang. 'Not far from here, actually.'

'That's all right then. I live over the shop, being the junior member of the practice, so if you just hang on a moment I'll nip up to my flat and bring you down a couple of rounds of bread and a cup of milk. Warm the milk and if he wakes in the night and seems too hot or too cold, crumble an aspirin in more milk and feed it to him on a teaspoon.' He hesitated, then smiled at her. 'Look, why not come up with me? It's a bit untidy but it'll be warmer than waiting down here, now the heating's off. Come on, just let me lock up.'

Nicola murmured her thanks; she was beginning to feel the strains of the day. Her legs and feet were numb with cold, she was draggled and disgusting from the rain and her struggle to reach the puppy and she was also terribly tired – exhausted, in fact. But it was real tiredness, the sort that hits you like a hammer and from which you can escape into deep, rewarding sleep, not the sort which drags at your limbs and dulls your mind but will never let you find forgetfulness in slumber.

'That's that.' The vet locked the door and shot bolts across top and bottom, then turned off the main light in the waiting room. He led Nicola into the short passageway between the two surgeries, across a room which looked horribly like an operating theatre, and out into a small yard. He crunched across gravel whilst Nicola limped painfully behind him – the feeling was returning to her bare feet – then the vet opened a door with a rattling bunch of keys and called over his shoulder, 'Forgive me for going first,' and Nicola mounted a short flight of stairs in his wake.

At the top there was a landing with three doors leading off. The vet opened the nearest and held it hospitably wide.

'My bolt-hole. Come on in and sit down – you *do* look tired – whilst I put the kettle on and warm some milk. Or if you aren't absolutely whacked, perhaps you could get me the loaf out of the bread bin and crumble a slice into . . .' he looked round wildly, then pounced on a blue cereal dish, '. . . into this, whilst I do the rest.'

The room was warm, a modern kitchenette equipped with gleaming white work surfaces, a new-looking gas cooker, a small fridge and a double-drainer sink unit with a disposal chute beside it. The red-tiled floor gleamed, the walls were tiled as well in a warm honey colour with pictures of harvest scenes in brown and gold. There was a sensible kitchen table in light pine, a matching bench, two tall kitchen stools with

61

scarlet leatherette seats and on the nearest work surface, a blue and white bread bin.

Approaching it with the puppy snugly tucked into the crook of her arm, Nicola saw a number of fat, white china jars with shiny red lids, each with its contents picked out in bold red letters. Sugar, Flour, Tea . . . A tall, thin jar announced that it held Spaghetti, another that it contained Dried Fruit. Nicola got the loaf out, took a couple of slices and turned to crumble them into the cereal dish. Without thinking she said impulsively, 'What a lovely kitchen; your wife must be the only woman on Harbour Hill with a modern sink unit!'

He was pouring milk into a pan, frowning, careful. He put the pan over the gas flame, then tested the warmth with the tip of his little finger. Finally, satisfied, he took the pan off the heat and turned to Nicola. He smiled and this time she noticed what a difference the smile made to his face. The rather severe lines beside his mouth disappeared, his dark eyes narrowed into gleaming slits, and she realised that despite his professional confidence he was quite young, probably still in his late twenties.

'I'm not married, despite . . . Ah, you've done the bread. Good. Supper up, young man!'

He came towards her, took the cereal bowl and added the warm milk to the crumbled up bread. With his head bent over the small task, Nicola was able to examine him more closely, seeing the thick, black hair cropped close to a nicely shaped head, the black eyelashes, longer than most, veiling eyes which she had just identified as being not dark but reddy-brown. His skin was clear, tanned from being out of doors a good deal, and his hands were wiry and strong, almost delicate for a man of his build.

'Not married?' Nicola echoed. 'But someone told me your wife ran the dog-training classes in the church hall.'

'Ah, I see I should have introduced myself. John Norrington's my boss, head of the practice. I'm Ian Frazer, the new boy. And I'm not married to the lovely Liz. Which reminds me, who are you?'

'Oh . . . Nicola Wharton. I work for Sneap, Paulett and Franks on Felbrigg Street and live in a flat further up the road. Look, thanks most awfully for the bread and milk, I'll bring the bowl back tomorrow . . .'

'No you won't, Miss Nicola Wharton, because he needs his nourishment warm, tonight.'

He set the dish on the kitchen table and took the pup from her. He tried to stand it down and it promptly keeled over sideways but he fielded it deftly and put the small, squashed-looking nose gently against the warm bread and milk. Nicola watched, fascinated, as the puppy began to buckle again and then twitched its nose a couple of times, gave another wheezy sneeze – and suddenly started to eat.

'Gosh!' Nicola said as the tiny creature frantically guzzled. 'Oh, gosh . . . wasn't he hungry?'

'Looks like it. And I'm the same . . . wonder if I've got anything in the pantry beside bread and milk?'

'We didn't even have that much,' Nicola was beginning when she suddenly gave a yelp. 'Oh dear, my Chinese meal!'

The puppy was cleaning the cereal bowl. Round and round its scrap of a tongue travelled, hopefully polishing. Ian Frazer laughed and picked the little thing up in one hand, rubbing its floppy black ears absently with the other.

'You'd got a Chinese meal in and then went out and rescued this fellow? Well hurry home, before it goes cold.'

'No, it wasn't like that. I ordered it at the Slow Boat, then found the puppy, and . . .'

'And forgot all about it. Look, tell you what, you stay here with the little'un and I'll go back to the Chinese in the car. Had you paid for your food?'

'Yes. They make you, fortunately,' Nicola admitted. She had no desire to find the Chinese mafia pursuing her for her debts!

'Yes, of course. Well, I'll pick up your meal, order for myself, and we can sit here and share the food. How's that?'

'It sounds nice. But oughtn't the puppy to be in bed?'

'He'll sleep sound wherever he is. Sit down and cuddle him up . . . I'll find you a bit of old blanket . . . and I'll be back before he's done more than snore a couple of times.' He looked at her narrowly. 'You look very tired still, it won't hurt you to relax here for an hour or so.' His glance dropped to her feet. 'Hell – where are your shoes, for God's sake?'

'On the beach,' Nicola mumbled. 'I took them off to go into the sea and didn't have time to put them back on . . . I just ran with him . . . I did so want him to live!'

'I'll take a look,' Ian promised. 'See you in about twenty minutes.'

Without demur Nicola sank into the comfortable cane chair with its soft scarlet and white cushions. The slight weight of the puppy on her lap was delightful; she curled a protective hand round him and felt the touch of his small, cold nose on her thumb. Was it possible to love at first sight? She had never believed it before but she loved the puppy totally, could imagine her devastation should he have died despite her rescue attempt. So little, so cuddly, so trusting!

When Ian came back, complete with shoes, she was all but asleep, her eyelids heavy with fatigue. She refused to put the sleeping puppy down despite his assurance that it would not wake, but ate her meal with a good deal of talk and laughter, over its sleeping head.

Ian made tea and they drank that, then he produced toffeed apples and a tin of condensed milk and they ate that. Nicola was quite ashamed of her hearty appetite but . . . goodness, it was gone eleven. Cinderella must have outstayed her welcome here in this lovely modern little flat, and would be missed up the road, as well!

When she lurched to her feet Ian insisted on driving her home, though Nicola protested that with her shoes restored to her she could very well have walked. They left the building and crossed the yard talking in hushed whispers, both, she suspected, a little awed by the strangeness of their meeting and the warmth of this sudden, unexpected friendship.

Ian drew the car to a halt outside Lavengro and got out, helping her to alight without disturbing the puppy. The rain had cleared and stars shone down out of a dark and sparkling sky. A smiling quarter moon swung lazily in and out of the scudding cloudlets, casting its silver light on the bulk of the house, making intricate patterns with the substance and shadow of the wrought-iron railings which surrounded the garden. A salt breeze stirred Nicola's hair, smelling of seaweed and sand and summer days, and for the first time since Roger had left her, Nicola felt beautiful.

Chapter Six

Ceri had still not returned by the time Nicola and the puppy went to bed. They started off conventionally enough with the puppy in an apple box lined with an old sweater and Nicola between the sheets, but although the puppy fell asleep at once it woke in the small hours. Nicola woke too as it stumbled drunkenly about the box, banging its little nose on the hard wood and raising its not so little voice in loud wails of protest.

'Hey . . . hush, you'll get us evicted,' Nicola whispered. She knelt by the box in the dark and put out comforting hands. Immediately a warm, wriggling little body used her hands to scramble onto her lap and then into her arms. And just when she was about to put it back to bed it heaved a deep, contented sigh and pushed its head snugly between her arm and her breast.

Only a sadist would have put it back in the box after that – it had suffered so dreadfully at human hands that Nicola could only marvel at its trust in herself. And, of course, climb back into bed again and snuggle down, curled round her small companion.

In the morning Ceri walked into her flatmate's room with a cup of tea, drew back the curtains and then stared; was Nicola cuddling a *muff* as she slept? But then Ceri went closer and the muff moved, gave the sort of squeaky grunt a teddy-bear gives when its tummy is pressed, and opened two round, bright eyes.

'My God!' Ceri said faintly. 'Nicola, is that . . . what *is* that?'

Nicola woke slowly, elegantly. She opened her eyes, smiled, stretched. Ceri was envious to see that no sleep gummed up those long, golden lashes, that she neither grunted nor groaned as she awoke. Even her hair looked nice, fanned out on the pillow like tassels of silk.

'What's what?' she said agreeably. 'Gosh, I don't think I moved all night I was so tired!'

'Under your chin,' Ceri persisted. 'That little . . . ratty thing.'

Nicola smiled again. It was a lazy, sleepy sort of smile, with a contentment quotient, Ceri reflected, which she had never before seen on her friend's face.

'It's my puppy,' Nicola said offhandedly. 'Someone tried to drown it, I waded into the sea and brought it out. I'm going to call it Zak.'

'A puppy!' Ceri put the cup of tea on the bedside table and squatted down beside the bed. 'Oh, the poor little fellow . . . Hello, Zak, I'm your flatmate, Ceri.'

'He says hello,' Nicola said. She sat up and the puppy wriggled away from her, yawning with much curling of a tiny pink tongue, stretching in the wholehearted way that animals favour. 'Do you like him?'

'Oh, *yes*,' Ceri breathed ecstatically. 'I've always wanted a puppy . . . But Nicola, we aren't allowed. You know what it says in the lease.'

'You wanted to get a cat. Well, I've got us a dog.'

'Yes, but Nicola, you said . . .'

Ceri remembered all too clearly what Nicola had said; she had not approved of them having a cat on the premises at all and had said that owning a dog was out of the question. But it seemed that Nicola had changed, not only her mind but her whole personality. She sat up in bed, reached for the tea, and then grabbed for the puppy as it crouched on the edge of the bed, clearly contemplating a suicide leap down to the floor.

'Just you stay here, young man,' she admonished, turning the puppy round so that it gambolled, falling over every third step, up the bed towards her. 'You're too little for a jump like that.' Addressing Ceri, she added, 'Oh, you mean the mice, I suppose. Well, I didn't think it was worth getting wrong with Mr Patani just to get rid of the mice, but then I hadn't met Zak.'

'And he's worth a row with Mr Patani?'

'Yes.'

Ceri looked at the odd little creature, now applying himself to sucking enthusiastically at the corner of the quilt. His eyes were half-shut and his paws moved rhythmically, pressing into the softness of the material.

'Hmm . . . well, I agree, he's worth some trouble. I think he wants some milk, can I get him some?'

'Feel free,' Nicola said generously. She sipped her tea. 'Take him into the kitchen with you if you want . . . We'll share him, shall we?'

'Oh, yes *please*,' Ceri said fervently. 'And if old Patani comes round we'll hide him. He's only small. What did you say his name was?'

'Zak.'

'Zak. Okay. Come with Ceri, little man.'

Ceri picked the puppy up and held him, warm and wriggling, under her chin. He felt lovely, better than a hotwater bottle on a chilly day. His tiny black nose, wet and cold, grazed her neck. A puppy! All her life she had longed and longed to own a puppy and now Zak was half hers! Father was always talking about having a dog one day, but somehow it had never come to anything – this was her chance to be a dog-owner at last! Damn old Patani and the shit-shovelling sister-in-law, damn the rules and regulations of the flat and the fact that the puppy would probably chew all their most precious possessions and widdle on the Patani carpets. What mattered was that he was theirs.

Ceri hurried into the kitchen and opened the fridge. She got out the bottle of milk, stood the puppy down, stared thoughtfully at the bottle for a moment, then poured a generous measure into a pan and put it on the stove.

Good thing it was Sunday! They would have a whole day to get him accustomed to their ways, a whole day to make him comfortable. A whole day to play with him!

By bedtime on Sunday evening, Ceri and Nicola knew what they had taken on. A bundle of fun, a widdler in corners. A doer of tiny snail-like curls of excrement wherever he chose to place them. A trusting, loving baby one moment, a squeaking, growling little horror who would jump up and ladder your tights or chew the toe out of your slipper the next.

'Can he sleep with me tonight?' Ceri pleaded, sitting cross-legged on the floor with Zak lying across one shoulder like a very small fur stole. 'Oh go on, Nicky, you had him last night!'

'Yes, but he ought to learn to sleep by himself. He should have his nice box in the kitchen, tonight.'

'Go on,' Ceri coaxed, red head tilted, green eyes ablaze with desire. 'Oh do say yes, Nicky . . . I'm twenty years old and I've never spent the night with a man, particularly not with a man-pup!'

'We-ell, he is awfully small to sleep by himself, I suppose. He really should be with his mum, still.'

'Great! Zakky-baby, you're in my room tonight!' Ceri struggled to her feet, the puppy still slung across her shoulder. 'Doesn't he sleep a lot, Nick? Do all puppies sleep so much, do you suppose?'

'I think they're just like babies,' Nicola said thoughtfully. Every time Ceri called her Nick or Nicky she had to fight a ridiculous desire to let a big, beaming smile spread across her face. No one had ever shortened her name before and she did like it! 'Well, if he keeps waking you up and crying, don't blame me. Want to take some milk with you?'

'Sure. I'll get a saucerful before we go off.' The puppy woke, digging its pinlike claws in, struggling to get down. 'No you don't, pupsy, you're coming to bed with Ceri!'

Exit one besotted female, Nicola mused as her flatmate left the room. What a dear Ceri was, and how well she had taken to the idea of keeping the little dog. At lunchtime, as they ate grilled chops and jacket potatoes, Nicola had begun to feel guilty about the presence of Zak in their lives. How would they cope, what would he do whilst they were at work, was she being fair to want to keep him? But even whilst she asked herself the questions, Nicola knew that nothing on earth would separate her from the puppy. For the first time since she and Roger had parted she felt secure, loved. Which was ridiculous, because the puppy could not possibly love her in the way Roger had, or rather in the way she thought Roger had.

But perhaps what she missed was giving love rather than receiving it? Or perhaps it was a bit of both, and the puppy had, in some strange way, fulfilled a need in her of which she had only partly been aware.

What would Milly say, though, if she knew that Nicola had got, not a young man but a young dog, as a Roger-substitute? Milly's approval had been important to her for almost twenty years, she could not now shrug it off so lightly. Nicola closed her eyes and leaned back in her chair. She could almost see Milly's face, the eyes which were always interested in everything fixed on Nicola, trying to understand, full of sympathy, amusement, warmth.

She'd think I was being sensible, not silly, Nicola told herself. She'd know that I've got to learn to live with myself first and other people next. She'd know, because she loves puppies and things too, because she's . . .

Because she's pregnant!

All in a moment, in less time than it takes to blink an eye, Nicola knew what had been different about Milly as she stood in the doorway of the Kett's Hill house the previous day. Her face had been rounder, her body rounder too . . . she could not be far along, could not possibly be . . . and Roger had looked so happy, so confident, yet when she, Nicola, had suggested a baby . . .

Nicola got slowly out of her chair and moved across the room, heading for the kitchen. Once there, she made herself Ovaltine and got a biscuit out of the tin for comfort. But she knew even as she did it, that she did not really need the comfort. So Milly was having a baby and Roger was obviously pleased. Very nice. It proved that he had not been in love with Nicola at all, otherwise he would not have said so firmly that he did not want children, preferred it to be just the two of them.

But Milly needs a baby, Nicola found herself thinking as she prepared for bed. Milly is self-confident, talented, extremely intelligent, she has a marvellous job, everyone loves her . . . but she needs a baby.

And I don't, Nicola thought, astonished. I really don't. But I think I did need Zak.

'If I had a typewriter of my own,' Ceri mused, 'then I could have a go at a story for a newspaper, or even for radio.'

She was in the bank, ostensibly paying in her cheque but really chattering to Tom. Tom, sitting behind the shock-proof glass ostensibly doing whatever tellers do to cheques, was really handing out advice in the generous way people do when others have a problem. Now, he raised his eyebrows, scribbled nothings on a piece of paper, and leaned closer to the glass.

'Have a go at what? My dear girl, you can't just type stories into limbo, and what does an ex-journalist know about writing for radio, anyway?'

'I'm still a writer, whatever they think, and if I got a really good story . . .' Ceri started obstinately, then broke off as Tom made a rude snorting sound.

'They wouldn't take it, not the *Chronicle*,' Tom observed. 'They'd send a real reporter to check it out and get his own view of it. Be realistic, Allen.'

'I *am* being realistic, Hetherington,' Ceri said crossly. 'When I say a story I don't mean a *story*, I mean fiction, or even one of those personal experience things . . . you know, you must have read something other than the headlines once, when you were at school.'

'Oh, sorry I breathe,' Tom said, grinning. He was a cheerful young man with dark curly hair, a spotty complexion and spectacles. He was also a fund of gossip and the sort of person who knows everything and everyone; he and Ceri had been on sparring terms ever since Ceri had moved into Cloister Row and opened an account with the bank on Lord Street. Once, Ceri reflected gloomily now, I was useful to Tom, a considerable source of reliable news and information, but now all I can tell him is who wants to sell a car and who's ringing up the paper about sacks of manure or paving slabs.

'I don't mind you breathing,' Ceri said generously now. 'Just so long as you don't think you know anything at all about writing for profit. Let me tell you I got this book off the market . . .'

'A book? You bought a book? Oh, heaven preserve us, I can just imagine what sort of a book that would be! All heavy sex and see-through undies . . . unless it was the story of Dauntless Dottie, the fifth columnist on the good old *Chronicle*, of course.'

'Don't be so bloody superior, Tom! Actually it was a book about writing for profit – mostly radio stories and talks but other things, too. And personal experience stories go awfully well.'

Tom chortled rudely.

'What, your personal experiences, Allen? I'd have thought Noddy and Big Ears cover that sort of market pretty well.'

'You don't know anything, *Hetherington*,' Ceri sneered, descending to lower-third talk. 'The story of my life would pin your ear'oles back a bit, I can tell you!'

'I bet it's like the story of mine; work, eat, sleep and work

70

again,' Tom said, suddenly serious. 'My landlady does a dream of a steak and kidney pudd . . . but that's about all she can do, between you and me.'

'And what else do you require of a landlady?' Ceri grinned as Tom chortled again. 'You're a wimp, anyhow – why do you live in lodgings when you could have a flat and please yourself a bit?'

'I'm a man, I am,' Tom said indignantly, flexing a non-existent pectoral muscle. 'Men don't cook and scrub floors and things, they get women to do menial work like that. Mrs Halesworth cooks whilst I torture my brain with studying.'

'What do you study? Form?'

'Oh, very witty! No, accountancy, actually. And photography. I haven't made up my mind yet whether to be a star of Ernst & Young or a second Lord Lichfield.'

'What's Ernst & Young?' the ignorant Ceri asked. 'As for Lord Lichfield, I thought that was the pub out on the Sheringham Road.'

'You never did . . .' Tom was beginning indignantly when Ceri saw, approaching him across the floor behind the counter, a plump, heavily-featured man she knew to be the manager. And what was more, she realised that a small but probably impatient queue of people had formed behind her during the course of her chat.

'Then that cheque won't have gone through the system until Monday?' Ceri said, rushing into the breach. 'Well, Mr Hetherington, that's too bad, the *Chronicle* have parted with the money yet I can't have it! How about a little bank loan, just so I can get my typewriter?'

Tom, quick on the uptake in certain directions, shook his head sorrowfully and spoke in a frank and friendly voice, quite different from the hissing mumble which he used to impart gossip.

'A bank loan, for the likes of you, Miss Allen? I should think it most unlikely. Why, the briefest perusal of your past dealings with us merely highlights the number of times you've been overdrawn. However, this month there are a few quid left in your account, so if you'd like to write a cheque against that . . .'

'No thank you, Mr Hetherington,' Ceri said disdainfully. 'Stuff your small cheques.'

Tom snorted again and the bank manager, who had probably not been paying either of them the slightest attention, stopped in his tracks. Behind her, she heard a quick intake of breath and a voice murmured, 'Steady, girl!'

Damn, Ceri thought, not only had the bank manager heard her last remark, so had the customer behind her. But Tom was covering up smoothly, nodding as though she had said something quite different, getting bags of tens out of his drawer and weighing them up. With the manager literally at his shoulder he spoke in tones of false bonhomie.

'There you are then, a fiver's worth of ten pence pieces. Thank you, Miss Allen.'

Ceri, grimly parting with a fiver and taking the heavy little bag of ten pences, smiled sweetly at Tom with murder in her heart. But you had to admire him, he had got himself out of a difficult situation and at the same time turned the tables on her very neatly. Just let him wait until she came in again though. She would bring with her a large sum in mixed small change and let him bloody well count every last penny!

She turned away and saw that the customer about to be served was Henry Johnson. As he moved forward to take her place he put a detaining hand on her arm.

'Ceri . . . can you hang about? I'd like a word.'

'Ah, you did wait!' Henry grinned at Ceri, standing rather apprehensively outside the bank in Lord Street. 'Have you got a minute? You see I couldn't help overhearing what you were saying to Tom and . . . oh damn, this is no place for a quiet chat. Care for a coffee?'

'Free sustenance is always welcome,' Ceri admitted. 'I wouldn't mind a scone, either, if you're in a buying mood. Only don't let's go to Styles, it always smells of fish and chips. Let's go to Sam's Place.'

'Sure; best coffee and scones for miles,' Henry agreed. 'Come on, then.'

The two of them hurried down Lord Street and into the Arcade, passing Archie standing behind his counter polishing a Georgian teapot and Dave redoing the window with his most expensive illustrated books. Ceri kept shooting sideways looks at Henry's craggy face so high above her own. Why on earth should he want to talk to her? Was it possible that Henry knew of a job for a young newshound? She always read the sits. vac. avidly, but no one ever seemed to want journalists.

Sam's Place was empty, Sam himself desultorily cleaning down tables, the kitchen staff cooking for the following day judging by the delicious smells which wafted through the kitchen doorway.

'How's it going?' Henry asked and Sam, with a grin at Ceri, admitted that things were pretty slow and, as yet, he had no need of extra staff but could cope with the customers himself. Ceri, who had worked for Sam in the past, pulled a face.

'But summer will come and now that you can't employ Anthea because she's full-time in the boutique you'll be happy to give me part-time work,' she prophesied and Sam, bringing the scones and coffee Henry had ordered, agreed that this was perfectly possible.

'But Ant was saying the other day that she doubts she'll be able to continue in the boutique much longer, now that her little boy's toddling,' he added, removing the menu and standing it on the next table to give them more room. 'He's into everything, is Kit – and scream? He sounds like a train in a tunnel when he's grumpy.'

When he had disappeared back into the kitchen Henry stirred sugar into his coffee and grinned a little self-consciously across the table at Ceri.

'Well! As I was saying, I couldn't help overhearing what you were telling Tom and I wondered . . . you see, it's like this. Keith and I bought an electric typewriter so that we could have our letters looking professional, we thought it would be quicker and so on. Only we can neither of us type and I gather you can . . .'

'Yes, I can, but I'm afraid I couldn't possibly afford to buy your machine,' Ceri said regretfully. 'You see, old Patani's rent is so high that most of my earnings just get swallowed up, and I do rather like eating . . .' she waved a scone in the air, took a bite, and finished thickly, '. . . which means no spare cash.'

'I rather got that impression. So what I thought was, why not trade? Barter? Swop, if you like? Your typing for the use of our machine . . . get it? If you would type our letters we'd lend you the machine free for as long as you wanted it.'

'You would?' Ceri felt a huge beam spreading across her

face. 'Oh, Henry, that would be wonderful! I'd really enjoy doing your letters, too, more interesting than everlasting adverts.'

'That's fine, then,' Henry said. 'It doesn't solve your cash-flow problem, but . . . You can't cook, I suppose?'

'I cook superbly,' Ceri said indignantly. 'Didn't you know I'd worked here, for Sam? Last summer it was and everyone does everything here, you know. A bit of waiting on, some cooking, sandwich preparation, barmaiding . . . oh yes, I can cook. With a recipe, of course. Why, though? You surely can't want a cook, just for the two of you!'

'No, of course not. Besides, Keith was a caterer, a chef, no less. He's worked in hotel kitchens all over the country in various capacities, head waiter, reception, the lot. No, what we want is someone to do plain cooking for the freezer, you could do that. And then we need someone to do things like changing the beds at the end of the week and cleaning down the rooms . . . but I don't suppose you'd be interested in that sort of thing. It only pays an hourly rate, it'll only be a sort of glorified Saturday job. How are you at decorating? Gardening?'

'Dogsbodying,' Ceri said joyfully. 'I'm marvellous at anything once I've been shown how, really. I'm what they call a quick study. Look, Henry, how many hours a week could you give me once you get started?'

Henry screwed up his eyes and gazed at the ceiling. Ceri felt she could almost hear his brain clicking up hours, sums, suggestions.

'We-ell, by then it could be a five-day week, I suppose, though you'd have plenty of time off say in the afternoons. Probably around fifty quid a week.'

'Through the books or on the side?' Ceri said practically.

Henry blinked.

'Would it matter? Either, I suppose.'

'If they give me the sack then I'll get the dole, and if you can pay me without it going through the books then I'll manage easy as easy. It won't be for long, either, because I'll soon start to make money from my writing,' Ceri said with the airy optimism of one who has never known anything but a regular salary. 'Until May what could I earn?'

'About the same working evenings and weekends, if you really can muck in and do all sorts of jobs,' Henry said after a moment's frowning thought. 'We can run to one other wage. Have you ever sailed?'

'No, but I'm a quick . . . what's so funny?'

'Oh nothing,' Henry said, trying to wipe off a broad grin. 'Only I don't think you can learn sailing just like that! Never mind, it seems you can do most things. Look, why don't you come up to Ambleside this evening and see the typewriter and we'll find you some hours which won't interfere with your job. Then if it goes okay you can think about making it more permanent. How's that?'

Ceri drained her coffee cup, chased the last few crumbs of scone round her plate with a wetted forefinger, then got to her feet.

'When I'm at your place, will you feed me? And can I bring Zak? Only puppies need company.'

'We'll feed you if you're working over a mealtime, and you can bring a puppy if it's housetrained,' Henry said. He stuck out a hand. 'Shake on it!'

They shook hands. Ceri walked out of Sam's Place ahead of him trying to control a huge smile, to sober up a bit, but it was impossible. A typewriter and freedom from the chains of Classified! It sounded like heaven!

'Why the sudden interest in cookery books?'

Ceri sighed and looked up from her perusal of a large copy of *Cooking for a Family*. She and Nicola, their evening meal eaten, were sitting in the living room with the telly flickering away unregarded and Zak on his back on Nicola's lap, having a pretend-fight with her fingers. Ceri was bathed and powdered, wearing a pair of faded pink pyjamas and slippers whose sorry state announced louder than words that there was a puppy in the house. She glanced across at her friend as the older girl spoke. Nicola, also ready for bed, looked wonderful in a blue velvet housecoat with a pair of unchewed mules on her narrow feet. It's always the same, Ceri thought miserably, no matter how hard I try, the best I can manage is wholesome. There is something deeply unsophisticated about me. But Nicola was glancing curiously at the cookery book and then at Ceri's face, plainly waiting for an answer to her question.

'I told you – I'm going to work for Henry and Keith and they want some plain cooking done.'

'And you said you could do it. You said you'd worked at Sam's Place last summer and were a brilliant cook,' Nicola reminded her. 'Besides, you said they didn't really want a cook or you'd have suggested they go for that girl in the Arcade who's got a baby . . . Andrea, was it?'

'No, Anthea. Poor old Ant, she's struggling to bring up Kit by herself and running that posh boutique in the Arcade, but she's well paid by the Bonners so I don't suppose she'd leave. And anyway, I can cook.'

'Oh?' Nicola tickled Zak's fat tummy, then squeaked as he lunged at her. 'I didn't know you owned a cookery book, to tell you the truth.'

'I've only owned this about two hours,' Ceri admitted. 'I nipped into Glenarvon Books and asked Dave, the feller in there, to find me something on plain cookery,' she waved the book, 'and he came up with this. It's all very simple and basic. No problem.'

'Hmm. Ceri, just how much . . .' began Nicola, only to be interrupted by the ringing of the doorbell. Ceri cast her book to the floor and got to her feet.

'Oh, damn! I wonder who it is at this hour? I wish to God I'd got a dressing-gown. Do you suppose it's Jenny, or Emma?'

Jenny and Emma were co-owners of the hairdressers', Waves. Their flat was on the same floor as Ceri's and a good deal of coming and going, borrowing and lending, was beginning to take place between the four girls.

'Bound to be. I mean, who else . . . ?'

'You never know,' Ceri said darkly, hitching up her pyjama trousers. 'It might be a mad axeman, or one of my suitors, or . . .'

'If you go and find out you'll know,' Nicola said with infuriating logic. 'Do hurry, Ceri, or whoever it is won't wait.'

Ceri sniffed.

'Well, that might be a good job. Fancy coming round at this hour, uninvited!'

She reached the sitting room doorway and peered across the hall at their front door as though expecting to be able to see through its solid pine panels. Nicola half got to her feet.

'Ought I to go? Only I feel stupid in a dressing gown at eight o'clock in the evening!'

'What about me? I'm in my peejays . . . suppose it's one of *your* suitors, whatever will he think?'

'I don't have any suitors,' Nicola said. 'Are you going to answer it or aren't you?'

'If we had a chain I could undo it and peer through the gap,' Ceri muttered, crossing the hall. She unlocked it, opened the door a crack – and was nearly knocked over by their landlord who entered as of right, the usual ear-to-ear grin missing, his face looking sad as an organgrinder's monkey.

'Come in, why don't you?' Ceri said to Gilbert Patani's back, for he was already walking towards the open living room door. 'Mr Patani, what on earth do you mean, coming round at this hour?'

Mr Patani turned back. The roguish smile appeared for a brief flicker.

'Gilbert, Ceri, if you please! I wish to be a friend to my tenants . . . Gilbert is my name. But I am disappointed in you, dear Ceri, most disappointed! My sister-in-law has brought a report . . .'

Ceri grabbed his arm, stopping him from marching into the living room. She scowled at him, trying to look angry and outraged and not as she felt, which was rather guilty and small.

'Is your sister-in-law a teacher, then? What sort of report? A school report?'

Gilbert blinked a couple of times, then tried to smile blandly, but Ceri could see that there was still puzzlement lingering.

'It is no matter, Ceri. She came to this flat today to clean up, and was nearly dead of fright . . . nearly dead of it, Ceri. There was an animal in your flat . . . now I know very well that you have closely read your tenancy agreement and you know that there is no animals allowed . . . under no circumstances are animals to be allowed in my properties. All my tenants know this.'

'Animals? Well, of course. Gilbert, we told you there were mice but you denied it. Oh well, if your sister-in-law actually saw one . . .'

'This was a *big* animal, Ceri,' Gilbert interrupted firmly. He held his hands apart to indicate a badger or a fully grown springer spaniel at least. 'She says you have an animal hidden away here.'

'That size? Gilbert, your sister-in-law must be muddling us

up with some other flat . . . no, don't barge into the sitting room, please, Nicola's ready for bed and . . .'

Too late. Gilbert strode into the room and stopped. Nicola sat there calmly, with Zak still supine on her lap. He looked adorable, all pink tummy and fawn and black fur, all tiny white teeth and round, trusting eyes, but to Gilbert he just looked illegal, Ceri could tell.

'And what is that?' Gilbert asked dramatically, pointing. 'What is that, Ceri?'

Ceri began to mumble something but Nicola cut in swiftly, her eyes fixed coldly on the landlord's face.

'This is a cat, Mr Patani. I think it fair to warn you that we intend to keep a cat and go on keeping a cat until you get rid of the mice. When you get rid of the mice then we'll get rid of the cat, but not till then. Is that clear?'

'A cat?' Mr Patani sounded incredulous, outraged . . . but also uncertain of his ground. Ceri, seeing him waver, leapt into the breach.

'Yes, a cat. The previous tenant had a cat to keep down the mice and you said nothing to him. So we intend to do the same.'

'A *cat*?'

'That's right, Mr Patani – Gilbert, I mean – a cat. And now, if you don't mind, Ceri and I are going to bed.'

Mr Patani turned. He looked puzzled, crestfallen . . . and then he swung round, the triumphant grin twitching at the corners of his mouth.

'But my sister-in-law, a most good woman, does not mind cats, and she said it was a great animal . . . she thought a wild sort of doggy . . . she said it would urinate on my floors and excremate in corners . . . my sister-in-law is not at all keen on dogs, so how can she keep an eye on your flat if you keep a . . .'

'Cat,' Ceri said quickly. 'He's a . . . an unusual breed of cat – have you heard of Siamese cats?'

Mr Patani, after some thought, agreed grudgingly that he thought he had heard of Siamese cats.

'Good. Well, this is an Icelandic cat, that's why it's got such thick fur . . .' Nicola made the sort of strangled sound that can sometimes be mistaken for a sneeze but Ceri recognised it unerringly as a smothered giggle. She scowled at her flat-mate but pressed on. '. . . and why it will grow rather bigger

78

than . . . than smaller cats.' More smothered giggles, but Nicola's head was bent over Zak, the long blonde hair swinging forward and half hiding him from the landlord's accusing gaze. 'So perhaps, in the circumstances, it would be better if you asked your sister-in-law not to snoop round our flat, even if she only does it to . . . to clean up. Right?'

'An *Icelandic* cat?'

'Mr Patani, are you stuck in a groove?' Ceri said impatiently. 'Thank you for calling, we do appreciate it.'

She hustled him out, locked the door behind him and listened to his footsteps as he descended the stairs. About halfway down the footsteps faltered and then stopped. Ceri could imagine the landlord standing there, frowning to himself, his lips forming the words 'Icelandic cat?' whilst his eyebrows drew together in an increasingly doubtful frown. She crossed her fingers that Zak wouldn't bark but there was still no sound from him when presently the footsteps resumed their descent.

Two minutes later, in the sitting room, she had the unusual experience of seeing Nicola not only laughing until she cried, but being thoroughly unsophisticated about it. She hugged the puppy, she hugged Ceri, and she laughed and laughed and laughed.

'My little Icelandic pussy,' she chortled over and over, until Ceri told her quite sharply that such a remark was liable to misinterpretation and then both of them laughed and laughed until Zak grew frantically over-excited and barked so loudly that, had Mr Patani still been within earshot, he would surely have demanded further explanations.

'How long can we keep it up, though?' Ceri asked at last, when they were in the kitchen making their bedtime drinks. 'He's bound to come round again, you know how incurably nosy he is.'

'If only Zak stops growing fairly soon we'll probably get away with it,' Nicola said thoughtfully, stirring sugar into her Horlicks. 'But . . . he is getting big, isn't he? He overflows his earth-tray in more ways than one, and his feet are huge – Ian says that's a sign of a biggish dog.'

'Ian?'

'Ian Frazer, the vet.' Ceri was interested to observe a faint pink flush stealing across Nicola's creamy skin. 'I'll tell him Zak is now an Icelandic cat and see if he'll back us up. I'm sure he will.'

'Oh, come on . . . a vet, tell a lie to save us bother? It doesn't seem likely.'

'I'm sure he would, he's awfully nice, but perhaps it wouldn't be fair to ask him. Tell you what, though, if Gilbert persists and doesn't believe Zak's a cat, we can say we're nervous of Harbour Hill after dark and we've got a dog to protect us. Well, we can when he's bigger, anyway.'

'Right. And in the meantime, let's get some sleep before we begin tomorrow's lying. Nick, can you cook?'

'Yes, of course, how do you think . . . yes, of course,' Nicola said. 'Just how much cooking did you do at Sam's Place, last summer?'

'Oh dear. Not much. Well, I chipped spuds and poached eggs and made toast. Could you teach me to do apple pies and things, do you suppose?'

'Easy-peasy,' Nicola said flippantly. 'Buy flour and fat and apples and we'll do one tomorrow after work.'

'Bless you, pretty lady,' Ceri said solemnly. 'I can't think who it was told me never to admit I can't do something, but I don't really like lying. It's your turn to sleep with Zak tonight, isn't it?'

'Well, he really ought to have his box in the kitchen now, like a big boy, but for one more night . . .'

'You'll be saying that when he's the size of a donkey and demanding a pint of ale instead of a saucer of milk for his bedtime drink,' Ceri prophesied. 'Good night, whacky Zakky . . . good night, kind Nicola!'

'I can't help it, I'll have to leave,' Anthea said sadly. 'Believe me, Diane, it's the last thing I want. I've been most awfully happy here. But you can see for yourself . . .'

She glanced expressively at Kit, howling and hiccuping in his playpen and still holding out sticky and hopeful hands towards the model gown with which he had just heaved himself almost over the top of the bars. The model gown bore unmistakable traces of its recent ghastly experience. Diane M'Quennell, who owned the Bonner boutique, sighed ruefully.

'Dear Ant, what's so wrong with a nursery school? Other mums in your position use them – women who aren't single-parent families do so in order to work and supplement the family income. Why can't you?'

Anthea felt her cheeks grow warm. How to explain? That she had one thing in her life which mattered overwhelmingly and that thing was Kit. Leaving him with anyone would simply mean she would not have her mind on her job and would worry constantly that he might imagine himself abandoned.

'It wouldn't be fair,' she muttered. 'Di, I'm terribly sorry . . . but you did say Helen would take over if I felt . . .'

'And you do? You really would rather leave?'

Anthea nodded, ducking her head, ashamed to meet her employer's eye. Eighteen months ago, when Diane had first offered her this job, it had seemed the most marvellous good fortune. But Kit was growing up, getting more difficult. Once he was in school it would be easier, but that would not be for years yet – and even then, there would be the holidays. No, the boutique would do better with Diane's friend Helen in charge and she, Anthea, would move on.

Chapter Seven

'If you ask me we're almost ready to roll,' Keith said.

He looked contentedly around the breakfast room with its warm, cream-painted walls, the floral carpet, the comfortable, saggy chairs and the darkly shining mahogany dining table. Here, everything spoke of a comfortable, easy occupancy. Books, business letters and personal correspondence were piled up on the tiny bureau. One wall was covered with photographs; of Henry aboard various yachts, of Keith at a number of social functions. The bookshelves on either side of the fireplace were crammed with shabby, much-thumbed volumes, the mantelpiece boasted ornaments; three tiny Chinese soldiers carved out of yellowing ivory, a turtle made of redwood and a long-necked Egyptian cat in honey-coloured onyx. Keith patted the turtle and smoothed the cat's slender back.

'The rest is posh I grant you, Henry, but this room is homey; just right for the two of us.'

He smiled affectionately at Henry, who grinned back. They had reached what Henry at least thought of as a sensible understanding. They would be close friends and partners, and they would both go their own way as regards personal relationships. Keith still hoped, though. Now that Ceri worked with them at weekends – and Keith thought Ceri a nice little thing – he was able to observe at first hand how totally uninterested Henry was in her. So it was not impossible, then, that Henry should turn, one day, to Keith. After all, Keith reasoned to himself as he buttered toast, it happened to me. At first I thought I had to love women, so I tried, but then . . .

'I agree. We needed somewhere of our own to relax away from the guests, and this is near the kitchen, so we can still keep an eye on what goes on. And the other rooms are just right; not too posh, like a big hotel, but good to relax in at the end of a hard day.'

Henry was right, Keith thought, going over to the Welsh dresser and putting more sliced bread into the toaster. What with their efforts and Ceri's, when they opened in a few days their guests would not be disappointed. The freezer and pantry were stocked with food and upstairs the beds were made up with brand-new sheets and duvets. They had two craft moored down in the marina, sturdy, reliable vessels with small cabins, a good spread of sail and plenty of room on deck. Henry had bought them after talking to Dick Tester of Great Yarmouth, who ran a successful sailing school there.

Keith had been a bit doubtful about approaching him; gays, he told himself ruefully now, are used to being snubbed. But Henry, who was not only the absolute opposite of gay but a seasoned yachtsman, had no such inhibitions and had gone over to see Dick sure of a welcome which, apparently, had not been wanting.

'Charming chap,' he had said genially that evening, as he and Keith discussed the day's events over a chicken marengo which Keith and Ceri had concocted between them. 'Didn't hesitate to recommend a boat builder, told me who he trusted to look his own craft over, advised me to get an advert in the local press as soon as possible. Even promised to pass our name to clients he can't take in August – they're at their busiest then, apparently.'

'Sounds super,' Keith had murmured. 'Is he nice-looking?' Henry snorted.

'Plain as a boot, just like me,' he said disapprovingly. 'Don't be flippant, old son.'

But Keith had not intended flippancy; it was honest interest, he told himself now, and what was wrong with that? Besides, Henry was not plain as a boot, he was strong and scarred and dangerous-looking.

'Put some toast on for me,' Henry said absently as Keith turned away from the dresser. He was reading a letter, frowning at it as though it contained unwelcome news. 'Oh the devil! Look, I'll have to nip over to Norwich today some time. Personal business. Sorry, but I can see it's unavoidable.'

Keith longed to ask what the personal business was, but told himself he knew better. Henry was not secretive exactly, but from time to time he received letters which made him frown and go quiet – or go off. Not for long, and he soon regained his usual cheerfulness, but it reminded Keith that his partner had a past which still had the power to draw him away from Haisby for short periods.

I'm lucky, Keith told himself as the two of them sat down at the table and began to eat their toast, I don't dwell on responsibilities, my past is past, I live for the now. If only Henry could see things my way!

'Ceri will be round later, won't she?' Henry said, munching toast. 'Get her to give Bentley's a ring, remind them that we'll be needing that dinghy now in less than a week. Tell them we'll call for it if they can lend us a trailer; that should hurry them up. And I wonder about asking Ceri if she knows anyone else who might give a hand at weekends.'

'Sure,' Keith said. 'Umm . . . will you be near any shops, in Norwich?'

It was the nearest he dared get to enquiring where Henry was going, but it availed him little.

'Shops? Bound to be. Why? Want me to pick something up whilst I'm there?'

'Please. Some . . . some root ginger, there's a health shop in White Lion Street . . .'

'Right.' Henry got up from the table and wandered over to the window. The breakfast room overlooked the back yard with a view of the dustbins and the washing lines. Another good reason for choosing to use it themselves. Henry took a huge bite of toast and spoke thickly through his mouthful. 'Pity the car isn't at her best . . . I can get a bus, though.'

'She'd make it, but if we really do have to tow with her next week perhaps it might be best to save her for that.' Keith hesitated, the words 'But if your trip into the city is urgent . . .' hovering, longing to be spoken. But he bit them back. No point in spoiling everything he was building up between himself and Henry – trust, affection, friendship.

'True.' Henry stretched and his tee-shirt shot up, revealing six inches of tanned and sinewy midriff. Keith looked away quickly, feeling his cheeks warm; you couldn't blame Henry, he just didn't know what he was doing to his partner! 'Well, I'll get off, then. See you later.'

'See you,' Keith echoed sadly.

Henry swung down Harbour Hill whistling beneath his breath. He was delighted with the progress they had made

84

on Ambleside, pleased by the fact that Keith, whilst admitting to homosexuality, had not tried to pursue it – or Henry – but had simply settled for platonic friendship, platonic partnership.

Perhaps I should persuade him to start meeting more people, Henry thought now, rather guiltily. Just because I'm not interested in a relationship that doesn't mean Keith can't enjoy one. It might stop his partner staring at him now and then with that moony look on his face.

Sometimes he wondered why he didn't snub Keith cruelly, once and for all. But he knew, really. In his heart he wanted someone to rely on him, someone he could look after, and Keith filled the bill. Henry still wasn't ready for the sort of reliance a woman tended to need, but someone less able, frailer than himself, who wouldn't make sexual demands, had begun to seem necessary to him. He thought, himself, that his feeling for Keith was more like a father's for his son. To Henry, Keith was a nice youngster who needed someone reliable to help him get by. The last thing I want is to jump into bed with him, Henry told himself, repressing a shudder. Poor Keith!

I wonder what would have happened if I'd stayed with little Fluff, Henry pondered as he strode down Harbour Hill. If she hadn't begun to get possessive I might have ended up married to her – what about that? But he knew it wouldn't have worked, not really. Sooner or later domesticity would have palled and he would have left. Sooner or later someone with more strength of character would have stolen him from under Fluff's nose.

Henry reached the swing bridge and crossed it at a fast lope. If he was to catch the early bus into Norwich he would have to get a move on!

Robin got off the train at Haisby station and looked around him. It was probably a nice sort of station really, the sort of station that a boy would spend hours dreaming about, if he were to spend his holidays in Haisby. He could imagine how excited he would have been had Mum been travelling with him – just the two of us, he thought hastily – how he would have helped her with the suitcase, putting down his own seaside impedimenta in order to do so, finding the tickets, having them clipped, hailing a taxi to take them to their boarding-house.

He had always been the man of the house, enjoying taking care of Mum. But that, of course, was now a thing of the past and even thinking about it made it hard not to cry a bit. Those days were over just because hateful, sneering Melvyn thought kids were a bind, and because she thought Melvyn wonderful Mum had changed towards her Robin, talked puzzlingly about 'a girl's other needs', whatever that might mean. So he had left and now, alone in a strange town, he found that he was tired, hungry and more than a little scared. Running away had seemed like a good idea at the time – it seemed like a good idea still, he told himself stoutly – but it had proved to be lonely and difficult work. He had only managed to get aboard the train by a dint of tagging grown-ups, pretending to be with them, and he bitterly regretted his hasty departure from Balham. If he'd had the forethought to pack even the smallest bag it would have given him some sort of credibility. But Melvyn was the pits and when Mum had actually moved him in, let him sleep in her room, he had known it was time to go.

He would have gone a week or more ago, but then he had not known anything about his father save that he existed. Mum had talked vaguely about a terribly handsome and charming man who had swept her off her feet and had then gone away. She seemed to bear no grudge for this desertion but told Robin that his daddy was a wandering spirit, always off on some wild-goose chase. She had said it not critically but admiringly, however, so Robin had always thought it would be nice to meet his father.

Gran was rude about his father, though. She always called Daddy 'im, and once Robin had heard her telling another nasty old woman that Robin had been love-begot. Weren't all children? But she had made it sound something which ordinary people avoided, a cause for shame.

Robin had asked around and found that those children begotten by love did not have a daddy, so Gran was wrong. And his father paid his mother every month . . . that was a recent discovery.

He had been left alone – ALONE! – in the house because Mum wanted to go out with Melvyn and their usual baby-sitter, Sandra-from-up-the-road, was not available. And Mum, who had said awful things about mothers who left small boys alone, had bought him some crisps and a bottle of coke and gone merrily off with that *pig's* arm around her shoulder and her blonde curls tickling his neck.

There was nothing on the telly, of course. Robin liked reading, but had read both his library books and knew his small stock of paperbacks by heart. Mum had one of those lovey-dovey things by her bed so he flicked through it but it was boring, all they seemed to do was talk, so he put it back and went into the study, then over to the bureau.

It was a dear little bureau with a roll-top which was locked, only Robin knew where the key was kept so he had it undone in a trice. He loved the pigeonholes with the coloured pencils, erasers, rubber bands, the long chains of paper clips, the little gold stud-things in the pot which looked like a light bulb. There were neat little bottles of white-out and thinners, though it had been ages since Mum used them because she had an electric machine now which did all sorts of clever things. But she hung onto her old typewriter in case of power cuts, she said. Mum was a typist, she worked through an agency and typed all sorts of things at home, so the bureau was work, not play. On the table next to it she kept her big machine and he wondered whether to take the cover off and use some of the scrap paper to have a go. Mum boasted about his typing but he could do with more speed and you only got that through practice.

He ignored the scrap paper in one of the pigeonholes but there was a little drawer somewhere where Mum kept her personal notepaper, which was pink with pictures of kittens in one corner. He had been abandoned, he was bored and lonely. Typing on a sheet of pink paper beautified by kittens seemed a small comfort, but better than none. And Mum guarded her personal notepaper because it was expensive, so if he used some it would jolly well serve her right for leaving him.

He spent a few moments tipping the gold studs out and making pictures with them on the leather writing pad, then he began to search for the drawer. It was here . . . no, it must be there . . .

He never did find the pink notepaper but he found something better. An account book. And some letters. In a shallow drawer with just room for them and nothing else.

You didn't read other people's letters, so he started on the account book. *Money for Robin* it said in the front. He went through it. Mum kept books beautifully, she worked on books at home too, and he was familiar with her neat writing and double-entry book-keeping, but this was very much simpler. Money was paid in quarterly and Mum used some of it and put the rest in a Post Office account.

When he had frowned over the account book for ten minutes he turned to the letters. Most of them were practical and boring and mostly from a firm of solicitors, who referred a lot to 'our client', but the last one explained everything.

It was from his father! There could be no doubt, though the writer did not state the fact in as many words. He simply said that he and a friend were starting a residential sailing school in Haisby-on-sea, where they were at present renovating an old hotel. The money might be a little less regular for two or three months but Mum was not to worry, things would soon be back to normal. He hoped she and the boy were all right, regards . . .

The boy! Me, Robin thought exultantly. Just when it seemed that his mother had lost interest in her son, a father had turned up and hoped he was all right!

He read the letter again, then looked at the heading. Ambleside Hotel, Harbour Hill, Haisby-on-sea, it said.

Slowly, Robin replaced the stuff in the shallow drawer and went to his own room. He took a long time getting ready for bed because he was thinking so hard.

Mum had said Daddy was away a lot. Well, he may have been once but he clearly wasn't now. There was no telephone number on the notepaper but perhaps he could write to his father, explain that he was being supplanted by the vile Melvyn? Or perhaps he could get his father to come back and kick Melvyn out . . . a glorious picture of Melvyn, screaming as he flew through the air, gave Robin his first real laugh for days . . . but it wasn't really practical. He did not want to share Mum with anyone, not even with Daddy, so that idea was a non-starter.

Mum came home after he was asleep and next morning at breakfast, though a little absentminded and singing rather more than usual, she seemed to have forgotten Melvyn. Robin went to school, came home for his tea, offered to wash up, and was told they were going to the cinema. He loved the cinema and got ready in the best of humours.

Melvyn met them outside. The three of them went in and

Mum and Melvyn held hands, whispered to each other and ignored Robin on the walk home as he trailed sulkily in the rear, hating Melvyn from the bottom of his heart.

It went on for several days, with Melvyn always turning up for tea and shouldering Robin aside. Then one morning he was there for breakfast, and when he had gone to work Mum had broken the appalling news.

'All boys need two parents, and your Daddy just won't take on the responsibility for you,' she said. 'Melvyn's a wonderful man, so big and strong, you and he will get along fine once you've accepted that he's here to stay. You see, darling, I *need* a man, I can't manage alone.'

Alone! She could say this to him, Robin, who had spent all his time, ever since he could remember, in being her little man, taking responsibility off her frail shoulders! It was unbelievable, but it was happening.

It sickened him. A strange curdling feeling which he had never felt before attacked his vitals. He was physically sick twice, on both occasions when he found Mum cuddling with Melvyn. Such a revulsion of feeling – he would as soon have cuddled a viper as Melvyn – had gone straight to his delicate stomach. And to add insult to injury Mum, who always told everyone about Robin's delicate stomach, was suddenly indifferent to his suffering, told him to grow up and act sensible for once.

It had been insufferable. Melvyn's smirk whenever Robin was told off was bad enough, but Mum, who had cuddled Robin, cooked his favourite food, taken his part, had suddenly changed. She grew cold, watchful, accusing him – with truth – of working against Melvyn, of trying to make trouble between them.

Sick, bewildered, suddenly unsure, there had been nothing Robin could do except leave and because of that lucky find in the bureau, at least he had a goal in view.

Haisby-on-sea and the Ambleside Hotel! He had left in the late evening because he could not bear the sounds coming from Mum's room . . . the gigglings, bedsprings twanging, squeaks and groans . . . and had spent an exceedingly uncomfortable night in a little park nearby, waiting for morning and the pursuit.

He had expected to be followed, caught, brought home. Instead, when he sneaked back to Scholar's Road, what did he see? Mum waving Melvyn off, Melvyn jaunty, his fair hair slicked down to his head, his unlikely tan gleaming with soap and water. Mum went in and closed the door, Robin knew she had not even checked his room. He thought about waiting until she did, but something told him that she would probably assume he had left early for school, and besides, he was going, wasn't he? Once he had gone how sorry she would be, how happily she would agree to kick Melvyn out in return for his own presence!

Defiance had got him to the station, onto a train for central London, onto another train for Norwich and finally, onto one for Haisby. Now, in Haisby itself, he was standing gloomily outside the station, wondering where he would get the strength to find Harbour Hill, let alone his father's hotel. This is my second day on the run, he thought pathetically. I haven't had a meal – not a proper one – since school dinner two days ago and I've only had water to drink. The money he had stolen from Mum's purse had been needed to pay train fares.

The station, he saw as he moved away from it, was at the top of a long, sloping road which led down into the town and eventually, to the sea. He could actually see the sea, very blue and sparkling under the azure sky, and it gave him strength to start the long descent. His father lived by the sea. Perhaps they would get on awfully well, perhaps he would take Robin in, no questions, and then how his mother would weep, how she would accuse him of being a traitor – and how he would once more demand Melvyn's absence as the price of his own return!

It was a good dream, good enough to get him down into the town, and then sheer interest kept him going, because it was a bright and breezy little town on this beautiful April day, people had smiling faces, the trees were coming into bud, there was blossom in the gardens and he smelt the gentle scents of spring as he wandered along.

Soon, however, he was into the town itself; the scent of flowers was overtaken by traffic smells and the salty, sandy, exciting smell of the seashore. Robin longed to go and paddle, to play on the beach, but he knew he would just lie down on the sand and sleep, so he continued doggedly on his way. Find a post office, or one of those town maps which says *You're here* and you'll find Harbour Hill, he told himself.

Look how well you've done so far, you're only ten and you've got to the right town, soon it'll be the right street . . . if you go down to the beach it'll be evening before you reach Ambleside Hotel.

Another dream began in his head. Suppose he fell asleep on the beach and was washed out to sea by the tide and drowned? Oh, then his mother would be truly sorry, she would hate Melvyn for ever – most satisfactory!

'My boy's body has been swept ashore?' she would say, her lower lip trembling and tears filling her big blue eyes. 'Oh, my dear, dear love, he did it for my sake! He was searching for his father so that I might be saved from Melvyn, this dreadful young man who was forcing me to marry him . . . it's just like dear Robin to do the practical thing! And now he's dead and I wish I were dead too! If only I'd listened to him, taken his advice, seen through Melvyn, as he did! And now it's too late, too late!'

He was on a busy street now, right in the town centre. His legs, rested on the train, were getting tired again. And he was so hungry he could have eaten the worst school dinner you could imagine – boiled skeletons followed by Death on the Alps – with relish. Oxtail stew and sago pud with jam were his particular hates, hence the cruel but not inaccurate nicknames.

Better ask, Robin advised himself. You'll look a real idiot if you faint or something . . . and anyway, Mum's probably alerted the police by now, they'll all be after you, they'll certainly take you home if you ask, or to your father's hotel.

It was a comforting thought. Robin looked carefully from one face to another and chose a nice one, a woman with fair hair pulled back into a jaunty ponytail. She was pushing a pram with a fat baby sitting up in it, its wide eyes regarding the world with approval.

'Oh, excuse me, I'm looking for Harbour Hill . . .'

'Harbour Hill. Ooh ah, got you. You want to go over the swing bridge . . . past both docks, pleasure craft on one side, trawlers on th'other . . . and you're there.'

She smiled and prepared to push on. Robin cleared his throat and trotted beside the pram.

'Please . . . where's the swing bridge?'

She smiled down at him good-naturedly. She appeared to

see nothing unusual in his rather grimy appearance nor in the fact that he clearly did not know one end of the town from the other. Robin supposed vaguely that holidaymakers were always asking directions.

'You come along of me, my man, do you're sure to get lost. Hold onto the pram, I'm going that way meself.'

Holding onto the pram, Robin felt uneasy for a moment. Was this pretty woman going to kidnap him? But a kidnap attempt with a pram as a getaway vehicle did seem unlikely, so he trotted on, smiling at the baby and playing boo with it.

'Whereabouts on Harbour Hill do you want?' the woman asked presently, as they turned yet another corner onto a long street busy with traffic and lined with tiny trees in wire enclosures. 'That's a longish road.'

Robin liked her voice. It was sort of cooing, and all her rounded 'o' sounds were 'oo' sounds. She made road sound like rude.

'The Ambleside Hotel,' he said, some obscure pride making him add, 'I know the people who own it.'

'Ooh ah? Them's the fellers what done the place up when it had bin let go, in't they? Now here we are . . . there's the swing bridge, go over there and keep on going up to the brow of the hill. Ambleside's on your right.'

'Thank you very much indeed,' Robin said with the punctilious politeness his mother had taught him, but also with heartfelt relief. He had good long sight and could see, from here, the words Harbour Hill on the far side of the bridge. 'Goodbye. Goodbye, baby.'

The woman turned away, pushing her pram back the way they had come. So she had gone out of her way to see him on the right road – true courtesy, Mum would have said. Or perhaps she would have said it once, Robin thought bitterly, but now all she seems to worry about is having everyone bow down and be polite to that Melvyn. The only good thing about Gran was that she didn't like Melvyn either; she called him 'that dretful, common young man', which Mum thought fearfully rude and Robin thought both accurate and fair.

Robin walked halfway over the swing bridge and then stopped and looked down on the boats in the harbour. He knew nothing about boats but they looked pretty, like a really good postcard, all different shapes and colours swinging gently on the water, their reflections forming and breaking up as they moved.

I wouldn't mind getting into one of those boats and cutting the ropes and drifting off, Robin thought. I could put up the white sail and away I'd go, until I was just a little speck against the horizon, and then they'd tell Mum I was lost at sea and she'd cry and cry . . .

This fantasy sustained him as he began to mount the long upward sweep of Harbour Hill. He passed offices, guest-houses, little shops, an amusement arcade, a betting shop, a café and an icecream parlour. One or two of the shops were open but the rest looked pretty dead. April, Robin concluded, was not really holiday time.

As he climbed, the properties became more spaced out, the gardens larger. But that was only on his side of the road, on the other side it was more commercial; he saw a small industrial estate with a sign over one of the buildings – *Haisby Chronicle*, it said.

Staring at the other side of the road made him less aware that he was nearing the brow of the hill, but at last he was there, no longer able to put it off. He let his eyes slide briefly right; yes, that must be it, a very large building half hidden by trees, all a bit wild though the grass had been cut and the beds edged fairly recently. Robin did a lot of gardening – had done a lot of gardening, he amended in his head – and he could tell that this was a tidying up of long neglect rather than the weekly manicuring of a lawn which, in summer, it had been his pride to carry out for Mum, in their shared patch.

But now he was actually here he found that he was not at all keen to walk up that short drive and ring the doorbell, announce his presence. Suppose his father was a wicked man? Well, no, that was a bit silly, a wicked man would not still be paying Mum to take care of Robin himself. But he could easily be bad-tempered, or simply too busy to listen to his son's tale of woe.

Robin leaned against the gatepost whilst he thought things out. After all, this whole thing was really meant to scare Mum into valuing him, that was all. It didn't really matter whether his father wanted him or not, so long as he never had to return to Melvyn. In the very heart of him, deep in his bones, he was afraid of Melvyn. Oh, the man had never hit him, but there was something sinister and cruel about him which told

Robin that unless he got rid of Melvyn he would live to regret it.

Really? Robin's ordinary voice asked his fantasy-mind rather sarcastically. *Are you going to tell me that you're really scared of Melvyn, that you really believe he'll do you harm?* And the answer was yes, he did believe it, despite only having evil looks and the odd spiteful remark to go on. I'm afraid of him and I think he hates me, Robin admitted – and as soon as he had admitted it, the enormity of what he had done, what he had still to do, overcame him. He was, after all, only ten.

Robin turned to face the gatepost and let the tears, which he had been suppressing for days now, flood into his eyes and down his cheeks.

Henry whistled as he climbed the long hill towards Ambleside. He had caught the bus, finished his business in good time and was now looking forward to a hot meal, a quiet evening watching a Western on the telly, and tomorrow, a gentle sort of day catching up with some gardening. He and Keith were still talking about cutting steps in the cliff so that their guests could climb straight down to the beach without leaving the property, but it looked less and less possible as they investigated the nature of the cliff itself. Keith had made him laugh last night by suggesting a slide – what a glorious swoop it would be – but in fact he feared they would have to give up the idea and continue to use the lane at the side of the property. However, there was nothing to stop them cutting a gateway in their quickthorn hedge so that guests could walk down across the garden, through the gateway and thence to the beach. Coming back, furthermore, after a long day of sand and sea, everyone would be glad of the short cut, especially since it meant they could avoid the steepest part of the lane.

Considering this, Henry walked briskly along until he reached the stone gateposts at the end of the short drive . . . and there was a small boy, clearly in tears, almost wrapped around the left-hand gatepost.

Henry cleared his throat. The lad did not move. Henry went over to him and put a gentle hand on one of the heaving shoulders.

'What's the matter, son?' he asked kindly. 'Lost, are you?'

Beneath his fingers the young shoulder stiffened; then a grimy, tearstained face was turned up to his.

'No, n-not lost,' the boy stammered. 'I-I'm going up to that house, there.' He gestured to Ambleside.

'So why not go? Why hang about? I live there myself, so we can walk up together.'

The boy's small face looked incredulously up at him for an instant, then he smiled uncertainly.

'You do? Oh, gosh!'

Robin walked along beside the man who, he now realised, must be his father. And his father had known him even before seeing Robin's face, he had addressed him as 'son'! He was nice, Robin decided, very tall and very tough, with big bones and a square jaw and a scar across one cheek. Not at all the type of man Mum usually went for. Not flashy, like Melvyn, but somehow solid and strong; dependable even, like a cowboy in a Western. But perhaps he had been flashy years ago, or perhaps Mum had only recently taken to admiring flashy men.

'Well? You're very quiet? Are you looking for a job, because you're a bit young!'

Robin laughed. His father knew, of course he did, but he would wait, now, until Robin actually told him of their relationship. And then . . . He looked around him. It was a super garden and the beach was only just over there. It was ever such a big house, there would be plenty of room for one small boy.

For Robin had felt safe from the moment that large and gentle hand landed on his shoulder. He had felt instinctively that this was someone who would never harm him, would take care of him like Mum had.

They reached the house, went round the side, crossed a paved yard and went through a back door painted a deep and glossy cream picked out with dark brown.

I'll tell him *now*, Robin kept saying to himself, first as they crossed the garden, then as they detoured round the house, finally as they entered the yard. But in the big, streamlined kitchen he turned, at bay, and faced his companion.

'I expect you're wondering who I am,' he said, and was surprised to hear how squeaky, suddenly, his voice had become. 'I'm Robin Truscott, and my Mum is Teresa Truscott.'

'My God!' his companion said. 'My God!'

*　　*　　*

'You could have knocked me down with a feather,' Ceri said comfortably, sitting in the kitchen at Lavengro with a plate full of tomatoes, cheese, baked beans and toast before her. She was going through one of her attacks of vegetarianism and would munch her way through fields of vegetables until the attack wore off. 'I was *amazed!*'

'Why? I thought you admitted that Henry wasn't queer, even though you thought Keith was,' Nicola said.

She was guiltily eating a pork chop though she did not think she could have faced lamb. It was bad enough being told at ten-second intervals that she was eating a little pink porker who had as much right to its life as she had, but it was springtime and there were lambs in the fields, with their sooty noses and high, baby cries . . . and then there was Zak, a baby-thing too, who might, in another culture, have been eaten . . . Nicola pushed her pork chop away and reached for the salad bowl. Whilst she was vegetarian Ceri always made a bowl of salad though she rarely ate more than the odd lettuce leaf.

'Oh no, Henry isn't queer . . . gay, I mean . . .' Ceri agreed, 'but I never thought he was the type to leave a wife and child; he's so responsible and steady, somehow.'

'He probably wasn't always,' Nicola said wistfully. 'He's older now, and that boating accident must have quietened him down, but he might have been wild, once.'

'I suppose he must have been. Anyway, it seems they've got things sorted out. The little boy is going to stay with them for a while. Apparently his mother's remarrying and the fellow doesn't care for Robin at all. Henry told me in the kitchen whilst I was making a fruitcake. Henry's thrilled, but Keith was rather tightlipped. And the kid's to call them Henry and Keith, not daddy or uncle, Henry says it's easier.'

'I wonder how long he'll stay for?' Nicola said idly. She ate a radish and then a spring onion and felt virtue rising up in her. No wonder Ceri took to vegetarianism, it made you feel such a goody-goody, she might try it herself some time. 'Surely he'll have to go back to school? Anyway, won't his mother miss him? I mean there were the two of them for so long . . .'

'It's odd, because from what Henry said I gather the mother doted on him until she met this guy, but now she

96

seems to resent the kid. As for school, Henry said they'll enrol him at the local primary; he can start when the Easter hols are over. He's a nice kid.'

'Yes, but even nice kids don't make life easier,' Nicola pointed out. 'And if Keith's jealous . . .'

'Jealous? A grown man jealous of a little boy? Oh no, he'll worship the kid once he gets to know him!'

'I'm not happy about it.'

Upstairs, in one of the small attic rooms, Robin slept at last. Henry had taken him into town and bought him some clothes and then he had had a bath and a meal, and had sat watching television until Henry had seen how tired he was and packed him off to bed. Now, in their small sitting room, the two men sat on opposite sides of the fireplace, staring at each other.

It was cosy with the red velvet curtains drawn, the fire starting to devour a fresh log. Yet the atmosphere was anything but warm. Keith's lip trembled, Henry saw impatiently, and his fingers plucked at his chair arm.

'Look, old lad, it's not for ever, it's just until things get sorted out! You spoke to the girl yourself . . . she's in a bit of a state, clearly she's scared stiff that she'll lose this fellow . . . Melvyn, wasn't it? . . . and the little lad's in a state too. Give them breathing space and he'll go home and she'll welcome him with open arms. Believe me, Kee, I know what I'm talking about.'

The nickname softened Keith, as it was meant to. He sighed deeply, shaking his head.

'He's a nice little boy, but . . . it's the extra responsibility, Hal, the fact that neither of us are used to a kid around the place. And he'll need a lot of attention, kids always do.'

'Of course, but I told you, he won't want to stay, not indefinitely. And we're going to have to get more staff, so we'll choose someone who's good with kids. As for responsibility, I'm happy to take that side of it on. And once the novelty wears off the lad'll be as keen to go back to London as you seem to be to get rid of him!'

It was jokingly said, but Keith rushed in at once, a faint flush staining his fair complexion.

'Henry! I'm not keen to get rid of him, but boys need mothers. Still, if you're right, by the time the hotel is up and running he'll be back in London. Isn't that so?'

'Probably,' Henry assured him. 'But we won't meet trouble halfway. If it looks like being too long a visit we'll have to talk again.'

'Right,' Keith said. 'Good. Perhaps we won't even have to bother with the school, then?'

'Probably not. But just in case, I'll have a word with the head teacher when I get a moment.'

'It doesn't seem necessary, if there's a chance . . .' Keith saw Henry's expression and the colour rose once more beneath his fair skin. 'Sorry, Hal,' he said humbly. 'I'm being a fool. We'll wait and see.'

Upstairs in his small bedroom under the eaves, Robin lay on his back and wondered why he was so extremely happy. He had always considered himself very lucky to be the man of the house, to be able to look after Mum, and here it had been made plain he would have very little official standing. If he stayed he would go to school, do his chores, play out, make his bed and help with the visitors when they had any. He would have pocket money, paid according to how much work he did, and all his big expenses would be shared out, he thought, between Mum and his father. Only he wouldn't call him Father or Daddy or anything, because their relationship had never included that title. No, they were just to be Henry, Keith and Robin, three fellows running a hotel.

So why the flooding happiness? He loved the hotel, of course, so huge and full of exciting possibilities, and the garden was brill! The girl, Ceri, who helped out was nice too, full of ideas. And of course having the beach just a short walk away would be dead good, particularly once he had made a few friends.

But the best thing about it was that he really liked Henry and Keith and he thought they liked him. And if he stayed here he would never have to face up to horrible Melvyn and he would never feel that awful, clawing jealousy which seeing Melvyn with Mum brought. He had lived in a flat all his life, with a share of a sooty London garden. Now, out there, was not only the beautiful garden and the beach, there was miles and miles of real countryside . . . and Ceri had a dog! When he had mentioned a dog, Henry had said they ought to have one too; it would keep undesirables away.

When I've got enough money from helping them, I'll buy them a puppy, Robin thought rapturously, and not altogether disinterestedly. How grateful they will be – and I'll feed it and take it for walks and love it most awfully. It will belong to all three of us, but it's bound to love me best . . . Oh, I'm so happy here! I never, ever want to leave!

Anthea pushed the pram across the swing bridge and admired the yachts swinging gently at anchor. Kit, sleeping for once, would have enjoyed them too, but Anthea was guiltily glad that the light of her life was, for once, slumbering.

She was going to apply for a job – not the first since she had told Diane she would leave by a long chalk. She had applied for work at a nursery school, a crèche, a holiday camp, a school . . . and all to no avail. Whether it was because she was unsuitable or whether it was Kit she had no idea, but she was still looking for a job, and getting increasingly desperate. Diane was far too kind to simply move Helen in, but she must be getting impatient as the weather improved and more holidaymakers came prowling down the Arcade. Some bought, but others were not prepared to wait for her attention whilst she coped with Kit and there was no doubt about it, when thwarted his shrieks were startlingly shrill.

But this job was different. For a start, she had heard of it through a friend. Ceri, the little girl from the *Chronicle* who had helped out at Sam's Place more than a year ago, when Anthea had been a part-time cook there, had told her about it.

'It's just two fellows, Henry and Keith,' Ceri had explained. 'Henry's son Robin is there too – he'd love Kit, I'm sure of it. And they do need someone who can cook and shop and manage things for them, poor dears!'

'It sounds ideal,' Anthea had said doubtfully. 'Only . . . I'm not very good with men.'

That was the understatement of the year, she thought ruefully now, pushing the pram up the steep hill. Men had always terrified her, even the mildest of them seemed a threat. Her father . . . But she turned her thoughts resolutely from her past, remembering how good and understanding Sam had been, how marvellously kind Archie in the antique shop was, how reassuring Dave from Glenarvon Books.

And Ceri had told her that Henry and Keith were nice to

work for, supportive and keen to make a go of their hotel. And she had offered to keep an eye on Kit should Anthea be unable to do so, which would be a great comfort.

So all in all, she was hoping Henry and Keith liked her and thought she could do the job. All in all.

Anthea pushed her pram onwards. And prayed. Let them like me. Let me like them. Let it all work out for the best, dear God! Oh, and let Kit go on sleeping until the interview's over!

Chapter Eight

'Ceri – come over here, would you, please?'

Ceri was talking to a farmer who had rung up to book advertising space for an open day he was holding and had stayed on the line to flirt decorously with her. Now, she glanced behind her and met the acidic eye of Karen Poole.

'Thank you for your advertisement; it'll be run as agreed,' she cooed into the phone. 'I'm afraid I have a call waiting on the other line. Good afternoon.' Beneath her breath she called Miss Poole fancy names, all of them insulting, as she took off her headset, stood up and moved over to where the older woman stood.

'Yes, Miss Poole? Can I help you?'

'Indeed you can. Come into my office.'

Ceri followed, outwardly calm, inwardly seething. It was too bad, the woman treated them all like recalcitrant school kids, and it wasn't as if they were busy. The end of the afternoon was near and somnolence hung over the girls, muting shrill voices, softening gossip. Even Ceri's neighbour, Alison, a girl whose range of sexual innuendo had to be heard to be believed, was apparently snoozing over her desk.

And there was I, minding my own business, Ceri thought crossly, following the older woman's outraged back. I'm the only person in the room actually taking money, and what do I get for it? Abuse, that's what I'll get. Well, I'm not standing for it, not this time.

And two minutes later, she was able to make good her promise. As soon as the supervisor began to hector and threaten, Ceri marched to the door of the cubicle and flung it open. Her colleagues should hear the whole thing firsthand.

'Miss Poole has just accused me of making private telephone calls in the firm's time,' she called to the suddenly interested faces surrounding her. 'She says I flirt with

101

customers and I should have been sacked weeks ago. She says the fact that I sell lots of advertising is just a fluke. Now we'll go on from there.'

'Shut that door at once,' the supervisor said. Her face was an unbecoming shade of puce, her eyes slits of spite. 'How dare you! I've a good mind to call Mr Mullins, he was the one who brought you in here . . .'

'He brought me in because no one will work here for a moment longer than they have to,' Ceri said firmly. 'This place is a hell-hole because you make it one. We all work hard for the firm and a fat lot of thanks we get!'

'How dare you! And shut that door!' Karen Poole tried to push the door to and Ceri hung grimly onto it, determined to keep it open.

'Shan't! Go on, you were saying . . .'

'Very well, if that's how you feel! You're an idle, worthless little gossip, you've never done a day's work in Classified and now you never will. You can leave!'

'Great,' Ceri said cordially. 'Cheerio, then!'

She was halfway across the room when a shriek from the supervisor's cubicle made her turn, brows rising.

'Did you screech?'

'Where are you going? And put that coat down!'

'You just fired me,' Ceri said. 'You do have a short memory, Karen – I think you ought to see a doctor!'

'You will obviously have to leave, but since you have to give me a month's notice . . .'

'Rubbish,' Ceri said cheerfully. 'If I was giving you notice of course that would be different, but you just fired me, remember?'

'I said you could leave, I didn't say you could go at once. But you needn't stay after Friday.'

'I shan't, because I'm going now,' Ceri pointed out, turning back to the door. 'Cheerio, all.'

'Ceri Allen . . .'

Ceri pulled at the door and it opened too easily. Someone outside was about to enter, so she stood back. Mr Mullins came in. He had a pile of papers in one hand and gave Ceri the sort of absent smile which means *Where have I seen that face before?* and is, from a once-close colleague, a none-too-subtle form of insult.

Karen, however, zinging across the room and clearly intent

on getting between Ceri and the door, seized the excuse of the boss's presence thankfully.

'Oh, Mr Mullins, I was very annoyed with Ceri, she's always taking personal calls on the phone and . . .'

Ceri, about to slip round Mr Mullins and escape, turned at that. The look on her face would have made a pigeon pale but Karen, poor fish, continued to burble.

'She's idle, a flirt, she's the sort of girl we can well do without –'

'And how, Karen Poole, did I get the prize last month for the biggest sales? Or did I charm men into buying advertising space? Because if so, you'd better go out and charm a few yourself – not that you could charm a man – snakes are more in your line, I daresay.'

'Mr *Mullins*,' shrieked the supervisor. 'Did you hear what she said? She's got to go!'

'I'm going; but not under false pretences,' Ceri said loudly. Her temper was hanging by a thread, she thought gladly; a thread which would presently snap. 'I'm a hard worker, I earn every penny of my money, and I earn it by selling advertising what's more, not by lolloping up and down the office shaking my tits and telling people off.'

Mr Mullins turned away. The back of his neck was a very dark red. He spoke without looking round.

'Ceri, come through to my office, would you? Miss Poole, perhaps it might be better if you stayed here.'

'That's libel!' Karen Poole said. 'She's libelled me, Mr Mullins, and you're a witness!' Her face was ugly with rage Ceri saw gleefully, and her eyes looked as though they might start from their sockets any moment and whizz across the room.

'I don't see how you can call it libel; it's a statement of fact,' Ceri argued. 'And from the back, Karen, your bum looks just like a jelly, all wobbly –'

'That's enough, Miss Allen. Follow me.'

Ceri, following, glanced behind her. The girls' faces, without exception, wore expressions of bliss. If I am sacked, she thought buoyantly, I've made a lot of people very happy – and one of them is me!

'What will you do, Miss Allen?' Mr Mullins had asked almost anxiously just before Ceri left the building for the last time.

'I feel Miss Poole was over-reacting a trifle, but you did take her up on it rather promptly.'

'I'm going to work as a freelance journalist,' Ceri said grandly. 'Once I leave here I'll have far more time to do my own thing.'

'Oh? But what will you live on?'

'The dole; you sacked me, you see,' Ceri reminded him. 'Well, not you personally, but the firm did. So they'll have to pay me the dole.'

'Not if you're sacked for misbehaviour,' Mr Mullins reminded her. 'Miss Poole is bound to say . . .'

'If she does, then, I'll have you for unfair dismissal,' Ceri assured her erstwhile boss. 'And I'll cite my sales figures as proof of competence.'

Mr Mullins sighed and wagged his head. They were standing in his office, Ceri booted and spurred so to speak and eager to be off, Mr Mullins clearly unsure what to do for the best. But apparently the thought of being sued for unfair dismissal decided him.

'No need for that; I'll speak to Karen,' he said. 'Well, you'll want to be off, then?'

'I do, rather. Can't wait to get to work on my latest piece, to be honest. And it won't be about working for the *Chronicle*; not yet.'

That had been a week ago. Right now, Ceri sat contentedly in the Ambleside office, bashing at Henry's typewriter and watching the words form on the page.

To her slight surprise, she had not as yet sold anything, but she was studying *Writing for Radio*, and was hopeful that any day now radio would realise that she was just the person they were looking for.

'I'm doing a piece on fashion to poke that Louisa in the eye,' she told Nicola severely, when her flatmate asked her what she was up to. 'But I'll have to do an awful lot of research or I don't think it will ring true. So I'm going to befriend someone in Chamberlains.'

Chamberlains was the only department store Haisby boasted. Nicola, however, looked doubtful.

'Chamberlains? Is their stuff haute couture?'

'It's haute enough for me,' Ceri said. 'Besides, they'll probably know the right names and things.'

To an extent she was right. The chief buyer in the ladies'

clothing department knew a thing or two, though she was, as Ceri said, old as the hills.

'I bet if she washed the make-up off her face at night her flesh would just crumble away like a mummy exposed to the air,' she said in an awed voice after a session with Miss Penelope Wittering. 'I have never in my life seen a face so smothered in pancake . . . and she had so much stuff on her eyelids she had to keep propping her eyes open with one finger.'

'Oh well, she's been there for ever so Wendy's mother says. Was she useful, though?'

'Enormously. She's lent me some magazines and advertising features, told me what to look out for, wrote names and things down . . .' Ceri consulted her notebook. 'A ravishing sweep of midnight blue velvet, with a crisp chiffon scarf, white with midnight-blue polka dots, around the neck,' she read out in a puzzled voice. 'I wonder what the hell she meant? And under that I've written Pierre Garden . . . suppose it should be Gardiner.'

'Fool! Pierre Cardin! Even I know that!'

'Is he a designer of haute couture? Thanks, Nick, I can see you're going to be a tower of strength. I say, you know your nightie?'

'Pretty but cheap and label-less,' Nicola admitted. 'Sorry, Ceri, I'm afraid I'm not in Louisa's league. But she's on the *Chronicle*, isn't she? I didn't think you'd try to write for them!'

'You're not? Oh well, never mind. And yes, Louisa's on the *Chron* and no, I'm not aiming the article at them. But when she reads it Louisa will be green with envy. I say, I suppose you wouldn't like to browse through *Vogue* and some of the other mags Miss Wittering lent me?'

'I'd adore it, actually. If you like I'll go through them and make notes so you can write descriptions of clothes without actually having to rack your brains.'

'You're a princess,' Ceri had assured her friend. 'Long may you reign – you can have Zak tonight.'

Thinking of these things now made Ceri, snug in the Ambleside office, look down at the box under her desk where Zak usually slept, only today Nicola had him. Ceri gazed at the box and thought of the puppy with all the fondness of a mother for a favourite child, and then returned her attention to the page before her.

'She's gone, Ces. She's got a lovely baby, a boy called Kit. I asked Hal, and he told her the job's hers if she wants it, and she does. Isn't that good?'

Wrapped in her dream of glorious glamour, Ceri jumped so high she hit about eight letters simultaneously and the typewriter beeped and flashed like an outraged virgin finding a man in her bed. Error, error! She turned and saw Robin in the doorway. Hovering. Nice kid.

'Hello, Rob; sorry, what was that?'

'I said your friend's got the job! And there are three in for lunch and Keith's done them meat pie and a big side salad and then a pud and coffee, and he says could you do with a coffee, because if so . . .'

'Anthea's got the job? Oh, Rob, that's wonderful. She's such a dear and the most marvellous cook. But I'm in trouble, I suppose. I should have been helping in the kitchen.' Ceri jumped to her feet. 'The trouble is when I start writing I forget all about time.'

'No, you're off duty from one o'clock and it's nearly two now.' Robin examined his wristwatch ostentatiously; it was a present from Keith and Henry for good behaviour and it meant that Robin could be told at what hour to leave the beach and return to the hotel once more. 'Henry's gone thundering down back to the marina and Keith said he did look in when he started the lunches and you were all hunched up and bashing away so he left you.'

'Good for Keith,' Ceri said from the heart. She knew too well how easy it was to become distracted, especially by food, but right now her tummy was singing a familiar song: feed me, feed me, even coffee would be better than nothing! 'Right you are, Robin, I'll just tidy away my stuff and be in the kitchen in two ticks.'

'I'll help,' Robin said. Ceri thanked him and the two of them scurried round turning the room back from a writer's den into a respectable office-cum-sitting room.

Ceri swooped on all the pages of manuscript which were all right and Robin picked up all the half pages, the scrumpled ones, the scrap, which had been chucked down on the floor by the impatient genius. He ended up, Ceri saw sorrowfully, with a considerably bigger armful than she, but at least what she had done was right, or seemed so now, at any rate. She smiled at Robin as he pushed the papers into the big folder for recycling and turned to her. He was an attractive little chap, sturdy and fair with round brown eyes and a freckly face on which the chubbiness of childhood was still discernible. He was also old for his age in a lot of ways, with an underlying streak of reliability and commonsense which Ceri had heard Henry saying was the result of having a featherbrained mother. If that's true, Ceri thought now, then perhaps having a featherbrained mother isn't such a bad thing. Certainly it produces a nice sort of child. But she thought, herself, that he had inherited his reliability straight from Henry.

'Thanks, Rob,' was all Ceri said, however, as the two of them left the room, shutting the door behind them.

In the kitchen, Keith looked up from setting out chocolate mint wafers in a silver dish.

'I thought they were only supposed to have them after dinner at night,' Ceri said accusingly. Keith fluttered his lashes at her and pouted.

'Oh you! You're as bad as hard old Henry – they're ever so nice, the Watsons, and since their son is the only one interested in sailing and we don't officially do lunches they'll pay extra for this . . . I thought it might be a good idea to spoil them a little. Then they'll tell other guests and we'll make a bit more money.'

'What about packed lunches? Henry was organising them when I came in this morning,' Ceri said, beginning to pour the coffee from the percolator into the delicate china cups. 'Do you charge extra for them?'

'Yes, but not enough,' Robin remarked before Keith could answer. Ceri caught the malevolent look cast at Robin by the older man and hid a smile. That kid had all his chairs at home, no question! 'They get oodles of grub, Ces, and they pay a measly two quid a head.'

'It doesn't seem much, but perhaps –' Ceri was beginning, when Keith leapt into the breach.

'When I do them they get a little prawn cocktail in a round jar, thin slices of roast chicken and a lovely salad, ever so nicely set out in the lunch-box, and crusty french bread with lots of butter. They have either a slice of rich fruit cake or Kee's carrot cake – I call it that because it's my very own recipe, Ces – and then a piece of fruit. Which may cost a little more than Henry's stingy sandwiches, but it makes a better impression.'

107

'Henry says –' Robin began, to be promptly snubbed.

'Oh, *Henry says, Henry says*,' Keith muttered. 'Henry says sandwiches are easier to eat when you're anchored off the coast, and he says we can't afford to keep losing cutlery, and he stopped me sending out a bottle of cheapo wine between four of them because he said he didn't want a tipsy crew. But of course Henry knows best!'

'He does,' Robin muttered as Keith, carrying the tray of coffee and mints, swept out. 'Henry's sensible. Sometimes Keith's really silly, Ceri. It's as if he doesn't know how important it is to make a go of this place.'

'And you do?' Ceri said, grinning at him. She poured herself a mug of coffee and stirred in sugar. 'Anyway, I daresay Keith knows all about catering.'

'Oh, sure. Only he wants to make a splash and Henry just wants to keep going and give people what they pay for. And I *terribly* want them to make a go of it so I can go on living here,' Robin said earnestly. 'You imagine, Ces, what'll happen to me if Keith spends all the winter money on chicken and champagne. Because we shan't have many guests in the winter, Henry says.'

'You really like it, don't you, poppet?' Ceri said. She picked up a chunk of french bread, tore it untidily in two and reached for a dish of salad. 'Don't tell, only I really am starving.'

'I won't tell,' Robin said. He took the remaining piece of french bread, filled it with salad and took a large bite. His voice, muffled by the food, continued. 'It's the best place in the world, I think. And this Anthea woman will do the right things, Hal told me so. He said she'd looked after a big old house and managed the money and everything. He said when he can't be here then she would do just as well, be just as careful. I asked him if Keith would mind and he said not, so that's good, isn't it, Ces? So you see, if your friend Anthea does what Hal says then we'll all be safe, the hotel and the sailing school and all of us. And besides, Mum *married* that beast Melvyn, would you believe? She actually married him, he's living in our lovely flat, so I can't go back, and anyway I'm going to have a puppy and Mum's ever so scared of dogs, even good ones, like Zak.'

'Zak isn't always good. Think of the begonias.'

Zak, unassisted, had ravaged a bed of begonias, not only tearing off every flower and almost every leaf but then digging with wild and happy abandon in the beds until every last corm had been disinterred, sucked and chewed, spat out and abandoned. He had trotted indoors, his black furry parts brown, his gold furry parts grey and his dear little rubbery nose wearing a conical cap of caked earth on its tip. Ceri had smacked and wept and rushed into town and withdrawn the last money in her bank account to buy more begonia plants, but she had realised she could no longer treat the puppy like a baby, to be petted, played with and occasionally reprimanded. He would have to be tied up whilst she worked, with brief excursions out to the long lawn for calls of nature.

'Oh, that!' Robin said airily. 'That was nothing, just high spirits. Besides, when the school holidays start I'll look after him for you. Until I get a dog of my own, that is, and then I'll look after them both!'

'Pour me a coffee, pet,' Keith said, swanning back into the room, very flushed and gratified. 'They complimented the chef and tipped the waiter.' He delved into his white coat pocket and produced a pound coin. 'Here you are, Rob – well deserved!'

'Oh gosh, lolly!' Robin exclaimed. 'Oh Keith, thank you *ever* so much for letting me wait on. Aren't they nice? A whole quid. Can I take it upstairs right now? I'll be down in two ticks, honest to God!'

'He's saving up for a dog for the two of you,' Ceri said mischievously as Robin disappeared through the doorway. 'It was nice of you to give it to him, Keith.'

'A dog? Oh well, it'll probably take him so long that he'll be back with his mother before he's saved enough,' Keith said optimistically. 'I know I grumble about him sometimes but he isn't a bad kid. And he earned that money. My dear, apart from the coffee he served everything, and a good job he made of it. Now! I know you're off duty, but if you'd be an angel and do the washing up then I could start tonight's dinner.'

'Sure thing,' Ceri said, glad to pay, however backhandedly, for her stolen lunch. Whilst Keith had been serving coffee she had devoured her salad sandwich and a slice of carrot cake. 'What are they having tonight?'

'Fresh salmon steaks. My own vegetable soup first, which is already made, and apple charlotte for pud. It's the charlotte I'll do now, whilst you wash up, and when you've finished at the sink I'll do the veggies.'

'You seem happy,' Ceri commented presently, clattering dishes in the sink whilst Keith sang softly to himself as he worked. 'I thought, earlier, that you weren't too pleased with life.'

Keith crossed the room and took down a pan.

'Ye-es, I do feel more cheerful,' he admitted. 'Did you hear the phone?'

'No, I didn't. Good news, was it?'

'Not exactly. Just an old friend. We're going out for drinkies tonight. Make a change for dull old Keith to get his leg loose!'

When the phone had rung, Keith, as Ceri had inferred, had gone across to answer it in no very pleasant mood. Life seemed to be all work, work, work, and mostly without benefit of Henry's company during daylight hours, now that they had guests, many of whom had come specifically to learn to handle a boat. As yet the boats were small but later, if all went according to plan, Henry would take people aboard the larger craft right up the coast as far as Scotland and the Western Isles, spending up to a fortnight away from home.

When Ambleside was still in the planning stage, Keith had agreed to all this, because he simply had not realised that he would be unable to go as well. He had visualised the two of them lounging on the deck beneath the northern lights, whilst Henry, out of the closet at last, held his hand and smiled into his eyes.

How different it was in fact! Keith was like the little woman left alone at home to slave over a hot stove; whilst Henry sailed off into the wide blue yonder Keith cooked, served, cleared away, washed up – and frequently collapsed on his bed after preparing dinner.

Ceri was a help, and the boy did his best. And now that Henry had employed this Anthea person things would undoubtedly be easier despite the presence of a boy of about two concerning whom Henry had been annoyingly vague. Yes, a single parent, no, not a young girl, a respectable spinster in her forties, he had said when Keith questioned him. She would cook, do the marketing, plan the housework. It would free Keith to help on board the boats at least three days a week. It would put an end to Keith's tiredness, the times when he felt drained and cross, wanting to quarrel with Henry for his lack of understanding.

So when the phone rang he snatched up the receiver and held it to his ear, though he remembered to coo into the mouthpiece; it would never do to offend a customer!

'Good afternoon; Ambleside Hotel. Can I help you?'

'We-ell, that rather depends. Don't tell me that isn't Kiwi Fell because I'd know that voice anywhere. Remember me, you handsome brute you?'

The teasing note was like a shot of adrenalin to Keith; it was like old times, when he'd had some sort of a social life, when he'd been in and out of Reynard's and the jazz club in Haisby, meeting people, searching for a soul-mate – it was like it had been before Henry!

'Yes, this is Keith,' he purred now. 'I wonder who can that be? Someone tall, dark and handsome? No-oo, I've got a feeling you're almost fair . . .'

The truth was, of course, that Keith was playing for time. He had no idea who his caller was, he just hoped he wasn't making an utter fool of himself over some dreary old queen who'd fancied him in the old days. There had been Alfie, the barman at the jazz club, who had been the eager recipient of Keith's favours for a whole month, and another man, Cyril, who was really *grim*, but he'd spent a lot of money and Keith had been kind to him, too.

'Kiwi, you don't remember my voice? Well, honey-bum, if you want to know who I am, come to the car park outside the jazz club this evening at nine, and we'll have a drink and a chat over old times.'

'*What* did you call me?' Keith said with pretended outrage. 'I can't believe my *ears*!'

'I'm not speaking from personal experience, not yet,' the voice said softly, with sufficient sexual innuendo in its velvety tones to send shivers down Keith's susceptible spine. 'I've always fancied you – you going to show?'

'Hmm . . . it's awfully tempting,' Keith mused. 'Can't you give me one teeny little clue?'

'Come and see, honey bum.'

The receiver went down with a final little click. Keith waited a moment, then replaced his own instrument. He was positively sparkling with excitement – he had made an assignation! Despite having come out of the closet years before he had never actually had an affaire and lately he had put sexual frolics out of his mind, hoping that Henry would fall for him.

But it was not going to happen. Lately, he had seen Henry mixing more and more comfortably with their guests, had seen him fussing round Robin just like a father would, and had acknowledged the truth of what Henry's attitude implied even though he never put it into words – that he, Keith, had better start searching for friends of his own, because Henry would never succumb.

On the other hand, he mused, going slowly back to the kitchen, his imagination still inflamed by that lovely sexy voice and the pictures it had conjured up, there's nothing like seeing something slip through your fingers to want it back. If Henry saw him with another guy then it might be the spur which would jolt Henry into his arms. He didn't believe it, but it was a better reason for keeping the rendezvous than sheer lust.

'I'm off now, Keith.' That was Ceri, heading for the back door. The kid had gone long since, probably back down to the beach since the sun was still shining. 'See you in the morning.'

'Oh, sure, Ces. Thanks very much.'

Alone in the kitchen, Keith continued to make his apple charlotte, but his mind was not on his work. What should he wear? The jazz club was a casual rendezvous but lots of gays went there and if he was really going to get back into the swing of things he ought to look his best. He had a pale blue linen suit which matched his eyes – would that be over the top for the jazz club, though?

Half an hour later, his cooking finished, he was upstairs having a rest on his bed when the sixty-four thousand dollar question occurred to him. Should he tell Henry or should he not? If he did not, then he could not pretend, even to himself, that he was hoping to make Henry jealous. But if he told Henry and nothing came of it he might look a fool. Which would he prefer?

I won't tell him now, he decided, on the verge of sleep. I'll wait until I know who phoned me and whether I want it to go further, and then I'll tell him.

Or perhaps, I will, anyway.

It was a fine night, the sky clear, the stars twinkling. Keith walked into town, enjoying the balmy breeze, the sea-scents of the beach blowing across the harbour. Even the salty tang from the fish wharves was pleasant on a night like this, with adventure ahead of him.

He had not told Henry about his caller; all he had said was that he'd decided to go down to the jazz club for a drink after dinner. He had asked Henry to accompany him but had not been surprised when the older man refused. Henry said he was going to watch telly with Robin and then have an early night. Oh well, each to his own tastes.

Once in Lord Street, though, Keith realised how long it was since he had been in town after six. There were crowds of young people, mostly girls at first glance, strolling up and down the pavements, ogling boys, patting their hair, gazing at their reflections in every window pane. He made his way swiftly amongst them, knowing himself an object of interest, seeing the girls look quickly at him, then at each other. He knew he was good-looking, that girls liked him . . . He flicked a lock of fair hair off his forehead, watching his reflection as the girls watched theirs. Yes, he looked good. Girls did not matter – but the sort of man who wanted Keith would expect him to look his best.

Outside the jazz club he hesitated, almost nervous. Suppose . . . oh hell, suppose he was wrong and it was Alfie? But what if it was? There was no law which said that, because he had flirted on the phone, he must now take the caller seriously.

'Hi, Keith; slumming?'

Keith spun round and felt his elbow gently grasped. Immediately, he knew who had called him. Ted Unwin. A blond guy with blue eyes set rather too close together and the sort of body-builder's torso which sent shivers down Keith's spine. He was in his late twenties, husky, smelling of aftershave and hair tonic, and his hand on Keith's elbow was strong, the fingers digging in just enough to make Keith feel vulnerable.

'Whatever do you mean, Teddy? I'm a big fan of the jazz club,' Keith said, looking at Ted through his lashes.

'Oh, yeah? You haven't been here much lately, old pardner. Too keen on husky Henry, so I've heard tell.'

'Henry and I are partners,' Keith said. 'Well, are we going in or aren't we?'

Ted said nothing but jerked his head and walked in. Keith followed. He can't help his eyes being too close together, he told himself, it's probably just inherited, it doesn't mean he's

113

sly. And doesn't he just radiate sexuality? Oh, I love a masterful man!

'What'll you have, Kee? I'm told you're anyone's after a couple of gins.'

'Who told you that, big boy?'

Keith had a Look which went with phrases like that; it was a long, slow, under-lid stare. He hadn't used it for years but he knew it made him look like a nineteen-twenties film star, knew that other gays liked it. Now Ted got the full candle-power.

'Whey-hey-hey!' Ted said. 'Never mind who told me, I just want to find out for myself. What's your fancy?'

To continue with the game Keith should have made some remark loaded with innuendo but just as he sought for it he saw Alfie, the barman, moving towards them.

'Gin and tonic please, dear,' he said, suddenly brisk. 'Shall I get us a table whilst you fetch the drinks?'

He moved quickly to the nearest table and stood by it, watching as Ted brought their drinks over, walking with a slinky, powerful stride. Ted sat down and gestured to Keith to follow suit. 'One g and t, one bitter.'

The bitter showed that Ted was the dominant one out of the two of them, the one who would take the lead. Keith shivered deliciously, wishing that they were in one of the quieter, less well-lit alcoves, but before he could say anything Ted reached up and took the bulb out. Now they were just two shadowy onlookers, watching the game of life as others chose to play it on the dance floor.

Keith leaned forward, elbows on the table, drink held between both hands, and pretended to watch two girls – or were they gays, in drag? – having a semi-serious fight over a pink mohair wrap. But really he was watching Ted. And Ted, he knew, was not even pretending to watch the floor, he was watching Keith.

Keith moved as if to get comfortable and found, surprise surprise, that his leg was now rubbing against Ted's and that Ted's arm had slid round his shoulders. Keith almost purred, resting his head, oh so casually, on Ted's arm, letting his hand fall, oh so accidentally, onto Ted's thigh, bulging beneath the silky material of his hand-stitched Italian slacks. It was wonderful to be admired, wonderful to be desired, too!

Ted leaned close and Keith moved too, believing the other

man was going to whisper something, but instead Ted's tongue came out, warm and wet, and dived into Keith's ear and his other hand abandoned the drink it had been holding and came round to seize Keith's shoulder, pulling him into a better position for this strange, inquisitive, wickedly arousing caress.

It had been so long! Keith was in ecstasy, ready to do anything that Ted should suggest. He was disappointed when Ted let him go and leaned back in his chair, eyes half-closed, nostrils flaring as he spoke.

'Well I never, what a hot-arsed little piece I seem to have found myself! And I thought you were going to tell me you weren't interested in anyone but husky Henry! Let's go somewhere more . . . more private.'

Ted held out a hand, Keith took it and they made their way out to the car park. After the heat in the club the night felt cold but it was not that which made Keith cling close to the other man as Ted led him over to an expensive-looking car and opened the passenger door.

'Get in.'

Keith, with a little shiver of happy anticipation, got in. The seats were upholstered in leopardskin and when Ted switched on the ignition the fascia sprang into colourful life, looking more like the instrument panel of a jet plane than a mere motor car.

The car began to move, purring over the asphalt of the car park. Keith, his voice deliberately trembling so that Ted would know excitement was spiced with fear, said, 'Oh, Ted, where are you taking me?'

Ted laughed and put out a hand to caress Keith's knee. He had hard fingers, Keith thought dreamily, yet though they were strong he just knew they would be gentle.

'I want to take you to my place . . . unless you'd rather go somewhere more exciting first?'

'Oh, your place, please,' Keith said. 'You – you will see me home again afterwards, won't you?'

He wondered for a moment if he had overdone the in-need-of-protection touch; you never knew, it could bring out the beast in a man. But it seemed he had hit it just right.

'Don't you worry, my little honey-bum; I'll take every care of you. Why, I'll see you right into bed!'

'Promises, promises!' Keith chirruped happily. He hugged

his knees as the big car purred out of town, into the deeper darkness where the street lighting finished. A country cottage, a feather bed and man in it who cared for him, who wanted him, would probably seduce him! He tried to raise a shiver at the thought of the seduction but it was not fear which made his skin prickle, his breathing quicken.

It was excitement.

Anthea sat in the kitchen of Cuttens Cottage, with the range open to warm the room, whilst Kit splashed in the baby bath. Her friend Mollie sat opposite, embroidering a length of white silk with cream and lavender pansies. Kit lurched, a great bow-wave of water sloshed onto the floor, and Anthea sighed as Mollie cringed into her chair, the material held possessively against her chest.

'Oh, Moll, I'm awfully sorry! Kit, you're a devil!'

Kit slapped the water with one hand, gurgled, and then said, 'Mum-mum-mum-mum! *Bad* Kick!'

'He's big enough for the upstairs bath,' Mollie grumbled, cautiously spreading her material out again. 'It's madness to try to wash him down here.'

'I know, but it's warm down here. The bathrooms at Ambleside have central heating though, so when I stay over I can bath him in a huge bath. And you'll be able to swim properly, Kit my boy,' she added, lifting her dripping son out of the water and depositing him on her towel-girt lap. 'Robin – he's Henry's son – is marvellous with him, loves helping me when I'm there. He said the other day he wished Kit was his baby!'

'Do you like it, then? At the hotel, I mean? When you told me you were going to work there, I had my doubts, but you seem to have settled in already.'

'Well, I have. Amazing, isn't it? The thing is though, that they're creating such a warm, friendly atmosphere, and the guests, even though there are rather a lot of young men, are either out of the house all day or else just don't seem to grumble.' She giggled. 'Except the day the tank burst, of course.'

'The tank burst? My God! What happened?'

'Well, Keith, he's the younger one, wept and wailed and tore his hair and said the whole place was falling round their ears. But I said I knew a really good plumber, the fellow who

116

did the work on the cottage when I first moved in, and Henry said to ring him, so I did. He came right away. And then Henry got someone in to make good the damage whilst the plumber put in a new tank, and we put the range out, because although upstairs there are geysers, downstairs the range heats the water. By evening everything was fine – Ceri and I had cleaned and dried things out, Robin had tucked Kit into the pram and gone off to the beach for the whole day, only nipping back at lunchtime so I could change Kit's nappy and see that he was okay, and the guests treated it like a joke . . . It could have been a disaster, but instead it was rather fun! And it was all Henry; he's an ideal boss, honestly.'

'Yes, but he's a man,' Mollie said as Anthea puffed powder onto a giggling Kit. 'You don't usually like men.'

'I know I don't, but Hal's a person first and a man next, if you understand me. Oh, Kit, stop wriggling, there's a good boy! And what's more, he does love Kit! He's teaching sailing most of the time, but no matter how tired he is when he comes in, if I'm helping to cook dinner he takes Kit up with him and chats away to him whilst he changes. Henry really is nice, Moll.'

'I'm glad you've fallen on your feet at last,' Mollie said placidly, stitching away. 'How about being a bridesmaid next spring, when Freddie and me get spliced?'

'Oh, I couldn't . . . I'm too old! But you can have Kit as a pageboy by then, I should think.'

'You'd make a super bridesmaid,' Mollie coaxed, but Anthea shook her head firmly.

'No, Moll, not me! It would be almost as bad as being a bride!'

Chapter Nine

'There you are! The final injection. So if you bring him back for a booster in twelve months time, he'll be vaccinated against some very nasty bugs.' Ian Frazer lifted Zak off the examination table and put him into Nicola's waiting arms. 'And how are things going back at the flat? Any more complaints from Patani?'

Nicola hugged Zak and considered the question, standing in the small surgery whilst next door Mr Norrington's deep, calming tones rumbled on above the yapping of some small but vocal dog.

'Things are going okay,' she decided at last. 'The sister-in-law hasn't been back and nor has Gilbert, but it's bound to happen one day, and then what shall we do?'

'Face him out,' Ian advised. He was writing out the vaccination certificate for Zak, presumably, to treasure. Nicola, who had parted with twenty-five quid for all this attention, just hoped that Zak appreciated what was being done for him. 'And if he still objects, send him to me. I'll say that dogs can be just as effective as cats in keeping mice under control, and tell him I'll report him to the public health people if he makes a fuss.'

'You wouldn't!'

'I would indeed. People like Patani get away with too much if you ask me. Nicola . . .'

'Yes?'

'I was wondering . . . Would you like to come out for a meal one evening? I really enjoyed that Chinese takeaway and we got on all right, didn't we, so I wondered . . . How about that South Pacific place, on the prom? They say if you like oriental food you should try their specials.'

'Thanks; but I'm not sure,' Nicola said cautiously, because she was not sure of anything, not any more. Ian Frazer seemed a nice enough guy, but she was doing so well right now, forgetting Roger, becoming closer to Ceri, realising that marriage, though a marvellous institution, is simply not the be-all and end-all of existence. Suppose she was fool enough to fall in love with Ian and he with her? It would not be long before Ian realised he was loving not a normal woman but a shell, a hollow thing. And Nicola had had more than her share of being hurt. Losing Roger and Milly in one fell swoop . . .

'I'm asking you to share a meal with me, nothing more,' Ian said almost sharply, as the silence between them stretched. 'I thought . . . I mean we're both newcomers to Haisby and I thought . . . But if you don't want to, it doesn't matter, I'm sorry I asked.'

Outside in the waiting room people shifted and sighed. Nicola could almost feel their impatience. Why on earth had she been so silly? She had hurt Ian's feelings and she hadn't meant to, it was just . . .

'I-I've had – I've been – It wasn't that – Oh, God! Yes, I'd like to come!' The words tripped over each other in her haste to make amends. She knew her face was red and buried it in Zak's neck, longing to escape from the embarrassment she had caused. 'It was really nice of you to ask and I didn't mean to be so rude.'

'You will come?' He was smiling, relief writ large on his thin, serious face. 'Well, that's great. And honestly, I'm not trying to start anything . . . Take care of Zak, he's turning out to be a sturdy little chap, you don't often find a cat as nice as him.'

Nicola smiled, murmured that she would take great care of Zak, agreed to be picked up at the flat the following evening at eight o'clock, and left. Walking back along the pavement, heading for home now, she wondered again why she hadn't just invented another engagement. She really did not think she could cope with another relationship just yet. All the subtleties of conversation, of not mentioning Roger, or Milly . . .

I'll give him a ring tomorrow and say I've changed my mind, she resolved desperately. After all, that was Zak's last injection. I shan't have to face him again.

She strode on and was almost at Lavengro when a voice hailed her.

'Nicola! Don't walk so fast, wait for me!'

It was Ceri, red-faced and panting, running up the road pushing her bicycle. Nicola obligingly slowed.

'Hey, Ces! Where have you been? I thought you were at Ambleside all day today.'

'I am, but Keith sent me out to buy leeks. He's doing them for dinner in a cream sauce. How's Zak?'

'Fine, he hardly seemed to notice the needle going into his scruff. I worked through my lunch hour so I could leave at four and came straight home for him, that's why we got one of the first appointments.'

'Great.' Ceri hesitated, looking across at Nicola with an expression which the other girl could not quite interpret. 'Guess who I met in town?'

'Not Gilbert the Grope?'

'No, thank God. Tom from the bank.'

'Oh?'

'He's a teller in the bank on Lord Street, he lives in lodgings. He's all right, is Tom, though he fools about a lot. Nicola, the thing is . . .'

'What on earth are you looking so guilty for?' Nicola said. 'You are allowed to speak to fellows, you know, if you meet them on the street.'

'Yes . . . well, I've asked him to have dinner with us tomorrow night!'

Almost without conscious thought a picture appeared in Nicola's imagination. Ceri and her bank clerk, staring starrily at each other, whilst between them, Nicola played gooseberry. I'd go mad, Nicola told herself, and decided then and there to meet Ian, after all.

'Grand. Because I'm having a Chinese meal with Ian Frazer tomorrow night.'

'Oh, Nick, how could you? I don't know what on earth to give Tom to eat and I don't know what to talk about! I've never had a meal with a guy, I was relying on you – I'll have to tell him I'm ill or something!'

They reached their gateway and went through it, Zak sitting up in Nicola's arms and beginning to try to bounce down onto the ground. Nicola suddenly began to laugh. She laughed so loud she made Zak bark and that made Ceri laugh too.

'Oh, Ceri!' Nicola said, opening the front door and ushering her friend up the stairs in front of her. 'What a couple of fools we are – I nearly told Ian I couldn't make it, and you're just as bad!'

'Well, but what am I to do?' Ceri wailed, getting out her door key and unlocking the front door. 'It's all very well for you, at least you've had fellers in your time.'

'Yes. And lost them,' Nicola said grimly. 'We'll both do okay if we just remember we're supposed to be enjoying ourselves. All right, Zak, you can go down now.'

The evening went quite well despite Ceri's fears. Tom arrived at the door with a box of chocolates, which seemed quite adult and un-Tomlike, and then he said he'd brought them because he wanted her acne to rival his, which somehow seemed much more typical and made Ceri giggle, and that went some way towards breaking the ice.

He was nice about the flat, too – and loved Zak. In fact he played with Zak for ages, until Ceri served up the curry she had made, and then they sat in the kitchen and ate curry and gossiped about the guests at Ambleside, the traders in Lord Street and other mutual acquaintances.

Tom fed Zak on the sly and so did Ceri, with the result that the puppy was unable to face his own meal and made sicky noises which had Tom and Ceri in fits. Ceri had made an apple and raspberry pie and a custard with hardly any lumps and Tom said that when he had a place of his own he would cook her his speciality – in fact it was the only dish he could cook – a French mushroom omelette.

'All gooey in the middle?' Ceri asked hopefully.

'Extremely gooey, masses of salmonella with every bite, to say nothing of those wild French mushrooms probably acting like Spanish fly,' Tom said with relish.

'What's Spanish fly?' Ceri said, and Tom went red around the gills and said he would tell her, one day.

This, of course, brought them round to Ceri's new career. Ceri really enjoyed telling Tom all about her efforts to become a freelance writer.

'The only field that's barred to me at present is frank discussions on sex,' she said gloomily, having gone pretty well step by step through her attack on the fashion scene, her attempts at a Morning Story and her grand success – a half-column about rearing puppies in *Good Housekeeping*. 'If only I had that sussed out I'm sure I'd make a fortune.'

Tom grinned at her.

'Tell you what, why don't we have a practice run?'

Ceri giggled.

'Fool! No, what I want is to have a bird's eye view of some-one really sophisticated, like Nicola, actually doing it. Properly, I mean. I could ginger up my short stories as well as my articles if I knew a bit more.'

Tom's brow rose.

'Do girls like Nicola do it differently from simple souls like you, then?'

Ceri felt her face crimson. She giggled again, but more uncertainly this time.

'Oh Tom, of course they must do! I expect I'd make an awful hash of it, I'm not at all experienced, you see. I've tried writing from what I've seen on the telly, but you never really see anything much, do you?'

'Not a lot,' Tom agreed. He leaned out of his chair and scooped Zak into his arms. 'Going to have a fight with Uncle Tom?' he asked. 'And then I must away; I've got another long, hard day tomorrow.'

'I'll walk you as far as the swing bridge,' Ceri said to cover some slight confusion. 'I usually take Zak out last thing, so he can do his little tiddles.'

'That's nice. And why don't we see a flick together next week, then I'll treat you to a cheap but sustaining snack at Joe's burger bar?' Tom suggested. 'You'd like that, it's real fast food, lots of onions and burgers simply oozing with beef.'

In ordinary circumstances Ceri would have reminded Tom pretty sharply that she was a vegetarian but as it was, overawed by the fact that Tom was almost asking her for a date, she merely mumbled that it sounded fine.

As she had suggested, Ceri walked down to the swing bridge with him, well muffled now against the bitterly cold wind which had sprung up. Zak came as well, on his lead because he was somewhat irresponsible still, and he did two puddles – Zak not Tom – which pleased her. Tom then offered to walk home with her, back to the flat, which made them both laugh and they parted more easily than Ceri had expected.

I never thought I'd be shy with Tom, she told herself as she and Zak walked extremely slowly up the hill, having watched Tom out of sight. Rather to Ceri's disappointment

Tom had not tried to kiss her or hold her hand . . . but then why should he? They were good friends, that was all.

The journey home took rather a long time since Zak's idea of progress was one step forward and two back the way they had come. Outside Bridge House he found smells so interesting that Ceri had to drag him past – all those tramps clearly left their mark – but after that he got a move on and they almost ran back to Lavengro.

Actually, Ceri was glad of Zak's company, small though he was. There were so many deep shadows, so many sinister patches of darkness between the pools of light cast by the streetlamps. Ceri trotted along, talking to Zak, reminding him that Nicola would be home quite soon and that he was to sleep with Ceri tonight since she had baby-sat with him whilst Nicola gadded off.

Ceri's imagination being what it was, she picked Zak up in the gateway to Lavengro and, cuddling him close for comfort, hurried at a near-run past the straggly bushes in which mad axemen dwelt and across the darkened hall where a ghoul lived behind the coat-stand, a very thin ghoul with great staring red eyes and skeletal fingers. On the first landing they avoided the tarantula which crouched in the corner and did not look up to where the Blob lived, hanging stickily from the ornate central light fitting which only worked when there was a z in the month.

They gained the safety of the flat at last though, and Zak accompanied Ceri on a tour of the premises, but there were no pigeons or spiders in the kitchen, no living dead lurched out of the wardrobe and there was no one at all in the loo, so Ceri rushed in there with a bursting bladder and almost forgot about being alone in the dark whilst her first wee since Tom's arrival rushed out. She could never have excused herself and used the loo whilst he was in the house – heavens, what a good job I've decided never to marry she told herself, swishing away, or God knows what would happen to my waterworks!

She was making cocoa and putting biscuits out on a plate when Nicola came home. They sat companionably in the kitchen discussing their evenings and scoffing at each other's fantasy fears.

Nicola, accompanied all the way home by Ian, admitted she hated dark bushes herself and Ceri said that as she came up the path towards the front door, she had almost convinced herself that she was being followed.

'It's no lie that we need Zak,' Ceri continued as they went into their respective rooms, she with the puppy warm in her arms. 'When I lived in town the dark never worried me; it seems much darker out here, somehow.'

'Never mind; light evenings are coming,' Nicola comforted her. 'Night, Ceri. Night, little Zak!'

The party that Henry and Keith had hoped to throw when Ambleside first opened had never come off. It had not been possible to hold it indoors because there was never a room which was not half-decorated or half-furnished, and the weather had not been reliable enough for outdoors. But now, walking down to the marina to get the boat ready, Henry decided what he would do.

Keith's twenty-ninth birthday was approaching and Henry thought it would be a good idea to combine the birthday party with a house-warming, though goodness knew the house was warm enough in that it was almost booked up for the season, more than they had dreamed in their first year.

And it was the sailing lessons which attracted them. Even the older ones, who didn't want to learn, admitted that they had rather hoped for the odd voyage along the coast and with the larger vessel still not much used for teaching, Henry was glad to take them, and glad of the recommendations which they handed out with so prodigal a hand so that already they were taking bookings from people who had 'heard from friends . . .'

The only points, really, on which he and Keith did not agree were the lavishness of Keith's catering and Robin, and both these things were easier now that Anthea worked at Ambleside.

She was a first-rate worker. Tall, thin, spinsterish, she moved quietly around the house, cooking, coping with the staff, seeing that Mrs Frett, who did the heavy cleaning, brushed under the beds and behind the wardrobes as well as in more obvious spots. Anthea wore a fawn nylon overall with white collar and cuffs and it was always spotless, and what was better, her diffident smile broke out whenever she caught your eye, warming you, making you feel wanted.

Under her quiet, unassuming rule the bills for marketing

fell dramatically and Keith's tendency to throw a fit if things went wrong calmed down to no more than a frowning mutter. Robin played with Kit, helped with the chores, fetched and carried, and somehow Anthea was always there, in the kitchen cooking, in the pantry writing lists for marketing, even in the garden, apologetically planting vegetables behind a rosy brick wall because it was such a marvellous spot for them.

And for the life of him, Henry could see nothing wrong with Robin living with them at Ambleside. But Keith moaned about the responsibility of a child when they were trying to run a business, how Robin's upbringing would interfere with their social life.

But it wasn't just the responsibility, Henry knew. Keith was jealous. He had flounced – there was no other word for it – into the kitchen a few weeks ago when Henry had been patiently ironing shirts – sailors are dab hands at small domestic tasks – and had pointed a dramatic finger at the door which had just closed behind Robin as he made his weary but happy way to bed.

'It won't *do*,' Keith exclaimed shrilly. 'No matter what you say, Hal, that kid is coming between us. We never have an evening for just the two of us any more, we help him with his homework, make his bedtime drink . . . And we have little enough time together in any case, now.'

'It's true we're awfully busy,' Henry agreed, reaching for another shirt and buttoning it up. He belonged to the school of thought which irons shirts on one side only, flat and buttoned, to ease the work load rather than produce the perfectly ironed article. 'But I don't see that Rob makes all that much difference – quite the opposite. He works hard for a kid and makes himself scarce when we want him to. Why, now he's in school, he brings friends back and plays out with them.'

'Yes, and you make them special teas and joke about the telly with them,' Keith said, his voice thick with resentment. 'It isn't the same, Hal. We're never alone!'

'Look, Keith, so far as alone goes, I think we're better not alone! I never talk about it, but you know very well how I feel. If you just mean alone to talk business, then what's wrong with now, when Robin's in bed and the girls have gone home? As for a social life, that really is up to you. I don't want to go out, but I'm a good deal older than you. There's absolutely no need for you to hang about the house when you've finished work for the day. Why don't you go down to Reynard's, or the jazz club? I'm happy for you to go, really I am.'

To Henry's secret surprise but real pleasure, the very next evening Keith had disappeared 'to have a drink with a friend'. He had come back late, with a sleepy, satisfied look on his face, and had gone straight to bed.

When this had happened five nights out of seven, Henry knew that Keith had taken his advice and found himself a friend. He was glad, knowing that this would make for a quieter, more peaceful life for himself, but he did hope that Keith was being sensible. Henry knew very litttle about the gay community, but he did know it was dangerous, healthwise, to mix with the wrong people.

He had a quiet word with Keith on those lines, but was told, by a rather shamefaced partner, that Keith was no fool, that he was not one for cruising or making himself cheap, and that his present 'friend' was a young man of impeccable background and high moral tone.

Just what sort of high moral tone could be held by one of Keith's gay friends Henry could not imagine, but he got the gist of it; Keith's friend, to put it bluntly, was not likely to pass on anything nasty. And probably, Henry told himself with stubborn optimism, they really were just friends; after all, it seemed to be common knowledge that Keith was gay yet though he had lived in Haisby for seven years there was no talk of a multitude of boyfriends.

I suppose I'm a careful type, Henry told himself, going down the steps onto the quayside, so I expect an equally responsible attitude from Keith. And I'm sure I won't be disappointed; he's a sensible little bloke.

Henry crossed the quay and stepped aboard *Sunny Saturday*. Yes, a birthday party was a good idea and he would be able to meet Keith's 'friend' and see for himself if he was a decent type of person. He wanted no risks for the lad. What was more, the weather had suddenly seemed to make up its mind to be set fair; they could have a beach-barbecue, which would save a lot of fuss up at the hotel itself. He strode across the deck, enjoying the bounce and give of the boards beneath his feet, and the soft water-murmur as the sea caressed the hull. This was the life – the best of both worlds! A boat, the sea, good companions, no hassle – a business he loved and a partner he trusted. And, of course, the kid.

The kid! Odd how attached he had become to Robin, though they had not known one another long. Robin didn't want to go back to London and Henry didn't want him to, either. It was not true that Robin got between himself and Keith but he certainly made it difficult for Keith to start the semi-flirtatious conversations which Henry had found so difficult and Keith had patently enjoyed. All in all, Robin was another good thing, a reason for Henry enjoying his sailing but never fretting to go off, to find tropic seas, desert islands. No, right here in Haisby was happiness enough. And when he got home tonight he'd wait until Keith had gone off and then he and Robin, and Ceri if she was around, would plan their party.

Anthea pushed her folding pushchair up to the bus stop after Henry had told her about the party with very mixed feelings. She had never yet attended a beach-barbecue, so she should be looking forward to it – she just wished she knew a bit more about what was in store.

'A great deal of work,' Henry had said cheerfully when she tried to get a bit more information. 'Don't worry, Ant, you'll have a good time despite being worn to a frazzle before the party even starts. Why the preparations alone . . . !'

'It's not that bad,' Ceri had protested, giggling. The three of them had been in the kitchen preparing dinner whilst Keith, in tails, swept regally to and fro, serving the guests with the help of the Saturday girl, Sarah. 'It's mainly meat cooked over a charcoal grill, Ant, and bread rolls and sausages. Fireworks, too . . . But as staff, we'll all have to nip around serving, I suppose.'

'You're guests, as well,' Henry had protested. 'Keith isn't twenty-nine every year!'

To Anthea's surprise, Ceri had given a muffled snort at that and Henry had grinned and shaken his head as though reprimanding himself.

'Silly thing to say . . . Go and take a look, Ces, see if they're nearly through with their starter.'

But now, reaching the bus stop with Kit still slumbering in the pushchair, Anthea drew her vehicle to a halt and bent down to pluck him gently out. The pushchair folded wonderfully small and the bus drivers were very helpful, there was scarcely one of them, now, who could not have folded and unfolded the pushchair as well as she, but she still liked to be able to get straight aboard and to stow the folded pushchair neatly in the space provided.

So, in a week she would be a guest-cum-worker at a beach-barbecue! She would stay the night, sharing Robin's room with Kit and Mrs Frett's daughter Heather who was Rob's best friend despite the disadvantage of being a mere girl. Robin would sleep on the put-u-up in Henry's room, though there were attics which, when they had been cleaned out and decorated, would do for live-in staff.

I really do fall on my feet, Anthea thought, as the bus drew ponderously alongside. It would have been hard to have to live in because she loved her cottage by the sea marshes, but she would have done it, to have a job where she could always be near the child. It had not been necessary, however; Henry was satisfied that she would manage the journey daily, only spending the night on occasions, like the barbecue, when she would be needed very late. Who could be luckier than me, Anthea thought, climbing onto the bus, working in a beautiful old house with friendly people like Henry and Keith?

'Hop you on, gal Anthea,' the driver said. 'Shove that there pushchair well in, do that'll trip people up.'

Complying, Anthea spotted her friend Lily and waved as she made her way up the bus. A beach-barbecue! Just wait until Lily heard!

Nicola was in the kitchen when Ceri bounced back from work with the party invitations.

'It's to be a surprise for Keith, because it's his birthday,' she explained, thrusting the bright yellow card into her flatmate's hand. 'Henry's awfully sensible, too. He's sent them all out with "so-and-so and friend", so you can take someone else.. Who'll you take, Nick?'

'Must I go, Ceri?' Nicola said doubtfully, looking at the invitation as though it had teeth and horns. 'I've only met Henry and Keith once, in the street.'

'Of course you must go! You're my friend . . . Besides, it's a barbecue on the beach, so Zak's invited as well. Oh come on, you've got heaps of friends. What about getting someone over from Norwich?'

'I suppose I could ask Milly . . .'

The words were out before Nicola could prevent them. She stopped short, appalled. What on earth had made her say anything so damned *naive*? As if she could possibly ask Milly! She must have a screw loose to let the thought cross her mind, let alone to vocalise it!

Ceri had never heard of Milly, knew of no reason why asking her was a bad idea, but she must have guessed there was something wrong, for she stared fixedly at Nicola.

'Who's Milly? Not that it matters. Nicola, why don't you ask Ian? He's taken you out a couple of times.'

'Ian? Oh no, I couldn't. He'd think I had designs on him or something! We're just friends, that's all.'

'Well, I'm going to ask Tom,' Ceri said. 'He teases me something rotten, but I like him. Anyway, he'll enjoy it, and although I daresay one of the *Chronicle* girls would go, I'd rather take a guy.'

Zak, waiting fairly patiently by the fridge for someone to make him his tea, suddenly realised that patience, whilst a virtue, wasn't getting him far and yapped sharply. He was getting awfully big, Nicola realised. Gone was the sweet little fellow who could have curled up in a milk saucepan. Today's Zak would have had difficulty in fitting inside a witch's cauldron!

'All right, old lad, I'll start your tea,' Nicola said, opening the fridge door. Zak's head promptly appeared in the aperture as he scanned the shelves for something he fancied. He fancied a sausage and he and Nicola both grabbed for it at once, Zak winning by a short head. He galloped off, the sausage gripped between his teeth whilst Nicola, who had planned a sausage sandwich whilst she created Zak's tea, followed with distressful cries. 'Come back, you greedy little bugger,' she shouted. 'How would you like it if I scoffed your food?'

'He'd swap it for a sausage any day,' Ceri said, when Nicola returned, sausageless, with Zak tucked under one arm. Zak was smiling. 'Come on, why won't you take Ian? I mean, if I'm taking Tom . . .'

'You and Tom must be closer than Ian and I.'

'Not true. But he does make me laugh. Doesn't Ian make you laugh? What about bringing some old boyfriends over from Norwich, then? We could share them out.'

Nicola began to shred white fish. Zak stood on end, a black

129

and gold sausage himself, peering hopefully up at her. He looked so sweet and so hungry that he might never have smelt the sausage, let alone devoured it.

'Boyfriends? Like the fishes in the sea, my child, one has to catch one's own. But you seem to have netted Tom pretty thoroughly.'

'No, that's where you're wrong,' Ceri said. She sat on the kitchen table swinging her legs, and began to peel the pile of onions Nicola had stood ready. 'Only yesterday I went into the bank and he was serving one of the girls, from Waves, the hairdresser's down the Arcade, and flirting like anything. And when she went he leaned across and said to me, "Doesn't she have a scrumptious little bum?" Now not the most insensitive person would say that to someone they . . . they liked.'

'Tom might. It strikes me that Tom's only comfortable when he's teasing someone; I don't believe you've met the real Tom yet, but you might, at the barbecue.'

Ceri sliced the first onion into rings and wiped her watering eyes with the back of her hand. Then she looked admiringly at Nicola.

'Do you know, you're a lot cleverer than you look. I think you've hit the nail on the head. Tom teases and jokes around because he's afraid that if he's serious . . . What is he afraid of, Nick?'

'He's afraid that if he's serious and shows how he feels, someone may hurt him by mocking him,' Nicola said. 'Lots of guys are like that – women, too, sometimes.'

'Me?'

'Well, no, I don't think you suffer much from an urge to be taken seriously. But I expect you have other hang-ups,' Nicola added, seeing that Ceri was about to think herself dubbed insensitive. 'And you don't much like it when people laugh about your writing, do you?'

'No. Tom's been hateful about my writing,' Ceri said broodingly. 'I don't expect you to understand this, Nicola, but every little article or story is like a part of me; when someone's rude and laughs and says I'm getting it all wrong, or such-and-such a person would never do that, I feel as if I've been kicked in the stomach. I ache inside for ages afterwards, and I keep reading it over to try to see what's wrong. But Tom . . . oh, he mocks all my stuff, whether it's fiction or a serious article.'

'I only know one writer,' Nicola said hesitantly. 'And she says no one should ever talk about their work until it's published and then they can read it for themselves. She's a really good writer, too, she's done telly scripts and stuff in the glossies.'

'Who is she? Where does she live? Oh, Nick, you don't know how wonderful it would be for me to meet a proper writer, someone who knows how I feel and could understand the things I don't, like why it is that bloody Marigold refuses to fall in love with Amos in my latest short story. I meant her to, I *commanded* her to, and I am the boss, after all. Yet she just will not.'

Nicola tried to suppress a grin, succeeded in suppressing a chuckle. It was too bad to laugh, when, as Milly often said, creative writing was such a difficult and lonely business. But somehow Ceri's small, freckled face, her wide, guileless eyes, made one want to laugh.

'Yes; I've heard Milly say that over and over,' Nicola said. Thoughtlessly as it turned out. 'She says that considering the characters are one's own creations, they don't treat their Maker with much respect!'

'That's it *exactly*,' Ceri said. 'Didn't you say something about bringing Milly to the barbecue? Because if so, I do wish you would. It would be such a help to me to talk things through.'

'I don't think she'd come,' Nicola said. 'You were right, I'll ask Ian. He'll enjoy it.'

'Oh! Then why don't you invite Milly over for a meal? I'll make it. Please, Nick, it would be such a help.'

'She wouldn't come,' Nicola said again. She could feel panic almost closing her throat. 'We didn't see eye to eye over something – we fell out.'

'You? I can't imagine you quarrelling with anyone that badly,' Ceri said. 'Are you *sure* she wouldn't come?'

Nicola, incurably honest, hesitated. She put the fish and puppy meal into a bowl, put the bowl on the floor, where Zak dived into it as though there were truffles below, and then walked over to the sink and rinsed her fingers under the cold tap. Finally, drying her hands on the roller towel, she answered.

'I don't know, she might. Milly's not like other people. But it would be awkward . . . although in a way I'd love to get in touch with her.'

There it went again, the stupid feeling that it couldn't possibly have been Milly who had let her down, the fault must lie in herself. And that feeling went hand in hand with the stupider one that she could not bear to lose Milly, because losing Milly was losing her childhood.

'Then why don't you? Is she single, like us? If so, she could spend the night – I wouldn't mind sleeping on the couch, she could have my bed.'

Nicola looked at Ceri's friendly, eager little face and knew that, unless she came clean, she would be fielding questions about Milly for the next ten years. She walked over to the table and picked up the bowl of onion rings. She fed them into the spitting fat in the pan and began, automatically, to turn them. Then she spoke, her face turned away, her voice almost abstracted.

'Yes, she's single, but she's living with a guy called Roger West, and don't suggest we ask him too, because he was my husband . . . still is, strictly speaking.'

There was a stupefied silence. Nicola turned and glanced across at Ceri. Her friend sat there, mouth at half-cock, eyes incredulously wide.

Silenced for the first time since we met, Nicola thought grimly. Well, well, well, I really must have fooled most people if Ceri never guessed.

'Your husband?' Ceri quavered at last.

'That's right.'

'But Nicola, I never knew you were married!'

'No. Well, I'm not, am I, not really. Because he's living with Milly Coppack.'

'And she . . . she's your *friend*?'

'Since we were in nursery school. Only it's awkward, now, because of Roger.'

'Oh, Nick!' Ceri's bright little face was awash with emotions, sorrow for her friend uppermost. 'What a beastly girl she must be, to steal a friend's husband! I bet you hate her, don't you?'

Nicola did not have to examine her heart for the answer.

'No I don't hate her,' she said slowly. 'I don't think Milly meant to fall in love with Roger, and of course Roger couldn't really have loved me, otherwise he wouldn't have gone with Milly, would he?'

'I don't know,' Ceri said wretchedly. 'Oh, Nick, I'm sorry

I asked stupid questions, I didn't mean to hurt you. It was just the thought of meeting a writer . . . My God, did you say Milly *Coppack*?'

'That's right. Do you know her?'

'Yes . . . no, but she writes a column in the *Evening News*, I always lov . . . I mean I always used to read it. And I've read one or two of her short stories . . . Still, she did a wicked thing to you, Nick.'

'Yes, she did, but perhaps I wasn't meant to be married, Ceri, because I don't think I was very good at it. I mean I loved my house, and being Roger's wife, and working out our budget and things like that, but I don't think I was much fun. I think I was boring. I mean Milly's marvellous, she's clever, always on the go, she loves life . . . Ceri, she's having a *baby*!'

'Serve her right,' Ceri said bracingly. 'She won't like that, I believe it's very painful and afterwards there are dirty nappies and snotty noses and all sorts. Probably Roger will get fed up with her, and move on to someone else!'

'When I said it might be nice to have a baby, Roger said he wasn't a child-lover and besides, we couldn't afford it,' Nicola said, her voice so low that Ceri had to lean forward to catch the words. 'So you see, Ceri . . .'

Ceri jumped off the table and ran to Nicola. She put both her arms round the older girl and hugged her, and Nicola, crying for the first time since she had lived in Haisby, was touched when she eventually broke free from Ceri's fierce embrace to find that Ceri, too, was crying.

'I hate them, Nicola,' Ceri said, gulping. 'They were cruel to you . . . Here!'

She picked up Zak, who had abandoned his long-empty dish and was gazing at them, wide-eyed and distressed, and thrust him into Nicola's arms. And the puppy, instinctively giving comfort, began to lick as much of her face as he could reach.

'You fool, Zak,' Nicola said unsteadily, smiling through her tears. 'Oh, what a little darling you are!' She turned to Ceri. 'And you, Ceri Allen, are another.'

'You're pretty nice yourself,' Ceri assured her. 'I'm glad you told me, Nicola. And I won't ask Tom to the barbecue, we'll go together, you and I.'

Nicola laughed again, but properly this time, with genuine amusement.

'Well, we'll see. The chances are that Tom will be invited anyway, but you and I will definitely go together.'

'And Zak,' Ceri reminded her, turning back to the stove. 'Oh my God, the onions are black!'

'And Zak,' Nicola repeated, still cuddling the puppy. 'We mustn't forget Zak!'

'As if we could . . . Nicola?'

'Yes?'

'If you're a married woman you must understand about . . . well, about what happens to men when they get all lovey-dovey . . . you know! I wish you'd explain, because Marion in Classified said that it was all about blood – that there were little veins and blood vessels in a guy's thing and when he got excited more blood rushed through and made it all hard. Is that *true*? And why does it have to be hard?'

'It's something like that,' Nicola said cautiously. 'Look, don't worry about it! It's all perfectly natural, really it is.'

'But how can I write love scenes, when I don't know what it is they *do*?' Ceri said, her voice laden with anguish. 'When Marion told me, I said it sounded like a sort of super-blush – you try taking a super-blush seriously!'

Nicola giggled.

'Ceri, one of these days you and I must have a serious talk; but right now, I'm going to answer Henry's invitation. And I am going to take Ian along, so you really must invite Tom.'

Chapter Ten

Ceri and Nicola need not have worried over who they should ask to the Ambleside party; a week beforehand half Haisby had been invited. Henry had to tell Keith about it once he realised how it was growing and it was a good thing he did, since it took Keith, Ceri and Anthea three days of hard work to arrange everything.

'But barbecues are supposed to be easy – just meat grilled over charcoal,' Henry said when he saw the preparations taking place. 'I've been to hundreds of them all over the world and meat and lobster and stuff are what we ate. Keith, this was supposed to give you pleasure, not hours and hours of extra work.'

'You can't ask a hundred or so people to a party and just provide steaks and lobsters, not in Norfolk,' Keith pointed out, laying wafer-thin slices of apple on pastry. 'Besides, you know how you nag about my champagne mentality, so this time I'm providing cheapos – salads, french bread, sausages and beefburgers grilled over the charcoal, with some of my own special veggie burgers for people like Ceri, who's a vegetable herself.'

'Vegetarian,' Ceri corrected. They were in the kitchen, Anthea and Keith cooking, and she and Henry peeling, chopping and doing what Keith had just called kitchen-maid jobs. Not that Henry minded; the two men had never been more in harmony. Ceri thought it might have something to do with Keith's increasingly successful social life. He hardly ever moaned about Robin now, and was far more relaxed over Henry being out on the boats.

'Yes, all right, vegetarian. And of course we'll provide jacket potatoes to cook on the bonfire and . . .'

'Bonfire?' Henry looked bemused. 'What's this about a bonfire?'

'A beach-barbecue would be pretty dull without a bonfire,

135

Hal,' Keith said reproachfully. 'It's something for people to gather round, and they push their own spuds into the embers and . . . Oh, well, wait and see. It'll be so successful the guests will clamour for one each week.'

Henry shuddered, but Ceri could tell he didn't really mean it, he was enjoying all the bustle as much as she was. Kit, bouncing up and down in the playpen on the other side of the kitchen was probably missing the attention usually lavished on him, but he seemed content enough, reaching for Zak through the bars and occasionally grabbing a handful of soft fur for a few moments.

'All right, I'll buy the fact that you need salads and stuff,' Henry said now. 'But what are you cooking? I mean, you don't cook salads, do you?'

Anthea, with her hair scraped back and one of Keith's big white aprons on, sniggered, but Keith turned to give Henry a pitying look.

'No, we don't cook salads,' he said patiently. 'But after our guests have had their savoury course they'll want something sweet to finish up with. Apple pie, or raspberry pavlova, or perhaps even fresh strawberries and cream, except that pushes the cost up a bit, so I'll probably go for a soufflé and a nice lemon meringue pie.'

'I see; nothing elaborate,' Henry said with heavy sarcasm. 'Just how much is this going to cost?'

Keith shrugged but looked evasive.

'A pittance,' he assured the older man. 'Tell you what, if they do like it, and I'm sure they will, we'll charge a fiver a head next time, and I promise on my word of honour that we'll make three quid each of that back.'

'When I suggested a party I didn't envisage –' Henry began, but was promptly squashed.

'Now, Hal, you suggested a barbecue, you said we'd invite heaps of people, I said I'd do the food. What's wrong with that?'

'Oh well – nothing, I suppose,' Henry said. He grinned at Ceri and she smiled back, being in the know in this instance at least. Henry intended to use the barbecue as an advertising feature, he had commissioned her to write it up for him and Tom was going to take the photographs. Far from being distressed at the number of people who were now coming and the amount of food which was being prepared, Henry thought it excellent publicity. But as he had said to Ceri, it would be fatal to tell Keith a thing like that.

'Before we knew it he'd have asked every soul in Haisby and would be buying steaks and champagne,' he told Ceri. 'He's a marvellous cook and a fantastic worker, but he's got this blind spot about profit and loss accounts.'

'It's because he's never worked for himself before,' Ceri said shrewdly. 'He's always been spending an employer's money so it didn't bother him. Think how sensible he was over the furniture and the decorating and the work on the garden – even the boats! He never said you should buy new, he was happy with secondhand. It's only with food that he goes a bit over the top. And Anthea's just the opposite; her father expected her to manage on almost nothing, so she did. And now, though the money's there, she still behaves with great caution.'

'That's very true; bright girl,' Henry had said approvingly. 'Now tell me how many hours you've worked this week.'

And now, with the party the following day, preparations were going on apace.

'Ceri, love, could you pass me the caster sugar? I can't bear to use granulated in something that has to be as light as a feather.'

Ceri put down the potato peeler but as she handed Keith the sugar, the telephone rang.

'I'll take it,' Henry said gladly. It was hot in the kitchen and the sun would presently move round, making it hotter still. 'I'll finish the spuds in a moment.'

'I thought you said we were having jacket potatoes,' Ceri remarked to Keith as Henry disappeared. 'So why must we peel such mounds of spuds?'

'Potato salad,' Keith said briefly. 'We'll need a good few onions, as well. Ant, when you've finished that meringue, pop on some gloves and do the onions, there's a dear. Thank God we can do the salads in advance, otherwise tomorrow would be hell, dear.'

Faintly, from the hall, Ceri could hear Henry's voice, then his footsteps, returning in their direction.

'Ceri? It's for you. Some chap called Durrant.'

Ceri sighed and headed for the door. She frowned at the telephone, then lifted the receiver. Who on earth could be ringing her here?

* * *

137

It was a warm, bright Friday evening and Nicola, in preparation for the party next day, was washing her hair. Ceri was due home from work any moment so she had made a large salad and cooked pasta with mushrooms in a garlic sauce. Now, with her head over the kitchen sink, she concentrated on getting her abundant locks squeaky clean.

As she washed, she thought about her day. It had been a busy one, with Mr Gregory coming in after spending the best part of the week with a client. He had been considerate as always, giving her the opportunity of doing the letters in her lunch hour or leaving them until the following day, but Nicola had felt it best to get them out of the way. She had nothing particular to do in her lunch hour and knew she would get time off in lieu, probably that afternoon. Mr Gregory had come and perched on her desk and dictated, and afterwards had gone and bought her sandwiches and a cream cake so that she could have a picnic whilst she worked.

He really was splendidly good-looking, with black hair cut close to a nicely shaped head and dark, intelligent eyes. But fortunately, handsome men were something Nicola avoided since Roger, so she had no trouble in being friendly but disinterested in her boss.

She had got through the letters speedily and as a result had left early, giving herself more time to prepare herself for the party next day. When the doorbell rang she actually considered not answering it; her hair was dripping, she was wearing a white bra and faded blue jeans, and if it was Gilbert the Grope she had no desire to wrestle with him on the doorstep, for she did not intend to let him in.

But on the other hand, Ceri was a past mistress in the art of losing her doorkey and it was just about time she came tootling back on her bike, with Zak sitting perilously up in the basket on the front. The peril came from the fact that he was now a very large puppy indeed, with what Ceri described as honking great feet and a deep, masculine bark. But he was still too little for the leap from bike to ground, so Ceri had to wobble along the road with an admonitary hand ready to snatch.

Yes, it was probably Ceri, Nicola decided. But even so, she took what you might call rearguard action. She wrapped her hair in a towel, ran into the bathroom and draped a second towel decorously round her bare shoulders, and then padded, barefoot, over to the door.

Once there, though, caution got the better of her.

'Ceri? Is that you?'

There was a pause and then a muffled female voice said what sounded like, 'No; it's Jenny.'

'Oh . . . hang on, whilst I unlock,' Nicola said briskly. She liked Jenny, a practical person who occasionally came in and cut their hair for nothing in return for a bit of typing or an apple pie. Ceri believed in barter, though it was a new concept to Nicola. 'Come in, Jen, I'm just . . .'

The door swung open and the words died on Nicola's lips. Facing her, smiling widely to be sure but with uncertainty in her eyes, was Milly Coppack.

'Sugar?'

'No, thanks. This is a nice little kitchen, Nicola.'

Milly was sitting at the table, elbows resting on it, whilst Nicola bustled round getting a cup of tea. So far, neither girl had said much. Nicola had invited Milly in, Milly had accepted, Nicola had offered tea, Milly had accepted. But the big question hovered, just behind the automatic politeness to a guest which had prevented Nicola from slamming the door smartly in her erstwhile friend's face.

That and curiosity, of course. And a sort of warmth, that Milly was here of her own accord, that she had actually searched for Nicola, that she must still care.

'I don't have any lemon,' Nicola apologised, adding milk to the cups. 'Ceri – she's my flatmate – doesn't have it in tea and somehow it's easier for both of us to take milk.'

'You never cared for lemon tea much,' Milly observed. Her bright, dark eyes were scanning Nicola as though she could see, by the sheer force of her interest, through the smooth mask of her friend's face to the thoughts in the mind underneath. 'You only drank it because I did.'

'Probably,' Nicola said. 'Would you like a biscuit?'

She remembered as she said it that Ceri had eaten the last of the ginger nuts this morning, instead of breakfast, and that there were no more biscuits in the flat. But she did not care, she knew Milly would refuse. Tea was one thing, eating the biscuits of someone you had . . . well, had wronged . . . was another.

'No, thanks. So this is where you went.'

The shrewd, amused eyes moved from Nicola and travelled

round the kitchen, taking in the cracked linoleum, the battered old ladder-backed chairs, the stained melamine table-top. Nicola thought of the kitchen in the house on Kett's Hill; the gleaming red floor tiles, the light oak units, the bunches of onions and herbs hanging a little self-consciously from the ceiling. Space, cleanliness, the sparkle of the racks of utensils, the copper-bottomed saucepans, each one lovingly cleaned and polished after every job. The window with its wide sill, crammed with all the silly little presents she and Roger had bought each other over the years. Weeping pierrots, china elephants, cats of every shape and size. Then there was the neat row of African violets which she liked because they didn't keep overflowing their pots or making demands, and the curtains, looped back with twisted silk ropes, the pattern carefully chosen to fit in with the rest.

Without looking round she could picture in her mind's eye the kitchen here, in Lavengro. The stained wooden draining board, all on the slope so that sometimes china slid gracelessly back into the washing-up water, and the sink itself which Mr Patani must have rescued from the Ark, so old and cracked and grey it was. The faded curtains which were just the wrong colour for the badly painted walls, the huddle of ill-assorted kitchen implements, saucepans, stained and holey tea-towels . . . The contrast was painful, yet somehow Nicola was not hurt by it. Her voice was steady as she answered.

'Yes, this is where I went.'

'Why didn't you go home? That's where we thought you'd go – I was really worried when I rang last week and your mother told me you weren't there.'

Nicola nodded; so Milly had traced her simply by asking Nicola's parents. But what did it matter, after all? She was not ashamed of her present living quarters, they were all she could afford. If anyone was ashamed it should be Milly, who had contributed nothing to the house on Kett's Hill, who had simply walked into perfection.

'So why here, Nicola? Why Haisby? Why didn't you stick around?'

Nicola had made the tea. Now she put a cup silently in front of Milly and sat opposite her, nursing her own cup. She found that she was oddly reluctant to speak; that the questions which had burned in her brain for months and months no longer seemed to matter.

'Stay? I had nothing to stay for, did I?'

'Well, you never know. I mean, Roger really loved you, you know. If you hadn't cut and run . . .'

'I didn't cut and run,' Nicola said untruthfully but with a sudden, deep conviction. 'I left because I'd had enough. I expect you think this flat is shabby, that my life is boring, but I love it, I've got a good job and I'm happy. What more could I ask?'

'You *left*? You didn't leave until you found he'd got someone else. Oh come on, Nicola, you aren't trying to tell me you were tired of Roger?'

The warm eyes smiled into hers; this was the friend who had been everything to her, Milly Coppack, her proudest possession. Milly was inviting her to say that she still loved Roger, that she still wanted him . . . and the old Nicola would have said what Milly wanted to hear. But not this Nicola. Not even, she realised, for the sake of getting Roger back.

'I didn't know I was tired of Roger until I moved out,' she said now, with an assumed frankness which she knew would fool Milly completely, because she had never been anything but straightforward with her friend before. 'It's all right, Milly, I don't grudge you any of it . . . certainly not Roger! I came round to see you one day a month or so ago, I thought we could have a chat, but Roger was home and it seemed cheeky . . .' she looked coolly at Milly, her eyes steady '. . . but now I realise I should have gone ahead and invaded your privacy, since you've not hesitated to invade mine,' she ended.

'Touché,' Milly said, throwing up a hand in a fencer's gesture. 'You think I shouldn't have come?'

'No-oo,' Nicola said slowly. 'If you wanted to see me again, why not? Only . . . it's over, isn't it, Milly?'

'Over? I don't know what you mean.'

'Oh, I think you do. You're so clever, Milly, you must know what I mean.'

'Look, why are we talking like this? I came to try to explain what happened, why I ended up with Roger when heaven knows I'd never shown any interest in him before. I was afraid you'd be bitter, think I'd done it for some obscure reason – spite, perhaps. But it wasn't like that, truly, Nicola. It was weird . . . one moment it was just a mad fling, an experiment you might say, and the next . . .'

141

'A mad fling? An experiment? Oh Milly, for goodness sake, what on earth is that supposed to mean?'

'I . . . wanted to find out what he was *like*, the man you'd decided to share your life with,' Milly said slowly. 'Before, you and I had been so close; then you married and Roger came between us. I was jealous of him but curious, too. Not just about what it was that had attracted you but . . . well, I wondered if I could have had him – you know, if I'd been around at the time. The pair of us always mucked about with the same crowd but I couldn't help noticing that the boys always went for you first, even if I ended up with them. Remember Stevie? You had him first, it was only after you'd ditched him that he attached himself to me.'

'You mean you weren't serious with Roger? That you were just playing when you started having it off with him?' Nicola felt colour flood her face; this really was absurd. 'Oh come on, Milly, credit me with some sense!'

'I mean just that,' Milly said stubbornly. 'I thought I could satisfy my curiosity about Roger and then go away again, and you'd never find out. Only . . . Roger was sweet, and we seemed to suit each other awfully well, and he didn't want me to go again, so I stayed, and . . . Oh, hell, Nicola, there have been times when I'd have given a lot for it never to have happened; I've really missed you!'

'I missed you, too,' Nicola said sadly. 'The odd thing is though, that the person I missed doesn't really exist, and I thought I knew her so well. My friend Milly would never have jeopardised my marriage from vulgar curiosity!'

'I didn't mean to,' Milly said earnestly. 'It was just a game . . . It seemed so unfair, you'd always had all the things I wanted and for all I knew you'd done it again. I had to make sure, you see. Only when I was with Roger it stopped being a game, something I could do and then forget. It got . . . well, serious.'

'I had the things you wanted? But Milly, you were always the one who came top of the class, won all the prizes, got the interesting jobs. I was just your shadow.'

Milly shook her head.

'Not true. Oh, sure, I'm clever – always have been. But somehow, you got what I wanted. First it was the Saturday job in the shop on the corner, then it was babysitting for that young couple in Eaton Rise, then you got into the lacrosse team at school . . . and after school you got Stevie, then Dick, then you got engaged to the handsomest man I'd ever seen, then you married him whilst I was still bumming around trying to make a name for myself . . . you had a lovely home, a good job with the Union, a settled future . . .'

'But Milly, you're famous! You could have married anyone!'

'I'm not famous enough, and I couldn't marry anyone, or at least I didn't think I could. So I tried with Roger just to see – and it worked too well. I would have backed out, honest, but Roger wouldn't. He was crazy for me.'

'You're trying to tell me that Roger insisted, when you would rather have left my marriage alone? Well, perhaps you're right, perhaps Roger was more to blame than you. I suppose he was in a way, since he was married and you were single. But it doesn't matter any more, Milly, it's too late! I've made my own life without you or Roger, and I'm happy! I made mistakes with Roger, but at least I'm honest enough, now, to admit they were my fault and to make sure I don't make the same mistakes again. If you and Roger are happy then I'm glad for you, but we can't change things.'

'I know we can't *change* things, of course I do. But why shouldn't we be friends still? After all, Nicola, it's been a lot of years. You're the closest friend I've ever had and I miss you hellishly. When odd little things happen, when something makes me laugh, I think *Just wait until Nicola hears that*, and when I remember I won't be telling you I get this horrid, hollow feeling.'

'I know what you mean; I suffered from it a lot, at first,' Nicola said. 'But it's part of the package I'm afraid, Milly, part of the price you pay for Roger.'

'But it needn't be, if we're sensible! We're living in the nineteen-nineties, when anything goes,' Milly said eagerly. 'We can still be friends, Nicola.'

'The three of us? Or should I say four?'

'Four? I don't know what you mean.'

'I mean the baby,' Nicola said patiently, and felt a stab of pain so acute that she almost gasped at it. Think of little Zak, she ordered herself; think of your little Zak! 'You know, Milly, the baby you're expecting.'

Milly stared. There was a look on her face which told Nicola that had Milly been a different sort of person she would be blushing. But Milly never blushed.

'Baby?'

'Yes. The one you're going to give birth to.'

Nicola let her eyes dwell on Milly's figure in its dashing scarlet and white smock and narrow black trousers. Pretty clothes, exciting clothes, but not the sort of thing Milly usually favoured. Clothes to hide, not reveal – and Milly had always been the sort of girl who thrust her figure at you, even though it wasn't a particularly good one by Nicola's admittedly exacting standards.

'You're guessing.'

'No. I knew it as soon as I saw you.'

Milly hesitated, then smiled. It was the first warm and completely genuine smile to cross her face since her arrival in the flat.

'Oh, the baby. Yes, I want the baby. I'm older than you, remember – twenty-five. I felt it was about time I had a baby and Roger agreed. I think the two of us will make a pretty baby because Rog is a great-looking guy, and I'm not so bad.' She grinned at Nicola. 'You aren't into babies, Roger said so . . . This will be one thing, Nicola, that I'll have done before you.'

'All right,' Nicola said. Thoughts chased themselves through her head, wanting to be spoken, were chased back again. So Roger thought she had not wanted a child, did he? Either Milly or Roger himself was a terrible liar. Nicola had suggested a child a couple of times – more – and on each occasion Roger had said he was sorry but they could not possibly afford a baby, not yet. But it was not worth mentioning, because now what Roger said and did was Milly's worry, not hers. 'Mind you, I have got a baby now, though he isn't mine.'

She was joking, but she was unprepared for the look which crossed Milly's face. It was a look of such rage, mixed with such a fury of despair, that it was almost frightening. For the first time Nicola realised that clever Milly Coppack had been jealous of Nicola Wharton all her life, and probably always would be. It had been possible for Milly to be her friend, to love her, in a way. But the jealousy had eaten away at Milly until, in the end, it had caused her to pursue Nicola's husband.

'You've got another man . . . well, I'm happy for you,' Milly said at last, but with that strange expression only beginning to fade from her eyes. 'Not that it's easy, mothering someone else's child. But I daresay you and your . . . your new fellow have considered that.'

'Yes,' Nicola said. It had been on the tip of her tongue to admit the truth – that her baby was a baby dog, not a baby child – but something stopped her. Why should she tell Milly anything? The other girl should not have come, it was none of her business whether Nicola had a man or a mouse, or a – a puppy!

'Fine. Then why don't we be really modern and go out together, in a foursome? After all, you and Roger will want to talk about a divorce. I'm a bit old-fashioned in that I'd like my baby to have a right to Roger's name,' Milly said. Now, her dark eyes almost pleaded with Nicola. 'Roger really does want to marry me, you know.'

'I'm sure he does,' Nicola said warmly. And found, to her own astonishment, that the warmth was genuine. She really did not mind in the least if Milly and Roger made it official. Why should I? I don't even want him back, she realised with amazement. I don't grudge him to Milly one little bit – and even the house . . . well, it was a lot of work, a lot of worry. In eight short months she had come to terms with herself almost without realising it. Nicola Wharton should never have married, she had not been ready for it. She had needed time in which to mature and now, thanks mostly to Milly, she had as much time as she wanted. And already, she realised, she was becoming a nicer person, less self-centred, more aware. In another year or two I'll make someone a good wife, she thought humbly. But not yet. I haven't had enough fun yet!

'Then you won't contest the divorce? You'll go along with it? And you'll come out with Rog and me?'

'I won't contest the divorce, but I won't go out with you either. Sorry, but I don't think it's a good idea to muddle my two lives. The old one didn't work, the new one will. So tell Roger to get in touch with me at work, we aren't on the phone here, and we'll sort it out.'

'I'll ring you,' Milly said eagerly, but Nicola shook her head.

'No. It has to be Roger. Where is he, by the way?'

'Oh, he's gone off to a sales conference somewhere. I didn't want to worry him by telling him I'd got your address and he won't be home until Saturday so I got on a train and came down here without telling anyone.'

'I see,' Nicola said, nodding. And see she did. Milly was by no means as sure of Roger as she made out, she had not wanted Roger to know where she had been. Why, she even wanted to arrange the divorce for poor Roger.

Poor Roger? But Milly is such fun, so intelligent, she can do anything she puts her mind to . . . Yes, but one of these days, Roger isn't going to like that, Roger likes someone dumber than him, someone he can patronise, her mind said, not critically but honestly. He did like his beautiful, dumb wife, he enjoyed showing her off, bossing her about, laughing when she got things wrong. How will he like being Mr Milly Coppack when they do the rounds of Milly's publishers? Poor Roger!

'I expect you're keen not to miss your train,' Nicola said now. She stood up and walked over to the door. She had put a shirt on when Milly first arrived and now she tucked it into the waist of her jeans. She was meanly aware as she did so of her tiny waist, of her gently curving hips, the slender length of her legs. She could see Milly getting up, bulky beneath the smock, her frizzy dark hair a bird's nest, her sallow skin sallower from the heat of the kitchen.

Milly is an ugly little thing, she realised with a pang. Oh, she's lively and clever and cute, but she really is ugly. Before the baby Milly had worn bright, shocking clothes and looked good, got away with it. But not any more, not now, with that big stomach poking out.

'It's been nice seeing you,' Nicola said, holding the front door open. 'Be happy, Milly.'

'But don't come back? Is that what you're saying, Nicola? Do the years mean nothing to you?'

'Oh yes, the years mean a lot to me; you're my childhood,' Nicola said cordially. 'But there are times when it's best to put one's childhood behind one. Perhaps one day, when we're older, we'll meet and talk about when we were kids, but for now we're best apart.'

'What shall I tell your mother? She's been awfully worried about you, she says you hardly ever phone.'

'I ring her up once a week,' Nicola said carefully. Of all the unlikely things to annoy her after so much that she could easily have found offensive, this unnecessary interference got her hackles right up. 'I don't think my relationship with my mother is any concern of yours.'

Milly, standing in the doorway, opened her eyes very wide and let her mouth form an astonished O to show her best feature, her white and even teeth.

'Nicola, how can you say that? I've always been so fond of your mother, she was so good to me when we were little. And she did say she was worried . . .'

'Then you must have felt guilty for worrying her,' Nicola said briskly. 'Poor Mum was so happy with my marriage to Roger, I never liked to let on how very unsatisfying it had become. But since you say she's been worried, perhaps I should go home so that I can explain.'

Milly's eyes opened wider and her teeth showed a little more. She looked, Nicola thought cruelly, like an overdressed rabbit.

'You found Roger unsatisfying? I just don't believe I'm hearing this. Your mother said you adored Roger, you were the perfect couple . . .'

'There you are, then, that proves I'll have to go home,' Nicola said with considerable satisfaction. 'But you needn't feel responsible for my marriage break-up, Milly, because it wouldn't have lasted much longer. Someone else would have come along.'

'Nicola, no matter how you feel about this new guy I can't believe −'

'Sorry, must go, I've got a date this evening,' Nicola cut in. 'Another time you must let me know you're coming. No, on second thoughts, don't bother. We won't need to meet again.'

'Oh, but −'

'Byee,' Nicola sang. 'Tell Roger to give me a ring some time.'

'Oh, but −'

The door shut, gently but firmly, in Milly's surprised face. Nicola stood just inside it and listened as first Milly stood there, breathing heavily, even muttering, and then began to descend the stairs.

When she could tell Milly was near the bottom of the flight Nicola rushed to the front window. She saw Milly, absurdly foreshortened, making her slow way down the garden path, out of the gate, along the road . . .

She'll get hot and cross going all the way home on the evening train, Nicola thought with unworthy satisfaction. She must have sold her car – perhaps they aren't quite so well off as I'd thought. I wonder what she'll tell Roger, though? I wonder if he'll ever know she's been to see me? But it didn't matter. What mattered was that she had laid the ghost of Milly Coppack once and for all. Milly was probably as wonderful as Nicola had always believed her to be, but she was also a spoilt and grabby girl who wanted what Nicola had and had taken it regardless of the consequences. And then she had realised what she had lost, which had been her one close friend, and she had come over to Haisby, hoping somehow to get the best of both worlds – to let Nicola see that Milly was the one, now, who had everything, and to get her closest friend back.

Some chance!

'Sorry I'm late,' Ceri panted when she hurried into the flat a good hour after Milly had left. 'You must have thought I'd fallen down the drain but actually I've been for an interview!'

Nicola, sitting on the kitchen table painting her toenails with pearly pink gloss, waved the brush vaguely in the direction of the cooker.

'Dirty stop-out! Zak, my dear little man, come to your mummy and give her a big hug! Your dinner, Ceri Allen, is in the oven. If you'd been a man I'd be in tears and the dinner would probably be ruined, but as you aren't, I kept it on a very low light and it's probably fine. It's Irish stew so just tip it onto the plate and eat it, all the veggies are in there.'

'Marvellous,' Ceri said, plonking Zak onto Nicola's lap and heading for the cooker. 'Oh God, I'm a veggie myself, Irish stew has meat in, I just know it does! And I've been for a job interview, Nick!'

'This Irish stew hasn't got any meat at all, because I did us two little ones, veggie for you and meat for Zak and me. Go on then, tell me about this interview.'

'Well, it was very odd, really. I'd sent in an article to the *Evening News* you see, just a short, chatty thing, women's page, I'd have thought. And the fellow rang me at Ambleside and asked if I was interested in doing a column for them, on the lines of the article I'd sent in. A twice-weekly column, Nick! And when I said yes I was interested he told me to hop

148

in a taxi and go round to his office right away! Thrills and spills, Nick, because of course I leapt into the taxi with Zak weighing a ton on my lap and never even thought of the white slave trade or drug barons until I was halfway to the city.'

'The city?'

'Interest at last! Yes, halfway to Norwich,' Ceri said triumphantly. 'Nick, I had the interview and it went really well. Mr Durrant told me what they want and I told him it would be a doddle, the sort of thing I love doing, and now I'm working in newspapers again!'

'What's the snag? There's bound to be one,' Nicola asked suspiciously, trying to paint her last toenail whilst cuddling Zak, a task many a professional contortionist would have found challenging. 'Go on; you got into this taxi and halfway to Norwich you thought about slavery and drugs. Why, for goodness sake?'

'Oh, Nicola, you must be half asleep! Because when a strange man rings you up and tells you to go somewhere at once by taxi and he'll pay, it's *always* slavery or drugs,' Ceri explained patiently. 'But in fact, it wasn't. It was this Mr Durrant from the *Evening News*, and he really did like my piece. He'd checked me out with horrible old Mullins though, who said I was okay!'

'He can't be quite so horrible after all,' Nicola observed. She waved her foot in the air a couple of times, then slid off the table and put Zak down on the floor. 'Get your dinner, Ceri, and I'll feed Zak.'

'He had a bite in the newspaper offices,' Ceri said cheerfully. 'Not the commissionaire, to whom we both took an immediate dislike on account of Zak hated his loud voice and I hated the way he leered at me. Mr Durrant took pity on him and fed him a Cornish pastie – Zak, not the commissionaire – which just shows he's a super bloke. As for old Mullins, he's really weird; apparently Mr Durrant rang him up to ask him if he thought I could do the sort of thing your friend Milly used to do, and he said he thought I could – after kicking me off his rotten little scandal sheet, the old louse!'

'The column Milly used to do? Don't say she's chucked it in!' Nicola scooped Zak's share of the stew into his little dish, added some puppy meal and put it on the floor, then stood watching raptly as Zak hoovered the food down into his small

149

stomach. 'Now why on earth should Milly give up her column?'

'She's started doing one for a London paper as well and Mr Durrant says he's not accepting a weak copy of what she sends to the London rag,' Ceri said. 'The only snag is that I'll have to go to Norwich twice a week to take my copy and to chat about the following week's work. So I'm going to make eyes at Tom's boss and see if I can get a loan, because I simply must have a car. In fact I told Mr Durrant I'd got one, but it was off the road because I wasn't using it right now.'

'What a porky,' Nicola said, pouring milk into Zak's bowl and watching it disappear as though a plug had been pulled out. 'Unless you've decided to put in for a car allowance and continue to ride your bike, which would be bound to end in tears.'

'Would I lie? No, by next week I'll have a car. Pity you aren't rich, Nick, because I could probably wheedle it out of you easier than the bank, but I'll be driving again soon, just you see. I say, this stew is brill, you and Keith are the only people I know who can make vegetarian food taste as good as beastly meat.'

'Thanks for the compliment, many congratulations on your job, and now let me tell you *my* news! Oh, by the way, does this mean you'll leave Ambleside?'

'Certainly not. Because you know I've got a feeling that my freelance stuff will really take off, once I'm doing the column. It often happens, apparently. And what's more Mr Durrant says if he needs someone at short notice to do a piece on Haisby, a sports event, or a murder, even, he'd pay me to get the story. Sorry, I digress – what was your news?'

'Milly came here today! If you'd been on time you'd have walked slap into her!'

'Gosh!' Ceri said, suitably impressed. She finished off her stew, patted her stomach and leaned back in her chair. 'Go on, tell me all about it!'

Sunny Saturday left the harbour with Henry at the tiller and Robin, for the first time ever, crouched in the well. There were two learners aboard, Jimmy and Steve Tilney, Jimmy was holding the jib-sheet in tight whilst Steve sat at Henry's elbow, listening.

'I want you to take over the tiller presently, Steve; and to steer towards that buoy, leaving it on the starboard side. Keep your eye on the masthead burgee; it shows you the wind's direction . . . You all right, Rob? Can you follow what I'm saying to Steve?'

'Sure, Hal,' Robin squeaked excitedly. 'The burgee's that little flag, isn't it?'

'That's right.' Henry turned back to tall, blond Steve. 'When we get past the buoy we'll go about to starboard. When it's time I'll shout. Now Jim, when we're ready to go about I want you to loosen the jib-sheet and be ready to pull it in on the other side. Clear?'

'As mud,' Jim said cheerfully.

'Steve, when I give the word you'll pull the tiller towards you and change sides. Duck your head or the boom will decapitate you. Got it?'

'Got it,' Steve confirmed.

The breeze was brisk, the sail roared as the wind cracked against it. The sea was noisy too, sizzling and creaming against the hull; Robin had to listen hard not to miss a word and was on his own personal high at the excitement of it, the wonderful sense of achievement he got whenever he did some small, menial task.

'Right, everyone?' The buoy slipped past the stern of the boat. 'Ready about! Lee ho!'

There was a scramble of activity. Steve brought the tiller up sharply and Henry and Robin scuttled to starboard, Henry shouting 'Well done!' against the crack of the sail and the blustering wind.

Jim pulling the port jib-sheet, swore as the starboard one wound itself round his leg, pulling him back the way he had just come. Henry, seeing what had happened, bawled to Jim to let go the port jib-sheet whilst Steve pushed his tiller hard down, taking the pressure of the wind off the sail.

Robin saw the problem and crouched in the bows, unravelling the rope from Jim's leg. Henry's laconic 'Well done, Rob!' brought a lump to his throat. He was one of them, almost a sailor!

'Let that be a lesson to you,' Henry said as the boat straightened up. 'Never just let go of a rope and turn away; always keep it under control. Now get that jib pulled in or we'll lose the wind. Steve, are you keeping your eye on the burgee? Make sure the wind stays on our starboard quarter, otherwise we'll gybe. Robin, old son, you look out for squalls. If you see a darker patch on the sea, sing out. All right?'

'All right,' three voices shouted.

'Good. Then who's for coffee? Pass us the flask, Robin old lad.'

Chapter Eleven

'Everyone got a spud? Good-oh . . . bring 'em here and I'll push them into the fire; they take a good hour, so how about another drink all round?'

Keith was in his element, Henry saw approvingly, enjoying both his role as host and as the birthday boy. He had never had so many cards and presents either, though a good few of the latter had taken the form of bottles of booze, most of which the donors would drink themselves before the night was out.

Keith was shovelling spuds into the embers with a long spoon lashed securely to a broom handle. Around him, their guests milled. It was ten o'clock and so far everything had gone according to plan. Ceri had gone from group to group taking names and getting reactions, and Tom had been close at her heels, snapping away with his professional-looking camera. Ceri had already arranged with her new employers that she would cover the event as a feature for the *Evening News*.

Ceri's note-taking had begun up at the house, where the presents had been opened and the magnificent buffet supper attacked for the first time. It would be finished off at midnight, before everyone went home. Now, Tom's camera had been put away along with Ceri's notebook; enjoyment was the order of the day.

Everyone had gone round the hotel, excepting the bedrooms, since they were full; the guests were all joining in and seemed to think themselves lucky to be able to share in such a local event. Even the couple in No. 4, inveterate grumblers, seemed to be enjoying themselves. It was clear the party was going to be a success. Now, with everyone gathered on the beach, the bonfire had been lit by the birthday boy, whose enormous smile underlined his personal enjoyment. He was, Henry saw, a really good host since his friend, a smooth young man called Ted, had been unable to get more than a few moments of his time, but now people were beginning to break up into couples or small groups he and Keith had their heads together.

Henry wandered over to where the big barbecue smouldered and helped himself to a homemade beefburger. He took a large bap already split, pushed the burger inside and added a couple of lettuce leaves and a big dollop of relish from the hostess trolley which stood incongruously nearby. Biting into his concoction he shambled over to Robin and sat beside him. Robin, also eating, turned an eager face towards Henry. Grease from the burger had run down his chin and there were smuts on his brow, but happiness shone from him.

'Hal! Isn't it *great*? Did you see my friend Clive? What a wimp, eh? His dad came for him at ten, said it was quite late enough for a child of his age. Gosh, I'm glad you and Kee never say stupid things like that!'

'Oh hell, I suppose we ought . . . but it's a special occasion and there's no school tomorrow.' Henry rumpled Robin's hair. 'Where's Ant?'

'She went up to settle Kit. Then she's coming back, because Mrs Frett's up there keeping an eye on things and she'll listen out for him. We're going to have our jacket spuds together and then a hot drink,' Robin explained. 'Hal, this is the best ever, isn't it? Tell me, are beefburgers nicest slightly burnt or slightly raw?'

'Slightly burnt, I think,' Henry said, having given the matter his serious consideration. 'Ah, here comes Anthea.' He smiled up at her, putting out a hand to pat the rock by him. 'Here we are, Ant, come and sit down; Rob will fetch your spud when it's cooked but in the meantime try some of that hot punch.'

Anthea settled herself on the rock, keeping a good foot between her and Henry; she was a person who liked a space about her, Henry knew.

'I don't drink much,' she said apologetically. 'Isn't this grand, Henry? We're all having the most marvellous time. It's a success with everyone, guests as well as friends.'

'True.' Henry took another bite of his burger and gestured with it, at the firm sand, the starlight glinting on the crests of the small breakers rolling up the sloping beach. 'With this on our side, how can we lose?'

*　　*　　*

As time passed and the booze began to run low, so, Ceri thought, the party began to degenerate. Not that she minded – quite the opposite. For a student of human nature who is in need of vicarious experience there is nothing like a beach-barbecue with a great many guests, most of whom know each other vaguely and, apparently, would like to know each other better.

For a long time she and Tom had gone the rounds, he clicking his camera, she taking notes. By the time they had sufficient material the light from the fire was just a rosy glow and the people lying about on the sand – frequently in pairs – did not want to be interviewed, far less photographed. So Ceri, starving as usual, had sneaked off to get herself something to eat.

There were still some burgers left and some sausages, plenty of French bread and different salads. Ceri piled her plate, with a stick of celery dividing the wheat from the chaff, or rather the meat from the veg, and then set off again to find Tom.

It was difficult to find anyone now, but she remembered vaguely where she had left Tom, and headed for the spot. On the way she passed a huddle which she suspected contained Nicola, judging by what looked like her flatmate's long blonde hair falling across a man's shirt. The man, Ceri supposed, must be Ian-the-vet, though she had little chance of positive identification.

She found her spot on the sand again quite easily and sat down. Tom was no longer there; had he gone for a wee? Very probably. Ceri had noticed a number of men sneaking guiltily off into the darkness earlier. She knew that men's bladders did not equal women's for sheer carrying capacity and besides, men drank beer which, it seemed, travelled almost non-stop from lips to loo. Still, Tom would find her again easily enough. Ceri squatted on the sand, put her plate on a flat-topped boulder and selected a veggie burger to beguile the next five minutes.

She was some distance from the fire now, feeling comfortably like a spectator, watching the small figures reeling across the lighted stage and quietly relishing the role of reporter once more. She had been out in the cold but now she was in again and very nice it was, too. She imagined her father's pride, her mother's smile when she told them that she was no longer with the local paper but actually employed by the *News*. And right now here she was, observing like anything, taking notes in her head so that she could write it all up later. In fact, with her mouth comfortably full she was lolling back on an elbow and pretending the whole thing was a play staged especially for her benefit when she saw, outlined against the bonfire's glow, a man approaching.

She was still squinting up at him, trying to decide who it was, when the man flopped onto the sand beside her, flung his arms round her and bore her to the ground.

Ceri's mouthful went down faster than she had intended, damned near choking her. She spluttered, squeaked, and then in the midst of panic and alarm, embarrassment and annoyance, she suddenly knew it was Tom and shoved him away as his mouth pecked at hers.

'Tom!' Ceri said reproachfully. 'I wasn't even sure it was you!'

'What *do* you mean? Sorry to abandon you, old Ces, but I was busting for a pee,' Tom said, looping an arm comfortably round her shoulders. 'How dare you kiss a stranger so passionately, then. Where's my grub?'

Ceri picked up the plate and put it down between them. Her heart was still jumping about all over the place. How could Tom be such an idiot and give her such a fright – she had a good mind to walk away from him now and never return. But he was all right, really, he was thoughtless more than unkind. She put out a hand to stroke his cheek but he was reaching for the food, carefully selecting from the carnivore side she was glad to see, mumbling with his mouth full that this was the best beach party he'd ever attended.

'Me, too,' Ceri said. What with all the darkness and the number of other people sprawled about, surely Tom would take the hint and start to make love to her? Oh, nothing too exciting, she told herself quickly. Just some nice kisses and a bit of cuddling.

Tom took a swig of beer and, regrettably, burped. Ceri saw that right now his mind was on the inner man and resigned herself to simply enjoying her food. After all, she reasoned, they had not known one another all that long; lovemaking would come, in time.

* * *

Further up the beach and in even deeper darkness, Nicola lounged against a rock and wondered where Ian had got to. No doubt he had just answered a call of nature, but he was being rather a long time about it and she was feeling a little lonely, a trifle neglected. The trouble was, of course, that when you've been married your expectations – or your body's – aren't simply satisfied by kissing and cuddling. Nicola, who knew very well that sex had not been particularly important to her during her marriage, now found that it was apparently something which her body, if not her mind, missed. And Ian, though a good friend, wasn't exactly setting the Thames on fire – he had only kissed her once, and it had been the gentlest and most platonic of caresses. So why didn't she go back to the bonfire, get herself some food to eat, and sit down somewhere different?

But it wasn't in Nicola to deliberately hurt someone and Ian was enjoying the party in his own way. So she leaned against her boulder and watched the small figures round the fire and saw that Keith and Henry, with Anthea hovering, were preparing to set off the fireworks.

She was still watching the preparations when Ian came back. He sat down beside her, then took her hand.

'Enjoying it, sweetheart?'

The endearment was such a surprise that Nicola jumped and, turning sideways, saw that Ian was looking equally surprised. Mortified, even. He opened his mouth as though to speak, closed it again, cleared his throat, and then pulled her roughly into his arms.

'Hey –' Nicola began, and found her protests stopped, gently but firmly, by his mouth. He kissed nicely, cool and soft and gentle at first but then slowly warming up, getting harder and hotter, more demanding, more exciting, until Nicola's mouth forgot that this was a young man she scarcely knew and was not at all sure she liked and allowed Ian liberties which, once, had been Roger's prerogative alone.

Cuddling came next. Hands smoothed, caressed, gentled her, and the body which held her was showing obvious signs of interest to which Nicola's body eagerly responded. She gasped, heart fluttering, when he began to kiss along the line of her jaw, across her slender collar bones, down to the smooth skin above her breasts. But he drew back here, though she could hear him breathing hard, could feel his

157

desire reaching out like a physical thing to her. And knew that she had been on the brink of letting him love her.

The tremendous fizzing crash of the first rocket brought them starkly upright, just in time, Nicola thought grimly, arranging herself decorously on the sand. The brilliance lit the scene, must have shown anyone interested that ice-maiden Nicola could have her moments.

Only no one was watching. Every face was turned towards the firework display, even Ian's. She could read his expression easily, despite the light in her eyes – it was pleasure mixed with guilt she decided almost scornfully. What was wrong with the guy? She leaned back a little, deciding miserably that she was just not desirable; simple as that.

The fireworks continued to zoom and sparkle and glitter and presently Ian took her hand once more. Absently, almost, he made little patterns on the palm with his forefinger . . . then turned to her, took both her hands, pulled her to her feet.

'Nicola, we've got to talk. Walk home with me?'

Golden and silver rain and what looked like gently falling snow lit up the night. Nicola, on her feet and turning away, hesitated, and gasps from all round showed that she was not the only one to be impressed. As the showers of colour gradually faded Nicola heard the hiss and sizzle of catherine wheels, pinned to a six-foot piece of two-by-four, beginning their first slow rotation. Should she go with Ian or should she stay here, amongst people she knew? After all . . .

'Nicola? Come up to my flat for a coffee, or we could walk into town, somewhere's always open on a Saturday.'

Nicola turned and looked up at her companion. He was not good-looking, though he had a neat, intelligent face. He was a Scot, a man of breeding and humour; she trusted him but did not know, yet, whether she wanted to get to know him better. Was it sensible – or kind – to go to his flat? Would it not be better all round to stay here and talk in the morning?

'Oh . . . I'm actually supposed to be with Ceri . . . but I suppose a walk along the beach . . .'

They set off whilst behind them, more fireworks spluttered and Henry's voice could be heard reminding everyone that there was still a lot of food to be eaten. Soon enough they were alone in the dark, Ian's arm round her waist, one thin hand comfortingly holding hers.

'Nicola; you think I'm a strange bloke. Cold.'

'No I don't. I'm supposed to be the cold one.'

'Och, you must do, everyone does. What I want to tell you is that you're a lovely wee girl and I – I like you right well, but until a year since . . .'

She knew what he had been going to say even as his voice faltered into silence. Was it not her story, too? Had they not been drawn together over the puppy, had she not even then thought it strange that a man of Ian's age should be alone, in a strange town, should not already have made a heap of friends?

'Me, too. Were you married?'

He gave a spurt of incredulous laughter, then squeezed her so hard it hurt.

'Engaged, and dreading telling anyone! You, too?'

'Married. Only he . . . went off with someone else.'

'Aye.' A moment of brooding silence and then Ian remarked with amusement suddenly evident, 'Mine went off with my best customer – a rich laird with a dozen fine hunters and a big old castle, a grouse moor – the lot. Would you believe I introduced them, hoped they'd get on?'

Nicola giggled. She returned the hug.

'Milly was my best friend, a TV presenter, a personality. Oh, Ian, it's great to tell someone!'

'Aye, great.' He pulled her to a halt in the windy darkness and kissed her. This time there was no holding back from either of them; they hugged hard, hard, their mouths took and received pleasure, discreet promises of things to come. 'Will we have a coffee at my flat?' Ian said at last, as they came up for air.

'Aye,' Nicola said, mimicking him sweetly. 'We will, laddie!'

The beach was quiet at last, and dark save for the faint glow from the dying fire. It was deserted too, at first glance. Ceri, leaning against Tom's shoulder, knew very well that they were the last. Alone on the shore, her writer's mind remarked romantically. Alone save for the frostily twinkling stars and the constant crash and surge of the ocean.

'Kissums!' Tom said, breaking the romance of the moment into a thousand pieces and giving Ceri's shoulders an amateurish squeeze. 'Ceri kissums Tom-kitten.'

'You revolting blob, there's absolutely nothing kittenish about you,' Ceri said severely, with a wobble in her voice, however. 'Besides, I kissed you just now.'

'You did not,' Tom said indignantly. 'I kissed you, but you kept moving your mouth away – or otherwise it isn't in the usual place. I got you on the nose twice, on the chin once, and God knows how many times under your right ear. Now I want a real, proper smackeroo.'

Naturally Ceri smacked him and naturally he promptly seized her, pulled her rather roughly against him, and began all over again trying to kiss.

In books it just happens, Ceri thought crossly, trying to line her mouth up with where she imagined his was and failing, judging by the pained squeak he gave as her head met his nose. The trouble with us being amateurs is that we're both relying on instinct, and it simply isn't enough. We need daylight, about three hours, and some sort of a homing device.

Unfortunately the mental picture this conjured up made her giggle and everyone knows that giggles are death to passion. Tom snorted, dived in, got her right eye, snorted again and then began to giggle as well.

'Ceri, *will* you stop messing about and hold still?' he demanded. 'What a fool you are, girl. I've a good mind to stop giving you all this excitement and go and find someone with a mouth about an inch under her nose and not round the back of her neck somewhere!'

'I'm sorry,' Ceri said remorsefully. The trouble was she had so enjoyed the party that Tom's fooling about seemed an anticlimax. But she had heard, just now, an embarrassed and desperate note in his voice barely hidden by the foolery and, being a kind girl, she turned towards him, closed her eyes and put her arms very tightly round his neck.

It was really odd what a little co-operation could do. Tom found her mouth at once, his own mouth firm, far more exciting than she had expected. Knowing, too. Considering they were both supposed to be such beginners, she thought presently, they were making a very good job of it. Tom kissed, moving his mouth on hers, and crushing her to him in a way which Ceri found not only exciting but also breathless-making. And then he somehow managed to get a hand round onto her neck, with the fingers pushing up into the curls on the nape, and his mouth did something very strange, something so exciting that Ceri's stomach skewered right through with a feeling she simply could not begin to explain. She only knew that she wanted to be a lot closer to Tom, that she resented the fact that they were both fully clothed, and that she did not intend to pull away from him, even when he released her to put a tentative hand on her small breast.

'Oh, Tom,' she muttered as he began kissing the side of her face and neck, little, sweet kisses which travelled across her skin surface seeming to drag warmth with them, so that she glowed beneath his mouth. 'Oh Tom, I do like you, I do like you!'

'Mmm, mmm,' droned Tom. 'Oh Ceri, let me . . . can't we . . . oh, my pretty little . . .'

Ceri opened her eyes – and shrieked. She clung to Tom, shaking all over, torn between terror and wild, inexplicable desire.

'Tom, there was someone watching us, one of those awful old tramps who hangs around Bridge House. Oh Tom, he had mad eyes. Oh please, let's go home!'

'Good thing it's a warm night.'

'Yes indeedy! Comfy, lover?'

Keith and Ted lounged in a tangled embrace in the back of Ted's station wagon. Ted had provided blankets and pillows and they could not have been more comfortable, as Keith had already remarked, had they been in bed at the Ritz. Now, at Ted's words, Keith rolled over and smiled into the other man's face; a smile lazy with contentment.

'Oh very comfy, Teddy-bare,' he purred. 'Teddy-bare makes Kiwi very comfy.'

'I do my poor best. What a night, eh, Kiwi?'

The two of them lay in each other's arms, Keith content, for he had still managed to keep Teddy at bay whilst enjoying a lot of what he would have termed innocent fun, though Ted had already called it a far less pleasant name. He thought Keith was a tease, playing hard to get, and Keith knew he had a point. Right now, however, they were both relaxed, even if Teddy was mainly happy because he was sure Keith was about to give in. He kissed the side of Keith's face hopefully.

'You're insatiable, you are!' Keith declared happily, patting Teddy's brawny shoulder. 'Poor Kiwi gets no rest!'

'Insatiable? You ain't had nothin', yet! C'mon, Kee, you know you're as eager as I am.'

'We-ell, this really isn't the time or the place . . . oh Teddy-bare . . . Now that's quite enough . . . naughty boy!'

The station wagon, parked in thick shadow at the side of the lane leading to Harbour Hill, lurched as Keith, laughing and dishevelled, tumbled out.

'See you tomorrow, you bad old Teddy-bare,' he said breathlessly, waving vaguely towards Teddy as he turned away. Was he being unfair to the other fellow? But the truth was he needed to be sure, and he was still not certain that Ted was right for him. After all, they had only been going out a few weeks. Plenty of time yet to make up his mind. Plenty of time.

Henry had walked past the station wagon and seen Keith and Ted cuddling, and he had not been pleased. Admittedly, his partner had behaved well all through the party, but fancy carrying on in the lane up which everyone must walk in order to return to the hotel! It was the sort of thing to put guests off, to say nothing of staff – and what he would have told Robin, had the boy noticed, he could not imagine.

At the time, however, he had just walked past; he could do nothing more without causing himself, Keith and Ted excruciating embarrassment. And back at Ambleside he found himself rushed off his feet, with only Anthea to help. She, poor soul, having settled Kit, seen Robin and Heather into bed and cleared up in the kitchen, found herself facing the guests alone.

Her relief at Henry's appearance was patent. The shy brown eyes lit up and the long, austere line of her mouth curved into the confiding smile which Henry thought her best point.

'Oh, Hal! The Grimmonds have changed their minds about sailing tomorrow morning, they said could you take them at two, instead. And No. 8 wants to skip breakfast because she's going to Mass, but said could she have something at about ten, when she gets back. And No. 4 have decided to be in to lunch after all.'

'Crumbs; all change,' Henry said absently. They were in the kitchen, Anthea making a pot of hot chocolate and setting biscuits out on a dish. 'Who's that for?'

'Anyone who wants it; I'm taking it through into the main lounge and leaving it in a prominent position,' Anthea said. 'I've noted all the changes in the diary, Hal, but it's a bit of a mess, I'm afraid. Isn't it odd how No. 4 seems to attract born grumblers?'

'So you noticed, as well! I put it down to being a family room, which is cheaper than the rest. And somehow there are people who are paying less than anyone else and instead of being thankful, they're so keen to get their money's worth that they pick on everything. What've No. 4 been up to this time, apart from deciding to eat in after ordering packed lunches?'

Anthea arranged the biscuits nicely, then turned to tick No. 4's demands off on her fingers.

'First, they claimed *she* was given a beefburger with no meat in; mistaken identity, I told her. She started to shout though, so I said if she had got the wrong sort I was very sorry, and passed on to their second moan, which was that the smallest boy queued up for sparklers but dropped them in the sea and when he went back for replacements Keith had run out.'

'My heart bleeds,' Henry said heavily. 'Not more, was there?'

'Of course; I was a captive audience, sitting at the desk changing the diary. The reason they wanted to come in for lunch tomorrow was that they'd got tired of everlasting ham, beef or chicken sandwiches. I didn't even try to point out that the choice is theirs and they know it, because they went rapidly on to the last point, which was that *his* yachting trousers had got snagged on a sticking-out nail aboard the boat, and he said he'd hand over the bill for mending and cleaning.'

'He may hand it over,' Henry said equably, stealing a biscuit from Anthea's careful display. 'That commits us to nothing. You trot off to bed now, Ant; I'll cope with everything else.'

'Well, I will if you're sure you don't mind,' Anthea said gratefully. 'Because I've promised Robin and Heather that we'll get up early and go down to the beach to search for rocket sticks.'

Henry followed her into the lounge. In one corner Mr and Mrs 4 sat over cups of coffee; they looked like a couple of would-be dynamiters, planning a big explosion. *He* had a

163

round, dissatisfied face and a whiny, fault-finding manner. He liked to wear a white linen cap askew on his thinning hair and his choleric temper showed in the flush of colour which rose readily to his cheeks and the way his dark eyes darted critically around. *She* was small, thin and wiry, a pushy woman with an aggressive voice who favoured baggy slacks and faded sweaters. Henry felt quite sorry for their two sons, who might have been decent kids in other hands.

Henry strolled over to them; they immediately stopped talking and looked up at him, their expressions defensive.

'Still up?' Henry said, smiling. 'Enjoy it?'

'Well, to tell the truth . . .'

'Jolly good,' Henry said hastily. 'I'm off to bed now, but there's hot chocolate and biscuits if you'd like some. Good night!'

Ahead of him, he could see Anthea's shoulders shake. Behind him, the occupants of No. 4 muttered what could have been a reciprocal good night. Henry yawned and headed for the stairs which Anthea was already eagerly mounting. It had been a good day!

It might have been embarrassing tackling Keith in front of the assembled staff and guests next day, but before Henry had decided what to do Keith himself made an opening.

'Want a stroll down to the beach?' Keith said when they'd finished breakfast. 'Do you know I was so late in last night that I never even saw you? Sorry, old chap.'

'That's all right,' Henry said. He saved the rest until they were actually walking down the lane and then, with Keith being very chatty, he was silent until they reached the spot where the station wagon had been parked.

Here, he stopped. He looked meaningly at the tyre marks, sunk deep into the soft sand by the side of the lane, and then at Keith, and his friend was nothing if not quick. He stared at Henry, then a flush crept across his face and he looked both defensive and what Henry described to himself as 'sickeningly coy'.

'Oh! You saw us when you . . . Oh *dear*; does that put the cat amongst the pigeons? I feel I've done *wrong*, yet you did tell me to find myself another friend.'

'True. And you haven't done wrong, exactly, Kee. But the boy could easily have been with me and . . .'

164

'Oh the boy, always the boy!' But Keith's tone was pettish rather than properly annoyed. 'If he saw anything I don't suppose he'd realise . . . and anyway, it was nothing, really, Hal; a tiny show of affection, just . . .'

'I'm sure that's all it was,' Henry said, trying to make it sound like a statement of fact and not a put-down and only partly succeeding. 'In fact Robin saw nothing, but what about the guests? People don't fancy having things like that thrust under their noses.'

'You mean that even if I'd been with a girl it wasn't the place,' Keith said shrewdly. 'You're right, Hal, and I'm sorry, really I am. Shan't do it again.' He giggled, casting another under-the-lashes look at Henry. 'Well, I *shall* do it again, but not right on top of the hotel.'

'Not al fresco at all, if you take my advice,' Henry said rather grimly. 'Stick to Ted's place.'

'Well, but the trouble is, Hal, if I go back to Ted's place he expects . . . well, more than I want to give, and suppose I fall in love with someone who hasn't got his own place? Is my room here totally out of bounds? Would cruel old Hal see me on the streets?'

'Cruel old Hal would indeed, if you try carrying on in the hotel,' Henry said crossly. 'It won't do, Keith. If you're going to start behaving like that then I'm off, and what's all this about falling in love with someone else? I thought you were the steady kind?'

'I am, in fact,' Keith said rather gloomily. 'But Ted wants a . . . well, a deeper relationship, and I'm not at all sure it's my scene. So I thought I might get about a bit without him, perhaps go to Norwich . . .'

'In the present climate I really hope you don't start cruising,' Henry said worriedly. 'And no more carrying on near the hotel, Keith. I won't stand by and see everything we've built up ruined. Clear?'

'As crystal,' Keith said humbly. He was serious for a moment, then brightened. 'I do believe, Hal, that you're just the teensiest bit jealous!'

And Henry's temper, which he had thought would never flare up over Keith's sexual mores, suddenly snapped. Perhaps it was missing a night's sleep, perhaps it was the way Keith was eyeing him, but his patience ran out.

'No, Keith, I'm not jealous, because I've had my fill of what

165

you coyly call "relationships",' he said savagely. 'I respect your right to find yourself a . . . a boyfriend, but for my part if I ever did want someone else, it would be a woman. So forget jealousy, old son!'

'There's one! Come on Kit, let's run!'

Robin, hand in hand with Kit, was searching for rocket sticks whilst Anthea and Heather competed with them for the biggest bundle. Now, seeing a beauty, Robin broke into a trot and Kit, giggling mightily, toddled along on his fat little legs, breaking into excited shrieks as Heather came thundering down the beach behind them.

'Go on, Kit, go on, you can win!' Robin shouted, seeing Heather tactfully slowing down. Kit ran past and fell over on top of the stick.

'Me got it! Got it, Mummy!'

Anthea, panting, flopped on the sand beside her son.

'Who's a clever boy, then?' She turned to smile at Robin. 'That was kind of you, Rob – and kind of you, too, Heather. Well, we'd better be getting back or the guests won't have their elevenses. Who's in, Rob, do you know?'

'They're mostly out, I think. Can't Mrs Frett manage the elevenses, just this once? We're having such fun!'

'We-ell . . . just this once we'll let your mum cope, Heather. Shall we have a paddle?'

'Race you to the sea,' Robin shouted at once, dragging off his socks and shoes. It was wonderful, he thought blissfully, being with Kit and Ant. Together, they were just like a real family!

Chapter Twelve

Ceri's trip to see the bank manager, which she had been anticipating with lively dread, turned out to be unnecessary. On Sunday Tom came calling for her very much in the style of the small friends of Ceri's youth. He stood outside the flat, raindrops pouring off his waterproofs, and announced that he could scarcely ask her to come out since it was raining stair-rods, but why didn't she ask him in?

'We could give your flatmate a quid and tell her to go to the cinema,' he suggested hopefully. 'Then I could get into practice with you, for later.'

'Nicola's training Zak to walk at heel,' Ceri said sadly. 'You can come in and watch if you like, but she won't take him out for a practical demonstration in this rain. I wonder why it rained today? Is it just that God can't see a Sunday without wanting to ruin it?'

'He'll strike you dead,' Tom warned, walking past her into the hall. 'I wonder if we might find a cosy bus shelter somewhere?'

'We'll sit and talk in the kitchen and I'll bake some scones for tea,' Ceri said, struck by inspiration. 'Nick's busy with Zak, she won't want to come through.'

'Oh. Right,' Tom said, and divested himself of his waterproofing in the hall, then kicked off his sodden shoes and followed her into the kitchen. Ceri installed him in a chair, switched the kettle on and went through into the living room. Zak, on a piece of string, was padding along directly behind Nicola, now and then breaking into a fast waddle so that his nose grazed the back of her knees.

'Who was it? He's doing ever so well now,' Nicola said, stopping to look round at Ceri so that Zak bumped into her and sat down hard, looking aggrieved. 'Oh sorry, Zak. Up you get, be a man!'

'It's Tom,' Ceri said. 'He's staying to tea because it's so wet. I'm going to make some scones.'

'My, aren't we getting involved,' Nicola murmured. She tugged at the string. 'Come on now, Zak – *heel!*'

'No we aren't, we're just friends,' Ceri told her back view. 'I'll bring you a couple of scones through when they're cooked.'

'Meaning don't just barge into the kitchen,' Nicola said, but she was laughing. 'Don't worry, Zak's lesson isn't halfway over yet. Now Zak, steady . . . and . . . *sit!*'

Ceri left the room as Zak's fast-growing bottom smacked obediently onto the faded carpet. In the kitchen Tom was reading a copy of the *Evening News* which Ceri had brought back from Norwich with her. It was Friday's, but that clearly did not bother him. He looked up as she came into the room.

'Hey, is this your paper? I say, you have gone up in the world! If you're going to work for them though, how will you get about? Buses, I suppose, because Norwich is too far to bike even for a true daughter of Cambridge! Well, I shall miss your funny face peering through my cash-point.'

'I'm not working in Norwich, fool,' Ceri said smartly. 'I'm doing a column; that means I do freelance work for the paper and they pay me for what they publish. And they only want me occasionally to cover this area, if something exciting happens in North Norfolk.'

'Oh. So you won't need transport, then.'

'In fact I will,' Ceri said, fishing flour, sugar and margarine out of the pantry and burrowing along the bottom shelf to find some sultanas. 'I have to go to Norwich twice a week and if something exciting happens here I've got to be able to get to the scene of the crime, faster than anyone else.'

'I see. What'll you do, then?'

Ceri emerged, pink-faced, clutching the sultanas and a small drum of cream of tartar.

'Do? Oh, you mean about transport. D'you think the bank would lend me some dosh?'

'They might, but . . . a car would be useful for me, as well. I mean I'm earning a reasonable whack and it'ud be nice to go up the city once in a while, or nip off home to the old ancestral. And the girl on the enquiry desk wants to sell her mini. It's old, but I've had a look . . . well, to be honest I got

Stuey from my lodgings to have a look and he said it's a good little motor, well worth what she's asking.'

'So are you going to buy it?' Ceri asked, mystified. She could not see where the conversation was leading nor why Tom was beginning to look as though his collar was too tight. 'If not, do you think I ought to see it and then try to bite your manager's ear?'

'Well, I thought we might buy it between us,' Tom said, blinking hard behind his glasses. 'Half and half, you know. Actually, I thought I'd buy it and charge you rent. Only until you'd paid your share, of course, and then we'd divide it as we needed it.'

'I say, that would be great,' Ceri said. 'It's very kind of you to think of it, Tom, because I was dreading facing your manager and having to tell lies to get the money. This way is much better – and I'll pay for my own petrol and try to drive carefully.'

'Is that a deal? Then I'll tell Marcia we'll have it and you can pick it up after work. Only are you insured and so on?'

Whilst Ceri mixed dough, rolled it out, cut it into rounds and put it on the baking tray the two of them discussed their incipient purchase. The car would be called Min and Ceri would have it when she needed it during the day, Tom in the evenings.

Ceri agreed to pay her 'rent' weekly, and Tom, eating raw dough, said there was more than one way of paying rent and if she cared to stump up a couple of dinners each week plus a never-ending supply of scones, he might see his way clear to letting her off one or two of her payments.

'How about a kiss a quid?' Ceri said hopefully.

'Sure; I'll kiss you now and you can pay later.'

They laughed together and the scones rose just as they ought and Tom ate six and Ceri three and neither of them had a pang of indigestion or a qualm over the cholesterol-heightening powers of scone-dough. Nicola was fed, the kitchen cleaned, and Tom and Ceri talked cars.

Outside, the dull day turned into a dull evening and then the streetlights flickered on around the harbour. Ceri looked out at the dismal scene and invited Tom to supper. Tom proposed to let Ceri make him an apricot tart, since she seemed so keen on the idea, but said he would go down to the Chinese and bring back a meal for all three of them. Nicola came in and talked to Tom whilst Ceri opened a bottle of her mother's apricots and made pastry, and the two of them played with Zak and Ceri saw how Nicola glowed and was glad that her friend was enjoying Tom's company and beginning to get over the traumatic effect of Milly's surprise visit.

And presently Tom put on his waterproofs and went out into the rain and the two girls laid the table and Nicola opened a tin of shrimps and hotted them up in butter whilst Ceri made a custard to go with the apricot tart.

'We're buying a car between us,' Ceri told Nicola as they bustled around. 'Tom's paying for it outright and I'm paying him back my half week by week.'

'The guy is smitten,' Nicola said gravely. 'Imagine anyone letting you drive their car, Ces!'

It had turned into a lovely Sunday.

When Keith told Ted about his confrontation with Henry he thought they would share a giggle over it, but instead Ted looked really angry. They were sitting on the couch in Ted's place, listening to records, and every now and again Ted's square, capable hand wandered over and gripped Keith's knee – hopefully, Keith knew.

'Why do you stay with the guy, Kiwi? Why don't you cut your losses and move in with me? I'd treat you good, you know it – we'd be a real couple. Imagine, being together every night . . . Why won't you? I tell you the guy despises you and besides, gays should stick together.'

'I'm not sure, yet,' Keith said patiently, not for the first time. 'Besides, the hotel's my work and my home, I can't just walk away from it.'

'You never should have taken on a straight partner,' Ted muttered. 'Now if you and I were there together . . .'

'Teddy, darling Teddy, what an *absurd* suggestion! Why, you're *awfully* successful, Trotters is the best male boutique for *miles*, and Hal and I are only beginning at Ambleside. Anyway, you don't sail and Hal is an absolute wizard at the wheel.'

'If I came in with you we could run it as an hotel,' Ted pointed out. 'Your money bought the place, Henry's only an employee when all's said and done.'

'No, that's where you're wrong. Henry and I went halves

to buy Ambleside, we shared the cost and the work of the conversion, and now we take the same sum of money out each month. And it's the sailing which brings them in, never doubt that.'

'But you help with the sailing, and your cooking brings the hotel guests back.'

'Yes, sure, I help, but I'm not a qualified instructor, not yet. And honestly, Teddy-bare, there's no question. Hal and I are partners, I only wish he could feel about me the way I used to feel about him – used, Teddy, you note! – but as a partner he's ideal. He's a tower of strength, a positive tower!'

'I daresay.'

Ted moved his hand from Keith's knee and put his arm round Keith's shoulders instead. He squeezed and Keith gasped and fluttered.

'Oh Ted, don't hurt your Kiwi! And you mustn't get cross 'cos though I'm fond of Hal I'm much *much* fonder of you. Only I'm *dependent* on Hal, lover, truly I am.'

He was. And despite a secret desire to go the whole hog with someone, he lied when he said he was fonder of Ted than of Hal. Hal had top place in Keith's affections and probably always would, though if he met the right man he was beginning to believe he would be able to enjoy a sexual relationship with him. Loving, he thought sadly, opens the door to desire, and just because the object of your desire isn't interested, that doesn't automatically close the door, with you safe on the further side. So in a way it was Henry's fault that his urge to come right out of the closet, to discover love for himself, had become such an overmastering one.

'Come to bed with me, Kiwi! Stay with me tonight and I'll prove to you that I can unlock the last itty-bitty defences you've put up against your lusty lover. Stay with me tonight, Kee!'

'I wish I could, Teddy-bare,' Keith whispered regretfully. 'How I wish I could!'

Keith walked up the drive that night in something of a quandary. Ted Unwin, it was clear, had not been entirely disinterested when he had persuaded Keith that they could become the perfect couple. Ted had seen himself taking Henry's place at the hotel, living very comfortably with a rich lover. Ted knew Keith was not wealthy yet, of course, but it was pretty clear he had faith in the hotel, faith in Keith's ability to make it a winner with or without Henry.

But Ted was mistaken, Keith thought with rare humility. I know my own failings too well. Left to myself, I would have made a pretty fair mess of the hotel already. Why must I always think so *big*, he brooded unhappily, crunching across the gravel. Why can I never see that to make money one must not simply pour more money out, one must budget? And it wasn't just that, either. Left to himself he would have let things slide, getting up later and later each morning, lunches would have been scamped, convenience foods used too often. He would not have thought to employ Ceri and Anthea, as Henry had, and would not have stayed on good terms with Mrs Frett, who had a broad sense of humour and a sharp tongue. Henry laughed and ordered her about; I'd sulk, Keith reminded himself.

So what must he do about Ted? It was becoming increasingly clear that Ted had an eye to the main chance and right now, he hoped to supplant Henry. When he realises he can't he may well turn nasty, Keith reminded himself. People did, perhaps gays more than others.

The sensible thing to do, then, was to end the affair before it caused pain. His own heart, he acknowledged ruefully as he unlocked the back door and slipped inside, had not been touched. He thoroughly enjoyed being made much of and admired but Teddy was too . . . too slick and dexterous for real love. Real love, for Keith, needed some of the old-fashioned, sterling qualities which Henry had in such abundance. Reliability, a sweet temper, a certain calm authority and the sort of patience which could deal with irate guests, sick employees and a split hot-water tank without once raising his voice.

Saint Henry? Rather not, Keith chuckled to himself as he quietly mounted the stairs. One of Henry's charms, for Keith, was his human touch, the way he cursed himself if his leg let him down or he could not heave on a rope with the strength he had once had. And he liked the way Hal would manoeuvre a situation to their own advantage, and the way he dealt with the boy.

Robin. Oh well, it wasn't so bad, having the kid living with them. He had to give Ted some of the credit for that – the miserable bitterness which had seized him whenever he saw his life drifting by had quite gone with Ted's arrival on the scene.

Still. Ted would have to go, and in fact when Keith thought about starting up another relationship he was quite surprised at the thrill which arrowed up his spine. He excused himself on the grounds that he had been alone for so long that naturally he could scarcely settle down with the first man who seemed keen on him. He did feel a twinge of guilt, though. Was he the faithless sort? But it didn't apply to him in the least, he had been celibate since Terry, and the love he had for Henry, a purer, cooler love than he had ever imagined himself knowing, would always be different from the love he had for others.

He had been friendly with several gays since Terry, but he had never met anyone he wanted to sleep with, not even to live with on a permanent basis. He had been too busy, and he had never found the right man, either. Until he found Henry, of course. Only Henry wasn't the right man because he would never – could never – reciprocate Keith's feelings. Well, he could put that right. He would go into Norwich and visit the clubs and dance halls and pubs which gays favoured. See if he could get friendly with someone who knew nothing about the hotel, or Henry.

Perhaps it would not work for him; perhaps he was not cut out for love. But he could give it a try.

'Soon it'll be the summer holidays and then my mum wants me to go back to London. Would you go if you were me?'

Robin and Heather Frett were playing on the beach, building a huge sandcastle which, presently, they would attack with stones and raze to the ground. Beside them, on a rug inside his playpen, Kit battered his building bricks with his learner-mug and occasionally toddled across and shook the confining bars.

Heather cooed at the baby, then sat back on her heels and considered Robin's question. She was a tall child for ten with round brown eyes, soft golden hair which was always escaping from the bows and slides her mother stuck into it, and slightly buck teeth. Robin secretly thought her beautiful but would never have confessed to it. She was just a girl. Still, she was fun to muck about with when his friend Clive was otherwise engaged – or so Robin told himself, kneeling on the sand and furiously digging a moat with one eye on Heather, to see if she was impressed by his ability as an earth-mover.

'Would I go back to London, do you mean? For the school holidays?'

'Yes. If it was your mum, would you?'

Once more Heather considered. She looked especially lovely when she was thinking hard, her long dark lashes half shielding her eyes, her rosy lips pursed in thought.

'We-ell, my mum's nice, I like being with her. Just for a day I'd go. But not for the school holidays; no way, man! Think what you'd miss!'

'What?'

'All this, for a start,' Heather said, with a gesture indicating the beach, the sea, the hotel perched on the cliff above them – even the baby in his playpen. 'And in the season the amusement arcades open. This beach is clean, too, so we can swim here when that's warm enough. And you're learning to sail – wish I could – and Kit's as good as your baby brother, and you like Anthea ever so . . . You wouldn't get me leaving all that!'

Robin blinked at the sudden revelation of his riches, but he smiled, too. How neatly Heather had put his own feelings into words! Mum could beg if she liked – he did not intend to waste his marvellous summer playing second fiddle to horrible Melvyn!

But it would not do to agree with Heather too quickly. He wanted her to realise he was making something of a sacrifice. He pulled a judicious face, squinting against the bright midmorning sunlight.

'We-ell, I might go for a weekend, I suppose. You're right, it would be too bad to miss all this. What's all the toys I want and visits to the zoo and the Tower of London and things, when I could be here?'

'Right, then. Can we have the packed lunches, please, Ant? One each for Keith and myself and the others for Nos. 2, 6, 14 and 18, today.'

Henry and Anthea were in the kitchen, Henry in his stained old yachting gear and rope-soled shoes, Anthea in her new overall, a pink and white checked garment which made her look more summery than the fawn ones. Anthea had been making pastry but now she ran her hands under the tap and produced the lunches, each one in a small carrier with the room number pencilled on the handle. We might have more than one Smith family, Henry had early explained, but we won't have two lots in one room!

'There you are; yours and Kee's on top. Is Ceri on this morning, Hal? Almost everyone who isn't sailing is in for lunch, and Robin's got his hands full with Kit, though Heather's a great help, bless her.'

'Ceri's on at eleven, Sarah's coming in at noon. Do you think you can manage? Only now the weather's so good and we're full, it's important to get as many boats out as we can. Dave from the Dolphin's taking *Haisby Maid* out tomorrow and Keith and I are both booked up all week . . . Will you be able to manage or do you need more help?'

'I can manage easily, so long as someone's around to keep an eye on Kit,' Anthea said, arranging crusty rolls on a tray. 'People are awfully good, I sit him in his highchair with his toys and whilst I'm dishing up Sarah or Ceri keep an eye, and during the meal I usually wheel him into the dining room and there's always someone who's happy to let him sit with them and chew on a rusk.'

Henry, who was rarely in at lunchtime, raised his eyebrows, then grinned.

'My God, every visitor has his uses! So even with a full dining room you can cope?'

'Yes, truly. So long as I've got Ceri too.'

'Anthea Todd, you're a wonderful woman!' Henry laughed as the colour rose in her cheeks. 'One of these days you'll be poached by a *real* hotel, and then what will I do? Is there a flask for me, by the way?'

'No; a can of pop,' Anthea said. 'I really envy you on a day like this – all that sun on the water! Be careful not to burn, though.'

'When we're not so busy I'll take you out on the water so you can see for yourself that it isn't just a matter of lolling on the deck in the sun,' Henry said, picking up the packed lunches and stowing them in a large plastic carrier bag. 'See you at dinnertime.'

Keith ran all the way down to the marina, but even so he was the last to arrive.

'I've got your packed lunch,' Henry said, handing it over. 'What went wrong?'

'Zak ate my shoelaces,' Keith said breathlessly. 'I had to use bits of white string. Who'm I taking?'

He was self-confident on the boats now, enjoying it every bit as much as he had hoped. Because he had not yet got his RYA instructor's certificate, he could not teach, so the second boat was let out to experienced people on a bare boat charter and Keith went along to keep an eye on things as the insurance company stipulated. He was familiar with the boat, had a good working knowledge of where they could safely sail, and if the crew got into hot water and needed help, there he was. He was studying for his certificate whenever he had time, but until he got it he simply enjoyed the company of his guests and sometimes learned from their experiences.

'You've got Jerry Wilson, Sam Bent and young Susan Stevens today; Sam and Sue haven't been on *Sunny Weather* before, so they're exploring below, but Jerry's on deck. Well, you'll be leaving now, so see you at dinner.'

'See you,' echoed Keith. He jumped down onto *Weather*'s deck and went below himself, into the tiny, cramped cabin, to stow away his thick jersey and the packed lunches in the lockers with the foul weather gear. The two *Sunnies* were not boats in which one expected to spend the night, they were small cabin sailers, but even so he and Henry had formed the habit of keeping gear aboard, in case they ever had to spend a night at sea.

Sue was fiddling with the tiny galley and turned to smile at him, suggesting that he might show off and make them a coffee once they were under way. Keith said he'd be happy to do so, but Sam, taking off his huge guernsey and shovelling it into a locker, shook his head.

'Too hot,' he remarked. 'Why not use the pop Anthea put into the lunch-bags?'

'Because it's for lunch,' Sue pointed out. 'Oh come on, Sam, it would be fun to have coffee at eleven.'

'If we anchor and we're hungry later, I'll really show off and make pancakes,' Keith said. It was his party piece and much appreciated after a hard day on the water. 'As for coffee, see how everyone feels by lunchtime.'

'Where are we going?' That was Jerry Wilson, the third

member of the party. He was tall and spare, with crisply curling black hair and a mischievous, tilted smile. He smiled at Keith now. 'How about Great Yarmouth?'

'Not even with a following wind, which we do have,' Keith admitted. 'But unless someone particularly wants to sail north, it's easier going south.'

'We'll go south,' Sam said at once. He clicked the locker and turned towards the companionway. 'C'mon, chaps, let's get away and out to the open sea!'

It was a wonderful day. The weather continued kind and Sam and Sue got friendlier and friendlier, until Jerry, with a grin and a wink at Keith, remarked in a low voice that he was downright glad the insurance company insisted on a member of staff accompanying the bare boat charters.

'I'd have looked a proper gooseberry, stuck out on the boat with the young lovers,' he commented. 'And those pancakes earned you your place aboard, young Keith!'

The two of them were lounging on the deck whilst Sam and Sue sailed the boat. Keith raised his fair eyebrows.

'Earned me my place, Jerry? I'm here to make sure you don't wreck *Sunny Weather*, not because I want to be!'

Jerry cocked his head to one side and smiled beguilingly.

'You mean you aren't glad to be out here? And in another few minutes it'll be our turn to sail!'

'Marvellous! Nothing nicer than tacking along the coast in a wind like this.'

And presently, Keith and Jerry took over whilst Sam and Sue lounged on deck. And it was fun; Jerry was good on the tiller and Keith was the instinctive sort of crew who does what he's told almost before the words are out of the skipper's mouth.

'We'd better all give a hand now or we'll be late for dinner,' Sue remarked presently, getting lazily to her feet. 'I know I had a huge lunch and I know I ate more than my fair share of those pancakes, but I'm starving!'

'Me, too,' Jerry called back. He glanced up at the sail, then pulled the tiller over. 'Ready about! Lee ho!'

They sailed along the coast in perfect amity, now one taking the tiller, now another. And presently, with Haisby in sight,

Keith went below to tidy himself up a bit and put on his shirt and was joined by Jerry, complaining that his shoulder blades were burning.

Keith was half into his shirt when he felt Jerry's hands on his bare shoulders. The other man swung him round until they were nose to nose, only inches apart.

'Keith? Doing anything after dinner?'

And all at once, Keith knew. How strange that he had not guessed before – it just showed how naive he was!

'Tonight, d'you mean? No, I don't think so.'

'Why don't we take a look at the town, have a drink? I've been so busy sailing I've hardly been out at all.'

The words were ordinary enough, but the glance which accompanied them spoke volumes to Keith. It said *I fancy you; any chance that you might fancy me, too?*

'That would be lovely,' Keith said. 'We could meet at the end of the drive at eight-thirty, say.'

'It's a date.'

As they sailed into the marina, tacking to make the most of breeze and currents, Keith could scarcely get over his luck. A marvellous-looking guy like Jerry – all the girls on the sailing course were crazy over him – yet he had picked Keith! And I never suspected for a moment that he was gay, Keith reproached himself; never let him see I was interested . . . which means he must be *very* attracted. He found himself watching Jerry covertly, approving the height of him, the slim hips, the broad shoulders, and the beautiful face with its dark, expressive eyes, its mischievous mouth. He imagined he could still feel Jerry's hands on his bare shoulders and shivered delightedly.

And now that he was aware, there could be no doubt that Jerry was smitten; he lost no opportunity of touching Keith, just a shoulder brushing a shoulder, or a knee touching under the cabin table . . . he helped Sue onto the quayside when they berthed, then made a joke of helping Keith too – and held him, for one heartstopping moment, in a brief, dangerous intimacy.

Because Jerry's not come into the open yet, not even as much as I have, Keith told himself. Jerry, during dinner, had definitely flirted with the wife of No. 18 and the prettier of the two girls in No. 6. But it's just a blind, Keith thought. Poor Jerry, he doesn't want to set tongues wagging, he wants to be socially acceptable, like everyone does.

I'll teach him, Keith thought nostalgically; I'll teach him about love, and desire . . . I'll show him that the relationship between us can be as beautiful and satisfying as any marriage.

Chapter Thirteen

'You'll have to say something to him; it isn't fair to simply go out with someone else.'

Nicola was lecturing Ceri as they cleaned the flat and Zak was prancing round them, making occasional dives at the brush and wrestling with the duster. The two girls had recently put down new lino in the kitchen and the resultant rush of house-pride to the head, as Ceri put it, meant that they took more pleasure in the place.

'But Tom isn't my *boyfriend* so why shouldn't I just go out with Fritz and see how I like him? Why should I tell Tom?'

'Because you're fond of each other and it's my belief that he'll be awfully hurt if he finds out about Fritz – why on earth can't you call him Hans, incidentally, since that's his name? – and you wouldn't want that, would you?'

'I don't know what I want,' Ceri muttered, applying wax polish to the round walnut table. 'Tom's so rude! He spends all his time putting me down and laughing at me, then he gives me a kiss on the nose and tells me I'm a funny little thing and goes off whistling. And . . . and I'd like to hear someone say, "Ceri, you're the prettiest girl I know" or even "Ceri, what a cute little nose!" instead of "Come along, zit-features" or "Move your butt, ginger!" Now Fritz is smooth, man!'

'Hans is smooth.'

'Hans that wash dishes can be smooth as your face . . .' Ceri carolled. 'He looks like a Fritz, he's got a long solemn face like Larry the Lamb's friend, that dachshund. His name was Fritz, wasn't it?'

'I don't know. But if he's so odd, why do you want to go out with him?'

'I *told* you; because I'm sick of being treated like a feed in a comedy routine,' Ceri said savagely. 'Tom can't be serious and it's exhausting, honestly it is.'

'Then tell Tom why you're going out with Fritz,' Nicola advised. 'Give him a chance to put things right, Ces. He *is* fond of you, I just know he is.'

'Huh! Bloody funny way to show it,' Ceri said breathlessly; she was putting all her energy into removing the polish. 'Well, all right, but I shan't give him details, I'll just say Fritz is taking me out to dinner tomorrow night.'

'Good. That's fair. Probably nothing will come of your date with Fritz anyway,' Nicola said. 'You can see what someone else is like and then go back to Tom.'

'Or not.'

Nicola raised her fair eyebrows, then snatched what was left of the hearth brush from between Zak's paws.

'Bad boy! Ceri, I don't understand you; why on earth have you suddenly decided you want Tom to be different? You've seemed quite happy with him as he is until now.'

'I've told you. It's all right for you, Nick, you know you're beautiful, but I don't know anything and I'd like to be taken seriously. I know I'm small and my hair's a funny colour and my nose is a funny shape and my eyelashes are white, I know I'm not pretty or clever or cute, but I don't want someone perpetually rubbing it in!'

Nicola sat back on her heels and blew out so that the hair overhanging her forehead stood out straight.

'You are extremely pretty, very intelligent and fun to be with,' she announced roundly. 'And anyone who says otherwise is a fool! If it's thanks to Tom that you think all that rubbish then the sooner you dump him the better.'

'Yes, that's what I think,' Ceri said with unalloyed gloom. 'I don't need putting down, I can do that for myself. And Fritz is so sweet and complimentary and . . . well, it sounds conceited, but so smitten!'

'There you are, then. Tell Tom and let him repent in loneliness, which is what he deserves. And now tell me what Fr – Hans, I mean – does for the *Evening News*.'

'He's not on the paper at all; I interviewed him – didn't I tell you? It made a jolly good piece as well, for all he looks so like a dachshund in the photograph that I nearly put "Woof woof!" as a caption.'

'No you didn't tell me and I still don't know what Fr – Hans actually does!'

'He's an engineer with Boston & James, in the city. But he

came first in a sail-board race on Oulton Broad, and I interviewed him for that. He looks awfully dashing from a distance,' Ceri added in an apologetic tone. 'If only he didn't part his hair in the middle!'

'He can't – no one does that any more, it went out with Oxford bags in the 'twenties, I'm sure.'

'Fritz does. Look, I can see my face in this table, so can we have lunch now?'

'Yes, I suppose so. When are you seeing Tom next?'

'After lunch. We're going swimming,' Ceri said. 'I'm going to wait until he's in his little cozzie, looking a complete prat, and then I'm going to say goodbye for ever.'

'Well, it will serve him right,' Nicola admitted ruefully. 'And maybe Fritz will be nice.'

'Hans, you mean,' Ceri said, grinning. 'Hans knees and boomps-a-daisy.'

'Talk about Tom – you're two of a kind!'

'I know; it's catching,' Ceri said gloomily. 'I say, I say, I say, who was that woman I saw you with last night? That was no woman, that was . . .'

'Shut up and lay the table,' Nicola said. 'Well, you always wanted to be a heart-breaker. My guess is you'll astonish Tom as well as break his heart.'

Ceri ran out of the sea and cantered up the beach, throwing herself down on her towel just as Tom, slower off the mark, reached her. She was panting, rubbing the water droplets off her face with a corner of her towel, enjoying the taste of salt on her lips, the langorous pleasure of relaxing after the vigorous swim. What a fantastic day – if only she wasn't going to have to spoil it!

'I love the sea when it's just that bit rough,' she remarked. 'Did you enjoy that swim, Tom?'

Tom draped his towel round his shoulders and began half-heartedly drying himself. Then he groped for his glasses and perched them on his nose, regarding Ceri through them.

'Sure did,' he said uneasily. 'What's up, Ceri?'

Ceri, who thought she had been behaving perfectly normally, blinked.

'What do you mean?'

'Well, you've been sort of quiet. And you know I enjoy swimming! So what's the matter?'

182

Ceri took a deep breath. Tom had not made a joke for all of fifteen minutes and he looked different with his hair sleeked down. And despite her rude words about his looking a prat in his cozzie actually he looked rather nice – taut and spare and fit. But still, she had promised Nicola.

'Nothing's the matter. But a fellow I met through the paper – he won a race at Oulton Broad last weekend – has asked me out. And I'm going.'

'Oh,' Tom said blankly. 'Who is he?'

'No one. Tom, I *told* you who he was, just the guy who won the sail-board race.'

'Yes, of course. Good-looking, is he? A mass of finely tuned muscles, like me?'

'Not particularly. But he asked me, and . . . well, I thought it would be fun.'

'Sure. But that doesn't mean you and me . . . You're going to come out with me again, aren't you?'

Ceri took a deep breath. She must be cruel to be kind, because she just knew it would do her good to be treated like a human being for a change.

'Well, no. I'm sorry, Tom, but I don't think I can go on. You're never serious and hardly ever polite, and I *know* I'm plain and not clever and I know my hair's ginger and I've got a million freckles, but Tom, it's all you ever say to me! And I really can't take it any more.'

There was a stunned silence. Ceri stole a look at Tom. All the colour whipped into his face by the swim had drained away. He did not look at all like himself.

'Tom? I'm really sorry, but can you understand? I need someone to be nice to me from time to time.'

Tom put a hand on her arm. It was a tentative gesture and it hurt Ceri, who had been pleased with the increasing assurance he was showing. But she must stick to her guns, she must!

'Ces? I don't mean . . . Dear God, the times the words have come into my mind, beautiful words which say just what I want to say. Only by the time they reach my mouth they've got twisted, somehow, and they're silly wisecracks, or smart alecky answers, and all the beautiful words have gone back inside my head.'

'Oh, Tom, if only I were older it probably wouldn't matter,' Ceri sighed. 'But right now I don't need put-downs and jokes

183

all the time. The guy I'm seeing tomorrow night doesn't joke at all and once that would have been awful, but now it just seems like a refreshing change!'

'I've hurt you . . . but Ceri, I want to *marry* you,' Tom muttered. 'I've never felt . . . I've never met . . . there's never been . . .'

'Marry?' Ceri laughed hollowly. 'Tom, I can just see it! On our wedding night it would be, *Well, well, so you are a natural red-head!* In the honeymoon hotel you'd tell everyone *She made me count her freckles last night, so we neither of us got a wink of sleep!* You'd look round our first home and say, *Have you burned my first meal yet, dear?* I couldn't stand it!'

'I'm sorry,' Tom said. He took his glasses off and rubbed his eyes, then pinched the bridge of his nose between finger and thumb. Sea-water ran down his face – or was it tears? 'Ceri . . .'

'Put your specs on,' Ceri advised him crisply. 'I'm only seeing this guy once. But it was only fair to warn you that it might easily lead to . . . to other things.'

'Ceri. Let me speak.' Still without replacing his glasses, Tom stared at her, right into her eyes. His own eyes, without the glasses, were really nice, a golden-brown colour, fringed with short black lashes. 'If I tear off all my outer layers of silliness, what will be left? Just a little nothing-guy quivering with fear in case he loses you, that's what. But Ceri, it's criminal that you thought yourself not pretty, when you're the prettiest, cheekiest, loveliest kid in the world – when your hair is soft as silk and smells of apple-blossom, when your skin is white as milk and the sun brings out a dusting of golden freckles . . . Oh, Ceri, you're funny and smart and twice as clever as me and I've loved you since the first day you walked into the bank and smiled at me.'

'Oh!' Ceri said blankly. 'Oh, Tom!'

'I'm half-blind without my specs, I'm the sort of guy who gets sand kicked in his face by the hero, I'll never make manager of the bank, you're my first serious girlfriend, I know how lucky I was to get you and it made me nervous, so I fooled around and fooled around . . . Ceri, let me love you!'

'Oh,' Ceri said again, but slower this time. 'Do put your specs back on.'

'No, I dare not. If you're going to walk away then I don't want to see,' Tom said wildly. 'Without my specs you're just a blur, but you're the blur I want to spend the rest of my life with . . . Ceri, don't walk away just because I couldn't be serious. I can be! Now that I know how you feel I will be!'

'How do I feel?' Ceri said curiously. Her voice did not sound like hers at all.

Tom put his arms round her and drew her close. He cuddled her and smoothed the hair off her salty face and then he kissed her salty lips.

'You feel soft and yielding and sweet as honey; you feel like the only person in the world who matters. You feel like my little Ceri.'

'Stop messing about; what did you mean when you said you knew how I felt?'

'You're serious. I thought you didn't want me to be serious so I mucked about all the time; I was afraid if I was serious you'd be embarrassed and leave me. But then you said you were going to leave me anyway and I could see I couldn't make things worse, so I let my serious side show. And you didn't kick sand in my face and walk away laughing.'

'No, I didn't,' Ceri purred, snuggling against Tom's nicely muscled chest. 'Oh Tom, I'm not afraid to say I love you now, for fear you'd make a joke of it.'

'I love you, tremendously,' Tom muttered. 'But you won't mind if I do muck around a lot of the time, will you Ces? Because it's the nature of the beast, I'm afraid.'

'I'd hate you to be serious all the time,' Ceri said stoutly. She kissed his neck, then opened her mouth and ran her tongue up to his chin. Tom swallowed convulsively and his grip on her tightened. 'But when it's just the two of us, I'd like it best if you didn't joke *too* much.'

'It's a deal,' Tom said jubilantly. He reached for his glasses and put them on, then looked at her through them, his beautiful eyes ordinary once more. 'Dear God, I called you a beautiful blur, but you're even lovelier now I can focus!'

'Oh, Tom, what a liar you are! But I do like it!'

The school holidays had come and Nicola was walking Zak along the prom, scene – though he was blissfully unaware of it – of his near-drowning. He was a big lad now, she thought, looking down at him, with the gangly legs common to most puppies of five months and the innocent eyes and engaging grin which had been his all his short life.

It was a fine evening, the sunshine falling on an almost empty beach, for most holidaymakers abandoned the sands after dinner and took to the town, instead. Nicola strolled along, knowing a moment of total happiness. Life was good. Ceri and Tom were reconciled and going about like Darby and Joan; work was going well – Mr Gregory had given her a rise and asked her out to lunch, and though she had refused, it was nice to be wanted – and even the flat had begun to look a bit more like home. Her chief worry, in fact, was a ridiculously personal one – her relationship with Ian Frazer. She liked him very much, was at ease with him and enjoyed his gentle caresses, though they had still not cemented their relationship by actually making love. Lovemaking was a tiny part of marriage, Nicola acknowledged, perhaps the easiest part to get right, yet she did feel that if they were unable to get it together in the first flush, with the forbidden fruit syndrome working on their side, then they were unlikely to make the earth move once they were married.

And marriage was definitely what Ian had in view. He had hinted at it, suggesting that she might go home with him, meet his people, see the part of the world which had produced him. She had not wanted to take him home, she knew that much, and rather resented his suggestion that she might go to Scotland with him. Why, for God's sake? And what was so marvellous about marriage? Neither of them had found it good, so why was he eager to repeat an experiment which had brought him nothing but pain?

But Ian's experience had not been of marriage; he and his treacherous lady had merely been engaged. He seemed to think that if they were married, if the knot was tied, then everything would go swimmingly, but it was barely a year since she and Roger had been living happily in the house on Kett's Hill, with no idea that their life was about to come crashing around their ears, and Nicola, once bitten, twice shy, could not forget the experience.

Yet when one door closes another opens, the saying goes, and in a way it had certainly happened for her and Roger. He had Milly, would soon have a child, and she had Ceri, her share of the flat, Zak her Icelandic cat – there had been no repercussions from Gilbert yet, she rather thought he would just let things slide – and Ian, who was kind, thoughtful and caring.

But he does not set me on fire, Nicola told herself sadly. Yet Ian was very eligible, only six years older than she, and he said he loved her and seemed to mean it.

Money did not really matter, but it would make Milly so cross if she knew how well Nicola was doing! Ian wanted to start his own practice. He talked of returning to Scotland, buying a big old farmhouse with lots of land and combining a vet's practice with farming or running a stables, all things which appealed to Nicola.

The question was, did she want to marry a second time, even if she suddenly found herself in love with Ian? It would mean changing her ways all over again. No more sloppy meals eaten in pyjamas, elbows on table, dog on lap. No more frank girl-talk, whilst she washed her hair and Ceri had a shower. No more slapdash cleaning, with a good go through once a month.

All my life I've lived in an ordered fashion until now, Nicola realised as she turned at the end of the prom and headed homewards. Mother liked the house to be just so, and Father went along with it – probably liked it too, for all I know. No mugs, they're for navvies, a nice cup and saucer never hurt anyone. Nicola, you aren't eating that biscuit *straight from the packet*, are you? Get a plate, there's a good girl. Cut the crusts off, dear – I know I'm old-fashioned but I like things nice. No, hang it up, you'll be grateful one day, it'll last you twice as long! Nicola, why on *earth* are you and your friend sitting on the floor? Animals sit on floors, dear. God gave you a sit-upon for chairs, not for floors!

And then Roger. I've put a row of hooks in the hall, darling – you hung your coat over my mac and I hate it all creased. I'm going to be late home tonight, could you run the mower over the back lawn? Yes, I did it two nights ago, but it grows like a weed . . . A dog? It wouldn't be fair to keep a dog, we're out all day . . . A cat's not quite the same. We'll have a kitten if you're set on it, but I might as well say straight out that I'm not keen on cats. Mother always thought I was allergic, I used to get a rash.

She had given in, of course. Over everything. Both at home and with Roger. And what had come of all her attempts to be what they wanted her to be? Sadness and misery, that was what had come of it; a conviction that she was in some way inferior, just a pretty face, a peg on which to hang expensive dresses.

And now? After nearly twelve months of freedom? She was a different person, she knew that. She had the sort of self-confidence which came from having faced up to life alone. She pleased herself, she took Zak in the park and ignored people who said dogs ought to be banished from public places. She told Ian she didn't want to go out if she felt like staying in, and he accepted her right to choose. She ate if she was hungry and did not eat if she felt full, even though it meant a mealtime might pass almost unnoticed. Snacks were spooned out of tins or packets, yesterday she had picked up a Smartie from the kitchen floor and popped it straight into her mouth, almost enjoying her phantom parent's gasp of protest.

So what about marriage, then? Odd, how she had once longed for it, feeling that it would fulfil her, prove her femininity and, of course, her desirability as a mate. She must have been mad! It had only proved that she could keep a house but not a man. And now, seen from the viewpoint of an observer and not a participant, marriage showed its true face. A Venus fly-trap into which the unwary wandered, only to find that it was not a simple and straightforward matter of drinking the honey, fertilising the plant. You had to risk the clinging properties of the trap, the sticky liquid which forced you in deeper than you wanted to go, which made leaving a nasty business, painful for both parties.

To marry again, then, after so short a period of freedom, was not a good idea. But poor Ian could not see it; he thought he loved her, and though she liked him very much she knew it was not enough. Besides, until they had lived together she would not know about Ian's obsessions or hang-ups, and he was a professional man, he did not want a relationship unblessed by church or state. And if you committed yourself to another person then the pain of parting would be as great whether you exchanged solemn vows or simple kisses.

But if they broke up, she would miss Ian a lot. Ceri had Tom, friends at work had their own lives. Only . . . she *knew* she did not love him! He was a better man altogether than poor Roger – how wonderfully easily now the words *poor Roger* came to mind – but he was too serious for her, too career-minded perhaps. Oh hang it, he wasn't . . . he didn't have that certain magic something which would have brought her eagerly to his side. If she settled for marriage to Ian, she thought suddenly, she would always dream about the man she had never yet met, always wonder what would have happened if she'd waited, bided her time.

Ceri and Zak were no problem. Trotting along in front of her now as they turned the corner into Harbour Hill and began the ascent, Zak would be as welcome in her new home, if she married Ian, as she herself would be. And Ceri would find another flatmate; it might not be long, anyway, before she wanted to move out herself, because if ever a couple appeared to be hearing distant wedding bells it was Ceri and Tom.

So it's really up to me, Nicola told herself. Whither I goeth, Zak goeth also. Ceri can cope. Ian needs me and Roger's got Milly. So why do I hesitate? Why don't I just say 'yes', and start making wedding plans? She had tried love and found it wasn't enough, so why not give respect and admiration a chance? But she knew, really. It was too soon. She liked being Nicola solo, Nicola independent . . . damn it, Nicola selfish! And she would not give it up just because Ian wanted marriage. Let him marry someone else, she thought recklessly, pushing open the garden gate. If he really loves me he won't try to hustle me, he'll understand that I need time. And if he doesn't, then balls to Ian!

'Zak, I'm not a nice person,' Nicola informed the puppy as the two of them mounted the stairs. 'But nice or not, I believe I've got a point; I do need time.'

Keith locked the bathroom door, turned on the hot tap and lit the geyser, watching with satisfaction as the water began to steam into the tub. He had a brand-new bottle of scented bath-foam which he would presently pour into the running water. Hanging on the back of the bathroom door were his good clothes, for tonight he and Jerry would meet at the Pleasure Boat night club in Norwich, and then they would have the whole night at an hotel! It will be like a honeymoon, Keith thought happily, splashing bath-foam into the tub. Two lovely people who enjoyed each other's company will take the plunge into a real relationship together!

He and Jerry had spent the last week of Jerry's holiday in a state of euphoria. Keith had been right, Jerry was untried, untested, only beginning to be aware of his feelings. For the first time in his life, Keith had led in a relationship, and had found it good.

He was a little worried over Jerry's tendency to flirt with any girl who so much as glanced at him; he suspected that, amongst gays, Jerry would flirt with any guy who glanced at him as well, but he could not complain. Had Jerry not chosen him? Were they not off together very soon, on what amounted to a honeymoon? Twin souls who had found each other at last and wanted to be together always?

Keith lay in the bath with foam up to his chin, and dreamed of the evening to come and the night to follow, and eyed his nice clothes. The Y-fronts with pictures of cuddly teddy bears all over them – bought as a subtle compliment to Teddy, they would give Jerry something to smile and tease him about – the pale blue sweatshirt with a caption reading *Love Games* across the chest. Pale blue linen trousers and his blue suede shoes completed the outfit, and he would take no nightwear because what was the point? He just knew that he and Jerry would have no need of nightwear in their ritzy hotel room!

But the water was cooling so Keith climbed out, towelled himself briskly, rinsed his hair over the basin and rubbed that dry too, then began to dress.

Downstairs, Robin would be doing his chores and Henry and Anthea would be clearing up after dinner. They would be helped by young Ceri since it was Keith's night off so he could take his time, enjoy his preparations. He shaved carefully, whilst clad only in the Y-fronts and his matching teddy bear socks. He cleaned his teeth next, applied a touch of after-shave, puffed talc under both arms and down his Y-fronts, smoothed handcream into his elbows, knees and hands, and then took a long look at himself in the full-length mirror.

He struck a model's pose first, then did a body-builder position, muscles flexed, lips set in a sneer. Then he checked that his teeth were not harbouring any fragments of food, that his tongue was a healthy colour, his nostrils clean. Only then, when he was satisfied with himself from the skin up, did he begin to dress.

By the time he descended the stairs he knew he looked good and thanked heaven that it was a fine evening. His off-white mac made him look like Humphrey Bogart – or did he mean Lauren Bacall? – but he looked more glamorous without it.

'How you doing, Robin?'

He and Robin met in the hall as the boy took the cleaned shoes back to the guests' rooms.

'Okay, ta. You look awfully nice. Have a good time. Henry says you won't be home until tomorrow lunch!'

'That's right. I'm going to have someone wait on me, for a change.' Keith looked inquisitively at the shoes. 'Smart – the cream and brown ones.'

'Do you think so? Hal called them brothel-creepers.'

Keith tutted. Henry was so full of don't say this, that or the other in front of the boy, then he went and said something like that!

'Well, you've made a good job of them, anyway. Finished for today, have you?'

'Sure have! All right if I go and watch telly now?'

Keith smiled. Henry was severe on the lad in some ways; no telly until all the chores were done, even if it meant Robin missing something he'd set his heart on. But it didn't seem to do him much harm, he was a good lad.

'Yes, run along then.' He felt around in his trouser pocket and produced a pound. 'Here you are.'

'Oh, Kee!' Robin's face shone. 'Gosh, thanks!'

'Kee-eeth!' That was Ceri, from the front garden. 'Car here for you!'

What timing! Keith had arranged with a friend who played in a dance band in the city, Lenny Walsh, to pick him up since Jerry would run him home tomorrow morning. He hurried across the hall and the car had only just drawn to a halt when Keith opened the passenger door and jumped inside. He waved to Ceri and then smiled at Lenny.

'I won't be coming back with you tonight, Len. I'm meeting a friend and we'll come home together.'

'Sure,' Lenny said easily. 'Good thing, in fact. I've told Sunny and Ellis that I'll take them home, which means their instruments, too. Be a bit of a squeeze.'

All the way to the city, Keith and Lenny talked in the casual, easy way of friends. Their discussion ranged from other members of the band, why one club did well and another badly, to the reasons for under-age drinking.

At Ramages, the club where Lenny worked, Keith got out of the car and made his way back onto the road. The Pleasure Boat was down by the river a bit further along, so he did not have far to walk. He strode out in the balmy evening air, humming to himself, looking at passersby under his lashes – handsome, plain, boring, he categorized them all as he passed.

He reached the Pleasure Boat a quarter of an hour before Jerry was due to put in an appearance. He felt diffident about entering since Jerry had paid for them both, but he could scarcely hang around in the road for fifteen minutes. He explained and they checked the membership and then waved him through, much to Keith's relief.

It was an impressive place. There was a glass roof over the whole area, so whether you were in the courtyard having a meal or dancing on the small dance floor, you would not risk a wetting. The courtyard was ringed with buildings, all with sliding glass partitions which could be closed in winter. One could wander through the bars, or dance, or sit and chat, but always, before you, you could see the river, the twinkling lights, the dark silhouettes of the trees against the dancing water.

Right now, however, most of the beauty and ingenuity of the Pleasure Boat was lost on Keith. He had not brought much money with him and drinks were extremely expensive. He knew that this was Jerry's treat, that his friend intended to buy any booze he consumed, so now he grudgingly bought a gin and tonic and sat at a table facing the entrance, waiting.

Some time later, stiffening with horror, he saw Teddy enter. He strolled across the dance floor, neatly avoiding the couples dancing, and appeared to see Keith for the first time. He came over, a big smile on his face.

'Keith, old lad! What a bit of luck; thought I was in for a lonely sort of an evening, and here you are, actually waiting for me!'

He giggled on a high, neighing note; he was clearly drunk already, Keith saw with disapproval. Oh, blow Jerry for being late, this might prove embarrassing!

'I'm meeting a friend,' he said stiffly. 'I'm sure he won't be much longer – he's late already.'

Teddy grinned knowingly.

'A friend, eh? Didn't know you had any, old lad . . . and why should you have friends, when you led me on and let me down and never even rang or wrote to let me know what I'd done wrong!'

'You hadn't done anything wrong, Teddy,' Keith said placatingly. He knew he had behaved badly and was ashamed of himself, but his friendship with Jerry had been so sudden, so unexpected, that he had simply forgotten Ted. What foul luck that he was here tonight, though! 'Look, you run off now and find yourself someone to – to –'

'Are you trying to insin . . . shin . . . Are you trying to say I'm *on the game*?' Ted said loudly, his voice growing almost shrill. 'Well, there's frenshi' for you . . . some price frenshi . . . Oh, look!'

Jerry, incredibly beautiful in a very macho dark suit, deep blue shirt, pale tie, was weaving his way across the dance floor towards them. Keith felt his heart give a little thump of pleasure. Jerry was here after all! Soon they would get rid of Teddy-bare and eat and then go – how could he bear to wait? – to their honeymoon suite! He stood up.

'Jerry, lovely to see you, my dear. Do sit down. Can I get you a drink?'

Jerry sat, stared at Ted, accepted the offered drink. Keith went to the bar but he was not a tall or pushful type and it took him quite a while to get the tequila sunrise which Jerry fancied, as well as his last few pennies. And when he got back to the table, neither Ted nor Jerry was there. He stared, then looked around.

At a corner table in an alcove so dusky that he could scarcely see them, Ted and Jerry sat, entwined. Keith could scarcely believe his eyes – this was not happening, it was some horrible nightmare! He walked over to the table, carefully carrying the drink, his face hot with humiliation. Was this a set-up? Had Jerry and Ted known each other all along, conspired to break his heart?

But Jerry smiled up at him and took the drink with a soft word of thanks, looking as though butter wouldn't melt in his mouth.

'Lovely, my favourite tipple! Sit down, Kiwi, and we'll all snuggle up together.'

It was a recipe for disaster, of course. A threesome is never comfortable, especially in such circumstances. Jerry was clearly very attracted to Ted, and finally it appeared that he could hide it no longer.

'Do stop scowling for a minute, Kiwi,' he said plaintively, standing up and holding out both hands to Ted. 'Teddy and I

193

are just going out to my car for something but you stay here, we'll be back in a brace of shakes. And remember, you and I will be off to our hotel suite soon, so don't grudge me a little time on my own to get to know Teddy here.'

He's a brazen hussy, Keith told himself, sitting alone at the table and fighting off tears. Oh, if only I didn't love him I could just walk away from here and keep my pride! But I most desperately want our night together! And after we've made love, when we're one, surely he'll be faithful, love me as I love him?

After half an hour he was called to the phone. It was Ted, giggling, covering the mouthpiece with his hand, but never well enough to shut out Jerry's voice.

'Kiwi? Lover boy's here, we're just going down to the chippy for a bite to eat, but we'll be back. Jerry says you're to wait, or no fun and games. Got that?'

Keith returned to his table in an evil mood. He was now all but penniless, he had no option but to make his present drink last until Jerry came back and then he wouldn't half sting his friend for his cruel neglect; it'll be tequila sunrises for me until the sun rises, he thought crossly, pretending to sip his drink. Oh, but poor Jerry, he's been trapped by Teddy – how he'll regret his cruelty later, when we're alone and I reproach him!

Time passed. Keith had no money now and his drink was finished. He had already ascertained that none of his friends were present. The place was crowded, yet apart from the departed Jerry and Ted, Keith knew no one.

The place was filling up, too. Keith, who had been sitting at a corner table, deliberately got up and took a seat nearer the dance floor, which was brightly lit and obvious. He would sit right here where he could be clearly seen, he decided angrily, and if Jerry came soon that would be all right, but if someone else wanted to be friendly, that would be all right too. If Jerry arrived and saw him flirting he would be served out for the misery he was putting Keith through!

'Nicola, dearest Nicola, would you do me a huge, enormous favour? I know it's my turn to walk Zak and normally I'd do it when I get home, but Tom's taking me out to a night club! He says we might be awfully late . . . Are you and Ian doing anything special tonight?'

Nicola was sitting in front of the mirror in her room applying mascara. Now she smiled at Ceri through the glass. Ceri thought wistfully that though she had done her best, she would never be able to compete with Nicola's creamy fair beauty.

'For you, anything!' Nicola said expansively. 'Actually, we're going out to a country pub for a meal, it would be nice to take Zak along with us; Ian never minds provided Zak doesn't try to make a meal of the handbrake. So you can count me in as baby-sitter tonight. Which night club, anyway? And why the sudden spending splurge?'

'The Pleasure Boat. Perhaps Tom is hoping to ply me with expensive liquor and persuade me to give my All,' Ceri said hopefully. 'Though on past experience it doesn't seem likely. No, it's because he got sent tickets for tonight so he can see whether he wants to become a member or not. He won't, but as he said, we might as well take a look. Do you like my dress?'

Ceri looked down at herself, at the goldy-brown dress clinging to her slight curves, the amber necklace, the dark brown suede shoes.

'You look lovely,' Nicola said. 'I've never seen you all dressed up, Ces – and how clever of you to choose that shade of brown.'

'It is nice, isn't it? But it wasn't really me,' Ceri said. 'I went to Bonner's in the Arcade, and Helen made me try on about a million things and thought this was best. It cost a lot, but if it seduces Tom into seducing me, it'll be money well spent.'

Nicola giggled.

'Why not just throw yourself at him and start tearing his clothes off?' she enquired. 'What about equal opportunities for women? A sort of do-your-own-seduction kit.'

'I'm too shy,' Ceri said. 'And I suppose Tom's saving himself for marriage, which is what I ought to be doing. Only I feel insulted that he doesn't ever have a go . . . And incidentally, I don't intend to *let* Tom seduce me, not if he pleads ever so. I just want him to *try!*'

'I see; a born-again tease. Fie upon you, Ceri Allen! And do come in quietly tonight, because if you wake Zak he wakes me –'

The doorbell's shrilling cut across the sentence and Zak,

stretched out on the bed, leapt to his feet uttering the deep, bewildered bark of one recently in dreamland.

'I'll come in quietly,' Ceri promised, hurling herself at the bedroom door. 'Sorry, must go, that'll be Tom and he's probably parked on the double yellow lines, he did last time and the traffic warden said . . . See you later!'

'I say, don't you look smart!'

Ceri's wild career had ended at the front door which she had opened to find Tom in a black dinner jacket and starched white shirt, a dark red bow tie nestling in the frill. Ceri had never seen him looking so formal, but as soon as he opened his mouth it was just Tom again.

'Oh, Ces, what a little cracker you are! That dress does things for me as well as you. Let's get a wiggle on, though. The mini's on a double yellow.'

'I guessed it. Some people have an affinity for double yellow lines and you're one of them. Why on earth didn't you bring it into the drive?'

'And risk being parked in by another tenant? Come on, run, we'll beat the traffic warden by miles if you'll just get a shift on.'

The two of them ran down the drive, with Tom leading because Ceri was not used to high heels. They burst into the road and Ceri groaned when she saw that the mini was not only on double yellow lines but also on the bus stop.

'That's a hanging offence so far as Blod the Sod is concerned,' Ceri gasped as they hurtled into the car. 'Don't you think, Tom, that residents ought to have a special parking permit? I mean why should we suffer three months of the year when trippers nab all our spaces?'

'Because they pay our wages,' Tom observed, starting the engine. 'I'm driving, as you can see, but I thought you might chauffeur me home if I get bladdered.'

'Bladdered, you uncouth pig you?'

'Oh, pissed, blotto – drunk, nitwit.'

'Thanks for the lecture; what if I get bladdered?'

'Women don't. Besides, you hardly ever drink more than one little fizzy thing with cherries in.' Tom revved the engine and charged down the road. 'Got to get a move on, mustn't miss all the fun!'

'Where are we going, then?'

'The Pleasure Boat first. Somewhere else later. The Pleasure Boat's the best, so they say.'

'I hope it isn't too expensive,' Ceri murmured doubtfully. 'I'm only working three days next week because the paper want me to do a story on the crab fishermen. I'm going out in a boat. It'll be a great experience. And I'm doing a follow-up of that hit-and-run incident out at North Walsham. I rather fancy myself as an investigative journalist.'

'It's *wildly* expensive; but since it's my treat, it's also my worry,' Tom said grandly, rather spoiling it by adding, 'And that's why we're going on somewhere else afterwards, because at the Boat's prices I shan't be able to get even slightly jolly.'

'I'll stick to Coke,' Ceri offered. 'I like it just as much as those little fizzy things with cherries.'

'Coke probably costs a couple of quid a throw at the Pleasure Boat,' Tom said gloomily. 'Have you eaten?'

'Of course I did. I can't go from lunchtime until ten at night without shoving something down to the inner Ceri. But only bread and butter and an apple. I thought we could get chips on the way home.'

'You are mundane, Allen, down-bloody-right mundane. This is a treat, remember? So I shall take you out for a slap-up feed, after the Pleasure Boat.'

Ceri hugged herself, beaming with pleasure.

'Oh, Tom! Where shall we go?'

'Somewhere pretty exclusive, I thought. There's a place out on Riverside Road. Mitch told me about it.'

Mitch was a teller in Tom's bank. He was a gangly youth who was magic with figures and had a great future, according to Tom.

'Oh well, if Mitch likes it it must be good,' Ceri said. Although she would never have dreamed of telling Tom, Mitch had made a pass at her recently in the swimming pool and she now regarded him more kindly. Not that one wants to have gangly youths pawing one below the waterline, she reminded herself severely, but at least it proved one was worth pawing. Ceri had once remarked that her looks were wholesome; perhaps I'm fraying round the edges at last, she had concluded whilst eluding Mitch's submariner gropings.

The roads of North Norfolk are good, particularly late in the evening when few tractors or herds of cattle are abroad.

197

Lights came towards them but they were few and far between. Ceri's day had started early and she was tired. Despite herself her lids kept drooping; despite herself her head kept nodding forward.

The little mini thundered on. The noise of the engine precluded quiet chat; only shouts could be clearly heard. Ceri told herself that she could not possibly sleep with the engine thundering and the wind shrieking in through the open window but it seemed she lied. Presently she sank into a light doze.

'Wake up, carrot-top.'

The words were accompanied by gentle shaking.

Ceri opened her eyes, unable at first to think where she was, and there was Tom's face above her, his glasses catching the light so that for a moment he looked blank-eyed, frightening. Then he moved and he was just dear Tom, gently scoffing at her ability to sleep anywhere.

'Oh Tom, I'm sorry, but I started work at six this morning so that Hal could have a lie-in, and I worked later than usual so that Keith could start his day off, and now the moment I sit down I want to fall asleep,' Ceri said distractedly, trying to get out of the car without undoing her safety belt and nearly strangling herself. Tom clicked the belt free, then pulled her into his arms.

'Have I ever told you you're adorable?' he demanded huskily. He kissed her mouth gently but with such controlled passion that Ceri shivered, suddenly very much awake.

'No, not often,' she murmured when her mouth was free. 'Oh Tom, it's lovely when you say nice things.'

Tom rubbed his cheek against hers, then stroked round her neck, up her jawline and round her ear.

'You know I hate to sound like a fool,' he muttered, still clutching her against him. 'But that doesn't mean I don't love you tremendously. Ceri, you're the best thing that ever happened to me, why don't we . . .'

A torch beam swung crazily across the front of the mini, then came to rest on the half-empty driver's seat, for most of Tom was sprawled over Ceri. Through Tom's open window a face appeared, sideways. It was large and bland and its mouth was set in a half-grin, showing horsy yellow teeth. It cleared its throat.

'*Excuse* me, sir, *if* you and the young lady wouldn't mind, you're supposed to park round the back.'

'I'm sorry, I'm just dropping my young lady off here to save her the walk. She's awfully tired.'

The face looked knowing.

'That's what they all say, sir. Now orf you go, sir, there's others waitin' for you to move along.'

'Damn the old fool,' Tom mumbled as he drove down to the car park. 'Never mind, littl'un, I'll park as near the front as I can.'

He found a parking slot and they locked the car and made for the club. At the arch, the face which had peered through the window winked at Ceri and raised a majestic finger to its cap when it caught Tom's eye.

'High-class bouncer,' Tom said. 'Probably got the real muscle hidden away so's not to put people off.'

Ceri, however, was too dazzled to listen. The courtyard, the dance floor, the twinkling lights in the great trees, all enchanted her. She clutched Tom's arm.

'Isn't it pretty! We could eat here if we wanted, there are lovely tables and waiters and things. Not that I want to, mind you. Can we look round?'

'Of course, but let's get a drink, first. I'll have a lager; what do you want?'

'Coke,' Ceri said diplomatically. 'Let's go to that bar, over there.'

It was a cosy little bar up a short flight of stairs but open to the courtyard. Ceri and Tom climbed the stairs and made for the bar, but halfway up Ceri poked Tom in the back.

'Look, there's Keith! Oh my God, on my night out the first person I see is my boss!'

Tom followed her discreet jerk of the head. There, at a table near the dance floor, sat Keith. He looked disconsolate but even as they watched a tall man approached him, leaned over the table and spoke. Keith looked up, oddly, Ceri thought, through his lashes. She did not recognise his Lauren Bacall.

'Is this a pick-up that I see before me?' Tom remarked. 'Well, at least we needn't go and sit with Keith now.' This as the man pulled out a chair and sat down. 'Where shall we take our drinks?'

'Down by the river,' Ceri said promptly. 'And after that, can we dance?'

'Of course. This is your evening. My desires are as nought beside your idlest wish.'

Ceri glanced at him as they retraced their steps but he was concentrating on not spilling his lager. Desires? What desires? It sounded hopeful, she thought.

Time passed and no Jerry appeared and Keith's self-pity increased. It was too cruel of Jerry, to stand him up in a place so smart, with drinks such a price. And how was he to get home? Lenny thought he was getting a lift, Henry wouldn't expect him till morning . . . What on earth was he to do, he couldn't even afford to ring Hal!

Yet he could not believe Jerry would really abandon him. He was teaching him a bit of humility, not dropping him altogether. Ever since Terry, Keith had always been the one to end a relationship. What had he done wrong this time?

When the tall stranger came over to his table and asked him for a light, Keith could have kissed him. He smiled his best smile, however, and said he wasn't a smoker, and then the other man introduced himself as Peter LeGrand and asked if Keith was alone.

'Well, yes and no,' Keith said guardedly. He had heard of queer-bashing – ghastly expression – and knew that to admit to being stranded here might be dangerous. But Peter pulled a sympathetic face and sat down, then asked him what he was drinking.

'Oh . . . I don't know whether I ought,' Keith said. 'If my friend arrives he'll be awfully cross to find me drinking with a stranger . . . but I'd love a g and t.'

Peter went and got the drink and came back with one for himself as well. He sat down by Keith and began to talk. It appeared he was an antique dealer, down in Norwich for an antiques fair and clearly lonely.

In response, Keith told Peter about his friend Jerry.

'I'm sure it's all some terrible mistake; my poor Jerry must have had an accident or been taken ill,' he said sadly, after explaining that he had waited for his friend for more than two hours. 'I'm penniless, stranded, but what about my Jerry, he might be hurt . . .'

'He'll be all right, he's probably involved in business, forgetting he's left a lovely little guy in the lurch,' Peter asserted, his large eyes moist with sympathy. 'Have another drink!'

Keith put a detaining hand on his arm.

'You're most awfully kind, but I must say no. I've had nothing to eat since lunchtime, I'll simply keel over if I drink any more and then who'll carry me home? But you have another.'

'We'll both have a meal,' Peter said at once. 'What do you fancy? They do a delicious starter – smoked salmon with scrambled egg. How about that?'

Keith, who adored smoked salmon but rarely got his teeth into any, agreed that it sounded delicious.

'Keep the wolf from the door until my friend arrives,' he said gaily. He hoped Jerry really would arrive, because he, Keith, would certainly not leave smoked salmon – and Peter – and go meekly off with him. No indeed! Keith was by now aware that he had been made a fool of and rejoiced to have found himself just the sort of friend he liked, attentive, amusing and generous.

Peter ordered and in due course the meal arrived. As they ate, Keith told his new friend a little about the hotel, though he did not say where it was. But he boasted a bit. After all, Peter would be leaving Norwich tomorrow, they would probably never set eyes on each other again.

'We must keep in touch,' Peter said, when their steaks arrived. 'It isn't every day I meet someone so easy to – forgive me – to love.'

'That's kind,' Keith said. It struck him for the first time that Peter had an enormous conk, a hooter which outhooted most. He found himself wondering if Peter's nose meant other parts of Peter were built on equally magnificent lines, and was glad he need not find out.

But as the wine sank in the bottle, as Peter plied him with port and liqueurs, it occurred to Keith that it might be fun to get to know Peter well. After all, he had planned a night on the tiles, what did it matter if he played love games with Peter instead of Jerry? He had fancied himself in love with a man who had turned out to be a fickle jade, why should he not find himself in love with thoughtful and generous Peter LeGrand?

'What do you think of Keith's friend?' Ceri said as they circled the dance floor. Tom's arms were round her waist, her hands

201

linked behind his neck; she felt a little shy at such closeness. 'I don't like the look of him much.'

'Great ponce,' Tom said. 'Eyes too close together. What a hooter, though; if he gets a cold I bet they have to evacuate the building.'

Ceri giggled.

'But Tom, he keeps putting his hand on Keith's knee – I *hope* it's his knee – under the table. Do you think they're old friends?'

'Possibly, but I don't understand gays. I can't imagine one bloke fancying another.'

'Keith is gay, then? I thought he was,' Ceri said. 'Henry isn't though – think of Robin.'

'Lord, I don't know, Ces! And Robin isn't proof of anyone's virility now. Men can change, I believe.'

'Can they? Don't you change, will you, Tom!'

'I certainly shan't,' Tom said huskily. He pulled her closer still. 'Oh Ces, do you know what I'd like to do to you?'

'No, what?' Ceri asked, trying to sound provocative. 'Do tell!'

'I'd like to kiss you!'

Although a trifle disappointed, Ceri raised her face to Tom's, lips parted, eyes shining.

'What's stopping you?'

Tom bent his head and they kissed. It was a satisfying kiss, for Ceri at least, though Tom uttered some frustrated moans and gripped her so tightly to him that she felt pleasantly threatened. Oh I do like Tom, she thought, returning his kiss fervently. Will it be soon?

'Well, Kiwi old chap, I'll have to love you and leave you, now,' Peter said at midnight, when the meal was over and Keith was relaxed and happy once more, with just the right amount of alcohol circulating in his bloodstream and a pleasantly full stomach. 'I'm off to a big sale tomorrow; can I walk you home?'

'I live in Haisby, down on the coast,' Keith said. 'Peter, I hate to ask, but could you possibly lend me the money for a cab? Otherwise I'll be sleeping on the pavement.'

Peter leaned across the table and brushed Keith's cheek with his fingertips.

'My dear old boy, this is absurd, if I hadn't had the odd

drink myself I'd run you home like a shot. And I'm not too flush with the old readies, having no idea I might need anything but my credit card. Look, can I offer you a bed until tomorrow morning? Then I'll run you home before I start work. There's only one bedroom, but you can kip down on the couch; no problem.'

Keith's pulses raced; only one bedroom? If he went back to his hotel with Peter he had no illusions about who would sleep where – could he bring himself to share a bed on such short acquaintance? Yet to insist on the couch would be a poor way to repay Peter's kindness.

'Well, if you're sure . . . it's very good of you, because you know what the police can be like if one of us is wandering the streets in the early hours.'

Peter nodded and stood up, putting a protective arm about Keith's shoulders as he did so. Keith had forgotten how tall he was. He had almost forgotten, too, how much he liked tall men.

'Right, that's settled. I rent a suite quite near here, so we'll walk, and then I'll make you a hot cup of cocoa and tuck you up until morning.'

Keith rolled his eyes up to meet his protector's. He felt so small and frail, so cherished!

'That sounds lovely, Peter,' Keith murmured, having a little trouble with his words, now. 'I'll repay you one day, you can be sure of that.'

'I *am* sure,' Peter said softly. 'I am sure, Keith.'

It was not far to Peter's suite, which was in a building overlooking the river. He led Keith across a foyer, up two flights of stairs and over to a door painted white and gold. It was an impressive door and Keith was impressed.

'This must cost you a bomb,' he observed, as Peter let them in. 'Fancy little Kiwi sleeping in such splendour!'

'Fancy,' echoed Peter; was that a trace of sarcasm in his deep, London-accented voice? If so, Keith put it down to the nervousness natural to one about to embark on a new relationship. 'Let's go straight to the living room, then I can make you a drink whilst you relax.'

He flung open another door. Keith stepped through the doorway, then stopped short. The room was not empty. It had two occupants, both seated on a luxurious couch, both smiling in his direction. Their smiles were enough to make Keith's blood run cold.

'I'm awfully sorry,' Keith said shakily, turning to Peter. 'I didn't realise you had company; I'd better go.'

Peter closed the door and turned to Keith. When he smiled his eyes seemed to creep closer to his enormous nose and his mouth looked wet and cruel.

'Say hello to Joe and Barney,' he said softly. 'Then we can all be friends together.'

Thoroughly uneasy now, Keith tried to smile naturally at Joe and Barney. Barney was black, with shoulders so square that they looked padded – only he was sitting in singlet and trousers so padding was out of the question. He had a bullet head, tiny little eyes and the broken nose and cauliflower ears of a less than successful boxer.

'H-hello, Barney,' Keith quavered. He looked back at Peter. Desperately.

'Say hello to Joe, now,' Peter said. Remorselessly.

Keith looked at Joe. He was another big fellow, but with narrow shoulders and a thin, sly face. His mouth was too big for the rest of him, a loose, slobbery mouth with rubbery lips over which his tongue kept passing. He had damp, restless hands with long fingers which plucked and twitched at the knees of his shabby jeans.

'Hello, J-Joe,' Keith stuttered. 'I really should leave now. I'll ring for a taxi and pay the other end. I'm sorry to have bothered you, Peter.'

Barney stood up, looming hugely over Keith, and picked him up as though he weighed no more than a child. Then he plonked him on the couch between himself and Joe. A big black hand caught at one side of Keith's lovely pale blue sweatshirt and heaved. Keith tried to grab it but other hands caught his wrists, pinioning them so tightly that he could not move. The sweatshirt was up over his head like a bag, he could see nothing, but he could feel their hands. They tore his trousers and Y-fronts off, making lewd comments on the teddy bears. His trainers and socks were pulled off, his feet trampled on. When he could feel air on his bare flesh he tried to rid himself of the blinding sweatshirt but once more his wrists were seized; this time they were tied, he felt the rope bite, and then hands were touching him, rubbing, arousing him despite his terrible fear, his complete revulsion.

'Don't, please don't,' Keith's voice squealed, but it was doubtful if any of the three heard; certainly they paid no attention. They were too busy arguing.

'I'll go first; I found him.' A hateful hand caught his penis, working on it so hard that Keith cried out. 'He's rather nice, isn't he? We're all going to enjoy ourselves tonight.'

'All but one,' a breathy voice said in Keith's ear as the sweatshirt was at last pulled from his hot and terrified face. It was Joe. 'All but one.'

Chapter Fourteen

The sky overhead was bright with stars when Ceri and Tom came out of the Pleasure Boat. It had been calm and still earlier but now a breeze had awoken, as if to blow in the dawn which traced a faint silver line to the east. Ceri leaned against Tom and gave a little shiver.

'Are you cold, love?' Tom's arm tightened about her. 'It was so hot in there!'

'Not cold; just excited and tired,' Ceri admitted. 'Thank goodness Henry said I could be late tomorrow; do you realise we'll be getting up again in four hours, and we aren't home yet?'

'And I had such nice plans for the rest of the night,' Tom said. 'Only the mini's so cramped.'

'True. Shall we drive to the chip shop, or walk?'

Tom laughed and hugged her tighter.

'Even the most enlightened chip shop closes at midnight; I doubt if we'd even find an Indian curry house open right now. Poor love, are you so hungry?'

They had eaten meat pies and jacket potatoes four hours ago, leaving the club for a cheap takeaway and then returning, replete. But Ceri nodded vigorously.

'Yes, starving – it's always the same when I'm happy, it goes straight to my appetite. Never mind, you can come back to the flat and I'll boil us eggs or something.'

They reached the car. Tom, who had kept off alcohol as soon as he discovered how much it cost at the Boat, put Ceri tenderly into the passenger seat and then got behind the wheel. There were a lot of people milling about, so Tom drove gingerly out into the road.

'Gosh, look at the queue for taxis,' Ceri said as they edged across the pavement. 'Do you suppose Keith's waiting there? If he is, perhaps it would be nice to give him a lift; it'll cost him the earth to get back to Haisby at this hour and he and Henry aren't exactly rich.'

'Oh, hell, must we?' Tom sighed but drove slowly along the taxi queue, then cheered up as he saw no Keith drooping in its ranks. 'Reprieve! He probably left ages ago, or he might be spending the night with big-nose.'

He revved the engine and drove on but presently he said crossly, 'Damn!'

'What's the matter?'

'We're going in the wrong direction. I drove along the queue, I should have turned right. I'll just back round in one of these side-streets or I'll get trapped in the one-way system and go miles further than I need.'

'I don't mind,' Ceri said sleepily. 'I love being a passenger for a change.'

'The sooner I get you home the longer we have to kiss good night,' Tom said practically. Ceri smiled.

'All right, reverse down this little road, it's private, but there's no one around to complain.'

Tom was backing gingerly down the narrow alley when Ceri suddenly said, 'Stop!' her voice squeaky with alarm.

Tom stopped.

'What's up? Broken glass?'

'No. Something . . . someone . . . we'd better look.'

Tom squinted in his mirror, then got out of the car.

'Good thing you noticed, Ces, I could easily have gone right over him. He's drunk, I suppose. Look, you stay there, I'll just move him into a doorway. He probably lay down with his meths and rolled into the road without realising it.'

Tom got out of the car closely followed by Ceri, whose newspaper instincts – or plain nosiness – would never let her be left out of anything. He took the still figure by the shoulders and started to try to lift it.

Terrifyingly, the figure screamed, a long shriek of anguish which, as Tom shot back, ended in a series of short, moaning grunts.

'He's hurt . . .' Ceri began, then clutched Tom's arm. 'My God! It's Keith! Tom, it's Keith!' She bent over the still form. 'Keith? What's happened? Were you run over? Don't worry, we'll get help right away!'

The man opened puffed and slitted eyes.

'Ceri? I . . . was . . . attacked.'

'I'll ring for the police,' Tom began, but was interrupted. Keith half sat up, groaned, then spoke.

'No! Not the police. Take me home. Take me *home*!'

With those words, as if it had taken the last of his strength, Keith collapsed back onto the cobbled street.

'Give me a hand, Ceri,' Tom said. He caught hold of Keith's shoulders as gently as he could, but Keith groaned and then the groans trailed off into whimpers. 'Take his feet, sweetheart. We'll soon have him home.'

It was a slow and painful business carrying Keith to the car and Ceri was terrified of hurting him, but they got him there at last and laid him on the back seat, without, so far as they could tell, Keith regaining consciousness at all.

'Hadn't we better get him to a hospital?' Ceri said, as Tom turned the car round and headed, fast, for the main road once more. 'He looks awfully bad, Tom. There was a lot of blood.'

'Better wait,' Tom said. 'It can be awkward with gays, sweetheart. And he was well enough to tell us where to take him, so I think we should do just that.'

'Yes, you're probably right,' Ceri said, turning round to stare at the figure on the back seat. 'But he's in a bad state . . .' She shivered. 'Oh Tom, I'm scared!'

'Me too,' Tom said frankly. 'But we'll be home in less than an hour, even though I'll drive slowly.'

Once they were on the Haisby Road Ceri had a better look and saw, with horrified pity, that most of Keith's front teeth were either missing or so blood-boltered that they were invisible against the dark of his gaping mouth. She looked further and harder, and saw that his wrists were deeply cut and bruised and his bare feet black and blue.

'Who would do that to him?' she whispered. 'You'd think he'd been mugged, but why would anyone mug Keith? He's not rich.'

'Richness is relative,' Tom said. 'He had decent clothing and perhaps a few quid; if you're on drugs and desperate for a fix I suppose you'll have a go at anyone.'

'Yes . . . but Tom, I think his wrists had been tied! We ought to get the police, truly we ought.'

'No. Look, sweetheart, have you ever heard of queer-bashing? Someone who hates gays may have done this.'

'Well, we're miles from the Norfolk & Norwich, but perhaps we ought to go straight to Haisby General.'

Tom shot a sideways look at her. It occurred to Ceri that her dear love looked almost guilty. He knows more than he wants to tell me, Ceri thought sadly, and perhaps he's right, because I'm out of my depth already; perhaps investigative journalism isn't for me.

She voiced the thought to Tom, who nodded.

'Dear Ceri, you aren't the only one, and you're right, I do think this is more than queer-bashing. You see, if he's been in some sort of gay relationship which went wrong, or if Keith tried it on with a straight guy by mistake . . . well, the police might say Keith was breaking the law as well. So we ought to do what Keith wants before we bring the police into it.'

'Then shall we take him to Ambleside? Henry's marvellous, he'll know what to do.'

'No, not Henry; it wouldn't be fair, with the hotel and the boy and everything,' Tom said slowly. 'If only we knew a doctor, but I've never visited my GP in Haisby, have you?'

'Jan!' Ceri said suddenly, her voice squeaking. 'Jan Bryant, who lives on the floor above us! She's a nurse! She'll know what to do. Nicola will fetch her for us.'

'You little gem, that's what we'll do. A nurse will know how to get him into hospital or whatever . . . Now keep your eye on him; I'll take every care.'

Tom drove slowly, his knuckles white on the wheel. They talked little, for Keith's moans were not conducive to light conversation. Once or twice Ceri spoke to their passenger, but he seemed not to hear. And then, halfway back to Haisby, Keith began to mutter.

'What have I ever done to you? Aargh, I'll die, you're killing me! Don't let him, please, please!'

After this Ceri tried to reassure Keith that he was safe, but he was far away in some nightmare world which knew nothing of Ceri or Tom or even the mini, bouncing its way nearer Haisby with every moment. And when Ceri began to sob Tom turned the radio on, so that Keith's tortured cries were drowned by music.

'What'll we do when we get back to Lavengro?' Ceri asked presently, as they drove slowly through the suburbs. 'Everyone will be asleep, and the two of us can't possibly carry him upstairs to our flat.'

'Can you wake Nicola? And that nurse? We should be able to get him indoors between the four of us.'

They reached Harbour Hill and just as they were passing Bridge House Ceri touched Tom's arm.

'Stop! Look, there's one of those tramps, he's still up. Couldn't he give us a hand with Keith?'

The tramp, a wild-looking character in a long black coat with a black hat pulled low over his brow, agreed to help, so it was the three of them, in the end, who somehow got Keith up the stairs and into the flat.

'I'll wake Jan,' Ceri said briskly. 'You tell Nicola what's happened. And then I'll make us all some grub!'

Jan was not as shattered to be dragged out of a deep sleep as some might have been, but that did not mean she was delighted. Hearing Ceri's breathy, garbled story, she got out of bed at once and began to dress, whilst wishing, not for the first time, that she had taken up some less traumatic profession such as steeplejacking or speed skiing. Still, it seemed to be a genuine emergency and she was willing to help in any way she could.

She went down to Ceri's flat to be greeted by the smell of sausages frying and by the bespectacled young bank clerk who she thought was Ceri's boyfriend.

'He's in here,' the young man said. 'Oh, I'm Tom Hetherington by the way. Have you met Nicola?'

Jan grinned at Nicola. What an incredibly glamorous girl the other was, even without make-up and in hastily donned jeans and shirt!

'I'm Jan Bryant. I've met Nick and Ceri often around the place,' she said cheerfully. 'What happened? No, don't explain now, tell me as I take a look.'

'Right. Nicola, could you give Ceri a hand?'

Nicola disappeared kitchenwards and Tom turned to Jan.

'I didn't like to say too much in front of Nicola but though I tried to tell Ceri he'd been mugged, I think . . . well, come and see. He's in a real mess but we didn't call the police because . . .' He opened the door and pointed to the figure on the couch. 'There.'

Jan had been studying earlier in the evening, delving deep into *Obstetrics for Nurses*; one look at Keith made her wish devoutly that she had been studying wounds, since despite knowing Keith was gay, she also knew he was most unlikely to go into labour. However, she had done her share of casualty

210

nursing so she stood over him, looking hard before she touched.

The first thing she noticed was that his arms were not in the sweatshirt arms, so the garment was acting as a sort of strait-jacket. Odd. Then she saw that his light blue trousers were unzipped and dappled with blood. He wore no socks or shoes and his feet were bruised and swollen. His face was badly cut though she could see no head injuries. She examined his scalp, gently probing; everything all right there.

Next she went to take his pulse and saw that his wrists had rope burns round them and had bled where the rope had chafed. And his fingers looked like his feet – swollen and black and split, as though they had been through a mangle . . . Looking closer, pulling down the sweatshirt, she saw more marks round his throat . . . What on earth had been going on?

'Help me get his things off, Tom,' she said at last. 'Let the dog see the rabbit.'

It was the jokey, jovial sort of thing the Casualty doctors said and Tom smiled dutifully, though he was very pale. He began to pull the trousers down . . . and Keith gave such a shriek that Jan heard, from the kitchen, the clatter of a pan hitting the floor. Ceri must have been as startled by the sound as she.

'You lift, I'll pull,' Jan said. She was beginning to guess why the youngsters had neither called the police nor taken Keith straight to hospital, but she had not expected the injuries to be as bad as this. She pulled as gently as she could but Keith cried out again, and then, as the trousers came away, blood cascaded down his legs, onto the couch, the carpet, Jan herself . . . Tom lowered Keith quickly but not before he had cried out again.

Jan could feel her face cold, drained of blood, but she was still in command.

'Help me turn him onto his face, gently,' she said.

Tom complied.

The two of them stared, aghast, at Keith's torn and bloodied body, so white and young and defenceless, laid out on the shabby old couch.

'He's been raped,' Jan whispered. She felt sick. She clenched her fists, digging her nails into the palms of her hands. 'Oh, Tom, someone's raped the poor bugger.'

211

'Yes, I thought . . . Jan, should we call the police?'

'Not the police,' Jan said quickly. 'Some of them are fine, but there are others . . . Look, I'll ring Dr Alex and get him admitted straight to the ward.'

'Who's Dr Alex? Can he take charge?'

'She's a woman, a very caring sort of person. She'll tell us what to do.' Jan turned and looked at Tom and saw that he was just as upset and bewildered as she. 'The truth is, Tom, I can't deal with this; I'm thirty-two years old but all of a sudden, I'm too young!'

'That's how I felt, and Ceri too, though she doesn't realise the half,' Tom assured her. 'What can they do for damage like that? Operate?'

'He'll have to be cleaned up and stitched, and X-rayed for internal bleeding,' Jan said. 'But the worst part will be the mental damage, I think. Well, you must have read how rape victims feel – just because Keith's a man that won't stop him feeling the same. But he won't get the sympathy, not from the police or the courts. Because practising homosexuals . . . Oh Tom, I know it's between consenting adults, but people will say he asked for it . . . Oh, *poor* Keith – it's not fair, is it, Tom?'

'No, it's not,' Tom said sombrely. 'I'll go and see Ceri whilst you call Dr Alex.'

In the kitchen Ceri was coping, but she was thoroughly relieved to see Tom appear. The tramp, whose name was Harry, was sitting at the kitchen table drinking tea and devouring sausage sandwiches as though he had not eaten for weeks. He was also staring fixedly at Ceri.

'Tom! Is everything all right?'

'Sure. That Jan is great; she's ringing for a doctor, one she works with at the hospital.'

'Oh, thank goodness, someone who'll know what to do. Will Keith be all right?'

'I'm sure he will. But everyone will have to be awfully understanding for a while.'

'Yes, of course. Victims of mugging have counselling sessions,' Ceri said wisely. 'Would you like some sausages, Tom? I didn't cook them all for Harry.'

'I wouldn't mind,' Tom said, and sat down opposite Harry. Ceri swung round to stare at him; he had sounded odd. But

212

then Nicola began to make bread and milk for Zak, who was whining plaintively at her bedroom door, and she dropped three more sausages into the hissing pan.

To do Harry justice, he behaved much more sensibly the moment he saw Tom. He drank his tea quickly and finished off his food. Long before Tom had drunk his own tea – his glasses kept steaming up – Harry was pushing back his chair.

'All right, was it?' Ceri said. 'You full up?'

'Full up,' Harry echoed, sounding regretful. He burped loudly. 'Shall I go now?'

'Sure,' Ceri said. 'I'll let you out.'

She went before him down the stairs and was conscious, halfway down, that the back of her neck was behaving in a very odd fashion, with the flesh prickling up into goose-bumps. Her neck, she concluded, did not care for the close proximity of Harry, harmless though the rest of her might consider him.

She opened the door to release the tramp – who shot out as though he had been imprisoned against his will – just in time to let the doctor in. Ceri might not have known the woman in the green mac was a doctor either, but she spotted the black bag and the woman smiled at her and then stared very hard at Harry as he whizzed by.

'Morning,' she said, as if it wasn't five o'clock with a milky mist hanging over the gardens but a perfectly normal time of day to be abroad. 'Who was that?'

'That was Harry, he helped us to carry umm . . . umm . . . into the flat, so I gave him some breakfast,' Ceri explained. She did not want to use Keith's name; she could hear a milkman clattering bottles nearby and the mist, she felt uneasily, might hide anyone.

'I see. Well, Harry's a wild-looking one.' The doctor followed Ceri up the stairs and into the flat, then paused. 'Where's my patient?'

'In the living room.' Ceri pointed at the closed door. 'Jan's with him.'

The doctor disappeared into the living room, closing the door behind her, so Ceri went back to the kitchen. Nicola was buttering toast and Tom was eating it. Looking down at him, seeing his tired, pale face and crumpled white shirt, Ceri's heart smote her. Poor Tom! Even his dinner jacket looked raffish at five in the morning, but he would have to be in the bank at nine, and he would not be able to tell anyone about his hectic night, either. Ceri knew that Tom, though a notorious gossip, would never break a confidence, and she felt strongly that what had happened to Keith came into that category.

'Look, Tom, why don't you go and have a lie-down on my bed? You look exhausted.'

'What about you? You're working this morning.'

Ceri groaned; she had forgotten that she was supposed to be helping Henry with the early shift.

'Then let's both have a snooze; Nicola won't mind holding the fort for a couple of hours, will you, Nick?'

'Not at all,' Nicola said. 'Off with you.'

Tom took Ceri's hand and together the two of them trailed across the hall and into Ceri's small room. They slumped onto the bed, too exhausted to feel embarrassed, and Ceri heaved a big sigh and snuggled up.

'Do you know I used to envy people who lived it up all night and now I'm one of them,' Tom murmured, putting his arm round her and tugging her close. 'A genuine stop-out, home-with-the-milk. Wait till I tell Mitch!'

'But not about Keith,' Ceri mumbled. 'That's a secret, isn't it, Tom?'

'Umm . . . what do you mean, love?'

'Well, they hurt him because he was gay, didn't they? And they were gay too, so they did awful things . . . there was blood . . . all the time I was cooking in the kitchen I kept reminding myself that I wanted to be an investig . . . one of those journalists who detect things, telling myself that this was a real opportunity to right wrongs and things. Only . . . Tom . . .'

'Yes, sweetie?'

'I feel horrid, somehow. Was it queer-bashing, Tom? Was that it?'

'It was worse, love. Look, you'll keep this to yourself, I know, but Keith was the victim of gang-rape.'

Ceri sighed tremulously.

'Oh, my God. What'll we tell Henry, Tom?'

Tom kissed the back of her neck and then moved reluctantly away from her warmth.

'Try to sleep; I'll be back in a tick,' he said softly. 'I'll speak to Henry, but first I'll check with Dr Alex. I heard the living room door open.'

He left and came back ten minutes later, when Ceri was so dopey with sleep denied that she could distinctly see two of him. He closed the door and came over and sat down on the bed. He looked better, less worried.

'There's an ambulance coming and Dr Alex will travel with him and see him into a side ward,' he said. 'We're to say that Keith seemed all right and insisted on being taken to Haisby. And it was queer-bashing. And now let's sleep.'

Ceri sighed and snuggled once more; and had obeyed his command before Tom's head touched the pillow.

Keith came dizzily out of a dark dream in which he struggled with his assailants and knew he would lose the fight, to find himself in a tiny, curtained room with a trolley covered with wicked-looking instruments nearby. A woman sat near the head of the bed in which he lay, looking down at something on her lap.

As soon as he focused on the trolley, a whimper escaped Keith's trembling lips; they had found a new way to hurt him, they would come through those curtains presently and they would . . . they would . . .

'Don't let them, don't let them.' He whispered the words, afraid They would hear his voice. And then the girl looked up and smiled and everything clicked into place. The girl was a nurse, he was in a hospital bed. He was saved! They would never find him here!

'Hello, Keith,' the nurse said quietly. 'Do you feel better? You've had surgery, so I can't offer you a drink yet, but would you like a mouthwash?'

Keith realised that he was terribly thirsty; he said as much, trying to lick his dry lips with a tongue like an emery board. He was still afraid, even though he was sure they couldn't get him here. But menace hovered . . . He would have liked to ask the girl to stay but she was getting the mouthwash and looked settled enough.

'Here you are.' The nurse held a metal dish under his chin and swilled out his mouth with pink fizzy water, then she cleaned his gums with little padded sticks and then she let him rinse out again. Keith began to feel more human, though still afraid of his own shadow.

'Where am I?' he said weakly as the nurse settled him back on his pillows.

'You're in Haisby General, in a side ward off Men's Surgical,' she said cheerfully. 'Your card says you're Keith Fell but that was about all your friend told us.'

'My friend?' Hideous fears raised hideous heads. 'Who . . . who was that?'

'Her name's Ceri Allen; she came along with the doctor to sign you in because she works for you. Have I got that right?'

Keith nodded, relief washing over him in waves. He had no idea how Ceri had come into it but she was a good kid . . . Oh thank God, thank God, he was back in Haisby, far from the city, he would be safe, he must be safe!

'She's nice, Ceri – is she your girlfriend?'

Keith felt his eyes grow moist. Every time he moved the pain in his rectum reminded him what he had suffered in the name of lust; he had been raped because he had gone with a stranger, hoping for sex. And now this nurse was asking him if Ceri was his girlfriend, making it plain she did not realise he was gay.

'No, alas. But she's a good kid. Can you tell me how she came to bring me in? I'd been at the Pleasure Boat, I can't remember much after that.'

'I believe she found you lying in the road. But she'll be in later, you can ask her yourself.'

Keith sighed and turned his head into the pillow. He was half on his side, with a bolster gently propping him up so that he did not touch his worst injuries. Now, he closed his eyes. He heard the nurse creep quietly away.

Alone, he began to remember. Not just the agony of the repeated rapes but what they had done with him afterwards. When he kept passing out they had grown frightened; he had come round once to hear them arguing. Joe wanted more but Barney said they'd all had enough and Peter was scared, you could tell from his voice.

'It's my bloody flat and he's my bloody pick-up; if it's traced back to anyone it'll be me,' he said. 'Let's dump him in the river.'

'If they find him they'll know it wasn't a mugging, not like he is,' Barney observed. 'Tell you what . . .'

There was whispering, and then they rolled him in a blanket and carried him downstairs, still only half conscious.

When they put him down cold air cut across him, like iced knives round his private parts, for he was not fully dressed. They rolled him out into the road and moved away, whispering again. Then they returned.

'Make it look like some bugger queer-bashing,' Peter said. 'Go on, Barney, you're the expert.'

The boots had thudded into his face, he felt again the screaming pain as his teeth smashed. When they untied him they trod on his hands . . . He had lost consciousness again, but the bursting agony of it was something he would never forget as long as he lived.

Yet now, lying in his hospital bed, what kept coming into his mind was not the pain or the terror of it, but just a question: *Why me?* Was it something I said, the way I looked, a mannerism which irritated beyond bearing?

A cool and sensible part of his mind knew that it was no such thing: it was nothing personal, it was just the way they were. The violence would probably have come even had he not tried to escape.

Yet he must bear some blame. Henry had warned him what happened to promiscuous men. But he *hadn't* been bad, he had been innocent, he had only wanted a bed for the night, because Jerry had let him down. *Why me?*

Keith shifted and the dressings tweaked at raw, stitched flesh. He screwed his eyes tightly shut, trying to stop himself from shouting. *Why me? Why me?* A part of him wanted to . tell Henry, to beg for sympathy. But another part was far too afraid. Henry had warned him of the dangers of cruising. If Henry had seen him making up to Peter that night, giving the other man his Lauren Bacall, pouting, smiling, he would say that in a way, Keith had brought it on himself.

He'll finish our partnership, Keith thought fearfully, and I couldn't stand that. I'd rather die . . . (*Why me? Why me?*) So I must let Henry think it was queer-bashing and he'll pity me and take care of me whilst I get my confidence back.

But Keith was sure that his desire for affairs had gone for ever. If only he could keep Henry's respect and retain his place in the hotel venture then he would be content for the rest of his life. No more fluttering eyelashes, no more being the pretty boy they all wanted. Just sensible Keith Fell, partner to sensible Henry and part-father to Robin, going about his business in the hotel, cooking in the kitchen, glad to be

217

alive, wanting affection, not sex; a safe life, not a gay one.

Keith shifted again, finding a whole new set of bruises, seeing his wrists multi-coloured, his hands blackened, the nails split. He winced, then found a cool spot on the pillow and tried to get some sleep. Later, Ceri would come, and later still, Henry and Robin. He was sure Henry would come. He must be strong for them, must not let them see how broken he was.

Presently, on the verge of sleep, he began to weep. Tears soaked into his pillow, stuck his fair lashes together. *Why me? Why me?*

Chapter Fifteen

'What's the matter, Ceri? I thought you and Tom were going swimming this evening?'

Nicola, cool and elegant in a green silk suit which had cost more than she liked to remember, paused in the hall. Ceri was sitting at the kitchen table, writing in a shorthand notebook.

'Oh . . . yes, we were. But I had this piece to finish so I rang Tom and put him off.'

Nicola wandered into the kitchen, sat down opposite her flatmate and removed the notebook from Ceri's grasp.

'Lies, all lies,' she said cheerfully. 'Life must go on, Ces.'

'What do you mean?' Ceri tried to grab the book back. 'You know I'm busy.'

'I know you've let what happened to Keith put you right off Tom,' Nicola said frankly. 'Just remember, flower, that for every man – or woman – who's raped, there are a thousand who live happily ever after. And be sensible. Who could be kinder or gentler than Tom?'

'It isn't that,' Ceri said. She had gone very red but she met Nicola's eyes frankly enough. 'It's not that I'm afraid of being hurt – good Lord, nothing's further from my thoughts – it's just that it makes the whole thing seem . . . oh, mucky, unpleasant.'

'You're condemning Tom to a life of celibacy because of what happened to Keith?' Nicola asked incredulously. 'Because a man dies running a marathon that doesn't stop people running for buses! Keith was hurt because of sex, that's what you mean, isn't it? Well, you've got it all back-to-front. Keith was hurt because he fell amongst thieves. And you mustn't muddle sex with love, either. I think what you and Tom have got is love, Ceri.'

'Yes, I know. And I'll get over it,' Ceri said, very much as though she were suffering from a common cold. 'You should have seen Keith last night though, Nick!'

'Poorly, was he?'

'Yes, but it was worse than that. Henry and I talked but I could see Keith wasn't listening, and then we left, only I went back because I'd forgotten my sweater, and he was lying with his back to me, and he was whispering something, over and over. "*Why me? Why me?*" And it upset me most awfully, to tell you the truth.'

'Yes, it would. But you simply mustn't let it. Look, Ceri, I'm going to ring Tom now and tell him to come straight round. Then I'm off; Ian and I are going into the city to see *Swan Lake* at the Theatre Royal.'

'Don't! I can't see Tom all by . . . Hang on, Nick.'

But Nicola was making her phone call.

'I've been a great help, Hal says so,' Robin told Keith, sitting on the end of his bed and absentmindedly eating grapes. Keith found it hard enough to eat his meals without having to get through the fruit as well, so he was glad to see Robin gobbling. 'We got through dinner a dream – Ceri's great, and Anthea's stayed over most nights, but Hal says he'd never have managed without me.'

'Good for you, then,' Keith said. He was feeling a lot better, even his nervous fears were easier to bear. 'I'm coming home soon, though. The consultant says I can leave at the end of the week.'

'Hal says if you come back by the weekend all his prayers have been answered,' Robin assured him. 'You've had a rough time, haven't you, Kee? Eleanor Braithwaite's mum is a cleaner here and she says they usually chuck people out after a few days! Mrs Braithwaite says you must have been real bad!'

'Very true,' Keith said. Mrs Braithwaite had introduced herself as soon as she realised who he was, leaning on her mop for what seemed like hours whilst she eyed him with lively and unabashed interest.

'Yes. Well, she would know; Eleanor says her mum's almost as good as a doctor. What have they done to you lately, Keith? They took your stitches out, didn't they?'

'Oh yes, but they do all sorts of tests. They take so much blood it's a wonder I'm not just an empty skin. And the X-rays! They've got pictures of my whole body!'

'How do they take blood? When I was a little baby they stuck a knife in my poor little heel and sucked the blood up with a tube thing. My mum told me. Did they stick a knife in your heel, Keith?'

'No, they tie a thing round your arm and then when the vein in your elbow swells up they stick a needle into it and suck up the blood,' Keith said with relish.

'Gosh! And they've done it more than once?'

'Lots of times. My arm was black and blue.'

'Cor! Did it hurt?'

Mindful of the fact that one of these days Robin might have to give blood, Keith shook his head.

'No, not really. And it's awfully important, they can tell if you've got wrong things in your blood and if you've got right things, too.'

'And is your blood full of right things?'

'Sure it is; and . . . Ah, here's Hal!'

Henry came down the ward slowly, looking grey with tiredness. He sat on the visitor's chair, then handed Keith a carrier bag with clean pyjamas and some rather good chocolates inside it.

'You look better,' he announced. 'God, I'm tired! Any news?'

'Home at the end of the week, unless something goes wrong, and it won't,' Keith said buoyantly. 'Shan't be able to do a lot, but I'll do whatever I can.'

'Just to have you there to keep the books up to date will be grand,' Henry said. 'Just someone else to answer the phone . . . You've been sorely missed, Keith.'

It was September, the hot dry summer was nearing its end and children were flagging on the beach, steering clear of the shops with their windows full of 'back to school' reminders. Ceri walked up Lord Street towards the bank, trying to make up her mind what to say to Tom.

The thing was, he had suggested they take a holiday together as soon as the season was over. He knew she would be busy with the hotel until then and had agreed to take his break late so that colleagues with children could have the school holidays off.

'We could have a lot of fun together, Ceri,' he had said only last week. 'We don't have much money, but a boat on the broads or a caravan further up the coast wouldn't break us. What do you say?'

A good deal of Ceri wanted to say yes, particularly the bit which was keenest to stop being the only person in the world who didn't know about sex. She and Tom had lovely cuddling sessions, but they always ended too soon for her – and, she suspected, too soon for Tom, as well. If they went away together, in a caravan or a boat on the broads, then they could really relax and . . . and . . .

And then her mother had rung up.

'Ceri, love, don't columnists ever get time off?' she had demanded hopefully. 'Longing to see you again I am, and your Da too. Couldn't you make time to come home for a few days, now? Give us something to look forward to, make the winter seem shorter, like.'

'Mam, you and Dad went merrily off to Crete in May, and you're going to Southern Spain in October . . .'

'Oh yes, love, but that's not family! Look, why don't I book us in to a good hotel in Haisby? We could see you, evenings. You might even get a few hours off, show us the sights . . .'

'I'll come home,' Ceri said at once. She had never thought it necessary to tell her mother about Ambleside; you could never tell with Mam. 'Would it be all right if I brought a friend?'

She had not realised she meant Tom until the words were said, but then she was glad. She loved Mam and Dad, she was proud of them and her home and her background; she was equally proud of Tom and she loved him, too. Why should three such well-adjusted, likeable people not meet?

Why, indeed? So here she was on this sunny September morning, hurrying along Lord Street and heading for the bank, to tell Tom he was invited to stay with Prof. and Mrs Allen for a whole lovely week!

She had to queue for Tom, but it was worth it to see his face light up when she grinned at him through his grill.

'Ceri! Want some dosh?'

'No. Well, I do, but not right now. When's your dinner hour?'

'I can get away in forty minutes, if that would suit you. Why? Anything happened? Made our holiday booking?'

'Well, almost,' Ceri said evasively. 'Just want to check with

222

you that it's all right. I'll meet you in Sam's Place in three-quarters of an hour; okay?'

'Fine. Since I've recently been paid we could afford the steak and kidney. My treat.'

'I am a *vegetarian*,' Ceri hissed, but with watering mouth. How she loved Sam's steak and kidney pie! 'You can eat loathsome meat; I'll have the pasta and mushrooms in a creamy garlic sauce. Yummy!'

It sounded as yummy as steak and kidney if you said it quickly, Ceri told herself, leaving the bank. And meanwhile, at a loose end, she wandered into the Arcade.

Dave grinned at her from the bookshop; when she had worked at Sam's Place she had often delivered his dinner, so she grinned back. In the beauty shop, Treat Yourself, Caresse, wearing a peach satin jump-suit which made her bum look enormous, was bending down to arrange the bottles and jars on the lowest shelf. Further along, Anthea's replacement, Helen, sat behind the counter in Bonner's Boutique. She half rose when she heard the door open, then sank back onto her seat.

'Oh, it's you, Ceri! Did you see the dark blue velvet skirt in the window? Isn't it gorgeous? By the way, how did that dress go down?'

'The goldy-brown one? Everyone loved it, thanks, Helen. How's business?'

'If you were still working at Sam's Place, I'd tell the truth and say slow, but since you aren't, we're doing nicely, thank you,' Helen said, giggling at her own joke. She was a pretty little blonde with blue eyes and a friendly smile. Ceri knew she had a boyfriend and was engaged to him but she seemed scarcely out of school.

'Your stock certainly has a quick turnover,' Ceri said, looking approvingly around. 'Not a garment I recognise.'

'Stuff always goes well in the season; then we stock up with autumn wear and it's slow for a bit, as though the customers just didn't want to admit summer's nearly over,' Helen said. 'Want to have a snoop at my autumn stock?'

'Well, I'm certainly not buying,' Ceri said. 'But I'd love to look round.'

Three-quarters of an hour later, Ceri was the owner of a delicious leaf-green linen dress with a mandarin collar and narrow skirt. It did exciting things for her eyes and hair and made the most of her small breasts. Helen, who really was an empty-headed little bimbo, Ceri thought, knew all there was to know about clothes.

Ceri had barely got into Sam's Place and ordered steak and kidney pie for Tom and garlic pasta for herself when Tom came through the doorway.

'I *say*! Who's looking a million dollars then?' Tom enquired, then spoilt it by adding, 'You weren't wearing that when you came into the bank just now, were you?'

'No, actually. And it cost a million dollars, dear Tom, which is why I've changed our holiday venue.'

'Oh? Not the broads, then? A caravan on the coast?'

'Cambridge,' Ceri said with her mouth full of pasta.

Tom paused with a forkful of food poised above his plate. 'Pardon?'

'Cambridge. The place of my birth.'

'Cambridge? A caravan in *Cambridge*? Why on earth . . . ?'

'Not a caravan, dolt! No. 32, Marlowe Drive.'

A sort of horrified comprehension began to dawn on Tom's homely features. Ceri suppressed a giggle.

'Oh? Who lives there? Is it a guest-house?'

'Yes, in a way. My parents have issued a kind invitation to us both to spend a week with them.'

'Oh, I see,' Tom said hollowly. 'It's . . . it's awfully kind of them, but . . . didn't we have other ideas?'

His smile was pleading, but Ceri hardened her heart. The fact that her own ideas had included a good few things which would be impossible under the parental roof was, she considered, something they would have to put up with.

'Yes, we did,' she said now. 'But we must bite on the bullet and say we'll go, Tom, or my parents will be hurt and I can't bear to make them unhappy.'

'Well, I don't see why. What about *my* family? You haven't met them, yet.'

'True. But they haven't invited us back, have they?'

'No, because they don't know you exist,' Tom said frankly. 'And before you attack me, I haven't told them about you because I'm superstitious; I can't boast about you until I've tied you to me with bonds of steel, or even gold, otherwise you'll flit off with someone rich and handsome. Know what I mean?'

'Yes, I know just what you mean,' Ceri said. She, too, had said nothing to her parents about Tom, in case he decided to go for someone tall and gorgeous, like Nicola. But since they were planning a holiday together . . .

She voiced the thought aloud and Tom nodded.

'You're right, of course. I can't expect you to marry me before we've met each other's parents. Tell you what, we'll go back to Cambridge for that week, and in the middle of it we'll whip over to Ipswich and you can meet my mother and my brothers and sisters. Not my father, since he fled the coop years ago, but those Hetheringtons who are still at home will be delighted to meet you.'

'Gosh! Now I know how you felt when I told you about Cambridge,' Ceri admitted, her stomach churning. 'It's strange, Tom, because shyness is a disease I have never suffered from, but right now I feel very shy indeed!'

Until the attack on Keith, Henry had scarcely realised how heavily he was beginning to rely on Anthea, but once Keith was out of the picture he could see not only how good Anthea was at her job but how extremely capable in other ways.

It was remarkable how she managed Robin, for instance, because she had never had much to do with small boys. Yet without even raising her voice, she seemed to command obedience simply by expecting it. And she was fun, too. She enjoyed doing most of the things the kids enjoyed – exploring the shore, teaching Robin how to cook simple dishes, playing involved games with bits of paper and matchsticks on rainy afternoons.

And considering how diffident she was, she dealt awfully well with the guests, revealing an unexpected streak of humour and the ability to smooth ruffled feathers and ease tensions. And Kit, who could so easily have been a nuisance, was a delight, eager to tag along anywhere behind Henry or Robin, sweet-temperedly accepting dismissal when it was necessary.

And even with Keith back from hospital, Henry found that he still needed Anthea. She was both sensible and supportive, seeing that Keith needed to feel his presence made a great difference, but also seeing that Keith was not, as yet, capable of much. Keith did the books, peeled vegetables, laid tables.

He helped Robin with his homework and sat by the telephone taking messages and making bookings. He did no heavy work, and no cooking, either. Not that it mattered; Anthea was proving to be a positive genius in the kitchen, though she was totally untrained and cooked by instinct.

And Henry thought Keith took too many baths. He understood that Keith had been made to feel dirty, that he needed to bathe constantly, but four or five times a *day*? It seemed excessive, even given the circumstances.

He worried about the nightmares, too. Some nights Henry spent as long waking his friend as he spent sitting patiently by the bed, waiting for the younger man to fall asleep again. And sometimes Keith was too scared to go back to sleep. He would sit up and talk, his eyes hollow with fatigue, whilst Henry dozed in a chair, unable despite his determination, to remain awake.

Keith was always worse on the days he went to Haisby General for his check-up. It was a small hospital on a quiet residential road, the atmosphere friendly rather than businesslike, and Henry thought Keith was lucky to see his consultant there rather than having to travel to Norwich.

Queer-bashing was an evil thing, Henry knew, as vile a show of blind prejudice as one could hope to find. But surely, despite his injuries, Keith should begin to recover both mentally and physically, soon? Henry was uneasily aware that he himself was changing; once, he would not have dreamed of sitting by a bloke's bed until he went to sleep. The old Henry, the tough yachtsman, would have scorned such weak behaviour, but he was different now, his imagination had begun to creak into active life. He could understand Keith's need for company and besides, Keith was younger than he, more like a son – more like Robin . . .

It was hard work running the hotel without his partner, though. He had expected Keith to get well sooner, but when he mentioned it to Dr Crown, their GP, he was told that these things often took years, that he must be patient. So Henry soldiered on, tolerating the extra work load. When Keith recovered Henry would be able to relax and take up his own life again. As it was he had to hire Dave from the Dolphin to take the bare boat charters, and to work like stink himself just in order to keep the place running. He was tired from morning till night, and sometimes the responsibility on his shoulders felt too much to bear. But he soldiered on. Keith would be better soon.

They had told Keith at the hospital that he must come for check-ups, and now they told him he was a high risk.

It had been a shock. Keith had just stared for a moment, before the tears had started . . . only he was strong enough, by then, to push them back until he was alone.

You mustn't cook for others, they had warned him, their faces serious. You should change your job. You must warn the people you live with and any sexual contacts you've made over the past few months . . .

No, not a death-sentence, the consultant had said at Keith's next visit. You've been infected by this virus and that simply means you are likelier to become a victim than the average person. That's all.

He stayed in bed for a few days, and took a lot of baths. But gradually increasing health allowed him to pick up his old life again. He was careful – always scoured his cutlery in boiling water, always kissed air above Robin's head when he said good night. Kept himself to himself, you might say.

He suffered, of course. Long walks on the beach with tears coursing down his cheeks – *Why me? Why me?* – and long nights when he either slept and dreamed horrors or lay awake, grey with fatigue, watching for the dawn.

It was hard to face the fact that it had been largely his own fault. He had fallen for the facile charms of Jerry Wilson, had hungered after a 'real relationship', and had gone with a stranger, knowing the dangers for someone like him. He had laid himself open for precisely what had befallen him.

But perhaps the hardest thing was that he could tell no one, not even Hal. It was his own dark secret and it was easy to become obsessive about it. You could have ten good years, the consultant said. Or months. Or weeks. No one knew when it would decide to take over his body, tired of its role of passive onlooker.

He knew he ought to move away. Not far, just away from Hal and Rob, because he loved them and loving them was a risk. He could get a clerical job, perhaps. He could get a flat, make a few friends . . .

The bubble always burst; how could he leave the town where he was known and loved, the hotel which he and Henry had striven over together? On his very worst days, when the man with the axe stood right behind him, he could escape by going up to his room, climbing into bed, and pulling the covers right up. Ambleside was his refuge, his safe house. Here, nothing could harm him. He would listen to the soft sounds of the girls cleaning the bedrooms, calling to one another, having a joke with anyone who could spare a moment. He heard the whirr of the lawn-mower, the clip-clip of shears, the feet on the gravel as visitors came and went, and knew himself safe.

Nowhere else was as good; he knew, because he had tried other places. He tried the harbour, which he had always loved, and was overcome by shivering so violent that he had been forced to return to the hotel. He tried sailing, but he froze to the mainsheet, suddenly certain that he was going to die right then and there. In crowds, every face, every pair of shoulders, belonged to one of the dreaded three. Only at Ambleside did he know himself to be perfectly safe, surrounded by love. Away from here he knew he would not last long. Leaving was too great a sacrifice, but he was careful, determined no one would share his fate. He would never be Henry's lover, but he was his true friend. They liked him, Hal and the boy; even Ceri liked him. Loved him, a little. He *could not* go!

'It's not a big house,' Ceri said to Tom as the mini ate up the miles between Haisby and Cambridge. 'But it's not small, either. You'll like it. And there are no dogs or cats because Mam doesn't like animals. The garden's lovely . . . there's a wall round, and trees, and it's quiet . . . You'll like Cambridge, everyone does.'

Tom patted her hand.

'Have a peardrop,' he suggested, holding out the bag. 'How much longer?'

'Half an hour,' Ceri said, without glancing away from the road, since she was driving. She was as edgy as he; more so. It was her home, her parents, who would presently be judged. Suppose they were found wanting?

'Half an hour; hmm, not long. Shall we have a meal now, then, so your mum won't have to cook?'

'No, certainly not! Mam would be hurt if she thought you didn't want to eat at our place.'

'It isn't that, I just thought . . .'

Ceri shook her head sadly at him. She knew very well why he was suddenly hungry, suddenly keen to save her mother trouble. He was dreading their arrival at Marlowe Drive.

'It's no good, Tom, we'll get there one way or another and Mam will have a meal ready. No use putting it off, and that's all you're doing, you know.'

'I never knew how hungry I was until now,' Tom said wistfully. 'But I expect you're right, no point in upsetting your Mam. I wish I'd thought to break a leg, then at least they'd have felt sorry for me.'

'Shut up, you fool,' Ceri said, giggling. 'Don't forget, we're going over to see your lot on Wednesday.'

'My lot? Thanks very much! Besides, Wednesday is a lifetime away. We could easily get knocked down or die of a palsy before Wednesday.'

'Things like that only happen when you want them not to,' Ceri reminded him. 'It's called Sod's Law. I say, I've had a brilliant idea – dead clever, too!'

'What? About going back to Haisby?'

'No, Tom, do stop it! On Wednesday, instead of seeing your mother and brothers, why don't we send them a telegram saying I've been called back to work urgently. Then we could just sneak off somewhere and have a lovely two days all by ourselves in a little hotel somewhere!'

But Tom, though his eyes gleamed, shook his head.

'Oh no you don't! If I have to stay in Marlowe Drive then you damned well have to visit Broughton Street; fair's fair, Ceri Allen!'

They were still arguing when they entered the city. Tom began to look round him with keen interest. He had visited Cambridge during his schooldays, but only the Arts Theatre on Peas Hill, so now Ceri took him past some of the more imposing colleges and noticed, with love and amusement, how quiet and still he grew.

'Not long now,' Ceri said gaily. 'Oh Tom, it'll be all right, they'll love you!'

Surprisingly, they did. Mrs Allen was so like Ceri – small, red-haired, cheeky – that Tom had no difficulty in liking her and showing it, and Ceri's father, tall, thin and scholarly, endeared himself to Tom by proving to be a great reader of detective stories. Since Tom had cut his milk teeth on Agatha Christie – his own phrase – the two men got on like a house on fire, particularly when the subject of sport came up.

'I never saw the *point* of rugger,' Mr Allen said plaintively, when a neighbour began to extol the sport. 'Why should one man want to hold onto a ball when fifteen others are prepared to use violence to take it from him?'

'I quite agree,' Tom said thankfully. 'Football's very similar, only not quite so disgusting. The times my glasses got ground into the mud you wouldn't believe, and my mum behaving like a lunatic on the touchline and threatening me with a hiding if I broke another pair.'

'Well, there you are,' Mr Allen said. He looked at Ceri over the top of his half-moon glasses. 'I was always glad you never had to play rugby at school.'

'I was glad, too,' Ceri murmured, winking at her mother. 'Not that I'd have minded fifteen husky males trying to . . .'

'That's quite enough of that sort of talk, dear,' Mrs Allen said blandly, but with a twinkle lurking. 'What ever will Tom think of you?'

Tom patently thought she was adorable. He loved her home, the square Georgian house set in its walled garden, the rooms well proportioned and airy, the furniture comfortable rather than smart, and he liked her parents, but Ceri herself he simply loved, from her topmost red curl to her small toes.

He liked Cambridge too. Ceri took him first on the tour her father advised, taking in King's College and its chapel, where Tom duly admired the medieval stained glass and the slender stone pillars frothing into fan vaulting above his head. He also admired Queen's, both the college and the cloister, St John's, Gonville and Caius and the view from St Mary's church tower. Game but exhausted, they did the rounds – cloisters, colleges, churches, chapels, a museum or two, even the Guildhall from the outside. They snatched lunch at the Mitre, Tom not daring to suggest that they linger when he saw how much there was still to see. On that first day it was to be gown rather than town and Ceri revelled in Tom's admiration, but the next day, ignoring the spires and magnificent buildings, Ceri took Tom to her Cambridge rather than her father's. They took a punt along the backs, taking turns with the pole so that Tom could show his skill (not much skill, Ceri remarked as they rammed the bank for the tenth time), and drew in under a willow tree, its leaves already beginning to turn to gold, for a stolen kiss or two. It was a lovely sunny day so they had a picnic on the river bank rounded off by the nicest icecreams Tom had ever tasted, and then they snooped round the new and secondhand bookshops around Trinity Street and ended up in the market square, where they got Mrs Allen an immense bunch of grapes and some autumn-scented chrysanthemums.

'Did you enjoy it?' Ceri asked late that night, as they tore themselves away from a convivial little pub in Grantchester and got into the mini. 'I don't mean here so much as everywhere, all day today,' she added.

'Loved it,' Tom said sincerely. 'Only . . . you won't be disappointed in my place, I hope? Ces, it can't measure up to this – nowhere could!'

'It's nice, isn't it?' Ceri agreed. 'But everywhere has something different. When term starts and you're having to shove through a pack of graddies and when the prices go up for tourists, well, then you can appreciate Haisby. It's so quiet and peaceful and there's always the beach. Everywhere's different.'

'I see what you mean; this is beautiful, but Haisby is, too,' Tom said. 'What'll we do tomorrow?'

On their last day they took Mr and Mrs Allen to Madingley for a pub lunch, then returned to Cambridge where Mr Allen insisted on buying them tea at Fitzbillies. Tom and Ceri ate cakes until they could scarcely move and then waddled along Pembroke Street, watching admiringly whilst Mrs Allen waxed lyrical on antiques and finally bought a small pie-crust table in glowing walnut for just about half the asking price and presented Ceri with it, 'for the flat'.

'Did you tell them we're going to get married?' Tom asked that night when, alone at last, they sat in the garden room with the glass doors open and enjoyed the sweet scents of dying summer. 'I haven't dared!'

'They'll say we're too young, but they'll be tickled pink,' Ceri prophesied. 'Oh Tom, Ipswich tomorrow!'

They reached Ipswich in time for lunch and whisked Mrs Hetherington out for a pub meal. This meant that Ceri met

231

Tom's mother before she had seen the flat which, Tom said, was probably an advantage.

'It'll look a bit small after Marlowe Drive,' he warned her. 'And a bit scruffy – there are so many of us!'

Ceri assured him it could scarcely look smaller or scruffier than Lavengro and then sat, heart hammering, in the mini outside the grocer's shop with its side passage which led to the flat above and waited.

Tom eventually reappeared towing a very large woman indeed. She had curly brown hair, shy brown eyes and a sweet, uncertain smile. Her bulging, billowing body was clad in a blue wool smock and her feet were pushed into cracked patent-leather court shoes. She smiled at Ceri, who jumped out of the car to greet her.

'It's nice to meet you,' she murmured, extending a hand fat as a pound of chipolatas. 'Our Tom said nothing – just like a man!'

'I suppose he didn't want us to have preconceived ideas about each other,' Ceri said with her frank and friendly smile. 'Where shall we go for lunch?'

They ate just a couple of streets away from the flat, in an attractive, timbered pub, and then returned to the flat. Mrs Hetherington was so shy, so hideously self-conscious about her weight, that she told Ceri she rarely went out of the flat and Ceri promptly told her that she would be expected, in future, to visit Haisby at regular intervals.

'Tom and I are hoping to share a flat, so we'll have plenty of room and you can teach me about housekeeping,' Ceri said, nobly not glancing around her at the signs which said plainer than words that Mrs Hetherington did not greatly care for housework. Everywhere was clean, she supposed doubtfully, but nowhere was tidy, and furniture polish had not been applied for years, judging by the state of table-tops and chair-backs. But Tom's younger sisters, Amy and Sally, were friendly, talkative girls of fourteen and fifteen respectively, and Tom's elder brothers, both married and living in a big estate on the outskirts of the town, were friendly too. Having observed Mrs Hetherington closely for a day, Ceri came to the conclusion that the only thing wrong with Tom's mum was too little money and too much time to dwell on her own – largely imaginary – faults.

'She ought to have a job,' Ceri announced as she and Tom

strolled along Butter Market, heading for Ancient House to see the beams and decorative plasterwork for which it was famous. 'She could do anything – be a school crossing lady, or a traffic warden . . .'

'My Uncle Bert's a traffic warden,' Tom cut in. 'I don't see Mum fitting into the uniform, but we'll ask him if you like. We can nip down Dial Lane onto Tavern Street. He does a sort of round trip, down Tavern, round Crown, and back to Carr. Want to meet him?'

'Is he nice?' Ceri said guardedly. An only child, she had been almost overwhelmed by the number of Hetheringtons lurking around the town. It reminded her, she told Tom, of visiting Llangollen, where it appeared her mother was related to at least half the populace.

'Very nice,' Tom assured her. 'Let's find him.'

Uncle Bert proved to be a spry and wispy man in his sixties with a singing Suffolk accent and a fund of stories connected with his work. He shook his head doubtfully over the thought of his sister cramming herself into uniform but said he would have a word with his sister-in-law, who was head cook at a local school, and see if she could fix Annie up with something.

'Only Mum doesn't know about it,' Tom pointed out, to be promptly squashed both by his uncle and his beloved.

'Mrs Hetherington has to be gently guided,' Ceri said tactfully, whilst Uncle Bert gave it as his opinion that Annie must allow an elder brother to know best.

'Force the issue, lad,' he said kindly. 'Take her to the school before you goes off to the seaside and she'll go like a lamb, you mark my words.'

It was all arranged in a rush for that very reason. Uncle Bert's sister-in-law was approached, got Annie Hetherington an interview at a school that had been, in her own words, 'let down that often by soma them flighty young things that they'd be rare glad of a solid woman with a bitta sense', and came up to the flat to break the glad tidings.

'And your Mum was really thrilled,' Ceri said, awestruck, as she and Tom sat outside the school whilst Mrs Hetherington talked to the head cook. 'She said she'd often thought it would be nice to work again.'

'That's Mum all over,' Tom said tolerantly. 'Wouldn't lift a hand unless someone told her to. That's what my father did for her. Convinced her she was useless and undesirable. Do you know, until he left she was a size sixteen? I mean, quite slim!'

Mrs Hetherington came out at that point, glowing with success. She had got the job, would start next Monday.

'We'll take you out to dinner somewhere nice, to celebrate,' Ceri said, giving Tom a quelling look, for he had planned a trip just for the two of them this evening. 'Where would you like to go?'

They went, after conferring, to Shotley Gate.

The evening sun was slanting gold across the land and Ceri was treated to the sight of the elegant concrete span of Orwell Bridge, surely the largest in East Anglia. After marvelling over it, and over the quiet mudflats of the estuary, they turned into the road they wanted. It passed through beautiful countryside. Pink-washed cottages with ancient thatch, farmhouses nestling in groves of autumn-tinted trees, churches reaching up slender spires to the clear Suffolk sky.

Through the village of Woolverstone, pretty as a picture, through Chelmondiston and past the Old Boot House, long and low and strawberry pink, looking as though it had grown beside the road, down into Shotley village itself and past the Rose, again pink-washed, with flowers everywhere and a pleasant garden, too.

'They do good food,' Tom said, but drove on, following the road right to where it ended, against the old stone wall overlooking the great estuary, with seabirds digging in the mudflats and the shipping in the docks at Felixstowe across the water plain to see in the thin, clear air.

Mrs Hetherington heaved herself out of the mini and went and sat at a picnic table to enjoy the view and Tom and Ceri, hand in hand, wandered along the shore path. They saw the Scandinavian Seaways ferry beginning to make steam and move slowly away from her berth, they saw lightships and yachts and coasters and all sorts, for Felixstowe is a busy port and Shotley Gate an ideal spot from which to observe.

'There's a seafood kiosk, only we're going to have dinner,' Ceri said wistfully, and Tom rewarded her with a tub of cockles which they shared as they walked.

'Blackberries!' she remarked presently, looking up at the high bank beside her.

Tom picked, Ceri ate, and now and again they kissed, con-

234

tentment with each other and with the evening an almost tangible thing.

They had a leisurely meal in a thatched pub, and Mrs Hetherington talked and talked about her new job and about how she had always loved kiddies and what a difference it would make to her life.

'You're giving Ceri a swelled head; it was her idea,' Tom said presently, and Ceri kicked his ankle and Mrs Hetherington said she would always be grateful.

'That's easy to get stuck in a groove at my age,' she observed. 'My, this is a nice place . . . I've lived in Ipswich all my life and never visited Shotley Gate before – but I shall again!'

On the way home, Tom detoured to take Ceri right round Ipswich, from Willis & Faber's monstrosity of black glass on the Franciscan Way to narrow, winding side-streets with ancient, beamed buildings. She saw a great deal of incongruity – two huge ugly tower blocks squeezing out a pleasant little church and glorious ancient almshouses in the shadow of a huge modern multi-storey car park – but it was a real town, not thinking self-consciously of tourism or holidaymakers, building anew or retaining the old to please itself, not others.

'Did you like it?' Tom said on the Saturday afternoon, as they set out for the long drive home. 'Did you like it as much as I liked Cambridge?'

'Yes, quite as much. As I said, everywhere's different and we're jolly lucky to have roots in two such different places. But Tom, I do love Haisby!'

'Uhuh, me too. But I guess we'll be in Haisby for a few years, yet.'

'Good. Only we've got our homes for holidays.'

Tom leaned over and squeezed her hand.

'That's it! And one day, when we've got a family and I'm a bank manager, perhaps we'll go back to one or the other.'

Their eyes met and they smiled blissfully. A family! Oh, boy!

Chapter Sixteen

When the sun came up, glinting over the sea, Henry sighed and got out of bed. The maddening thing was he had gone to bed tired last night yet he had slept only fitfully, waking finally as dawn greyed the east knowing that sleep had eluded him once and for all.

He was less worried than he had been about Keith, but he was still uneasy. His partner had gone for his check-up yesterday, talking too loudly, laughing at everything Robin said, until Henry could have screamed at the tightening tension. *Why* was Keith still having such frequent check-ups? Sometimes Henry suspected that the hospital had found something wrong. But then again surely Keith would have told him?

Still, Henry consoled himself as he padded quietly towards the bathroom, he really is better. A nightmare is a rarity now, he still has a bath morning and evening but that's not unreasonable, and he's tackling more work, though he leaves the cooking to someone else.

Keith had come back from the hospital in an odd sort of mood, though; optimism mixed with unease was the closest Henry could get. They had done extra tests, he explained when Henry asked how he had got on; tests which might easily mean his visits could go down to one every six months. Keith did his best to look confident, but Henry could tell that he was still worried. I suppose I've no right to examine his feelings, Henry told himself, shaving in the small, speckled mirror, it's Keith who knows what's going on and he hasn't said the test results could be bad. And since he'll get the results this morning, at least he won't have long to worry.

Henry turned on the geyser, accustomed now to its violent behaviour, and splashed a hand under the hot tap, then got into the water. There was nothing like a nice bath to start the day off right – ever since the accident he had loved a bath because the warm water seemed to have a therapeutic effect on his injuries. Warmth got his arm and leg moving after the inaction of the night and worries which had loomed large seemed to shrink. Keith's strength, Henry decided, was returning with every day that passed. They had a good life here, it would get better. Before you know it, he told himself, you'll actually have time to enjoy life instead of working and worrying all the time. Why, look at last night! Keith, who had hung around the house ever since his accident, had decided to have an evening out. He left the hotel at about nine with the express intention of going down to the Dolphin for a drink, and it had been past midnight before he returned. Henry had heard him stealing up the stairs and smiled indulgently; good old Keith, tiptoeing about to make sure everyone got a decent night's sleep!

The warm water was insidious, though, and Henry had to jerk himself awake and start washing, otherwise he would have been there till breakfast time. I'll be well away today, he told himself, vigorously pumicing his heels. Oh yes, by the time Keith gets back I'll have got through most of my work. It's time we talked.

The previous evening Keith had been so determined not to spend all his time worrying about the next day that going down to the Dolphin seemed a very good idea. It would take his mind off things and prove he was himself again.

That was why he chose the Dolphin. A pub where everyone went, not just one section of the public. If there were gays in there, they would be in search of a drink and pleasant company, not other gays.

And he was right. He saw Nicola and her young man, talking earnestly at a corner table overlooking the long drop to the beach below – the windows of the Dolphin were all but at the edge of the cliff. He said hello to Fred, who delivered greengrocery to the hotel each day, and chatted to the barman, Dave, who helped with the sailing school during their busy times.

He left before time was called though, because it was a good walk back to Ambleside and he still had a healthy dread of drunks, and knew he would have to pass several pubs on his way home.

He walked slowly along Lord Street, not thinking of anything much. He had passed the pubs, still pulsing with music and talk, and was level with Styles, the big fish and chip shop, when a dozen people spilled onto the pavement in front of him, talking and arguing.

Keith hung back, then followed at a discreet distance because the party happened to be heading his way. Trippers, Keith guessed, searching for somewhere to lay their heads. He hoped they got fixed up before they reached Ambleside, he could hear the guffaws and see the horseplay; not the sort of clientele he and Henry wanted.

Nearing the swing bridge, several people peeled off from the main group. Over the swing bridge, more left, heading up Weyham Road. Only three now, going in the same direction as he, illumined by the faint streetlights.

'If only you'd *thought*, fellers, we could've been tucked up by now,' a nasal, familiar voice was complaining. 'We'll try one more, then we'll go back.'

Keith felt sick and his knees wanted to buckle. He was peering ahead, trying to tell himself it was his imagination, when the biggest man turned his head.

Barney. Unmistakable, a nightmare come true.

'Look, we're three guys wanting a bed, Peter, that's what puts folk off. We can try one at a time, or go back to the prom, like I wanted.'

The three turned and Keith fled. They were after him! They must have seen him earlier and had been playing cat and mouse with him and now they would kill him!

He reached Lord Street without once stopping, mindless with terror. Halfway along he glanced back – and saw or imagined three figures, hurrying in his wake.

Panic led him. Down Church Street, then left into Cloister Row – my God, a dead-end! If they'd seen . . . He forced himself between the wrought-iron railings into the church-yard, then threw himself down behind the biggest tombstone. His heart was beating deafeningly. There was a rustling – they had found him!

It was a cat. Long, green eyes widened with surprise as they met Keith's frightened gaze, then the cat stalked deliberately over to him and began to weave around his head, pressing itself against him. It was only scent-spreading, Keith knew, but – it felt like a friend.

'Pussy? Anyone out there, puss?'

The cat, as if it had understood every word, left him and stropped itself against the tombstone, then peered round the corner. It came back to Keith, purring louder than ever. It looked back; its glance said, *No one there; why the fuss?*

It was a quiet night with almost no wind. If Keith listened he could hear the shush and murmur of the sea, the soft sounds of the town settling for sleep. A child cried and was hushed in one of the flats above Cloister Row. A dog whined in its sleep. A taxi cruised along Lord Street, hoping for a last customer.

Keith stood up. He looked around. No one. Only the cat and the church and the deep black of the sky overhead, pierced with stars.

He had meant to hail a taxi but by now his paranoia was such that even a taxi might have contained the three men, so he walked. Hugging the shadows, starting at every sound, he made his way back through the sleeping town.

He reached Harbour Hill without seeing a soul, walked up it, arrived at Ambleside. The drive was very dark, a tunnel between the trees and bushes. He ran, scattering gravel, thundering along, his heartbeats deafening.

He reached the front door, fumbled his key into the lock, darted in, slamming the door behind him.

The loving-care of the house closed round him, like the hand of God. The very smell of it spelt safety – floor polish, Robin's bathtime soap, Henry's practical aftershave and the faint smell of good food.

For a moment, Keith could not move; he just stood there whilst fear drained out of him and confidence took its place. He looked around the hall, at the black and white marble tiles which took so much keeping clean, at the richly coloured rugs, bleached into black and white now by the thin moonlight. He was home. He was safe. The three men might have followed him, they might be lurking outside. But this house would keep Keith safe.

He crossed the hall and hurried up the stairs to his bedroom. He drew the curtains, first looking out at the moonlit loveliness of the garden below him. Safe. Safe!

Home is the sailor, home from the sea. Keith undressed, put on his pyjamas, lay down in bed. Nowhere else in the world could have welcomed him as this house had, tonight. He could never go away, never leave it, no matter what they said at the hospital tomorrow. In his small attic room Robin slumbered, and Henry slept too, in his own bed. The three of them were making such a good life for themselves, why should it ever be different? He, Keith, was beating his fears, with the help of the house and the other fellows. All would be well, Henry and Robin would help him, would never let him be hurt.

Keith turned on his side and slept quickly, easily. His dreams, for once, were kindly.

'Morning, Ceri! What a wind, eh? Good job we invested in that tumble drier because sheets pegged to the line this morning would be in Holt by this afternoon!'

Ceri grinned at Henry, then raised her eyebrows at Keith.

'Morning, Hal! I say, Keith, you're awfully smart this morning. Business meeting?'

'Hospital appointment,' Keith said briefly. He was eating egg and bacon with a hearty appetite.

'More tests?' Ceri pulled a sympathetic face, hanging her anorak on the back of the door. 'Poor you.'

'No, just results, today,' Keith said. 'Nothing to worry about and won't take long, so I thought I'd catch a bus to Norwich afterwards and see our solicitors. We both agree we could do with another boat for next season so I'm going to have a word with the Session Holiday people.'

'Can I come?' Robin put in. He scattered cornflakes into a bowl and poured milk on. 'I wouldn't mind a day in the city. It is half term, after all.'

'Not today, Rob,' Keith said. 'I'd love to have you with me, but it's not a good idea for you to hang around the hospital, they can be ages and you'd get most awfully bored. Be good though, and we'll go swimming when I get home this evening.'

'Right on,' Robin cheered. He crunched an enormous mouthful of flakes. 'Did you *hear* that, Hal? You going to come too? It'll be dead good with all three of us!'

'I might,' Henry said. 'I might, at that.'

Keith's smart dark suit, the white shirt, the red tie, made Henry unhappy, worried him in some obscure way. Sometimes he wished he were a more cerebral character, less a man of action. If he had been, surely he would have under-

240

stood more easily how Keith felt, would have been able to help his partner? Deep thought had never come as easily to him as simply getting on with the job. Moving around the kitchen preparing his own breakfast, watching Ceri as she served their half-dozen guests, he decided that what was worrying him was not just the untypical dark suit, it was something much more basic. But what it was he could not imagine. And a stupid tag niggled at Henry's mind. *Nothing in his life became him like* . . . Like what? Like a dark suit, a red tie? And anyway, why should he think that merely because Keith had dressed smartly and joined them for breakfast, things might have changed in some subtle way?

Henry struggled to get his thoughts into useful channels and in the end he was more or less successful. He decided that Keith was trying to show them that he was no longer a mental or physical wreck. Now he would take decisions and pick up the reins of the partnership once more. He might be worried about the tests, but with his new attitude, his new suit, he would take in his stride whatever the world flung at him, and conquer it.

Outside, the wind rose to a fresh crescendo of sound and Ceri rushed to rescue her bike, which had blown over. Keith got his mac and set off down the drive with Robin prancing along beside him. Robin was going to visit his friend Heather.

All will be well, Henry told himself, greeting Anthea cheerily as she came briskly in through the back door, Kit snuggled down in his pushchair out of the wind. So if he believed it, why did he have this hollow ache in the pit of his stomach, this sense of a storm to come?

Keith had woken that morning to the howling wind and for a moment it had intensified his sense of safety, of the house being like a lover, holding him. But then he remembered the tests and doubt trickled coldly into his mind. What would they tell him? Not the worst, surely? He felt *well*, better than he had done for ages, and far more capable. After the terrors of the previous night he had decided to become a different person, someone who would be a help and a comfort to Henry and Robin, not a drag. He would work harder, pay his way, suggest that since he was now so adept at doing the Ambleside books he might earn money by doing the same for other small businesses. And whatever happened at the hospital today he would take in his stride.

When breakfast was over he set off down the drive with Robin beside him, jumping and darting and jabbering non-stop. He dropped the boy off at Heather's home and continued on, to the hospital. It was a long walk but he enjoyed it, though with reservations; he always hated his hair being blown about.

He was one of the first to arrive in Outpatients. The nurse was a pretty, dark-haired girl who knew him well by now. She smiled at him.

'In good time today, Mr Fell! You shouldn't have long to wait, you're first on the list.'

'That'll be nice,' Keith said cordially. He picked up a magazine and sat back in his maroon plastic armchair. 'Might even be home in time for lunch.'

'In and out in no time,' the girl assured him. 'You'll be home for your elevenses today, mark my words.'

Keith left the hospital half an hour later. He came out of the consulting room and went straight through the main entrance. A tune was running through his head and now and then he tried to hum but it refused to be brought in to the open save as a miserable, off-key mumble.

He walked down to the prom and then along it, scarcely noticing the force of the wind though it was violent still. On the beach below him sand-devils hissed, turning any innocent piece of paper they met to emery board, embedding their stinging grains in unwary legs.

What a devilish day, Keith thought absently. A ship at sea would not stand much chance, it must be a force twelve gale at least. No day for going into the city; I'll go straight home, get some lunch and chat to Henry, he told himself. Good thing I've no need to be out on a day like this.

Which made it even stranger when he did not turn off the promenade and go round by the harbour and over the swing bridge. He could have done, he meant to, but instead he turned right round and retraced his steps. It was a harsh, buffeting wind but he thought he would rather be out here fighting it, than indoors with time to think.

Keith knew you could walk right along the shore until you reached the next coastal village. He had often meant to do so and now, suddenly, it seemed a good idea. When he reached the end of the promenade he simply went on walking. He continued along the shaley path between the sand dunes and then began to ascend the cliff.

The power of the wind was quite frightening up there, but Keith found it exhilarating. He shouted into it and tried to sing his beautiful tune and this time it did not sound quite so bad, mainly because he could not hear it – the wind snatched the notes from his lips – but Keith did not realise that. He thought he was hearing in reality the notes he heard in his head and was satisfied.

Lunchtime came and Keith was alone in the breathless wilderness of the undulating cliffs. Below him the shore looked no more than a sandy path, the waves little ripples. But he did not look below much, having no liking for heights. He kept his gaze ahead and now and then he checked his wristwatch, because he wanted to get home in time to make himself useful. But when it was time to go back it seemed such a shame . . . Henry wouldn't be expecting him, he might as well keep on. And the wind was still unconquered, still giving any gull fool enough to take wing a hard time. I'll beat the wind, Keith thought. I'll just keep on walking until it stops because it can't keep this up for ever, it's got to die down sooner or later, but I can walk and walk.

It was dusk before he decided to turn back. He had walked the entire day, eating nothing, drinking nothing, and not thinking. But it was growing dark so he struck inland, found a telephone box and phoned Ambleside. Robin answered, his voice squeaky with importance.

'Hello, Rob, it's Keith. Tell Henry I'm going to be late and not to wait up. I'm with a friend, I'll be back in time for breakfast. Tell him I'll get his tea tomorrow morning, for a change.'

He meant to go to the pub for a meal, but the wind was still blowing hard and he did not want bright lights or company. If he gave up now, let the wind beat him, then it would be just like all the other things he had tried to do, only to find himself not able to achieve them. It would be like the platonic friendship he could not keep, the child he could not father, the fight he now knew he could not win. But this walk against the wind was a battle in which he could triumph; in one small way he could prove who was boss.

So Keith turned away from the pub and its beckoning lights

and set off along the cliff path once more, to continue his struggle against the wind.

It was midnight before the gale began to ease, and then he realised that it was changing direction. It was blowing on his back now, urging him on, helping him home.

This would never do; he wanted to fight the wind, not be pushed along by it. Yet he was very tired and it was easier to give way, to head for Haisby once more.

But as soon as he started, with the wind balmy on his back, he knew that returning to Haisby was wrong. He had meant to go far away and take his secret with him. He could never go back, now, to the rambling old hotel on the cliffs, to his dear loves, Henry and Robin. He could never chaff with the barman at the Dolphin, or tease Ceri, or play with Zak. It was all over for him . . . *They are not long, the days of wine and roses* . . . When next day's dawn broke, he intended to be far away, out of reach.

It was a long walk though, even with the wind on his side, now. It was six o'clock when he saw Haisby's dimming lights loom and looking east, he knew that dawn was not far distant. The stars were paling, the moon no longer looked like a big white penny and the wind, though it moaned around the eaves, was no longer a wild animal snatching the gulls from the sky.

Walking cat-quiet through the deserted town he wondered where he should go, what he should do. He wished he had something valuable to leave the world, a beautiful tune, a lovely poem to tear at the heart-strings. But he could do good, just by . . . well, just by leaving. It was more, he knew, than many could say.

In the quiet night, he looked at the town and saw it was beautiful, loved it for the way it had accepted him. He did not hurry now, he strolled; along Lord Street, up Harbour Road, past the fish wharves where he saw a thin and solitary cat sitting on an empty fish box grooming herself. He crossed the swing bridge, seeing the yachts swinging at anchor in the marina, hearing the soft clunk of the rigging as it twanged to the wind's breath.

He was on Harbour Hill now and it seemed that everyone slept. And at last he knew what he would do.

He, too, would sleep. It would be easy to sleep, to end the

heartache and the thousand natural shocks that flesh is heir to. He would be doing Hal and Robin the best favour one man can do for another; to leave whilst the party is still going on so no one sees him slip away.

If he stayed, what misery he would bring, what a depth of pain and sorrow! They would take Robin away, and he knew how very fond of the boy Hal had become. So he would go, taking his own path to that undiscovered country from whose bourn no traveller returns.

But how? Should he simply walk into the sea? But he might start to swim; he was a strong swimmer and even though the waves were high, he might survive.

He continued up the path until he came to the lane which led down beside the hotel. He walked down it, very softly, until he reached the gate. There he stopped, to look at Ambleside for one last time, to see whether anyone was awake in that rambling pile.

No lights. Henry's window ajar, the curtains swaying softly in the breeze and Robin's room uncurtained, so that he would be up betimes. He looked higher, automatically checking; yes, Henry had got Anthea and the baby to stay; the attic which she used when she slept over had its window open and its curtains closed. All was well, then.

Before he had thought Keith had slipped through the gate and into the garden, was actually heading towards the house. He stopped in his tracks and stared hard at the hotel, at the dream which he and Henry had fought to make a reality. What was it he had said once? Some half-remembered quotation he had recited to Henry . . . Oh yes, it was one of those rather twee sayings J. M. Barrie had put into Peter Pan's mouth – *life must be an awfully big adventure*. Only it wasn't life, was it? No, he had it now, he even remembered being a bit taken aback by it at his first theatre visit. *Death must be an awfully big adventure* – that was it!

And then he knew. Long ago he had joked with Henry about the cliff-fall, saying that they should tell guests it was called ·Lovers' Leap, and recite an apocryphal tale about lovers who had leapt to their deaths, long ago, rather than be parted. It would not be so bad, perhaps, if you flew, like they had done in *Peter Pan* when little Keith had been about six.

Keith's breath began to come faster. A drop, a quick

plunge, and there would be no telling what had happened, no rumours, no stories circulating. The cliff was known to be dangerous, crumbling. Keith would be sleep-walking, or he would have turned the wrong way – it didn't matter. What mattered was doing it before his courage failed and he set in train the long, painful business of dying.

The light was strengthening. The sky in the east was silver now, and the silver, where sea met sky, was tinged with pinkish gold. He climbed the fence which he and Henry had erected to keep people away from the drop, then had to smile at himself when he fastidiously dusted the dew-damp knees of his dark suit. How strange was his mind, which could tidy up trousers knowing they would presently be considerably ruffled by the beach below!

He was still smiling as he came to the edge; it must look like an accident, he must take some of the crumbling cliff with him as he went. Kneeling would probably be best, that way he could be sure . . .

He knelt on the very edge of the grassy drop just as the first golden rays of the sun crept over the horizon. For a moment he just stared, seeing as if for the first time the beauty of the world, smelling the fresh salt sea, hearing all about him the cries of sea birds welcoming the new day. It seemed . . . oh, it seemed an awful waste! Any moment now, though, Henry would be drawing back his curtains, getting ready to face the day, strolling down the garden to glance at the sunrise before starting work. He must not be here then, he could not bear that Henry should see him fall!

A gull swooped low over the cliff, then shied away as something plunged past it, cracking into the smooth boulders on the beach below with a sickening thud.

Keith felt the rush of wind, heard the squawk of the gull . . . felt the impact.

He had a moment of doubt, of cruel, stabbing pain. And then it was dark.

Chapter Seventeen

Henry had gone to bed late and for once he slept like a log, scarcely stirring until the alarm went off at half past six. And then he lay there for a moment, wondering whether Keith really would bring him his tea, today.

He had probably meant it, but he must have been pretty late last night since Henry had not gone up until well after midnight. He'll be sleeping like the kid he is, Henry thought wryly, climbing out of bed. Poor little bugger, he's had a rotten time, but now he's got the test results perhaps he can begin to live again.

Heading for the bathroom, padding along the lino . . . straight past Keith's door, resisting the temptation to go in, dig him out of bed to get that cup of tea. Wondering about giving Robin a discreet shout, because today would be a quiet one, workwise, and the sun was already climbing. There was no reason why they should not have that swim, he and Robin, even if Keith had forgotten his promise to the kid yesterday.

He bathed and dressed, shaved in the spotted mirror, made his way back along the corridor, paused outside Keith's room. To wake or not to wake? Perhaps he would just check; if Keith was already awake there could be no harm in reminding him of his promise to Robin . . .

The door opened silently, and Henry put his head into the room, mouth already forming the first words.

Empty. Bed not slept in. Curtains still back.

The dirty little stop-out, was Henry's first, surprised, thought. Then he frowned and stroked his chin. Odd. Keith had been so responsible lately, so sensible. He had said, loudly and often, that he was going to concentrate on work, leave social life alone . . .

Henry continued down the stairs feeling a deep unease. He reached the kitchen, put the kettle on and then strolled out into the morning.

247

It was a marvellous one, the air fresh after the storm, the wind gentle, caressing his cheek. Sunshine spilled, gold as honey, onto the russet roofs of the outbuildings, touching the autumn-tinted trees with magic. The sky above was blue and bisected by gulls' wings.

Forgetting his worries – and the kettle – Henry walked down the garden, every step shaking the dew from the grasses. He loved being the first one to step on the lawn, to make footprints in the carpeting dew.

Not today, though. Today someone had been before him. Like an Indian tracker, Henry bent over the narrow footprints, heading right across the lawn, making for the cliff. Who was trespassing so early? No, it wasn't a trespasser, it was probably one of the guests. Not Robin, they were too large for Robin's footprints. Nor Keith, because Keith had not come home last night.

Henry followed the footprints. They led to the fence. He leaned on it, where the footprint-maker had leaned earlier; the dew which stood in shining drops along the top fencepost was cleared here, from another's arms.

Beautiful! The sun coming up, just a deep gold sickle no wider than a fingernail, pouring colour over the awakening sea. The waves were still fierce after the gale, the crash and the drag of pebbles exhilarating. We *will* bathe, Henry decided, the sea will be just right by about eleven, Robin deserves a little treat now and then and so do I – it was half term, after all.

He looked down at the grass on the other side of the fence and saw that the footprints continued . . . they led straight to the cliff-edge. Oh dear God, and there were no prints returning!

He ran all the way down the lane, feet slithering in the sand, heart pounding. One part of his mind remarked severely that he was out of condition; it was about time he took some regular exercise instead of just talking about it. The other part was dreading what he would find.

He reached the beach and ran along it, slipping and slithering on wet stones. From quite a distance he could see the huddle sprawled on the big, flat pebbles, he fancied he could even see a scarlet tie around its neck, or was it . . .

He knew it was Keith before he was near enough to recognise the familiar face, the cluster of fair curls, but nevertheless when he fell to his knees beside the crumpled figure
only a part of his brain acknowledged that it was he; the other
part still professed ignorance . . . until it could no longer
deny what it saw so clearly.

'Keith? My God, you're hurt! Hurry someone, hurry, he's
badly hurt . . . he's broken . . . there's blood!'

Anthea woke early, as she always did, because as soon as it got
even slightly light Kit began to purr and murmur to himself,
playing with the bars of his cot, or his fingers and toes, or just
sucking his thumb so noisily that no one within a few feet of
him could possibly have remained asleep.

However, there was no real need to get up at once. Not
today. She was actually on the spot, instead of ten miles or
more down the coast, and for five minutes she lay quiet,
revelling in the comfort of the divan bed, the warmth of the
blankets.

But after that five minutes she found herself getting out of
bed, because one's body clock is an awkward creature and
takes no heed of holidays or lie-ins and her body clock had
announced in no uncertain terms that it was time she had a
wee and afterwards made herself a hot cup of tea to start the
day right.

So Anthea felt for her slippers, slid her feet into them, and
glanced across at Kit. He was absorbed; indifferent to her. It
was the same at home, he seemed quite resigned to her getting up first and getting all ready for the day ahead before
picking him out of his cot. Good little fellow, she thought
thankfully, whisking her long cotton dressing-gown off the
back of the door. First she would visit the bathroom – she
picked up her underwear and a baggy tracksuit which she
wore a lot at home – and then, dressed and respectable,
she would go down and get that tea. She might even get Hal
a cup, spoil him for once, because she knew very well that
however tired he was he would never let her overdo it, always
reminded her – as if she needed reminding! – that Kit must
come first. It was high time, Anthea concluded, that someone
did something for Henry, for a change.

She was not long in the bathroom; she had bathed the night
before, so it was a cat's lick and a promise, a dab of the hair-

brush on her hair, and then a quiet trot along the corridor and down to the kitchen.

The first thing she noticed was the kettle, boiling its head off, and then the open back door. She pulled the kettle off the heat, saw that the pot, with tea in it, stood ready, and smiled to herself. That would be Hal – always first up, always busy. She wondered vaguely where he had gone to, then made the tea, put the cosy over it and left it to brew whilst she examined the morning.

It was a grand day, absolutely grand! For a moment she felt quite homesick for her little cottage, the marshes at her door, the cry of the gulls as they circled over the mud in the creek. But then she crossed the yard and went down to the long, sloping lawn which led to the cliff, because she knew that the coast here would be almost as beautiful as her sea marshes, in its own way.

She saw Henry at once. He was running towards her like a mad thing but he did not see her, he was concentrating on getting to the side gate and into the lane in the shortest possible time. Anthea frowned. Odd! She glanced across the lawn and saw the footprints crossing it – he had gone right down to the fence then, and leaned over it, looking down . . . What had he seen, to send him off at such a pace?

So far as Anthea could be fond of a man, she was fond of Henry. He was kind, thoughtful and undemanding. He did not frighten her with displays of temper or hassle her by being too friendly. And he loved Kit with a straightforward affection which Anthea recognised and appreciated as being entirely unassumed. Henry loved all kids, from babyhood to teenage.

And now he was in trouble. There had been a desperate fixedness in his pale face, and he had run with all of him, not at an amble nor even a canter, but at a heedless gallop, so that he had run across a newly dug flowerbed and through the shrubbery, scarcely noticing the plants he trampled nor the branches which tore at him.

Almost without thinking, Anthea followed. She did not run at first, but as though Henry's going had left urgency in the air, presently she began to hurry. She ran fast, her long legs picking up the rhythm quickly, her head down, her long arms scooping at the air, never heeding the soft sand in the lane nor the steepness of it as it neared the beach. Hal was a good man, who gave freely of himself, her confused thoughts reminded her. He was in trouble and she was on her way to give him a hand.

She ran on, slithering down the cliff path, landing with a thud on the beach. Now she could see Henry to her left, crouching over something crumpled up on the sand. She ran harder.

Keith's head was at a weird angle and a trickle of blood had run from the corner of his mouth across one cheek. His limbs were jammed into broken-doll positions by the force of the fall and his eyes were closed, demure as a dead dove outside a poulterer's, Henry found himself thinking, even whilst frantically shrieking to the indifferent wind for help.

He was getting up when he saw a figure approaching him across the sand. It was Anthea, he recognised her at once. Henry knelt down again, stupidly feeling that he should make Keith look better before the woman reached them. Uselessly, he brushed back Keith's hair, tried to mop the blood which had run from his mouth.

As he did so, an odd thing happened. The heavy lids opened and for a tiny thread of time Keith looked out of his shattered body at his friend. And then, just for an instant, his mouth jerked into a lopsided smile.

'He's alive!' Henry shouted, his voice cracking. 'He's alive. Get help, get a doctor. Hurry!'

He looked wildly round to where Anthea's small figure was growing larger and saw that her face was white and her eyes widening with horrified understanding.

Henry looked down at Keith's face once more, resting now in the crook of his arm. The smile had gone, the mouth hung slack and the eyelids were closed. He began to rub Keith's limp hands, as though such an action might help to restore the lost life. He could feel tears in his eyes and forced them back, determined that no one should have cause to despise his weakness. Then he saw a movement on the other side of Keith's body.

It was a tiny kitten, white and tortoiseshell, its big golden eyes fixed on Henry. As he looked, it opened its mouth and miaowed, then came over to him. It was so small it could scarcely walk on the soft sand, yet still it butted its head against Henry's arm and gave its plaintive, hungry cry.

Henry lay Keith gently down, then picked up the kitten.

As Anthea reached them he held it out, trying to force his face into normality, trying to smile.

'Ant, old dear, Keith's taken a nasty tumble, he must have missed his footing trying to rescue the kitten. I'm afraid . . .' His voice broke, then rallied. 'I'm afraid there's not much anyone can do, but could you ring for an ambulance? I'll stay with him until you get back . . . I'll stay . . . oh, my God, Ant!'

Anthea was on her knees by him. She patted his arm timidly, then turned to look down at Keith. Henry tried to hide the wretched, useless tears which had begun to run down his cheeks, turning his head away. Anthea was so shy and awkward, she would be horrified to see him weep.

'It's all right, Henry,' Anthea said, her voice calm, almost authoritative. 'You're his friend, you mustn't leave him, but I'll get help immediately . . . Oh, poor little Keith! Look, I'll run like the wind and send someone back at once. Shall I take the kitten?'

Her voice was steadier than his, but Henry no longer cared. Out of her own deep insecurity, Anthea had still found, from somewhere, the maturity to comfort him, and the courage to face his pain without flinching.

'No, I'll keep the kitten here; I want everyone to know that Keith was trying to rescue it . . . I don't want any talk about . . . He'd had a bad time, poor little bugger . . . For the boy's sake . . .'

Anthea gripped his hand very tightly for a second, then stood up. He watched her running, not like a girl but like a professional runner, her stride effortless.

He watched her out of sight. What had she been doing on the beach? Surely she could not have got a bus in from her cottage so early? Then he remembered she had stayed over and was incredibly thankful, so glad she had been on hand. What would he have done had there been no one to answer his cry? He sat down on the sand beside Keith's body, the kitten held close to his face, and smoothed its soft baby-fur. It kept turning in his grasp to look up at him with its huge amber eyes. He felt its body begin to reverberate, a big purr for such a tiny scrap.

It was not long before Anthea was back; this time she had a flask of tea and she made him drink some, not being bossy, just being sensible, almost motherly. He found that he

wanted to talk, to explain what had happened, a sort of rehearsal for when officialdom arrived, and Anthea listened, her
expression serious, and when the doctor and ambulancemen
arrived she was calm and competent, backing Henry's story,
explaining that the cliff was crumbling, that Keith had tried
to rescue the kitten . . .

Henry was still numb, appalled by the speed with which
things had happened, but he was doing well until the doctor
asked for Keith's full name.

'Keith Fell,' Henry said. 'Oh, sweet Jesus . . . Keith Fell
. . . Keith fell, Keith fell . . .'

But he was all right when he saw Anthea was crying, because comforting her gave him something to do, and Henry
had always needed something to do. When the time came for
the body to be moved, he walked with his arm gently support-
ing Anthea up the long, sandy lane back to the hotel, and if
he was crying inside, if his voice sometimes shook a little,
what was shameful about mourning for a friend?

Later in the morning, when statements had been taken and
the body had gone, when Anthea was supervising the cleaning staff and Henry and Ceri were in the kitchen preparing
the vegetables for lunch, a constable came to the door.

'There was a witness, sir,' he announced, when Henry
asked what he wanted. 'Would you like to have a word?
Seems he's a neighbour of yours.'

He led Henry and Ceri round to the front drive and there
stood Harry, a scarecrow figure in his tattered black coat.

'Harry? Can you tell us again what you saw this morning?
The gentleman who fell came from this house.'

Harry shuffled closer. Ceri, standing by, caught hold of
Henry's fingers in her small, warm hand.

'He's not all there, Hal,' she whispered. 'But I don't think
he'd cause any trouble.' To Harry she said gently, 'It's all right
you know, Harry, no one's angry with you, just tell us what
you saw.'

'Saw 'im,' confirmed Harry after a long pause. His nose was
running and he wiped it on his coat-sleeve. 'Saw 'im come orf
the cliff.'

'Did he fall, Harry? Was he trying to rescue the kitten?'

There was another long pause while Harry assimilated what
he was being asked. Beads of sweat broke out on his narrow

forehead whilst he struggled to produce the answer that was expected of him.

'Yers. Fell. Dived, like. Reachin' down for the little 'un.' He pointed to the kitten, now cuddled in Ceri's arms; his fingernails were long and gnarled, yellowish. 'Some earth come too.'

Henry exhaled long and gently; so it was true! No matter what despair and misery had come to Keith from those confounded tests, he had not been trying to kill himself, he had fallen to his death.

'Thanks very much, Harry,' Ceri was saying earnestly. Henry echoed her words and then the two of them and the kitten returned to the kitchen. Henry slumped into a chair, his mind buzzing. What was it he had been thinking yesterday, when he had seen Keith in his dark suit, his white shirt and red tie? *Nothing in his life became him like the leaving of it*. That's right, it was from *Macbeth*, he remembered doing the play for an exam many years ago, and suddenly he became convinced that the words were not only apt, but true. Whatever it was politic to say and believe, he knew that Keith had died to save Henry himself and young Robin from the pain that would have lain in store for them, had Keith lived.

A good end, then. A good man, in the end.

Henry got up from the chair and headed for the pantry. It was time to start getting lunch and he was grateful for his good staff, for marvellous Anthea and even for young Robin, as they buzzed round him, keeping the world at bay, allowing no interloper in.

Except for grief. No one could keep grief out.

Chapter Eighteen

Ceri's grief at the funeral was unassumed; no one could have worked with Keith and not grieved for him, and she was so sorry for Henry and Robin! And then, as though they did not have enough to bear, Henry called her in to the staff sitting room the following morning and told her, his face grey with strain and unhappiness, that he could no longer promise that there would be a job for her at Ambleside.

'I'm no good at the books, Keith's always done them, so it will take me all my time just to learn how it all works,' he started off. He was sitting in an armchair one side of the fireplace, Ceri had taken the other. The informality of their surroundings made conversation easier, Ceri supposed, but she could not help remembering the times she had come in for a chat, to find Keith perched on one chair, Henry at the table, Robin playing with cars on the rug. Keith's presence must haunt Henry, she thought.

'You could get someone else to do them, only not me,' Ceri said. 'And anyway, winter's coming; it's the best time to learn how to do anything, with fewer guests.'

'Yes. We'd planned to do long weekends, combining some sailing with good food, perhaps some walks and some of the theory of yachting in the evenings. With Keith to provide the good food . . . But Ceri, I don't know that I can cope, alone.'

'Anthea's a marvellous cook; she would take it in her stride,' Ceri reminded him. 'And weekends would mean she could let Robin keep an eye on Kit whilst she worked.'

Henry shook his head. He looked down at his knees, deliberately avoiding Ceri's eye, she thought.

'Robin won't be here, you see.'

'He won't be *here*? Oh, but he's such a good boy, such a help, surely you'd not want to send him back to . . . to that woman?'

Henry continued to stare down at his faded jeans but he smiled faintly at Ceri's vehement tone.

'I wouldn't send him back, not for anything. But his mother won't leave him here because I'm . . . I'm not married, and people would talk. She's the sort of person who cares a great deal about her image, and whilst it was apparently quite acceptable for the boy to live with his father, it's simply not done for a boy to live with a solitary male.'

'But . . . but it was Keith who was gay,' Ceri said, totally perplexed. 'I don't understand; what difference does it make that you're one man, instead of two? I mean you're his *father*, Hal; you've got rights!'

It jerked Henry's head up; he stared at Ceri, then he shook his head.

'I'm not Robin's father, Ceri. Robin is Keith's son; I thought everyone knew!'

'*Keith's* son? Oh, but . . . I mean everyone assumed .'. . Keith was gay and he didn't seem particularly keen to have Robin living here. Are you *serious*?'

'I wish I wasn't. Keith moved in with Teresa – he called her Terry – when he was no more than a kid himself. His father was ex-army, the sort of man who couldn't bear to think he had produced anything that wasn't one hundred per cent fighting, snarling male. Keith adored his Dad, and tried his best to become what he wanted. He chose Terry because she was clinging and feminine, but when she told him she was pregnant he cut and ran. He knew by then that he could never be the man his father wanted.'

'Oh, poor Keith,' Ceri said sorrowfully. 'We thought he was jealous because you and Rob hit it off so well. Was it really because he wanted Rob to love him best?'

'No, alas, you had it right the first time. But he grew fond of Robin, though he really wasn't cut out to be a father. And I am – I love kids. To be honest it's taken the fun out of it, to know it'll be just me. Working for Robin, watching him grow, made it worthwhile.'

'And you've spoken to that Teresa?'

'Yup. She never knew Keith was gay, incidentally, and she'll never learn the truth from me. And to do her justice, she said if I was engaged to a suitable sort of woman she'd let him stay because Robin's happy here and was miserable in London.'

'Suppose you got a motherly housekeeper in?' Ceri said, clutching at straws. 'Wouldn't that do?'

'I doubt it. It's respectability Teresa's after, you see. And what with that and everything else, I thought I'd probably put Ambleside on the market and move on. It always seemed too good to be true. We were so happy, with Ant as fond of Robin as I am of Kit, and the guests so pleasant, the staff friendly and helpful . . . and Keith, of course, to stand by me when things went wrong.'

'You're just depressed and still sad from losing Keith,' Ceri said bracingly. 'Sleep on it, Hal; things will look better in the morning.'

'Oh, I'll give it a few more days,' Henry said. 'Robin's leaving at the weekend – would you believe, Ces, that she isn't even coming down to pick him up? She told me to put him on a train, went on about how self-reliant he is, what a little man. I nearly threw up – it was talk like that which brought Keith to . . . to that bloody cliff.'

'Don't worry,' Ceri said abstractedly. 'You've not said anything to the rest of the staff yet?'

'No. Fair's fair. I'll tell Ant next, and she can tell the others that things are in the melting pot. I won't quit until the season's bookings are finished, but once that happens then I'll start looking round.'

'Fine,' Ceri said, getting to her feet. 'Where's Ant now? I'll wheel her in.'

'Give me half an hour, I've got some calls to make.'

'Right.'

Ceri left the sitting room and hurried in search of Anthea. She found her folding the used bedding for the laundry which called later. She smiled at Ceri, leaned over to write on her pad, then raised her eyebrows.

'Everything all right?'

'No, it's not,' Ceri said definitely. 'Ant, we must talk. Can you put that lot down and give me your undivided attention for a few minutes?'

Henry was sitting at the desk when Anthea knocked and entered the room. He smiled at her, aware that it was a poor effort but wanting to put her at her ease, for Anthea looked so anxious and unhappy that even Henry's own problems suddenly shrank to size. When he thought about it, poor Anthea had given up a job as manageress of a boutique to come here, and he was about to tell her that she would soon be job-hunting once again! And what was more, he realised that he would miss her and the baby almost as much as he would miss Keith and Robin. She was a poppet for all her awkwardness, and worth her weight in gold both as a manageress and a worker. But he might get a quick sale for the hotel, might be able to hand on the staff intact; he must tell her that.

'Ah, hello, Ant. Everything all right?'

'Ceri told me, Hal. I-I'm most awfully sorry.'

'Oh, she did? Well, I ought to be cross with her, but actually, I'm relieved. Believe me, it isn't the sort of news which gets better with repetition, and I've not told Robin yet. I'm dreading it, he's bound to think I'm letting him down and he's been let down quite often enough, in my opinion. He's a bright kid; it didn't take him long to realise his father didn't want him really, any more than his mother had.'

'Yes. Hal, Ceri thinks . . . she thinks I ought to tell you a bit about me and Kit.'

Henry, who had often wondered, nodded encouragingly. 'All right, go ahead.'

There was a long pause whilst Anthea slowly went dark red and examined her thin, work-worn hands with extreme attention; the sort of attention which Henry had lavished on his jeans, he realised, whilst telling Ceri how things stood.

'Ant? Look, if you'd rather not . . .'

'No, it's all right. I promised Ceri. A bad thing happened to me, a man . . . Ceri says he abused me. But a good thing came out of all that fear and pain, because I had Kit. His father was . . . but he's dead. Gone. And children are awfully important, aren't they, Hal? I know how you love Robin, it's how I love Kit. And I thought perhaps we could . . . could help one another, you and me.'

'You help me a lot already, Ant,' Henry said gently. 'You're a tower of strength.'

'I do try. And I'll willingly take on the paperwork, because I had to do the books for Bonner's Boutique, the VAT and everything – wages, buying, the lot. But I do love your Robin – and he is yours, even if Keith was his father, because you see my Kit's father could never have been . . . I mean, he had no share in Kit at all, not any share at all . . .'

She stopped, red-faced, on the point of tears, but still

struggling to make her point. Henry leaned forward and patted her arm.

'I believe I know what you're trying to say,' he said slowly. 'You're saying that one earns a relationship with a child by one's behaviour, by the giving or denying of love. You're saying that Robin was more mine than Keith's because I loved him and willingly made sacrifices for him, whereas Kit's father never loved anything, and therefore had no rights to his son. Is that it, Ant?'

'Yes,' Anthea whispered. 'It was the same for me. My mother loved me, but my father hated me. I never felt like his daughter; just like a barely tolerated servant.'

'So you want me to keep Robin? Dear Ant, if I could I would, but his mother . . .'

'Ceri said if you were getting engaged to someone . . . then she'd let you.'

'That's right,' Henry said. 'Only . . .'

'I'd pretend, if it would help.'

Henry was so astonished, so profoundly moved, that for a moment he could only sit, staring at Anthea with rounded eyes. Anthea, who was so shy, who had been so ill-treated by men that she was in agony whilst in their company, was willing to make such a sacrifice? He felt his eyes moisten and once more he put out a hand, as timidly as though she were a wild creature, and patted her arm.

'You really would? But Ant, suppose we had to make some sort of promise of a wedding in the future? My dear, I couldn't ask such a sacrifice.'

'You wouldn't want to marry me,' Anthea said, not humbly but practically. 'But you've been very kind to me, and most awfully good to Kit. When he's bigger, Kit will need someone like a father to play with him, teach him to swim and sail. Would a pretend be wrong, then? When Ceri told me, it seemed . . . well, it seemed like a solution for both of us.'

'It would be more than I'd dared hope,' Henry said. 'Only if we . . . well, if we *did* go through with a pretend engagement or even a marriage, would you mind living in? Because we'd better be businesslike, having got this far. You see, I need a partner, here. Someone to take charge and take decisions, too, whilst I'm out teaching. Someone who can manage the hotel side of the business, see to the guests' comfort, cope with the staff, take the bookings, do all the things, in fact, that you and Keith shared between you whilst I was on the boats.'

'We'd need another full-timer,' Anthea said thoughtfully. 'Just a girl, probably, who could keep an eye on Kit whilst I was cooking. And if she could type then that would be useful, because we'll lose Ceri, you know. Her column is thriving, she keeps getting sent off on reporting jobs, and when she and Tom marry she'll want work with more conventional hours, I imagine.'

'You could have Keith's room instead of the attic one,' Henry said. He felt wonderful, as though someone had given him a new lease of life. 'You're a natural gardener, too – your vegetable patch could have kept us in runner beans and winter cabbage, and even the flowers you planted have done well. I know you can't possibly tackle the full garden,' he added hastily, 'but at least you'd know what to tell a gardener to do, which is more than I could. Only . . . what about your cottage?'

'I'd keep it for days off and holidays,' Anthea said promptly. She had clearly given the matter a good deal of thought. 'There are two bedrooms, so if you and Robin wanted a rest, you could come and stay. Robin's often said he wished Kit and he were brothers, and he'll love the cottage, anyone would. I wouldn't sell it, anyway, because when Robin's grown up and you don't need me any more . . . well, I'll have somewhere to go.'

'And you really will do it? Tell people we're engaged and move into Ambleside? So that I can keep Robin, and the sailing school, too?'

'If it'll work I'll do it,' Anthea said. The hot, uncomfortable colour was fading from her cheeks, she was beginning to look more like her usual self. 'Do you want me to ring Robin's mother, or will you?'

Nicola finished the letter she was typing, ripped the page neatly out of the machine and read it through. When she was sure it was all right she separated the two copies, fed an envelope into the machine and typed the name and address on it. She was putting the letter with the others on the right of her machine when the door opened and Mr Gregory's dark and handsome head appeared round it.

'Finished those letters, Nicola?'

'Yes, they're all done,' Nicola said cheerfully, picking up the pile and getting to her feet. 'I was just about to bring them through for signature.'

She and Mr Gregory were alone in the building, since he had been out with a client until late and had then returned with a good many letters needing to be typed up. Nicola had agreed to work overtime since Zak was with Ceri up at Ambleside today and they would be working late, too. She enjoyed her job and had no objection to working late one night and leaving early another, but since she had asked for the next couple of weeks off she did want to get Mr Gregory's work as up-to-date as she could before she left.

'Don't bring them through, I'll sign them here,' Mr Gregory said, getting his gold pen out of an inner pocket. 'I'll give you a lift home, shall I? I know you don't worry about walking up Harbour Hill as a rule, but it's late and dark and I'd rather see you to your door.'

'Thanks very much,' Nicola said, touched by his concern. He was a nice person to work for, thoughtful and generous, but their social lives had never touched, she had not seen him at parties, in pubs, pools or beaches. She supposed vaguely that it was because he lived inland, about fifteen miles away, but never let it bother her. Mr Gregory was tall, dark and extremely handsome, which meant by definition that he was also married, and the sort of man she most definitely did not intend to get to know.

'And where are you going on holiday next week?' he remarked idly as he saw her out to his car, parked – illegally – right outside the office. 'We'll miss you – the other two will have their work cut out to keep their heads above water with you away.'

'I'm going to Scotland,' Nicola told him. 'With Ian Frazer, the vet.'

'Really?' Mr Gregory opened the passenger door, saw Nicola into her seat, and then closed it and walked round to the driver's door. He slid behind the wheel, adjusted his belt and turned the car very neatly considering the narrowness of the street. 'Does this mean you and he . . . ?'

'No, not necessarily,' Nicola said, not pretending she did not understand. 'We're good friends, but Ian wants me to meet his parents and see where he was brought up.'

'And that's not significant? I only ask because I've been

hoping you're settled in Haisby. It doesn't need me to tell you that you're a valued employee, I'm sure.'

Valued and underpaid, Nicola thought ungratefully. Why couldn't the firm run to a word-processer, if they valued their staff so much? Or at least to a first-class electric typewriter!

'I think I'll be in Haisby for a while yet,' she said however. 'Ian's a junior partner, you know – he wouldn't just go, even if we did decide to get married and go back to Scotland.'

'Is it on the cards? Marriage, I mean?'

Nicola subjected Mr Gregory's arrogant profile to an affronted stare which he was probably unaware of in the darkness. Still, anyone was entitled to ask, she supposed.

'I'm not sure, Mr Gregory. I'm fond of Ian, but . . .'

'You've had a bad experience,' Mr Gregory murmured. 'You aren't the only one . . . Did you know my wife had left me? I've been living alone in a family-sized house for two years, now.'

'I'm sorry,' Nicola said feebly. No one at work had said a word – surely they must have known?

'That's all right, I'm beginning to pick up the pieces. It gives one's self-confidence a rap, though – to know you haven't lived up to expectations.'

'Yes,' Nicola agreed fervently. 'But I thought only girls felt like that!'

'Nope. It can happen to anyone.' The long car drew up outside Lavengro. 'When you come back, Nicola, would you come out to dinner with me, one night? I'd like to chat, get to know you a bit better.'

'Ye-es, thanks very much,' Nicola said slowly. 'If . . . if I decide not to . . . well, if Ian and I are going to get married I suppose it might be a mistake to . . .'

'I know what you mean.' Was there the trace of a smile in his voice? 'We'll play it by ear, shall we?' He got out of the car and went round to open her door. 'Have a good break, and come back to us refreshed.'

'Oh yes, thanks, see you in a fortnight, then,' Nicola gabbled. She was suddenly sure he was going to kiss her and she simply could not face that sort of a relationship, not with Ian so . . . so . . .

But her fears were unfounded.

'Take care,' Mr Gregory said, getting back behind the wheel. He raised a hand, the engine roared, and he was gone.

Nicola headed for Lavengro, getting her keys out of her handbag as she walked. She wondered what it would be like, kissing Mr Gregory. What it would be like dating him, come to that. Oh, she liked Ian, they got on well, but she was still full of doubts over marrying anyone.

Still, Scotland would be fun, and though it was almost November, Ian had promised her autumn colours the like of which she had never seen before.

Running up the stairs, she began to sing beneath her breath. She was very happy.

It was cold on the shore, but Anthea was well wrapped up and so was Kit, roosting in her arms now because the sea marshes were no place for a pushchair and Kit's small legs had taken as much as they could on the long walk over the marshes and down to the sea.

Am I mad? Anthea wondered as she turned for home, seeing the setting sun slanting long red-gold rays across the marsh, turning Cuttens Cottage into something so beautiful that it looked like an old oil painting. How could I have agreed to leave all this, to live under someone else's roof, just so that one small boy won't have to spend the rest of his life resented?

Because that would be Robin's fate if he returned to his mother, she was sure of it. I spent too much of my childhood being resented, derided, ever to let it happen to anyone else, she told herself defiantly now. How could I have faced Kit if I'd let Robin, who is as good as his big brother, down, when I could have saved him?

And Robin was a bright lad; he had not been told the fate in store for him, but he had guessed. The joy and relief on his small face – so like Keith's, once you knew – had been reward enough when he had heard that Anthea and Kit were moving in, that there would be no big change in his small life.

'We'll be a real family,' was his constantly reiterated theme and that alone should have been enough to make up to Anthea for her sacrifice.

And it wasn't just Robin, of course. She was proud of Ambleside and her position there and downright fond of Henry. What was more, she trusted him. He would accept her offer on her terms and never try to change her; they would keep the engagement fiction going as long as they could and if that no longer satisfied Robin's mother then they would marry, because Anthea knew very well that Henry didn't love her, though he respected and liked her. Thus there would be no fear of him expecting a physical relationship – a shudder ran through Anthea at the thought – and the closeness of a business partnership, whilst she could never have tolerated it with anyone else, was perfectly acceptable with Hal as the other half.

It was heavy going across the marsh though, and Anthea stood Kit down for a moment, breathing deeply. Kit, apparently having regained his energy during his brief rest, promptly set off, splay-legged, towards the channel and Anthea, laughing at his pudgy, adorable determination, set off in pursuit. She caught him up easily enough and held his hand, steering him away from the sunset-reflecting water, the bobbing boat, the squabbling gulls.

So she would be in Ambleside five days a week – so what? She would be here for at least two, probably with Kit and Robin, possibly even with Henry as well, once the hotel became established. We'll have fun, she dreamed, heading for home once more. Family fun, the sort I've never known, the sort Robin wants so desperately. The four of us, waking in the mornings to the cry of the gulls, the soft marsh sounds. Going to sleep with the wind in the eaves, the distant roar of the surf. Their time here would be all the sweeter because it was short, longed-for interludes in the stern business of earning their livings.

They reached the dusty lane which separated the marsh from Cuttens Cottage. Once more, Anthea swung Kit up into her arms.

'Home, home, home for tea,' she sang, breaking into a trot. 'Lovely yellow fish and bread and butter for Kit and Mummy! Or a boily egg and soldier-boys. Which do we like best, today?'

'Brem-buppy,' Kit shouted. 'Kit wants brem-buppy!'

'Kit's a thundering great idiot,' Anthea said happily. 'Boily egg or yellow fish, dunderhead?'

'Brem-buppy,' Kit roared, between giggles. 'Kit wants brem-buppy!'

The two of them disappeared into the picture-book cottage. Just the two of them. Soon to be four.

* * *

264

'It's all worked out beautifully, and it was my idea in the first place,' Ceri said contentedly, leaning back against Tom's shoulder. 'Anthea's engaged to Henry, with a little sapphire ring and everything, That Woman has agreed to let Robin stay, and we're all working like stink to make it a success. Dave from the Dolphin is coming in full-time next summer and Anthea interviewed a nice kid called June who will be YTS and nanny and things . . . so it looks as though my job's safe for a while at least.'

The two of them were sitting on the couch in the living room at Lavengro. Tom had only just arrived and apart from an unworthy delight in Nicola's absence, had hardly had a chance to open his mouth. Now, however, he pulled Ceri onto his lap and began to cuddle her.

'It all sounds very satisfactory. Everyone likes Hal, and Anthea's a brick. But tell me, where's Nicola now?'

'Oh, somewhere in Scotland. She's having a good time, but I don't know that anything will come of it, though he's most awfully nice. I really thought they'd get it together, but now I'm not so sure. She's rung me at work twice and both times she wanted to know about that Gregory fellow she works for . . . Pretty suspicious, if you ask me. Anyway, I said I'd do her rotten spying for her, so I have, and his wife left him just over two years ago, took their little girl and went off with a local businessman, said she was sick of never seeing Gregory except briefly at breakfast. They'd been married six years, so imagine that, Tom! I mean, that's weird!'

'Weird yourself. Then if Nicola isn't back for another week, why don't I stay the night?'

'If you stay, she'll probably row with Ian and turn up at midnight,' Ceri said gloomily. 'Anyway, I thought we were going to get married.'

'So we are, because I want you to darn my socks as well as pander to my wicked masculine urges, but I don't really see the harm in a little rehearsal,' Tom said, doing a bit of rehearsing there and then and paying very little attention to Ceri's wriggles and squeaks. 'Think, Ces, if Nicola really does leave, you'll be landed with all the rent to pay yourself!'

'No I wouldn't, because I'd soon find someone else to share.'

'You've found me,' Tom said at once. 'I'd give Mrs Halesworth notice tomorrow and move in with you. You must be lonely here right this minute without Nicola.'

'True. She offered to leave Zak, but it seemed awfully mean – he is her puppy, really. So she took him, which means I really am alone,' Ceri confessed. 'But since we're getting married you'll have to sleep in Nicola's room, Tom – no sneaking into my bed in the early hours!'

'As if I would!'

Ceri smiled sweetly up at him and Tom smiled sweetly down at her. As if he would – since he had every intention of joining Ceri in bed long before the early hours!

And presently Ceri, snuggling as close as she could get to Tom, made an interesting discovery.

'Tom,' she declared. 'I do believe you're blushing!'